Bijiao Wenxue

比较文学

教育部教学改革重点项目

——「文化原典导读与本科人才培养」成果

曹顺庆　徐行言　主编

文　宇　靳明全
杨亦军　赵渭绒　副主编

高等院校汉语言文学专业系列教材

重庆大学出版社

内容提要

本教材从“比较文学学科内涵与发展脉络”出发，加上影响研究、平行研究、变异研究、总体文学研究这四大研究领域，组成五大板块的理论架构。在内容处理上采用以理论概述为引导，以原典为支撑的模式，每一节均辅以两到三篇原典的节选。原典又分为理论经典和研究范例两类，前者多为比较文学发展史上具有代表性的名篇，后者则为中外学者开展比较文学个案研究的经典之作。考虑到本课程对学生跨语际实践能力的特殊要求，本教材对英文文献大多直接选用原文而非汉语译本，以便使学生能直接领略原典的魅力，并提升英语阅读水平。有条件的学校可藉此开展双语教学。

图书在版编目(CIP)数据

比较文学 / 曹顺庆，徐行言主编. —重庆：重庆大学出版社，2016.2

高等院校汉语言文学专业系列教材

ISBN 978-7-5624-9672-4

Ⅰ.①比… Ⅱ.①曹…②徐… Ⅲ.①比较文学—高等学校—教材 Ⅳ.①I0-03

中国版本图书馆 CIP 数据核字(2016)第 028493 号

比较文学

曹顺庆　徐行言　主编

策划编辑：贾　曼　雷少波　林佳木

责任编辑：李桂英　　版式设计：雷少波

责任校对：张红梅　　责任印制：赵　晟

*

重庆大学出版社出版发行

出版人：易树平

社址：重庆市沙坪坝区大学城西路 21 号

邮编：401331

电话：(023) 88617190　88617185(中小学)

传真：(023) 88617186　88617166

网址：http://www.cqup.com.cn

邮箱：fxk@cqup.com.cn (营销中心)

全国新华书店经销

万州日报印刷厂印刷

*

开本：787mm×1092mm　1/16　印张：19.5　字数：359 千

2016 年 5 月第 1 版　　2016 年 5 月第 1 次印刷

印数：1—3 000

ISBN 978-7-5624-9672-4　定价：39.00 元

总序

这是一套以原典阅读为特点的新型教材，其编写基于我们较长时间的教改研究和教学实践。

有学者认为，中国当代几乎没有培养出诸如钱锺书、季羡林这样学贯中西的学术大师，以至钱锺书在当代中国，成了一个“高山仰止”的神话。诚然，钱锺书神话的形成，“钱学”（钱锺书研究）热的兴起，有着正面的意义，这至少反映了学界及广大青年学子对学术的景仰和向往。但从另一个角度看，也可以说是中国学界的悲哀：偌大一个中国，两千多万在校大学生，当钱锺书、季羡林等大师级人物相继去世之后，竟再也找不出人来承续其学术香火。问题究竟出在哪里？造成这种“无大师时代”的原因无疑是多方面的，但首当其冲应该拷问的是我们的教育（包括初等教育与高等教育）。我们的教育体制、课程设置、教学内容、教材编写等方面，都出现了严重的问题，导致了我们的学生学术基础不扎实，后续发展乏力。仅就目前高校中文学科课程设置而言，问题可总结为四个字：多、空、旧、窄。

所谓“多”，是课程设置太多，包括课程门类数多、课时多、课程内容重复多。不仅本科生与硕士生，甚至与博士生开设的课程内容也有不少重复，而且有的课程如“大学写作”“现代汉语”等还与中学重复。于是只能陷入课程越设越多，专业越分越窄，讲授越来越空，学生基础越来越差的恶性循环。其结果就是，中文系本科毕业的学生读不懂中国文化原典，甚至不知《十三经》为何物；外语学了多少年，仍没有读过一本原文版的经典名著。所以，我认为对高校中文课程进行“消肿”，适当减少课程门类、减少课时，让学生多有一些阅读作品的时间，是我们进行课程和教学改革的必由之路和当务之急。

所谓“空”，即我们现在的课程大而化之的“概论”“通论”太多，具体的“导读”较少，导致学生只看“论”，只读文学史以应付考试，而很少读甚至不读经典作品，以致空疏学风日盛，踏实作风渐衰。针对这种“空洞”现象，我们建议增开中国古代原典和中外文学作品导读课程，减少文学史课时。教材应编写简单一点，集中讲授，不要什么都讲，应倡导启发式教育，让学生自己去读原著、读作品。在规定的学生必读书目的基础上，老师可采取各种方法检查学生读原著（作品）情况，如抽查、课堂讨论、写读书报告等。这既可养成学生的自学习惯，又可改变老师满堂灌的填鸭式教育方式。

所谓“旧”，指课程内容陈旧。多年来，我们教材老化的问题并没有真正解决，例如，现在许多大学所用的教材，包括一些新编教材，还是多年前的老一套体系。陈旧的教材体系，造成了课程内容与课程体系不可避免的陈旧，这应当引起我们的高度重视。

所谓“窄”，是一个亟待解决的问题。自20世纪50年代以来，高校学科越分越细，专业越来越窄，培养了很多精于专业的“匠”，却少了高水平的“大师”。现在，专业过窄的问题已经引起了国家教育部的高度重视。拓宽专业口径，加强素质教育，正在成为我国大学人才培养模式的一个重要改革方向。中文学科是基础学科，应首先立足于文化素质教育，只要是高素质的中文学科学生，相信不但适应面广，而且在工作岗位上更有后劲。

纵览近代以来的中国学术界，凡学术大师必具备极其厚实的基础，博古通今，学贯中西。而我们今天的教育，既不博古，也不通今；既不贯中，也不知西。这并不是说我们不学古代的东西，不学西方的东西，而是学的方式不对。《诗经》《楚辞》《论语》《史记》我们大家多少都会学一点，但这种学习基本上是走了样的。为什么是“走了样”的呢？因为今天的教育，多半是由老师讲时代背景、主要内容、艺术特色之类“导读”，而不是由学生真正阅读文本。另外，所用的读本基本是以“古文今译”的方式来教学的，而并非让同学们直接进入文化原典文本，直接用文言文阅读文化与文学典籍。这样的学习就与原作隔了一层。古文经过“今译”之后，已经走样变味，不复是文学原典了。诚然，古文今译并非不可用，但最多只能作为参考。要真正“博古”，恐怕还是只有读原文，从原文去品味理解。甚至有人提出，古文今译而古文亡，一旦全中国人都读不懂古文之时，就是中国文化危机之日。其实，这种危机状态已经开始呈现了，其显著标志便是中国文化与文论的“失语症”。更不幸的是，我们有些中青年学者，自己没有真正地从原文读过原汁原味的“十三经”或“诸子集成”，却常常以批判传统文化相标榜，这是很糟的事情，是造成今日学界极为严重的空疏学风的原因之一。传统文化当然可以批判，但你要首先了解它，知晓它，否则你从何批判呢？“告诸往而知来者”，“博古”做不好，就不可能真正“通今”。

那我们在“贯西”上又做得如何呢？在我看来，当今中国学术界、教育界，不但“博古”不够，而且“西化”也不够，准确地说是很不够！为什么这样说呢？详观学界，学者们引证的大多是翻译过来的“二手货”，学生们读的甚至是三手货、四手货。不少人在基本上看不懂外文原文或者干脆不读外文原文的情况下，就夸夸其谈地大肆向国人贩卖西方理论，“以己昏昏，使人昭昭”。这种状况近年来虽有所改善，但在不少高校中仍然或多或少地存在着。一些中文系学者仍然依赖译文来做研究（我并非说不可以参照译文来研究，而是强调应该尽量阅读和参照原文），我们不少学生依然只能读着厚厚的“中国式”的西方文论著作。在这种状况下怎么可能产生学贯中西的学术大师？

这种不读原文（包括古文原文与外文原文）的风气，大大地伤害了学术界与教育界，直接的恶果，就是空疏学风日盛，害了大批青年学生，造就了一个没有学术大师的时代，造成了当代中国文化创新能力的严重衰减。

基于以上形势和判断，我们在承担了“教育部教学改革重点项目——文化原典导读与本科人才培养”的教改实践和研究的基础上，立足“原典阅读”和夯实基础，组织了一批学科带头人、教学名师、著名学者、学术骨干，为培养高素质的中文学科人才，群策群力，编写了这套新型教材。这套教材特色鲜明，立意高远，希望能够秉承百年名校的传统，再续严谨学风，为培养新一代基础扎实、融汇中西的创新型人才而贡献绵薄之力。

本教材第一批共九部，分别由各学科带头人领衔主编，他们是：四川大学文科杰出教授、教育部社科委员、985 创新平台首席专家项楚教授，四川大学文科杰出教授、教育部长江学者、国家级教学名师曹顺庆教授，原伦敦大学教授、现任四川大学符号与传播研究中心主任赵毅衡教授，以及周裕锴、谢谦、刘亚丁、俞理明、雷汉卿、张勇（子开）、李怡、杨文全等教授、博士生导师。

本丛书第一批九部出版以来，被多所学校选作本科生、研究生的教材，或者入学考试的参考书目，读者反响良好。目前第一批已经全部安排重印或者修订，以期精益求精。同时，在出版社的倡议和推动下，我们启动了第二批教材的编写工作。此次编写依然由我担任总主编，在第一批书主编的基础上，第二批书的主编人员既有著名学者、美学家冯宪光教授，也有一些中青年专家，如四川大学文新学院的傅其林教授，四川大学海外教育学院的刘荣教授。需要特别指出的是，第二批的编写工作与第一批不同，在主编及编写人员的组织遴选上不限于四川大学，而是将兄弟院校中一些有专长、有影响的学者邀请来一起做。如，四川师范大学文学院院长李凯教授、西南交通大学艺术与传播学院徐行言教授、西南民族大学文学院院长徐希平教授、西南大学文学院副院长肖伟胜教授、成都理工大学传播科学与艺术学院院长刘迅教授、西南财经大学邓时忠教授等。相信通过这些新生力量的加入，丛书第二批将更能代表和体现教学的需要，更好地服务教学实践。

曹顺庆

2014 年 7 月于四川大学

前言

和中文专业其他各科的教材一样，比较文学的教材即使称不上汗牛充栋，也早已不胜枚举了，其中不乏经典和富有创意的版本。再编一种新的，不会是重复劳动吗？其必要性何在？这也许是不少教师和读者会提出的问题，也是我们在承担编写工作之初，不断叩问自己的问题。然而，在终于完成本教材的编写，即将付梓的今天，我们完全可以理直气壮地说，这的确是一部不一样的教材。

从中学到大学，同学们接受过各种各样的原理和概论。当我们为了应付考试，去背诵那些枯燥的理论要点和结论时，往往并不知晓它是如何产生的，它经过怎样复杂的探索和变迁，其间有哪些不同的方向，哪些争论与分歧，它们分别有什么价值，产生过什么样的精彩的华章，或者还存在哪些限制和不足。我们更无从了解的是，这些理论或方法是如何运用于实际的研究和阅读活动中，又是怎样有的放矢地解答那些无限丰富又千差万别的文学实践中提出的问题的。之所以如此，是因为我们传统的教学目标便是在一个既定的理论架构下，尽可能将现有的理论成果整理为简明扼要的观点和论据，把它们条理分明地传达给学生。一个不争的事实是，长期以来，我们的理论教学满足于知识的灌输，对于知识的生产与知识的应用都关注得很不够。于是，同学们都满足于知道现成的观点和结论，而不去探究其中的“为什么”和“怎么样”，更难以体会到理论探索过程中思辨的魅力与求知的趣味。造成这种现状的原因之一，是现有的教学体系使学生远离了原典，即使有课外阅读的要求和愿望，也常常由于找不到合适的读本或缺乏相应的规范与考核而流于形式。因此，他们也就很难从课程学习中收获思维的启迪和治学的方法。

本教材系列的改革方向正是在中文专业的理论课教学中把原典选读直接纳入教学内容，使学生能够从课程学习过程中直接窥见理论的来源和应用的典范，让他们更多地领略到原创性知识的生产过程，以及优秀学者是如何运用理论与方法去探究和回答实际问题，继而推动理论发展的。因此，本教材尽可能将传统教材的原理和知识部分压缩到最小的比重，而将更大的空间留给原典选读和经典的研究范例的学习。相信这将有效地加大课程的知识容量，开阔学生的学术视野，有助于增强他们阅读、思考与分析批判的能力。

本教材在理论框架上借鉴了“十一五”国家级规划教材《比较文学教程》（曹顺庆主编）的基础架构，即从比较文学的学科内涵与发展脉络切入，再以影响研究、平行研究、变异研究、总体文学研究四大研究领域为线索组成五大板块，每章内部再按照研究视角和方法的不同分别组成基础单元（节）。在单元的体例上则采用以理论为先导，以原典为核心的编排模式，每一章节在简略的理论知识概述之后，均有两到三篇原典作为支撑。每节文末还推荐了两到三种中外文论著作为延伸阅读材料，供同学们课外选读，以引导学生进一步拓展阅读面。

考虑到比较文学是一个实践性很强的学科，其特点是较少抽象的理论推演，却依赖于大量的个案研究与实证分析，因而我们在原典的选择上，分为理论经典和研究范例两类，前者多为比较文学发展史上具有里程碑意义的名篇，后者则为中外学者开展比较文学个案研究的典范之作。考虑到本课程对学生跨语际实践能力的特殊要求，本教材对英文文献大多直接选用原文而非汉语译本，以便使学生能绕过翻译媒介可能带来的变异，直接面对原文，领略经典的魅力，并藉此提升自己的英语阅读水平。总而言之，让学生尽可能多地接触原典，正是本教材编写的初衷。

本教材是一部集体合作的成果，编写团队包括来自 9 所高校的 20 余位教授和博士。编写采用分工合作的方式，先由徐行言主编和 4 位副主编分别组编各章的书稿，并按章进行初步统稿，然后由徐行言统筹全书，包括对各章格式的调整规范，并对部分内容进行了修改补充；最后由曹顺庆教授统审全书。

全书各章节编写的具体分工如下：

第一章统筹　徐行言（西南交通大学人文学院）
第一章第一节　徐行言、张宪军（西南交通大学人文学院）
第一章第二节　邓建华（西南交通大学人文学院）
第一章第三节　阮航、胡星灿、曹瑶瑶（西南交通大学人文学院）
第二章统筹　靳明全（四川大学文学与新闻学院）
第二章第一节　靳明全
第二章第二节　翁礼明（内江师范学院文学院）
第二章第三节　杨先明（贵州师范大学求是学院）
第二章第四节　管新福（贵州师范大学文学院）
第三章统筹　支宇（西南交通大学人文学院）
第三章第一节　支宇
第三章第二节　向天渊（西南大学新诗所）
第三章第三节　马建智（西南民族大学文学与新闻学院）
第三章第四节、第五节　支宇
第四章统筹　赵渭绒（四川大学文学与新闻学院）
第四章第一节　曹顺庆、赵渭绒（四川大学文学与新闻学院）
第四章第二节　曾昂（四川大学文学与新闻学院）
第四章第三节　曾宪文（四川文理学院文学院）

第四章第四节　梁昭(四川大学文学与新闻学院)

第五章统筹　　杨亦军(四川师范大学文学院)

第五章第一节　邱永旭(西华师范大学文学院)

第五章第二节　杨亦军

第五章第三节　欧震(四川师范大学文学院)

在这里,我们要对大力支持并积极参与本教材编写工作的各位专家、教授和青年学者表达由衷的谢意,正是你们的创造性工作为我们完成这一部富有探索性的教材提供了品质保障。我们还要衷心感谢重庆大学出版社为本教材的编写提供的支持和帮助！期待着我们共同的成果能够得到广大师生的认可和方家的指教。

编　者

2015 年 9 月

目　录

目 录

第一章　什么是比较文学

什么是比较文学，这个问题也许并不像“什么是文学”那样深奥和玄妙，但同样蕴含着深厚的内涵和丰富的思辨。它要求我们回答——这个学科研究哪些对象，运用什么方法，解决什么问题，它与其他学科的关系和区别是什么，以及它的成果将会对我们的文学创作、文学研究、文学传播与交流产生怎样的启示与影响。然而从比较文学诞生之日起，对这些问题的回答就充满分歧和论辩，伴随着人们对其学科性、合法性的质疑之声。而在比较文学界，往往也因学派与方法的不同，会出现相互矛盾的答案。比较文学学科正是在这样的质疑、对话和发现中实现不断发展创新的。本章旨在通过对比较文学发生与发展历程的追溯，帮助我们理解比较文学研究所面对的基本问题。

第一节　比较文学的诞生背景

在比较文学作为一门学科诞生之前，“比较文学”作为术语就已产生，最早出现于法国两位中学教师诺埃尔和拉普拉斯合编的《比较文学教程》(1816)中，但这只是一部来自不同时期和国家的文学作品选集，并未涉及比较文学的方法与理论。使这一术语得以流行的，是法国文学批评家、巴黎大学教授维尔曼(1790—1870)。1827 年至 1830 年，他在巴黎大学开设比较文学性质的讲座——关于 18 世纪法国作家对于外国文学与欧洲思想影响之考察，他在讲授中曾几次使用“比较文学”和“比较分析”等术语，两年以后他出版了渗透了大量欧洲意识的讲稿《18 世纪法国文学综览》，为“比较文学”术语在实践中找到安身立命之所。以后他又出版了著作《批评哲学的比较研究》，作者由此获得“比较文学之父”之尊号。稍后，安贝尔(1800—1864)接替维尔曼的工作，在巴黎大学开设“各国比较文学史”的讲座，并讲授“论中世纪法国文学同外国文学的关系”，他还著有《各种诗歌的比较研究》。此后，基内(1803—1875)在里昂大学作了名为“比较文学”的讲座。1865 年后，“比较文学”作为专门术语而被普遍接受。1871 年，大批评家勃兰克斯开始在丹麦讲授具有比较文学性质的课程，在后世的学者看来，其代表作《19 世纪文学主潮》正是比较文学类型学研究的典范。1877 年，第一本专业杂志《世界比较文学》创刊于奥匈帝国的克劳森堡(今罗马尼亚克卢日)；1886 年，德国学者科赫创办《比较文学杂志》。同年，时任新西兰奥克兰大学教授的英国学者波斯奈特出版世界上第一部讨论比较文学理论的专著《比较文学》，开始确立“比较文学”的方法论基础和研究框架。1900 年夏，欧美学者在巴黎举行国际讨论会，“各国文学的比较史”成为会议重要议题，会议还呼吁建立国际比较文学学会。

19 世纪 70 年代以来，随着比较文学研究在欧洲的关注度日益增加，比较文学作为一门独立学科的地位开始逐渐形成。1871 年，意大利的那不勒斯大学给著名批评家桑克蒂斯提供比较文学教授职位；继之都灵大学、俄罗斯的彼得堡大学以及丹麦的哥本哈根大学也设立了同样的职位。1888 年，普鲁士的布雷斯劳大学①聘用科赫为比

① 该校所在城市布雷斯劳现属波兰，更名为弗罗茨瓦夫。

较文学教授;1891 年,布拉格大学设立比较文学教授职位;1897 年,法国的里昂大学为戴克斯特(1855—1927)设立比较文学教授职位,他开设的讲座课程是“文艺复兴后日耳曼文学对法国文学的影响”。到 20 世纪初,巴黎大学、斯特拉斯堡大学和法兰西学院也相继设立了比较文学的教授职位。

在美国,哈佛大学 1897 年为马什设立比较文学教授职位。他分别面向本科生和研究生,主要讲授“中世纪欧洲文学比较研究”“欧洲中世纪史诗的起源和发展”“来源于凯尔特人的传奇与诗歌材料和它在中世纪叙事诗中的处理”等课程。1899 年,哥伦比亚大学开始设立同样的职位,伍德佩雷和斯宾加恩先后担任此教职,后者在该校英语系首次开设了比较文学课。

与此同时,比较文学的研究成果也得到越来越广泛的承认。1895 年,戴克斯特以《卢梭与文学世界主义之起源》的论文获得学位;同年,瑞士学者贝兹以《海涅在法国》的论文获得博士学位。接着贝兹又于 1897 年至 1899 年间,在编写《比较文学史》的同时,整理出版了包含 3 000 个条目的《比较文学书目》。贝兹去世后,在比较文学领域贡献卓著的法国学者巴登斯贝格又将其修订为具有 6 000 项条目的《典据史》,并于 1904 年署名贝兹印行。由此,比较文学已成为在各国的本土文学和国别文学研究之外的一门独立的学问。

到 20 世纪初,比较文学研究进一步延伸到日本、苏联、印度、中国等国家和地区。巴登斯贝格和弗里德希合编的《比较文学书目》(1950)收录文献 3.3 万种,1954 年国际比较文学学会成立、1958 年美国教堂山会议首次实现美国比较文学研究者和欧洲学者的正式对话之后,比较文学研究队伍日益壮大,著述更丰富。

尽管比较文学的术语和学科体系的形成都是近 100 多年间的事,但在文学研究中运用比较法却在欧洲有着悠久的历史传统。比较方法的渊源可追溯到古希腊、罗马时期。古希腊著名文艺理论家亚里士多德在《诗学》中运用了求同辨异的比较方法,分析史诗、悲剧与喜剧等不同文类的异同。罗马帝国时期,由于古罗马文学有意借鉴和模仿古希腊文学(如维吉尔创作《埃涅阿斯记》时有意对荷马史诗的模仿,写成世界文学史上第一部“文人诗史”),古罗马作家或理论家自然经常比较两个时代、民族和语言等在文学上的异同。例如,诗人贺拉斯以古希腊诗歌为典范,广泛吸收了希腊抒情诗的各种格律,成功地运用于拉丁语诗歌创作,达到了相当完美的程度,把罗马抒情诗创作推向了高峰,并在其《诗艺》中论及艺术与摹仿的关系,把希腊、罗马文学两相比较,号召作家们“日日夜夜把玩希腊的范例”,他把维吉尔比作荷马,将普劳图斯与阿里斯托芬进行了比较。罗马修辞学家昆提利安在《演说术原理》中曾非常细致地比较了古罗马演说家西塞罗和古希腊演说家狄摩西尼的异同。理论家麦克罗皮斯也探讨了维吉尔诗歌对希腊史诗的模仿与从属关系。此后这种比较方法相沿成习。

中世纪时，意大利著名文学家但丁在其学术著作《论俗语》的第九章，把奥克语的古法国文学和奥依语的普罗旺斯文学加以比较。文艺复兴时期，面对新发掘出来的希腊、罗马的古典文艺，意大利的人文主义者深受影响，进行了比较研究，在一些问题的看法上发生分歧，形成保守派与激进派，这两派之争一直影响到17世纪法国的“古今之争”。

18世纪以后，随着资本主义的不断发展，西方各国之间，甚至东西方国家之间的政治经济与商业的联系大大加强，文化交流日益频繁，而且成为影响各国文学发展的重要因素。在这种情况下，任何国家文学的发展也不可能脱离国际环境与异国影响，广泛的文化交流使得各民族文学之间互相联系、互相影响，诱发了人们比较研究的意识并且能够提供比较研究的参照系。

18世纪兴盛于法国的启蒙运动使欧洲各民族之间的接触更加活跃。当时，法国是思想文化的中心，各国纷纷向法国学习，英国和德国也因其优秀的思想文化成就开始受到法国人的瞩目。当时，文学作品的翻译大量涌现，法国启蒙思想家的作品被译成各种文字，传遍欧洲，莎士比亚的戏剧不但被翻译成各国文字，而且占据了各国舞台；作家和作品之间的相互借鉴和影响成为普遍现象。在这种历史条件下，文学之间的对比研究自然比前代更为丰富，欧洲范围内的思想和文学的超国界说和“文艺的共和国”的观念随之出现。

18世纪至19世纪初，德国的莱辛在《汉堡剧评》中比较了亚里士多德和法国古典主义的理论，认为古典主义理论对《诗学》的诠释是偏颇的。莱辛认为，德国剧作家应该师法的对象不是伏尔泰、拉辛、高乃依等法国古典主义作家，而是英国的莎士比亚。而在《拉奥孔》中，莱辛则是以诗与画的差异为切入点，进行了文学与美术两大文类的比较。奥·威·施莱格尔在柏林开设的“关于美文学和艺术讲座”从总体上描述了整个西欧的文学史，他把西欧文学分成古典的和浪漫的两部分。在《论戏剧艺术和文学》一书中，他进一步说明古典的文学和艺术是机械的、造型的、有限的、简单的、封闭的、文类分明的，而浪漫的文学艺术却是有机的、如画的、无限的、复杂的、不断发展的、文类混杂的。依据这样的原则，他比较了古希腊罗马的文学、中世纪文学、文艺复兴，以及17—18世纪西欧各国的文学，而把古罗马文学、17世纪欧洲各国文学看作古典的文学。1827年1月31日，在与爱克曼的谈话中，歌德提出：“我相信，一种世界文学正在形成，所有的民族都对此表示欢迎，并且都迈出令人高兴的步子。在这里德国可以而且应该大有作为，它将在这伟大的聚会中扮演美好的角色。”他在世界视野中关注民族文学，这就使文学的天地由民族拓展到世界，从而预告了养润民族文学个性、冲决狭隘民族藩篱的“世界文学”的出场。此时,从世界文学的角度来研究各国文学的相互联系,比较其异同,就成为一种必然的趋势。

在法国,孟德斯鸠曾比较不同节奏语言的诗歌,试图通过这种比较研究制订出总体文学诗歌格律的理论。伏尔泰则写了《论史诗》一文,采用比较古代和近代各个国别文学中史诗类型的方法,以提炼史诗类型的本质因素,从而综合制订出总体文学史诗类型的理论。中国的元杂剧《赵氏孤儿》传入欧洲之后,他将此剧与欧洲同类剧本作了对比,认为中国杂剧更富于美好的“理性”,有许多“合理近情”的原则,并按照自己的启蒙思想和理性原则,将其改编为《中国孤儿》。狄德罗的《理查逊颂》则把英国的理查逊与法国的拉辛相比较。司汤达的《拉辛与莎士比亚》在拉辛、莎士比亚等的比较中批驳古典主义,鼓吹所谓的“浪漫主义”,并初步确立了文学中现实主义的概念和理论原则。斯达尔夫人的《从文学与社会制度的关系论文学》通过对莪相和荷马诗歌为代表的北、南文学的比较,不仅指出北方文学饱含激情的忧郁与海滨、风啸、灌木、荒原以及多雾的气候有关,而南方文学充满欢快的明媚却与“清新的空气、丛密的树林、清澈的溪流”以及明朗的气候相关,她还说明:“北方文学与这一地区的各民族对哲学的关注和对自由的向往紧密相关,而南方文学则与该地区各民族对艺术的热爱和安居乐业的向往紧密相关。”她的这一论著和《论德国》一起对后来法国的比较文学起了开拓性的作用。

19 世纪盛行于欧洲的浪漫主义文学思潮对比较文学的形成也有较大影响。第一,浪漫主义秉承歌德提出的“世界文学”观念,接受了斯达尔夫人注重文学发展和社会状况之间的相互关系的理念,要求用历史比较方法代替古典主义纯文学批评的思想,强调描写异国风光,表现异国情调,颇为注意文学的国际性。第二,浪漫主义作家向往中世纪,重视民间文学。他们大量搜集中世纪故事和民间文学作品,这不仅促进了民间文学的整理、研究工作,而且促进了民俗学的兴旺发展。而民俗学的发展,导致对文学更大规模的比较研究,对比较文学的形成起了促进作用。

到了 19 世纪,随着各国之间的政治、经济、文化交流的发展,各个学科都出现了“比较热”。自然科学中以比较解剖学发端,陆续形成了比较生理学、比较胚胎学。接着波及人文学科,出现了比较语言学、比较神话学、比较宗教学、比较哲学等。各种各样的比较研究著作也纷纷问世:生物学方面有居维叶的《比较解剖学》、布朗维尔的《比较生理学》、科斯特的《比较胚胎形成学》;神话学方面有阿贝·特莱桑的《历史上的比较神话学》、缪勒的《比较神话学》;哲学方面有德热兰多的《哲学系统比较史》;爱欲研究方面有德·维耶的《比较爱欲学》;美学方面有索伯里的《比较绘画和文学教程》;宗教学方面有缪勒的《宗教学导论》。

加速和互联网时代不同区域与民族间文化交流的拓展，比较文学将展现出更加广阔的前景。

【原典选读】

比较法与文学（节选）

◉波斯奈特

【导读】哈钦森·麦考利·波斯奈特（H. M. Posnet，1855—1927），英国比较文学学者，1855 年出生于北爱尔兰的安特林郡，1872 年入都柏林大学三一学院学习希腊和拉丁文学，1877 年获文学士学位，因学业出众，荣获金质奖章并留校工作。1881 年起负责编辑《爱尔兰代表评论》杂志。翌年，发表了学术论文《伦理学、法理学和政治经济学中的历史方法》，并获得文学硕士学位。1884 年，发表题为《李嘉图的租金理论》的论文，同年获得法学学士和法学博士学位。此后，他大部分时间从事讲学，1900 年，在《现代评论》杂志上发表题为《比较文学的科学》的论文。

波斯奈特 1886 年出版的《比较文学》是世界上第一部论述比较文学理论的专著。包括引论、氏族文学、城市国家、世界文学和国别文学五个部分，共 18 章，另有前言和结束语。在这本专著中，波斯奈特把"比较的"与"历史的"看作同义语，对文学的本质、相对性、发展的原理、比较研究等许多问题作了精辟的阐述，该书的重要创见在于触及了世界文学的多元起源问题，认为世界文学起源自四大古老文明希腊—罗马、希伯来、印度和中国；从这四个文明古国的文学中，归纳出各自的世界文学精神；认为文学的发展与社会进化同步，是从简单向复杂、从城邦到国别再到世界的发展过程。本书所选的《比较法与文学》(*The Comparative Method and Literature*)系波氏《比较文学》著作的第一部分第四章 21—24 节，谈论了"比较法"对于文学研究的方法论意义。■

§ 21. The comparative method of acquiring or communicating knowledge is in one sense as old as thought itself, in another the peculiar glory of our nineteenth century. All reason, all imagination, operate subjectively, and pass from man to man objectively, by aid of comparisons and differences. The most colourless proposition of the logician is either the assertion of a comparison, A is B, or the denial of a comparison, A is not B; and any student of Greek thought will remember how the confusion of this simple process by mistakes about the nature of the copula (cart) produced a flood of so-called "essences" (*pvatat*) which have done more to mislead both ancient and modern philosophy than can be easily estimated. But not only the colourless propositions of logic, even the highest and most brilliant flights of oratorical eloquence or poetic fancy are sustained by this rudimentary structure of comparison and difference, this primary scaffolding, as we may call it, of human thought. If sober experience works out scientific truths in propositions affirming or denying comparison, imagination even in the richest colours works under the same elementary forms. Athenian intellect and Alexandrian reflection failed to perceive this fundamental truth, and the failure is attributable in the main to certain social characteristics of the Greeks. Groups, like individuals, need to project themselves beyond the circle of their own associations if they wish to understand their own nature; but the great highway which has since led to comparative philosophy was closed against the Greek by his contempt for any language but his own. At the same time, his comparisons of his own social life, in widely different stages, were narrowed partially by want of monuments of his past, much more by contempt for the less civilised Greeks, such as the Macedonians, and especially by a mass of myth long too sacred to be touched by science, and then too tangled to be profitably loosed by the hands of impatient sceptics. Thus, deprived of the historical study of their own past and circumscribed within the comparisons and distinctions their own adult language permitted, it is not surprising that the Greeks made poor progress in comparative thinking, as a matter not merely of unconscious action but of conscious reflection. This conscious reflection has been the growth of European thought during the past five centuries, at first indeed a weakling, but, from causes of recent origin, now flourishing in healthy vigour.

When Dante wrote *De Moquio Vvlgari* he marked the starting-point of our modern comparative science—the nature of language, a problem not to be lightly overlooked by the peoples of modern Europe inheriting, unlike Greek or Hebrew, a literature written in a tongue whose decomposition had plainly gone to make up the elements of their own living speech. The Latin, followed at an interval by the Greek, Renaissance laid the foundations' of comparative reflection in the mind of modern Europe. Meanwhile the rise of European nationalities was creating new standpoints, new materials, for comparison in modern institutions and modes of thought or Hentiment. The discovery of the New World brought this new European civilisation face to face with primitive life, and awakened men to contrasts with their own associations more striking than Byzantine or even Saracen could offer. Commerce, too, was now bringing the rising nations of Europe into rivalry with, and knowledge of, each other, and, more than this, giving a greater degree of personal freedom to the townsmen of the West than they had ever possessed before. Accompanying the increase of wealth and freedom came an awakening of individual opinion among men, even an uprising of it against authority which has since been called the Reformation, but an uprising which, in days of feudal, monarchical, and "popular" conflict, in days when education was the expensive luxury of the few, and even the communication of work-a-day ideas was as slow and irregular as bad roads and worse banditti could make it, was easily checked even in countries where it was supposed to have done great things. Individual inquiry, and with it comparative thinking, checked within the domain of social life by constant collisions with theological dogma, turned to the material world, began to build up the vast stores of modern material knowledge, and only in later days of freedom began to construct from this physical side secular views of human origin and destiny which on the social side had been previously curbed by dogma. Meanwhile European knowledge of man's social life in its myriad varieties was attaining proportions such as neither Bacon nor Locke had contemplated. Christian missionaries were bringing home the life and literature of China so vividly to Europeans that neither the art nor the scepticism of Voltaire disdained to borrow from the Jesuit Premare's translation of a Chinese drama published in 1735. Then Englishmen in India learned of that ancient language which Sir William Jones, toward the close of the eighteenth century, introduced to European scholars; and soon the points of resemblance between this language and the languages of Greeks and Italians, Teutons and Celts, were observed, and used like so many stepping-stones upon which men passed in imagination over the flood of time which separates the old Aryans from their modern offshoots in the West. Since those days the method of comparison has been applied to many subjects besides language; and many new influences have combined to make the mind of Europe more ready to compare and to contrast than it ever was before. The steam-engine, telegraph, daily press, now bring the local and central, the popular and the cultured, life of each European country and the general actions of the entire world face to face; and habits of comparison have arisen such as never before prevailed so widely and so vigorously. But, while we may call *consciously* comparative thinking the great glory of our nineteenth century, let us not forget that such thinking is largely due to mechanical improvements, and that long before our comparative philologists, jurists, economists, and the rest, scholars like Reuchlin used the same method less consciously, less accurately, yet in a manner from the first foreshadowing a vast outlook instead of the exclusive views of Greek criticism. Here, then, is a rapid sketch of comparative thought in its European history. How is such thought, how is its method, connected with our subject, "Literature"?

§ 22. It has been observed that imagination no less than experience works through the medium of comparisons; but it is too often forgotten that the range of these comparisons is far from being unlimited in space and time, in social life anil physical environment. If scientific imagination, such as Professor Tyndall once explained and illustrated, is strictly bound by the laws of hypothesis, the magic of the literary artist which looks so free is as strictly bound within the range of ideas already marked out by the language of his group. Unlike the man of science, the man of literature cannot coin words for a currency of new ideas; for his verse or prose, unlike the discoveries of the man of science, must reach average, not specialised, intelligence. Words must pass from special into general use before they can be used by him; and, just in proportion as special kinds of knowledge (legal, commercial, mechanical, and the like) are developed, the more striking is the difference between the language of literature and that of science the language and ideas of the community contrasted with those of its specialised parts. If we trace the rise of any civilised community out of isolated clans or tribes, we may observe a twofold development closely connected with the language and ideas of literature—expansion of the group outwards, a process attended by expansions of thought and sentiment; and specialisation of activities within, a process upon which depends the rise of a leisure-enjoying literary class, priestly or secular. The latter is the process familiar to economists as division of labour, the former that familiar to antiquaries as the fusion of smaller into larger social groups. While the range of comparison widens from clan to national and even world-wide associations and sympathies, the specialising process separates ideas, words, and forms of writing from the proper domain of literature. Thus, in the Homeric age the speech in the Agora has nothing professional or specialised about it, and is a proper subject of poetry; but in the days of professional Athenian oratory the speech is out of keeping with the drama, and smacks too much of the rhetor's school. Arabic poets of the "Ignorance" sing of their clan life; Spenser glows with warmly national feelings; Goethe and Victor Hugo rise above thoughts of even national destiny. It is due to these two processes of expansion and specialisation that the language and ideas of literature gradually shade off from the special language and special ideas of certain classes in any highly developed community, and literature comes to differ from science not only by its imaginative character, but by the fact that its language and ideas belong to no special class. In fact, whenever literary language and ideas cease to be in a manner common property, literature tends either towards imitation work or to become specialised, to become science in a literary dress—as not a little of our metaphysical poetry has been of late. Such facts as these bring out prominently the relation of comparative thinking and of the comparative method to literature. Is the circle of common speech and thought, the circle of the group's comparative thinking, as narrow as a tribal league? Or, have many such circles combined into a national group? Are the offices of priest and singer still combined in a kind of magic ritual? Or, have professions and trades been developed, each, so to speak, with its own technical dialect for practical purposes? Then we must remember that these external and internal evolutions of social life, take place often unconsciously, making comparisons and distinctions without reflecting on their nature or limits; we must remember that it is the business of reflective comparison, of the comparative method, to retrace this development *consciously*, and to seek the causes which have produced it. Let us now look at the literary use of such comparison in a less abstract, a more lifelike form.

When Mr. Matthew Arnold defines the function of criticism as "a disinterested endeavour to learn and propagate the best that is known and thought in the world," he is careful to add that much of this best knowledge and thought is not of English but foreign growth. The English critic in these times of international literature must deal largely with foreign fruit and flower, and thorn-pieces sometimes. He cannot rest content with the products of his own country's culture, though they may vary from the wild fruits of the Saxon wilderness to the rude plenty of the Elizabethan age, from the courtly neatness of Pope to the democratic tastes of today. M. Demogeot has lately published an interesting study① of the influences exerted by Italy, Spain, England, and Germany on the literature of France; our English critic must do likewise for the literature of his own country. At every stage in the progress of his country's literature he is, in fact, forced to look more or less beyond her sea-washed shores. Does he accompany Chaucer on his pilgrimage and listen to the pilgrims' tales? The scents of the lands of the South fill the atmosphere of the Tabard Inn, and on the road to Canterbury waft him in thought to the Italy of Dante and of Petrarch and Boccaccio. Does he watch the hardy crews of Drake and Frobisher unload in English

① *Hutoire dee Litteratures ibrangere* (Paris, 1880).

port the wealth of Spanish prize, and listen to the talk of great sea-captains full of phrases learned from the gallant subjects of Philip Ⅱ.? The Spain of Cervantes and Lope de Vega rises before his eyes, and the new physical and mental wealth of Elizabethan England bears him on the wings of commerce or of fancy to the noisy port of Cadiz and the palaces of Spanish grandees. Through the narrow and dirty streets of Elizabethan London fine gentlemen, with Spanish rapiers at their sides and Spanish phrases in their mouths, pass to and fro in the dress admired by Spanish taste. The rude theatres resound with Spanish allusions. And, were it not for the deadly strife of Englishman and Spaniard on the seas, and the English dread of Spain as the champion of Papal interference, England's Helicon might forget the setting sun of the Italian republics to enjoy the full sunshine of Spanish influences. But now our critic stands in the Whitehall of Charles Ⅱ., or lounges at Will's Coffee-House, or enters the theatres whose recent restoration cuts to the heart his Puritan friends. Everywhere it is the same. Spanish phrases and manners have been forgotten. At the court, Buckingham and the rest perfume their licentious wit with French *bouquet*. At Will's, Dryden glorifies the rimed tragedies of Racine; and theatres, gaudy with scenic contrivances unknown to Shakspere, are filled with audiences who in the intervals chatter French criticism, and applaud with equal fervour outrageous indecencies and formal symmetry. Soon the English Boileau will carry the culture of French exotics as far as the English hothouse will allow; soon that scepticism which the refined immorality of the court, the judges, and the Parliament renders fashionable among the few who as yet guide the destinies of the English nation, shall pass from Bolingbroke to Voltaire, and from Voltaire to the Revolutionists. We need not accompany our critic to Weimar, nor seek with him some sources of German influence on England in English antipathies to France and her revolution. He has proved that the history of our country's literature cannot be explained by English causes alone, any more than the origin of the English language or people can be so explained. He has proved that each national literature is a centre towards which not only national but also international forces gravitate. We thank him for this glimpse of a growth so wide, so varying, so full of intricate interaction; it is an aspect of literature studied comparatively, but, in spite of its apparent width, it is only one aspect. National literature has been developed from within as well as influenced from without; and the comparative study of this internal development is of far greater interest than that of the external, because the former is less a matter of imitation and more an evolution directly dependent on social and physical causes.

§ 23. To the internal sources of national development, social or physical, and the effect of different phases of this development on literature, the student will therefore turn as the true field of scientific study. He will watch the expansion of social life from narrow circles of clans or tribal communities, possessed of such sentiments and thoughts as could live within such narrow spheres, and expressing in their rude poetry their intense feelings of brotherhood, their weak conceptions of personality. He will watch the deepening of personal sentiments in the isolated life of feudalism which ousts the communism of the clan, the reflection of such sentiments in songs of personal heroism, and the new aspects which the life of man, and of nature, and of animals—the horse, the hound, the hawk in feudal poetry, for example—assumes under this change in social organisation. Then he will mark the beginnings of a new kind of corporate life in the cities, in whose streets sentiments of clan exclusiveness are to perish, the prodigious importance of feudal personality is to disappear, new forms of individual and collective character are to make their appearance, and the drama is to take the place of the eurly communal chant or the song of the chieftain's hall. Next, the scene will change into the courts of monarchy. Here the feelings of the cities and of the seigneurs are being focussed; here the imitation of classical models supplements the influences of growing national union; here literature, reflecting a more expanded society, a deeper sense of individuality, than it ever did before, produces its master-pieces under the patronage of an Elizabeth or a Louis Quatorze. Nor, in observing such effects of social evolution on literature, will the student by any means confine his view to this or that country. He will find that if England had her clan age, so also had Europe in general; that if France had her feudal poetry, so also had Germany, and Spain, and England; that though the rise of the towns affected literature in diverse ways throughout Europe, yet there are general features common to their influences; and that the same may be said of centralism in our European nations. Trace the influence of the Christian pulpit, or that of judicial institutions, or that of the popular assembly, on the growth of prose in different European countries, and you soon find how similarly internal social evolution has reflected itself in the word and thought of literature; how essential it is that any accurate study of literature should pass from language into the causes which allowed language and thought to reach conditions capable of supporting a literature; and how profoundly this study must be one of comparison and contrast. But we must not underrate our difficulties in tracing the effects of such internal evolution on a people's verse and prose. We must rather admit at the outset that such evolution is liable to be obscured or altogether concealed by the imitation of foreign models. To an example of such imitation we shall now turn.

The cases of Rome and Russia are enough to prove that external influences, carried beyond a certain point, may convert literature from the outgrowth of the group to which it belongs into a mere exotic, deserving of scientific study only as an artificial production indirectly dependent on social life. Let an instrument of speech be formed, a social centre established, an opportunity for the rise of a literary class able to depend upon its handiwork be given, and only a strong current of national ideas, or absolute ignorance of foreign and ancient models, can prevent the production of imitative work whose materials and arrangement, no matter how unlike those characteristic of the group, may be borrowed from climates the most diverse, social conditions the most opposite, and conceptions of personal character belonging to totally different epochs. Especially likely is something of this kind to occur when the cultured few of a people comparatively uncivilised become acquainted with the literary models of men who have already passed through many grades of civilisation, and who can, as it seems, save them the time and trouble of nationally repeating the same laborious ascent. The imitative literature of Rome is a familiar example of such borrowing; and that of Russia looked for a time as if it were fated to follow French models almost as closely as Rome once followed the Greek. How certain this imitation of French models was to conceal the true national spirit of Russian life, to throw a veil of contemptuous ignorance over her barbarous past, and to displace in her literature the development of the nation by the caprice of a Russo-Gallic clique, none can fail to perceive. In a country whose social life was, and is, so largely based on the communal organisation of the *Mir*, or village community, the strongly-individualised literature of France became such a favorite source of imitation as to throw into the background altogether those folk-songs which the reviving spirit of national literature in Russia, and that of social study in Europe generally, are at length beginning to examine. This Russian imitation of France may be illustrated by the works of Prince Kantemir (1709-1743), who has been called "the first writer of Russia," the friend of Montesquieu, and the imitator of Boileau and Horace in his epistles and satires; by those of Lomonossoff (1711-1765), "the first classical writer of Russia," the pupil of Wolf, the founder of the University of Moscow, the reformer of the Russian language, who by academical *Panegyrics* on Peter the Great and Elizabeth sought to supply the want of that truly oratorical prose which only free assemblies can foster, attempted an epic *Petreid* in honor of the great Tsar, and modelled his odes on the French lyric poets and Pindar①; or by those of Soumarokoff, who, for the theatre of St. Petersburg established by Elizabeth, adapted or translated Corneille, Racine, Voltaire, much as Plautus and Terence had introduced the Athenian drama at Rome. As in Rome there had set in a conflict between old Roman family sentiments and the individualising spirit of the Greeks, as in Rome nobles of light and leading had been delighted to exchange archaic sentiments of family life and archaic measures like the Saturnian for the cultured thought and harmonious metres of Greece, so in Russia there set in a conflict between French individualism, dear to the court and nobles, and the social feelings of the Russian commune and family. The most ancient monuments of Russian thought—the Chronicle of the monk Nestor (1056-1116) and the *Song of Igor*—were as unlikely to attract the attention of such imitators as the *Builinas* and the folk-songs; and among a people who had never experienced the Western feudalism with its chivalrous poetry, to whom the Renaissance and Reformation had been unknown, came an imitation of Western progress which threatened for a time to prove as fatal to national literature as the imitation of Greek ideas had proved in Rome. In this European China, as Russia, with her family sentiments and filial devotion to the Tsar, has been called, French, and afterwards German and English, influences clearly illustrate the difficulties to which a scientific student of literature is exposed by imitative work out of keeping with social life; but the growing triumph of Russian national life as the true spring of Russian literature marks the want of real vitality in any literature dependent upon such foreign imitation.

§ 24. These internal and external aspects of literary growth are thus objects of comparative inquiry, because literatures are not Aladdin's palaces raised by unseen hands in the twinkling of an eye, but the substantial results of causes which can be specified and described. The theory that literature is the detached life-work of individuals who are to be

① The son of the fisherman of Archangel did much, no doubt, to create national literature, especially by his severance of the old Slavon of the Church from the spoken language; but his works contain evidences of French influence in spite of his national predilections.

worshipped like images fallen down from heaven, not known as workers in the language and ideas of their age and place, and the kindred theory that imagination transcends the associations of space and time, have done much to conceal the relation of science to literature and to injure the works of both. But the "great-man theory" is really suicidal; for, while breaking up history and literature into biographies and thus preventing the recognition of any lines of orderly development, it would logically reduce not only what is known as "exceptional genius," but all men and women, so far as they possess personality at all, to the unknown, the causeless—in fact, would issue in a sheer denial of human knowledge, limited or unlimited. On the other hand, the theory that imagination works out of space and time (Coleridge, for example, telling us that "Shakspere is as much out of time as Spenser out of space") must not be repelled by any equally dogmatic assertion that it is limited by human experience, but is only to be refuted or established by such comparative studies as those on which we are about to enter.

The central point of these studies is the relation of the individual to the group. In the orderly changes through which this relation has passed, as revealed by the comparison of literatures belonging to different social states, we find our main reasons for treating literature as capable of scientific explanation. There are, indeed, other standpoints, profoundly interesting, from which the art and criticism of literature may also be explained—that of physical nature, that of animal life. But from these alone we shall not see far into the secrets of literary workmanship. We therefore adopt, with a modification hereafter to be noticed, the gradual expansion of social life, from clan to city, from city to nation, from both of these to cosmopolitan humanity, as the proper order of our studies in comparative literature.

(Hutcheson Macaulay Posnett. Comparative Literature. Memphis: General Books LLC™, 2012.)

比较文学的目的、方法、规划(节选)

◉艾金伯勒

【导读】雷内·艾金伯勒(Rene Etiemble, 1909—2002),通译艾田伯,法国著名学者、作家、文学评论家。他毕业于巴黎高等师范学院法律系,曾先后在美国、墨西哥和埃及等国家任教多年,国内曾执教于蒙彼利埃大学和巴黎大学,自1956年起,接任巴黎大学比较文学研究院院长,比较文学首席教授,直至1977年退休。作为比较文学学者,他的代表性学术著作有《比较不是理由》(1963)、《面向全球的比较理论》、《(真正的)总体文学论文集》(1974)、《世界文学论文集》(1982)、《中国之欧洲》(1988、1989)、《世界文学新论》(1992)等,其中《中国之欧洲》荣膺首届巴尔桑比较文学基金奖。他具有宏阔的东方视野和浓厚的"中国情结",除了《中国之欧洲》外,写过《孔子》(1956)、《耶稣会士在中国》(1966)、《我信奉毛泽东主义的四十年》(1976),在索邦大学开设过题为《哲学的东方》(1957—1959)的课程,组织翻译了《水浒》《红楼梦》《金瓶梅》等中国古典名著。他在《比较不是理由》一书中提出“比较文学是人文主义”的观点,他主张把各民族文学看作全人类共同的精神财富,看作相互依赖的整体。《导读》所选章节为该书的第三部分,着重批评了法国学派从实证主义出发进行的影响研究只注意文学作品外部诸关系的偏向,主张把历史主义的影响研究和美学评价的平行研究相互结合,将案卷研究与本文阐释结合起来,将社会学家的审慎与美学家的大胆结合起来,进行新的探索。

历史主义与文学批评

是的,不管调和者作出怎样的努力,今天,在整个世界范围内,比较文学由于存在多种倾向而被划分开来,有时是被撕裂开来,其中,至少有两种倾向彼此极少谅解,一种倾向坚持认为,由于这门学科实质上是与历史研究同时产生的(甚至到了这样一种程度:似乎孟德斯鸠和伏尔泰因为对历史发生兴趣,同时也就规定了比较文学的某些原则),它一定是,而且也只能是文学史的分支;这里的“文学史”是就其依据、注重事实(événementiel)的意义上来理解的,这是他们今天的说法,如果照我的说法,是就其堆积遗闻轶事的意义上来理解的。另一种倾向认为,即使两种文学并不存在历史的联系,对这两种文学根据各自用途发展起来的那些文学类型进行比较仍然是有理由的。借用哈佛大学的讲授中国文学的哈埃妥厄教授(James Hightower)的话说,“甚至完全排除了直接影响的可能性”,比较文学不仅仍旧是可能的,而且事实上特别能激发思想。

历史主义者

某一阵营里聚集着这么一些人,他们以为,或者说自称他们是在把朗松①的历史方法运用于比较文学。但是他们老是忘掉它的实质,那就是,对这位最正统的文学史经典的创立者来说,历史方法远不能构成文学教学的本质特性,而只能够、事实上也只应当构成探讨文学的一种方法。这一点在朗松著名的《法国文学史》这部支配了我们的教学长达半个世纪的书中讲得很清楚。然而,这部书的用意却一直没有得到正确理解。人们是否读过书的序言?不管怎样,下面这段文字很值得推敲:

> 所以,我想不出一个人学习文学除了想提高自我修养外,还能出于什么其他理由;除了他喜欢它外,还能出于什么其他原因。无疑,那些打算当教师的人必须使他们的知识系统化,使他们的学习遵循一些方法,和那些仅仅作为文学的“业余爱好者”

① 朗松(Custave Lanson,1857—1934),法国文学史家。

> 的人们相比，需要在他们的学习中运用更加精确的（如果他们愿意的话，我想说更加科学的）概念。但是，决不能忽视这两点：其一，如果他不能首先努力去培养学生对文学的鉴赏力的话，他将是个蹩脚的文学教师……其二，如果在成为学者前，他本身并不是个“业余爱好者”，那么，对于如何使他的教学富有这方面的成效，他就会不得要领。

你“成为学者之前”就一直在正确地阅读。普雷沃（Jean Prévost）就把自己说成是“诗歌的业余爱好者”。普雷沃这位人文学者不仅翻译西班牙、英国、德国、现代希腊的诗歌，而且还在一位中国文学家的帮助下，借助一些拙劣的法文译作，翻译中国诗歌。普雷沃的杰作之一《诗歌爱好者》使他跻身于比较文学的忠实的解释者，也就是说，比较文学的忠实的信徒的行列；所以能这样，是因为这位作家能够遵奉朗松提出的那些要求，他第二次世界大战期间在里昂曾为一部著名的、出色的论述“司汤达的创作”的论文进行答辩，而同是这位作家，对一些中国诗人喜爱得如痴如醉（像他自己说的那样）。

在被盗用了的“朗松主义”的名义下，那些最低能的，因而也是最顽固的效颦者们，追随那位老一代的大师已有半个世纪，却仿佛他提出的先决条件是失效了的：对他们来说，那些最没有价值的文献汇编、遗闻轶事、附属文件构成了比较学者的工作的核心部分；无论怎么说，这些也是他们的范围以内的唯一的工作。某些法国学派的代表人物机械地将这种走了样的“朗松方法”运用到比较文学中来，而在朗松看来，历史的、信实的、确凿的研究是文学研究的前奏，作家欣赏的前奏［并且同时保证“业余爱好者”免受妄自尊大的批评，有关这类批评，勒梅特尔（Jules Lemaitre）以及其他许多文学方面的报刊撰稿人在当时提供了出色的然而是令人沮丧的例子］。这些热心分子自作主张，把文学研究，甚至比较文学划入历史研究的范围。不过，甚至像让-马里·伽列这样眼光敏锐的大师，故世前不久在同意为基亚的《比较文学》撰写前言时，也犯了同样的错误。虽然急于想继巴登斯贝格和梵·第根之后划定我们学科的范围，他在下面这些话中还是没有给出这样一个定义，使我们确实应当称之为“法国式的”正统：

> 比较文学是文学史的分支，它研究国际性的精神联系，研究拜伦和普希金、歌德与卡莱尔、司格特与维尼之间的事实联系，研究不同文学的作家之间在作品、灵感，甚至生活方面的事实联系。
>
> 它不是主要探讨作品原有的价值，而是着重关心一些国家和作家如何改造他们借用来的东西……说到底，比较文学不是美国学校里教的那种“总体文学”。它最终可能导致总体文学的产生；对某些人来说，它必须这么做。但是，像人文主义、古典主义、浪漫主义、现实主义、象征主义这样的大略的平行关系（还有共时性关系，synchronisme），因为系统性过强、时空延展太开而有化成为抽象空泛、主观臆断的东

> 西，只剩下些标签的危险。尽管比较文学能够领出条通向这些综合的路来，它本身并不能完成这些综合。

并不是说所有这些话在我看来都应当受到批评。为了把这些观念引向荒谬（但毕竟，这些观念往往是文学史家杜撰出来或加以系统化的），我从我们的历史学者的教科书里收罗了所有适合归类的欧洲前浪漫主义的题材："自然""情与景""爱情与激情""宿命""敏感性""过去的时光""古代遗迹"，等等；随后我在蒙特贝里埃（Montepelier）大学开设了十八世纪末叶欧洲前浪漫主义的课程。我讲授了一门再正统不过的课，最后，我用这些话作结语："我想指出，所有我用来评述欧洲前浪漫主义的诞生的引语均出自中国诗歌，从生活在纪元前的屈原到宋代。"我是以这种方式在为伽列的审慎辩护，并且为那些人辩护（同时也偷偷捅了他们一拳），他们认为，作家之间、流派之间或文学类型之间的"事实联系"的历史并没有穷尽我们这门学科的内容。原因在于，如果说我能够引用公元前和公元后十二个世纪的中国诗歌来解释十八世纪的前浪漫主义的所有题材的话，显而易见，这是因为那些形式存在着，类型存在着，不变因素存在着，一句话，有人存在，文学也就存在。

批评家

确实，像美国的雷内·韦勒克以及其他地方的许多人，他们是对的，这些人认为，比较文学史的研究与文学的比较研究是不一样的；文学是寓于人的自然语言之中的诸形式的系统；文学的比较研究不应局限于"事实联系"的研究，而必须尝试把研究导向对作品的价值的思考，甚至于（为什么不呢?）对作品进行价值评判，也许，依我的看法，它甚至应力图对新的价值标准的精心确定作出贡献，这些价值尺度和我们今天还靠它们度日或者说正因为它们我们才陷入险境的老的一套相比，在某种程度上要较少主观臆断的成分。

和让-玛丽·伽列一样，我相信，鉴于比较文学目前还处于童年时期，它还不能加入歌德的"世界文学"或美国的"总体文学"中去，事实上也不能加入到苏联的那个"世界文学"中去（我的苏联同行阿尼西莫夫最近告诉我说，莫斯科科学院正在编写一部"世界文学"史）。但我确信，它一定会将我们引向这种世界文学。我赞成雷内·韦勒克的意见：除非历史研究（法国和苏联学者们有理由重视它）的根本目的是使我们最终能来谈论文学，甚至总体文学、美学、修辞学，否则，比较文学注定会长时期完成不了自己的使命。德·多尔（Guillermo de Torre）的疑虑是有充分理由的，他感到奇怪，在当今的所有学科中，跟歌德说"世界文学"时设想的极相符合的那门学科怎么会不是比较文学呢。由于"总体文学"暗示出一般性，也就是近似的观念，这个提法让那些注重细枝末节的历史学者望而生畏；这一点是可以理解的。但当巴达庸反对这一提法时，谁又会对他这种相似的顾虑感到费解呢？他写道："比较不过是我们称之为比较文学的那门学科的方法之一，而这个名称是相当词不达意的。我常常私下里想，总体文学是个较好一些的提法，而我马上就意识到采用这个新名称会带来的一些弊病，它会使人们只顾到一般原则，而不再去考虑那些活生生的作品之间的具体关系了。”

“给这门学科的词汇以更纯粹的意义”

最杰出的法国比较学者对我们学科的名称提出了疑问，由此看来，那些人是对的——而且这样的人很多——他们坚持认为，今天比较文学的首要任务是给这门学科使用的术语下定义，而首先是给它本身下定义。西欧比较学者正在计划制订和出版一部我们学科的术语词典，词典中对那些使用得极为频繁，同时也极无分寸的词的意义将从历史的角度加以澄清；在这一时刻，我们很愉快地获悉，在社会主义国家的科学院的主持下，于布达佩斯筹备组织的比较文学大会宣布了三项课题作为大会讨论的三个部分：1. 比较文学当前面临的问题；2. 在文学史中运用的术语的形成和变化；3. 东欧文学的历史和比较的探讨：制订一部这些文学的比较史是否可能和必要？第一个部分是考察我们学科的对象和方法，第二个部分正确地强调了它的任务中的一项，它的未来还有赖于这些任务的完成。在了解下述情况方面，比较学者的地位不正是得天独厚的吗？——一旦我们进入抽象的领域，一种特定的语言的概念极少能与另一种语言的概念相一致；或确切地说，它们是部分一致的，每一个概念都由几个不同的外语的概念的一些部分组成，后者随所论及的那个语言而变化：在德语中，Volk 充满着感情色彩和种族意味，而这在我们的 people（人民）这个词中是不包含的。Völkisch 根本不是 populaire（大众的）的意思，倒是增添了一层 rassisch 的含义，这是一个可以翻译为 racial（种族的）的准科学概念；这个词中的浪漫主义的和左派的色彩没有挽回它在纳粹影响下背离原意，转向可怕的“种族主义的”这个规范意义的厄运。在历史方面，德国古典主义与法国古典主义很少共同的特点，然而在美学方面，他们的确具有某些共同的特征。对我刚刚提到的在古代中国找到了欧洲前浪漫主义的所有题材这一点从历史方面又何以解释呢？而在美学方面，它们之间的类同之处迫使人们对此加以思考。这样，我们就得确定，在这种情况下，用“浪漫主义”这个名称是否还妥当。

而当我们碰到像“现实主义”，以及它的别称“批判现实主义”“社会现实主义”这样的词时，我们面对着一个谜。不管从意识形态上说是属于社会主义世界还是属于资本主义世界，专家们在过去的三十年里对这些词的含义一直争论不休。随着日丹诺夫主义的结束，也许可能在某一天看到他们达成一致。这一点在布达佩斯是以这种方式显示的：一些教授对卢卡契发表保留意见时，主要是抱怨这位理论家在拿巴尔扎克和托尔斯泰——唯一可敬的现实主义作家——与自然主义作家左拉作强烈对照时做得过火了（这使我回想起这位匈牙利批评家大约三十年前在我面前展示的类同的两个辉煌场面：《安娜·卡列尼娜》和《娜娜》中的赛马场面；自然主义遭到痛斥，而现实主义得到赞许）；而且，一些民主德国和波兰的比较学者已经认识到，“现实主义”这个词被滥用了、歪曲了，已经失去了一切意味。路易·阿拉贡不久前在布拉格发表的演讲也许与这种令人庆幸的逆转不无关系；路易·阿拉贡于 1953 年在西欧创立了“社会现实主义”的理论，而到 1962 年，他作出了对这个问题的重新思考，这为他赢得了声誉，鉴于这一点，人们可以认为，全世界的比较学者在每个术语的规定含义方面将能够很快获得统一；这并非是天真幼稚的想法。

（于永昌，等. 比较文学研究译文集[M]. 戴耘，译. 上海：上海译文出版社，1985.）

【延伸阅读】

1. Steiner, George. 何为比较文学[M]//*No Passion Spent*. New Haven: Yale University Press, 1996:142-159.

《何为比较文学》一文收录在乔治·斯坦纳的散文集《未耗尽的激情》中，该文是作者多年教学及研究的思想核心。在文章中，作者开门见山地点出“比较”在人文艺术学科的重要性，但同时否认了现行的比较文学“方法论”，他认为“方法论”只有在科学领域有确凿的意义和可证伪的标准，但在人文学科领域却难以实现。因此，作为学科的比较文学应关注三个领域，首先是翻译研究，其次是文本在时空中的传播与接受，最后是主题研究。作者强调，只有在比较文学学科领域，这三方面才会形成创造性的互动。

2. 曹顺庆. 比较文学学科史[M]. 成都：巴蜀书社，2010.

全书分三编，内容主要涵盖比较文学学科发展的三个阶段。第一编关注以“法国学派”为代表的影响研究时期，同时涉及德、英、俄等国的比较文学发展状况。第二编聚焦以“美国学派”为代表的平行研究时期，同时介绍了平行研究的特点及局限。第三编侧重以“中国学派”为代表的跨文明研究时期，主要探讨了中国和日本等国家或地区，在面对比较文学学科中存在的“西方中心主义”倾向，所作出的积极回应。书中特别提到了比较文学的“史前史”，论述了在比较文学学科形成之前，存在于不同国家文化史中的比较渊源和方法。

3. H. J. Schulz, P. H. Rhein. *Comparative Literature: The Early Years* [M]. North Carolina: The University of North Carolina Press, 1973.

舒尔茨和雷因主编的《早期比较文学论文集》是一本侧重于比较文学资料汇编的论文集。书中主要收录了比较文学渊源和发展时期的相关资料，对比较文学学科建设提供资料和史实方面的支持。值得一提的是，书中收录了 7 段歌德对“世界文学”的论述。尽管歌德最早提出“世界文学”，但其有关探讨均散落在论著、书信、对话和日记中,这本书的出现很好地弥补了这一缺憾。这7段短论除了一篇出自J.P.艾克曼的《歌德谈话录》之外,其余6篇均摘自《歌德全集》,在一定程度上还原了歌德对"世界文学"的构思和探讨。

第二节　比较文学的发展阶段

从比较文学作为一门学科出现以来,贯穿整个比较文学发展史的一个核心问题就是这门学科的命名困难,以及由此而来的对于这门学科研究范围的界定及其方法论。换言之,比较文学发展的三大标志性时期:欧洲阶段、美洲阶段与亚洲阶段,都始终面临这样的问题,由于各学派立场与研究旨趣各异,他们也分别给出了自己的答案。而这一节所选三篇文献也充分说明了这一点。巴登斯贝格文章的英译名与韦勒克的文章如出一辙,张隆溪所总结的钱锺书有关比较文学的讨论,在题目上就澄清"比较文学"与"文学比较"这一比较文学学科最易让人产生的误会。

一、欧洲阶段

尽管比较文学的历史在西方文化体系中可以追溯到古罗马时期,但是作为一门近代学科而诞生,法国学派功不可没。这个学派的一系列代表人物,都前赴后继的为比较文学获得其学科独立性而努力。法国学派的特征一般被概括为"影响研究",即法国作为一个文学大国对于其他欧洲国家或其他文明体系的文学所产生的影响。影响研究立足于文学传播、接受的事实基础上,更接近于文学史研究。其代表人物包括巴登斯贝格,他创办了《比较文学评论》这份法国最重要的比较文学杂志,先后在法国和美国教学,在研究方法上始终强调论证的科学性与明晰性,并一直坚持编撰比较文学书目索引;梵・第根(Paul Van Tiegehm,1871—1948)则在其经典论著《比较文学论》中全面阐述了法国学派观点,其中包括对比较文学的学科价值的强调:比较应摆脱美学的含义而取得科学的含义,提出将文学研究划分为国别文学、比较文学、总体文学三大范畴;卡雷(Jean-Marie Carré,1887—1958)对于比较文学的定义,更为强调国别文学之间的"精神联系",并开创了法国学派的一个崭新领域——形象学;基亚(Marius

François Guyard，1921—　）的观点则对其学术前辈的理论进行了某种糅合，认为比较文学的研究领域既包括媒介学、文类学、主题学，又包括国别文学彼此之间的精神联系。重视事实联系固然是法国学派最明显的特征，但绝非法国学派的全部。从以上的简短介绍即可看出，它充满活力，一直在不停地探索新的研究领域；更为重要的是，法国学派在其发展进程中始终关注的一个问题就是争取比较文学的学科独立性，即它特定的研究领域、特定的方法论，以及与之密切相关的比较文学的学科价值，为比较文学的学科发展作出了巨大贡献。韦勒克认为法国学派在进行着类似“文学外贸”的学术活动，这样的讽刺是有失偏颇的。

二、美洲阶段

第二次世界大战以后，美国成为比较文学研究的中心。1952 年《比较文学与总体文学年鉴》在美国创刊，按年总结比较文学发展的成绩与问题。1962 年，美国比较文学学会正式成立。以韦勒克与雷马克为代表的美国学派，既开启了比较文学发展的新阶段，也开拓了这一学科新的研究领域。韦勒克与沃伦合著的《文学理论》一书，曾将文学研究分为三大领域：文学史、文学理论与文学批评。虽然这三大领域之间有所重合，但它们之间的区别更为明显。法国学派已经明确宣布他们的研究是文学史研究的一个分支；而美国学派的研究更倾向于文学理论。韦勒克的代表性论战文章《比较文学的危机》是美国学派崛起的标志之一。文章题目其实不尽准确与完整，作者想说的并非是比较文学这一学科走到了尽头，他针对的完全是法国学派实证主义的方法论，巴登斯贝格在美国教书时受到的排斥就充分说明了这一点：他的美国同行完全不能欣赏他对考证的专注，反而认为这种烦琐的考证会损害这门学科。法国学派从肇始之初就强调比较文学研究的科学性，被其明确拒之门外的美学，在深受新批评理论影响的美国学派这里却大受欢迎。与重视事实联系的法国学派不同，美国的比较文学学者更注重的是对无事实联系的文学现象进行比较，由此论证文学的某些普遍性规律。

美国学派的代表人物分别是韦勒克、雷马克（Henry H. H. Remak，1916—2009）与奥尔德里奇（Alfrod Owen Aldriage，1915—2005）。韦勒克本人就是新批评的代表之一，而新批评的主张是注重文本细读与文本审美特质的发掘，并认为这是真正深入文学内部、有关文学的本质性研究。除了本节所选取的文章之外，上文提到的韦勒克与沃伦的《文学理论》一书中也有不少章节是有关比较文学的。另一位重要学者雷马克所写的《比较文学的定义与功用》（*Comparative Literature: Its Definition and Function*）一文被广为引用，该文甚至被美国学派奉为圭臬。虽然这篇文章在题目上和巴登斯贝格和韦勒克的文章很像,但他的文风与内容都与韦勒克大相径庭。韦勒克在语言上得天独厚的优势淋漓尽致地反映在他的文章之中,他详尽地考察“比较”与“文学”二词渊源;而雷马克的文章则更为实际地针对美国学派的具体研究领域,除了法国学派所开辟的国别文学间的研究之外,他特别开辟“跨学科”这一全新疆域,法国学派所固守的两国之间的文学关系(大部分情况下仅仅指法国和其他某个国家)的研究,就这样被拓展到多国别文学之间与学科之间。简言之,美国的比较文学研究具有他们的法国同行所没有的理论雄心:通过这样的研究途径来探知文学的本质和普遍性规律。美国学派的终极问题正是文学是什么而不是比较文学是什么;奥尔德里奇的贡献则在于,将美国学派标志性的研究方式“平行研究”详加定义,并在研究方法上倡导注重文学的审美性与精神性特征的阐释学、符号学等理论。美国学派的崛起与发展,同时也是比较文学学科本身的重要发展阶段。比较文学研究的两大研究领域:多国别间文学研究与跨学科研究也由此确立。尽管有学者指出,美国学派的研究范围过于宽泛以至于有消弭学科界限的危险,但应该看到,看似宽泛的研究有一个共同的旨归:文学的特性或本质。不过,进行平行研究要特别注意进行研究对象之间的“可比性”论证。

三、亚洲阶段

从20世纪70年代以来,比较文学学界有一批新的学者加入,他们既包括在美国、加拿大工作的一些华裔学者,如刘若愚(James J. Y. Liu,1926—1986)、叶维廉(1937—)和余宝琳(Pauline Yu,1949—)等,也包括中国内地以及港澳台的一些学者。对于在海外工作的华裔学者而言,中西比较是一项必须承担的工作:如果他们要对读者或学生讲解中国文学,势必要使用西方语言特别是英语去言说中国传统文学;另外,由于这样的言说让他们处于一个中西之间的位置,他们获得了一种前所未有的视野,这种视野是那些隶属于欧洲文化圈的比较文学学者所没有的,也是中国传统文学的学者所没有的。这种特殊的处境,既为他们的理论探索带来极端的困难,也为他们的工作带来意想不到的张力与生机。比较文学学科本身也由此获得了全新的发展。其中刘若愚出版于1975年的《中国文学理论》(*Chinese Theories of Literature*)一书,在研究旨趣上和美国学派的平行研究是完全符合的,但是由于他是根据艾布拉姆斯的四要素对中国文学理论分别进行梳理,首先就预设了艾布拉姆斯理论的普适性,以及在中国传统语境中也有“文学理论”。这些不足之处都受到了后继学者的批评。但这充分说明了中西比较是一个全新的领域,美国学派固有的方法已经远远不能适应这一领域的复杂性。刘若愚的著作开启了中西之间的对话,尽管这种对话是不充分的,是以一方的强势与另一方的迎合为代价。叶维廉的《比较诗学》一书提出“文化模子”理论,显然意识到了刘若愚的局限,更强调不同文学本身的文化立场,对中西比较中的“西方中心主义”更为警惕。但过于强调中国文学与西方文学的异质性,又难免有矫枉过正之嫌。在这一批海外华裔学者的带动之下,又有相当数量的欧美学者投入了中国文学研究的领域,如宇文所安(Stephen Owen)、苏源熙(Haun Saussy)、浦安迪(Andrew H. Plaks)等人。

中国比较文学的发展肇始于20世纪初。由于特定的历史语境,西方文化在当时的权威地位,当时学者的研究方式多为“以西释中”,并借以探究民族兴衰之症结,如王国维的《红楼梦评论》一文。这一阶段的中西比较远非单纯的学术研究,其背后有当时中国知识分子为传统把脉问诊的深切焦虑:中国文化到底在哪里出了问题?这绝非一个学理性问题,因为它蕴含了一个基本预设:西方文化就是人类文化发展的必然方向。为这种焦虑支配的中西研究不仅缺乏学术研究所要求的客观公允,更以西方文学为标准,提出了很多伪问题,如中国为何没有悲剧,中国为何没有史诗等。这些伪问题日后以不同的形式出现在很多当代西方学者的著述之中,可谓“西方中心主义”在中国学者身上自觉的发生与呈现。

在这种语境下,钱锺书先生于1948年出版的《谈艺录》显得非常独特。首先是这部著作的写作方式:它以传统诗话的形式写成。这种写作方式,早已为深受西方文化影响的同代学者所不取;殊为可惜的是,在以后的中国比较文学研究史上也未曾再出现过。不仅空前,也可谓绝后。这部著作的独特之处还在于:广涉欧美文学理论,借以谈论中国古典诗歌。这本著作昭示出中西诗学对话的一种范式,一种以中国文学为本位的、深入且无隔膜的对话。这场对话的成功在于,钱锺书先生对于中国传统文化的信心,并将自身的写作毫无顾虑地置于这一传统之中。由于这种信心,以及与这种传统的紧密关系,这部著作尽显学术写作的雍容优雅,不仅没有王国维等学者的焦虑症,也没有困扰后来学者的“失语”问题。

中西文化之间的异质性远远超过了相似性,透过纷繁复杂的文学现象而直接深入文学理论的比较研究是中西比较的一条可行的途径。比较诗学就是比较文学学科亚洲阶段的突出成果,其代表性学者有王元化、杨周翰、张隆溪、曹顺庆等。如前文所述,可比性问题在美洲阶段已经成为一个焦点,在中西比较的领域中更是学者们必须加以论证的首要问题。但这种“可比性”问题,并非单纯地针对两个具体的研究对象或个案,而是指中西文化传统之中有关文学的讨论,是否可以形成对话。上文中提到的余宝琳等学者就曾经指出,即使是 Literature 这一西方概念也不能直接与中文的“文学”一词画等号,因为两者都因其地域、时间的不同而形成不同体系。但是这样一种强调中国文学特质的观点，在逻辑上也有很大的漏洞：无论西方的 Literature，还是中国的"文学"，都并非是一个普适性的概念，而仅仅是歌德所谈论的"世界文学"中的一个分支而已。尽管一个普适性的文学概念还有待对各个不同传统的文学现象详加研究，但是人们仍然能够在"世界文学"的框架之下谈论中西诗学。当然，比较文学的亚洲阶段不仅仅包括中西诗学，还包括中国与其他国家的文学关系史研究，如季羡林的《中印文化关系史论文集》，也自然包括亚洲其他国家，如日本、韩国在比较文学领域所取得的成就。

以上是对比较文学学科发展的一个简单概述。从上文列出的欧洲阶段、美洲阶段与亚洲阶段可以看出，作为一门学科的比较文学极具活力，在不断拓宽其研究领域的过程中焕发新的生机。与韦勒克划定的文学史、文学理论与文学批评三大传统的文学研究领域不一样，比较文学可谓文学研究中最具问题意识的学科。三大阶段的发展，既是比较文学学科史的一部分，也是世界各国学者面对比较文学这一崭新的研究领域作出不同应对的一个过程。无论是法国学者强调的不同民族文学间的影响研究，美国学者强调的平行研究与跨学科研究，还是中国学者努力耕耘的中西比较诗学的跨文化对话研究，每个阶段的发起人都有自身特定的文化立场与文化语境，这使得他们在投身比较文学研究时不能因循老路，不能人云亦云，说他人的语言，而是要在"对话"中发出自己的声音。随着参与者越来越多，或许比较文学的研究终将汇成世界各文学、文化传统的多声部合唱，人们对于"文学"，甚至对于人类本身的精神文明，也终将获得越来越深透的认识。这一前景是可以预期的，因为伴随着这门极具特质的学科发展进程的正是研究者们视野的不断拓宽：从法国到其他某个国家到多国家之间（西方文化传统），再到亚洲与欧洲之间。这门学科的中国参与者们还将在从事中西比较或中印、中日、中韩比较的过程中，不断地返回自身的文化传统，就自我的文化归属做重新的打量与思考。

【原典选读】

比较文学：名称与实质（节选）

◉巴登斯贝格

【导读】巴登斯贝格（Fernand Baldensperger，1871—1958）是比较文学法国学派的奠基者之一。《比较文学：名称与实质》（*The Name and Nature of Comparative Literature*，原文为法文），代表的是比较文学学科发展的欧洲阶段。该文是巴登斯贝格为《比较文学评论》的创刊号撰写的发刊词。由于"比较文学"作为一门学科的名称不尽精确，容易让人产生误解，他特别强调了作为一门学科的比较文学的独立性：缺乏“论证的明晰性”的文学比较是完全不值得认真对待的。比较的目的在于揭示某些不易为人察觉的文学间的关系，而这些文学间的关系则是文学史的重要环节，这构成了比较文学的学科独立性。巴登斯贝格还特别提出一种危险的比较：在民族主义的情感下抬高本国的文学创作，并在国别文学之间树立屏障，阻碍彼此的沟通与了解。显然，他推崇的是一种超越了国别界限的文化观，希望人们能用赫尔德与维柯的将人类文明成果视为一个整体的精神，客观地研究文学之间的关系史。显然，巴登斯贝格并没有美国学者攻击“法国学派”的法国中心主义，反而具备的是超越了小国范围的“欧洲主义”的情感。■

一

……仅仅对两个不同的对象同时看上一眼就作比较，仅仅靠记忆和印象的拼凑，靠一些主观臆想把可能游移不定的东西扯在一起来找点类似点，这样的比较绝不可能产生论证的明晰性。……

三

人们不厌其烦地进行“比较”，难免出现那种没有价值的对比；在这一百五十年里，人们比较了什么？怎么比较？在那些习惯的方法——美学批评、教条主义的批评、心理分析批评、历史批评和编年史的方法——之侧，比较文学以怎样的形象出现呢？有时她被认为有野心，不知趣；有时她被迫沉默寡言，但是她的姐姐们从来没有能够把她变成“灰姑娘”。从十八世纪末开始，无论在文学实践还是在文学理论的历史范围内，这方面都已发生某种奇异而有教益的演变。

起初大多数的情况是这样：爱国主义的敏感性把原来学说上、习惯上和趣味上的对立情况加深了。国别文学一被唤醒，意大利人、法兰西人、德国人和英国人，各自玩弄了一种归根结蒂为了鼓励本国文学创作的手段，今天，当这些作品开出丰硕果实的时候，他们又尖刻地将它们的价值进行比较，而这些价值又往往是无法估量的，他们这样做是为了证明什么？证明莎士比亚的成就高于或低于高乃依；证明现代的古典主义是否真正的古典主义；证明法兰西人绝不可能了解但丁。……赫尔德和维柯，他们将文艺复兴以来从未被人遗忘的思想明确起来，把各国人民的语言、文学和精神状态当作一个整体来看待，因而有机地用一些决定因素来制约精神生活，通过这样的方法，把比较工作从由于人们的偏爱而把它作为理由和论据的贫乏的教条主义之中拯救出来。从那以后，人们就可以用历史的批评方法对文学现象进行比较和对照……因此，艺术的相对性（随着它的广泛运用，创作的活力能从中得到鼓励）能在1880年取得胜利，就是由于人们对比较作出了新的努力。

在斯达尔夫人、贡斯当、司汤达、《地球》杂志、歌德和曼佐尼那里都显示了这种努力；同时被日益激起的“环境”决定论，也逼使艺术史接受那些不严谨的系统化理论。……

四

……虽然丹纳某些无可争议的真理和若干非常鲜明的观点仍可得到保留，但是他的主要理论已被削弱。居约的“美学情感”，B. 克罗齐所偏爱的“艺术表达”的优越性，用他们自己的方法，后来都有助于文学可能性更灵活的观点获得自由的发展。然而，为了解释文学现象，布吕纳介却重新采用了若干已经陈述过的观点，并将它们用一种严密的逻辑武装起来，提出了他的体裁演变的理论。这个理论将各民族集团重新活动起来并相互沟通；它假设有一个欧洲整体，这一整体主要组成部分之间确实能够相互发生影响，尤其是靠一些比种族和环境的狭窄决定论更高的形式。在这里，“时代”因素变得那么严厉，以致只需丹纳理论中的第三要素，差不多就足以让文学发生“演变”。这一活动，是为了体现“体裁”存在，它的范围远不限于单独一个国家，而是在各国文学之间建立依附关系，因此，如果谈到悲剧体裁的演变，可将意大利对法国的影响写上一章，如果论及历史小说，可写上英国对法国的影响……

毋庸置疑，这种文学上的达尔文主义，在一种单一的流传范围之内可以起作用，也常常得到证实；但是这里所引证的生存竞争，必然导致一种体裁通过借用或竞争加强它的生存力。

五

从那时起比较文学就出现了两种主要方向，这两种主要的活动能够开阔人们的视野，打破了以传统研究为天经地义的偏见，那种传统的研究，只着眼于一系列具有象征意义的名篇巨著。

其中一个方向在我国以加斯东·帕里斯为主要代表，外国的学者也极感兴趣，这一研究致力于将文学赖以生存的各种主题归并为单纯的传统要素……

另一种研究方向是在一系列国家的文学作品之间展开并明确那些显而易见的相互关系；在某些趣味、表达方式、体裁和情感演变之中，它要发现一些借用的现象，并确定大作家所受的外来影响。……

探讨文学“主题”的起源和最初含义怎样？……从本质上来说，这种比较文学着眼点是在于追溯一些简单的形式，而不是去发掘和确定一种独特的创造性，无疑地，它是在美学中，表达方式的个性权再次受到肯定的时候，去孜孜以求若干被人所遗弃的成分……

……应该是，除了让体裁发生“演变”（简单地说就是变化）之外，还要让观点、读者、“对象”和“主题”统统来一个“演变”，这样才能取得与过去的事实比较接近的看法。P. 布尔热曾经注意到，一部作品过了二十年，就不再是原来的作品了，这种看法有一定的道理。仅仅从这一考虑出发，“运动”——布吕纳介明确地感到在回忆往事时，必须让形式和思想的生命受制于它——才有可能不至于过分地歪曲事实真相。……

于是比较文学渐渐地成了一种“遗传学”，一种艺术的形态学；我所要说的是，它拒绝接受一切已被肯定的作品和已有的声望，更加有意识地将自己置身于后台，而不是在剧场里……

六

……同样，在我看来，这就是“新人文主义”的准备工作，在今天还支配着我们的危机过去以后，比较文学的广泛实践尤其可以促成这种“新人文主义”：“比较主义”的努力所要达到的，是一种仲裁，一种清算，它将为新的、人道的、有生命的、文明的信念开辟道路，我们的这个世纪是能够再次做到这一步的。……

（于永昌，等. 比较文学研究译文集[M]. 徐鸿，译，王坚良，校. 上海：上海译文出版社，1985：31-48.）

比较文学的名称与实质

◉韦勒克

【导读】美国学派的杰出代表韦勒克（René Wellek，1903—1995），捷克裔美国人，当代著名的文学理论家、批评史家和比较文学家，曾任耶鲁大学比较文学教授，美国比较文学协会和国际比较文学协会主席。他的《比较文学的名称与性质》（*The Name and Nature of Comparative Literature*）一文，代表的是比较文学学科发展的美洲阶段。本段节选自该文的英文原文。本文显示了作者渊博的学识与高超的语言能力，他宣称自己采用的研究方法为词典编纂学和历史语义学，实际上就是采用了共时与历时的方式，对于本学科名称所涉及的几个关键词 comparative、literature 以及 comparative literature 详加考辨，如文学一词在法语中很长时间都指的是“文学研究”，分析它们在西方各主要文化传统中的历史演变；另外，文中还深入分析了法国学派的代表人物基亚所提出的一些重要范畴：Comparative Literature、Universal Literature、International literature、General literature 及 World literature，整篇文章理路清晰，以语言学上的多重证据不容置疑地论证了比较文学学科名称足以成立。作者的渊博学识则表现在对本学科发展史的全面细致的掌握上。如果想要知道比较文学史上的诸多“第一”：第一位使用比较这个词的作家、第一个以比较文学为书名的著作、第一位使用“比较文学”这一术语的学者、开设这门课程的第一位教授等，都能够在这篇文章中找到答案。这篇文章成为比较文学学科史上的名篇是有着充分理由的。■

The term "comparative literature" has given rise to so much discussion, has been interpreted so differently and misinterpreted so frequently, that it might be useful to examine its history and to attempt to distinguish its meanings in the main languages. Only then can we hope to define its exact scope and content. Lexicography, "historical semantics," will be our starting point. Beyond it, a brief history of comparative studies should lead to conclusions of contemporary relevance. "Comparative literature" is still a controversial discipline and idea.

There seem no particular problems raised by our two words individually. "Comparative" occurs in Middle English, obviously derived from Latin *comparativus*. It is used by Shakespeare, as when Falstaff denounces Prince Hal as "the most comparative, rascalliest, sweet young prince," Francis Meres, as early as 1598, uses the term in the caption of "A Comparative Discourse of Our English Poets with the Greek, Latin and Italian Poets." The adjective occurs in the titles of several seventeenth—and eighteenth-century books. In 1602 William Fulbecke published *A Comparative Discourse of the Laws*. I also find *A Comparative Anatomy of Brute Animals* in 1765. Its author, John Gregory, published *A Comparative View of the State and Faculties of Man with Those of the Animal World* in the very next year. Bishop Robert Lowth in his Latin *Lectures on the Sacred Poetry of the Hebrews* (1753), formulated the ideal of comparative study well enough: "We must see all things with their eyes [i. e. the ancient Hebrews]: estimate all things by their opinions; we must endeavor as much as possible to read Hebrew as the Hebrews would have read it. We must act as the Astronomers with regard to that branch of their science which is called comparative who, in order to form a more perfect idea of the general system and its different parts, conceive themselves as passing through, and surveying, the whole universe, migrating from one planet to another and becoming for a short time inhabitants of each." In his pioneering *History of English Poetry* Thomas Warton announced in the Preface to the first volume that he would present "a comparative survey of the poetry of other nations." George Ellis, in his *Specimens of Early English Poets* (1790), speaks of antiquaries whose "ingenuity has often been successful in detecting and extracting by comparative criticism many particulars respecting the state of society and the progress of arts and manners" from medieval chronicles. In 1800 Charles Dibdin published, in five volumes, *A Complete History of the English Stage, Introduced by a Comparative and Comprehensive Review of the Asiatic, the Grecian, the Roman, the Spanish, the Italian, the Portuguese, the German, the French and Other Theatres*. Here the main idea is fully formulated, but the combination "comparative literature" itself seems to occur for the first time only in a letter by Matthew Arnold in 1848, where he says: "How plain it is now, though an attention to the comparative literatures for the last fifty years might have instructed *anyone* of it, that England is in a certain sense far behind the Continent." But this was a private letter not published till 1895, and "comparative" means here hardly more than "comparable." In English the decisive use was that of Hutcheson Macaulay Posnett, an Irish barrister who later became Professor of Classics and English Literature at University College, Auckland, New Zealand, who put the term on the title of his book in 1886. As part of Kegan Paul, Trench, and Trübner's International Scientific Series, the book aroused some attention and was, e. g., favorably reviewed by William Dean Howells. Posnett, in an article, "The Science of Comparative Literature," claimed "to have first stated and illustrated the method and principles of the new science, and to have been the first to do so not only in the British Empire but in the world." Obviously this is preposterous, even if we limit "comparative literature" to the specific meaning Posnett gave to it. The English term cannot be discussed in isolation from analogous terms in France and Germany.

The lateness of the English term can be explained if we realize that the combination "comparative literature" was resisted in English, because the term "literature" had lost its earlier meaning of "knowledge or study of literature" and had come to mean "literary production in general" or "the body of writings in a period, country, or region." That this long process is complete today is obvious from such a fact that, e. g., Professor Lane Cooper of Cornell University refused to call the department he headed in the twenties "Comparative Literature" and insisted on "The Comparative Study of Literature." He considered it a "bogus term" that "makes neither sense nor syntax." "You might as well permit yourself to say 'comparative potatoes' or 'comparative husks.'" But in earlier English usage "literature" means "learning" and "literary culture," particularly a knowledge of Latin. *The Tatler* reflects sagely in 1710: "It is in vain for folly to attempt to conceal itself by the refuge of learned languages. Literature does but make a man more eminently the thing which nature made him." Boswell says, for instance, that Baretti was an "Italian of considerable literature." This usage survived into the nineteenth century, when James Ingram gave an inaugural lecture on the *Utility of Anglo-Saxon Literature* (1807), meaning the "utility of our knowing Anglo-Saxon," or when John Petherham wrote *An Historical Sketch of the Progress and Present State of AngloSaxon Literature in England* (1840), where "literature" obviously must mean the study of literature. But these were survivals; "literature" had assumed by then the present meaning of a body of writing. The *Oxford English Dictionary* gives the first occurrence in 1812, but this is far too late: rather, the modern usage penetrated in the later eighteenth century from France.

Actually, the meaning of "literature" as "literary production" or "a body of writings" revived a usage of late antiquity. Earlier *literatura* in Latin is simply a translation of the Greek *grammatike* and sometimes means a knowledge of reading and writing or even an inscription or the alphabet itself. But Tertullian (who lived from about A. D. 160 to 240) and Cassian contrast secular literature with scriptural, pagan with Christian, *literatura* with *scriptura*.

This use of the term reemerges only in the thirties of the eighteenth century in competition with the term *literae*, *lettres*, *letters*. An early example is François Granet's series *Réflexions sur les ouvrages de littérature* (1736-1740). Voltaire, in *Le Siècle de Louis. XIV* (1751), under the chapter heading "Des Beaux Arts," uses *littérature* with an uncertain reference alongside "eloquence, poets, and books of morals and amusement," and elsewhere in the book he speaks of "littérature légère" and "les genres de littérature" cultivated in Italy. In 1759 Lessing began to publish his *Briefe die neueste Literatur betreffend*, where literature clearly refers to a body of writings. That the usage was still unusual at that time may be illustrated from the fact that Nicolas Trublet's *Essais sur divers sujets de littérature et morale* (1735-1754) were translated into German as *Versuche über verschiedene Gegenstände der Sittenlehre und Gelehrsamkeit* (1776).

This use of the word "literature" for all literary production, which is still one of our meanings, was in the eighteenth century soon nationalized and localized. It was applied to

French, German, Italian, and Venetian literature, and almost simultaneously the term often lost its original inclusiveness and was narrowed down to mean what we would today call "imaginative literature," poetry, and imaginative, fictive prose. The first book which exemplifies this double change is, as far as I know, Carlo Denina's *Discorso sopra le vicende della letteratura*(1760). Denina professes not to speak "of the progress of the sciences and arts, which are not properly a part of literature"; he will speak of works of learning only when they belong to "good taste, and to eloquence, that is to say, to literature." The Preface of the French translator speaks of Italian, English, Greek, and Latin literature. In 1774 there appeared an *Essai sur la littérature russe* by N. Novikov in Leghorn, and we have a sufficiently local reference in Mario Foscarini's *Storia della letteratura veneziana* (1752). The process of nationalization and, if I may use the term, aesthetization of the word is beautifully illustrated by A. de Giorgi-Bertòla's *Idea della letteratura alemanna* (Lucca, 1784), which is an expanded edition of the earlier *Idea della poesia alemanna* (Naples, 1779), where the change of title was forced by his inclusion of a report on German novels. In German the term *Nationalliteratur* focuses on the nation as the unit of literature: it appears for the first time in the title of Leonhard Meister's *Beyträge zur Geschichte der teutschen Sprache und Nationalliteratur* (1777) and persists into the nineteenth century. Some of the best known German literary histories carry it in the title: Wachler, Koberstein, Gervinus in1835, and later A. Vilmar and R. Gottschall.

But the aesthetic limitation of the term was for a long time strongly resented. Philarète Chasles, for example, comments in 1847:"I have little esteem for the word 'literature'; it seems to me meaningless, it is a result of intellectual corruption." It seems to him tied to the Roman and Greek tradition of rhetoric. It is "something which is neither philosophy, nor history, nor erudition, nor criticism-something I know not what: vague, impalpable, and elusive." Chasles prefers "intellectual history" to "literary history."

In English the same process took place. Sometimes it is still difficult to distinguish between the old meaning of literature as literary culture and a reference to a body of writing. Thus, as early as 1755, Dr. Johnson wanted to found *Annals of Literature, Foreign as well as Domestick*. In 1761 George Colman, the elder, thought that "Shakespeare and Milton seem to stand alone, like first rate authors, amid the general wreck of old English Literature." In 1767 Adam Ferguson included a chapter, "Of the History of Literature," in his *Essay on the History of Civil Society*. In 1774 Dr. Johnson, in a letter, wished that "what is undeservedly forgotten of our antiquated literature might be revived," and John Berkenhout in 1777 subtitled his *Biographia Literaria, A Biographical History of Literature*, in which he proposed to give a "conscise view of the rise and progress of literature."The Preface to De La Curne de Sainte-Palaye's *Literary History of the Troubadours*, translated in 1779 by Mrs. Susanna Dobson, speaks of the troubadours as "the fathers of modern literature," and James Beattie in 1783 wants to trace the rise and progress of romance in order to shed light upon "the history and politics, the manners and the literature of these latter ages." There were books such as William Rutherford's *A View of Ancient History, Including the Progress of Literature, and the Fine Arts (1788)*, *Sketches of a History of literature* by Robert Alves(1794), and *An Introduction to the Literary History of the 14th and 15th Centuries* (1798), by Andrew Philpot, which complains that "there is nothing more wanting in English literature" than "a history of the revival of letters." But we may be surprised to hear that the first book with the title *A History of English Language and Literature* was a little handbook by Robert Chambers in 1836 and that the first Professor of English Language and Literature was the Reverend Thomas Dale, at University College, London, in 1828.

Thus the change in meaning of the term "literature" hindered in English the adoption of the term "comparative literature," while "comparative politics," prominently advocated by the historian E. A. Freeman in 1873, was quite acceptable, as was "comparative grammar," which appeared on the title page of a translation of Franz Bopp's *Comparative Grammar of Sanskrit*, *Zend*, *Greek*, *etc.*, in 1844.

In France the story was different; there littérature for a long time preserved the meaning of literary study. Voltaire, in his unfinished article on *Littérature* for his *Dictionnaire philosophique* (1764-1772), defines literature as "a knowledge of the works of taste, a smattering of history, poetry, eloquence, and criticism," and he distinguishes it from "la belle littérature," which relates to "objects of beauty, to poetry, eloquence and well-written history." Voltaire's follower, Jean-François Marmontel, who wrote the main literary articles for the great *Encyclopédie*, which were collected as *Eléments de littérature* (1787), clearly uses *littérature* as meaning "a knowledge of *belles lettres*," which he contrasts with erudition. "With wit, talent and taste," he avows, "one can produce ingenious works, without any erudition, and with little literature." Thus it was possible early in the nineteenth century to form the combination *littérature comparée*, which was apparently suggested by Cuvier's famous *Anatomie comparée* (1800) or Degérando's *Historie comparée des systèmes de philosophie* (1804). In 1816 two compilers, Noël and Laplace, published a series of anthologies from French, classical, and English literature with the otherwise unused and unexplained title page: *Cours de littérature comparée.* Charles Pougens, in *Lettres philosophiques à Madame xxx sur divers sujets de morale et littérature* (1826), complained that there is no work on the principles of literature he can recommend: "un cours de littérature comme je l'entends, c'est-à-dire, un cours de littérature comparée."

The man, however, who gave the term currency in France was undoubtedly Abel-François Villemain, whose course in eighteenth-century literature was a tremendous success at the Sorbonne in the late twenties. It was published in 1828-1829 as *Tableau de la littéature française au XVIIIe siècle* in 4 volumes, with even the flattering reactions of the audience inserted ("Vifs applaudissements. On rit."). There he uses several times *tableau comparé*, *études comparées*, *histoire comparée*, but also *littérature comparée* in praising the Chancelier Daguesseau for his "vastes études de philosophie, d'histoire, de littérature comparée." In the second lecture series, *Tableau de la littéature au moyen age en France*, *en Italie*, *en Espagne et en Angleterre* (2 volumes, 1830), he speaks again of "amateurs de la littérature comparée," and in the Preface to the new edition in 1840, Villemain, not incorrectly, boasts that here for the first time in a French university an attempt at an "analyse comparée" of several modern literatures was made.

After Villemain the term was used fairly frequently. Philarète Chasles delivered an inaugural lecture at the Athénée in 1835: in the printed version in the *Revue de Paris*, the course is called "Littérature étrangère comparée." Adolphe-Louis de Puibusque wrote a two-volume *Histoire comparée de la littérature française et espagnole* (1843), where he quotes Villemain, the perpetual Secretary of the French Academy, as settling the question. The term *comparative*, however, seems to have for a time competed with *comparée*. J.-J. Ampère, in his *Discours sur l'histoire* de la poésie (1830), speaks of "l'histoire comparative des arts et de la littérature" but later also uses the other term in the title of his *Histoire de la littérature française au moyen age comparée aux littératures étrangères* (1841). The decisive text in favor of the term *littérature comparée* is in Sainte-Beuve's very late article, an obituary of Ampère, in the *Revue des deux mondes* in 1868.

(René Wellek, *Discriminations: Further Concepts of Criticism*, New Haven and London: Yale University Press, 1970.)

【研究范例】

钱锺书谈比较文学与文学比较（节选）

◉张隆溪

【导读】本文节选自著名学者张隆溪的《钱锺书谈比较文学与文学比较》，阐发的则是比较文学学科发展的亚洲阶段的思想方法。张隆溪是哈佛大学比较文学博士，瑞典皇家人文、历史及考古学院外籍院士，香港城市大学比较文学与翻译讲座教授，教育部长江学者。张隆溪早年在北京大学就读和工作期间，曾当面受教于杨周翰、钱锺书、朱光潜等著名学术大师，因而对钱先生关于比较文学的见解有深刻的领悟。《钱锺书谈比较文学与文学比较》一文梳理了钱先生关于比较文学性质与研究方法的真知灼见。全文脉络清晰，简单易读，篇幅较短。作为学贯中西的大家，钱锺书先生有关比较文学的论述处处结合中国比较文学新领域的开拓，比如近代史之前的中西交流，西方文学中所反映出来的中国元素，再如五四之后积极接受西方影响的中国文学创作也是比较文学的好题材；相比更为重要的领域则在于中西之间的翻译实践、翻译研究以及比较诗学。钱锺书先生尤为强调的是有关"比较文学"的实践性研究，希望学者不要仅仅停留在对中西比较的学理性的讨论上。■

比较文学在西方发展较早，它的史前史甚至可以追溯到古罗马时代，而作为一门学科，也从十九世纪三四十年代就开始在法国和德国逐渐形成。比较文学是超出个别民族文学范围的研究，因此不同国家文学之间的相互关系自然是典型的比较文学研究领域。从历史上来看，各国发展比较文学最先完成的工作之一，都是清理本国文学与外国文学的相互关系，研究本国作家与外国作家的相互影响。早期的法国学者强调 rapports de fait［实际联系］，德国学者强调研究 Vergleichende Literaturgeschichte［比较的文学史］，都说明了这种情况。钱锺书先生说他自己在著作里从未提倡过"比较文学"，而只应用过比较文学里的一些方法。"比较"是从事研究工作包括文学研究所必需的方法，诗和散文、古代文学和近代文学、戏剧和小说等，都可以用比较的方法去研究。“比较文学”作为一个专门学科，则专指跨越国界和语言界限的文学比较。钱先生认为，要发展我们自己的比较文学研究，重要任务之一就是清理一下中国文学与外国文学的相互关系。中外文化交流开始得很早，佛教在汉代已传入中国，而马可·波罗(Marco Polo，1254？——1324？)于元世祖时来中国，则标志着中西文化交流的一个重要阶段的开始。《马可·波罗游记》在西方发生巨大影响，在整个文艺复兴时代，它是西方最重要的、几乎是唯一重要的有关东方的记载。研究马可·波罗的权威学者本涅狄多(I. F. Benedetto)曾把马可·波罗的《游记》与但丁《神曲》和托马斯·阿奎那《神学总汇》(*Summa Theologica*)并举为中世纪文化的三大“总结”，并非过奖。在《神曲·天堂篇》第八章，但丁描写金星天里一个幸福的灵魂为欢乐之光辉包裹，如吐丝自缚的蚕，这个新奇比喻毫无疑问是来自中国文化的影响。……

外国文学对中国文学的影响，是还有大量工作可做的研究领域。自鸦片战争以来，西学东渐，严复、林纾的翻译在整个文化界都很有影响，而五四以后的新文化运动，更有意识地利用西方文化、包括俄国和东欧国家文学的外来影响冲击封建主义旧文化的“国粹”。鲁迅、郭沫若、茅盾、巴金、郁达夫、闻一多以及活跃在当时文坛上的许许多多作家、诗人和理论家，都从外国文学中吸取营养，做了大量翻译介绍外国文学的工作。郭沫若自己曾说他写诗受泰戈尔、歌德和惠特曼影响……因此，比较文学的影响研究不是来源出处的简单考据，而是通过这种研究认识文学作品在内容和形式两方面的特点和创新之处。

就中外文学，尤其是中西文学的比较而言，直接影响的研究毕竟是范围有限的领域，而比较文学如果仅仅局限于来源和影响、原因和结果的研究，按韦勒克(René Wellek)讥诮的说法，不过是一种文学“外贸”(the “foreign trade” of literatures)。比较文学的最终目的在于帮助我们认识总体文学(littérature générale)乃至人类文化的基本规律，所以中西文学超出实际联系范围的平行研究不仅是可能的，而且是极有价值的。这种比较唯其是在不同文化系统的背景上进行，所以得出的结论具有普遍意义。钱锺书先生认为文艺理论的比较研究即所谓比较诗学(comparative poetics)是一个重要而且大有可为的研究领域。如何把中国传统文论中的术语和西方的术语加以比较和互相阐发，是比较诗学的重要任务之一。……

各国文学要真正沟通，必须打破语言的障碍，所以文学翻译是必然的途径，也是比较文学所关注的一个重要方面。钱先生在《林纾的翻译》(见《旧文四篇》)一文中，对文学翻译问题提出了许多见解，认为“文学翻译的最高标准是‘化’。把作品从一国文字转变成另一国文字，既能不因语文习惯的差异而露出生硬牵强的痕迹，又能完全保存原有的风味,那就算得入于‘化境’”。钱先生在谈到翻译问题时,认为我们不仅应当重视翻译,努力提高译文质量,而且应当注意研究翻译史和翻译理论。在各国翻译史里,早期的译作往往相当于译述或改写,以求把外国事物变得尽量接近“国货”,以便本国读者容易理解和接受。严复译赫胥黎《天演论》,态度不可谓不严肃,“一名之立,旬月踟蹰”,但实际上加进了许多译者自己的阐释。林纾根本不懂外文,他的译作是根据别人的口述写成,遇到他认为原作字句意犹未尽的地方,往往根据自己作文标准和“古文义法”为原作者润笔甚至改写。英国十六、十七世纪的翻译,这种改译的例子也很多……

比较文学在我国真正引起学术界的普遍注意,可以说是最近几年内的事,而一旦大家注意起来,希望促其进一步发展的时候,对于比较文学的性质、内容、方法等理论问题,就有探讨的必要。钱锺书先生借用法国已故比较学者伽列(J. M. Carré)的话说:“比较文学不等于文学比较”(La littérature comparée n'est pas la comparaison littéraire)。意思是说,我们必须把作为一门人文学科的比较文学与纯属臆断、东拉西扯的牵强比附区别开来。……事实上,比较不仅在求其同,也在存其异,即所谓“对比文学”(contrastive literature)。正是在明辨异同的过程中,我们可以认识中西文学传统各自的特点。不仅如此,通过比较研究,我们应能加深对作家和作品的认识,对某一文学现象及其规律的认识,这就要求作品的比较与产生作品的文化传统、社会背景、时代心理和作者个人心理等因素综合起来加以考虑。换言之,文学之间的比较应在更大的文化背景中进行,考虑到文学与历史、哲学、心理学、语言学及其他各门学科的联系。因此,钱先生认为,向我国文学研究者和广大读者介绍比较文学的理论和方法,在大学开设比较文学导论课程,是目前急待进行的工作。同时,他又希望有志于比较文学研究的同志努力加深文学修养和理论修养,实际去从事具体的比较研究,而不要停留在谈论比较文学的必要性和一般原理上。正像哈利·列文(Harry Levin)所说那样,Nunc age:是时候了,去实际地把文学作比较吧。

(读书,1981(6):132-138.)

【延伸阅读】

1. Henry H. H. Remark. *Comparative Literature: Its Definition and Function* [M]. Carbondale: Southern Illinois University Press, 1961.

本文是亨利·雷马克,甚至是“美国学派”理论的核心所在。在文中,作者全面阐释了平行研究的立场,认为比较文学暂且还不是一个拥有严格规则的独立学科,而是一座把那些本质上有关,而表面上分开的各个领域联结起来的桥梁。因此,比较文学应从不同领域的方面来扩大研究范畴。文章探讨了民族文学、世界文学和总体文学的区分，并强调比较文学的研究者应该越过区分，多去涉猎别国文学或者和文学有关的其他领域。

2. 乌尔利希·韦斯坦因. 比较文学与文学理论[M]. 刘象愚，译. 沈阳：辽宁人民出版社，1987.

该书是韦斯坦因以1968年德文版的《比较文学导论》为基础删减、修改而成的。作者特别在序言中强调了变动的原委，指出德文版遵照克罗齐和韦勒克的观点，认为比较文学没有自己的方法论，只能作为文学史和文学理论的一个特殊分支。而在这本书中，他不仅修正了原来的观点，而且强调了比较文学的学科意义。全书共分七章，分别探讨了比较文学的定义、渊源、背景和方法论等相关问题。

第三节　比较文学的学科性质

比较文学作为一门独立的学科，已经有一百多年的历史，国内外学者曾对它做过多次界定，但至今仍没有一个为大家公认的科学定义。这不仅因为比较文学学科处在发展过程中，尚未建立一套严密的科学体系，更因为它是一门开放型、交叉型的学科，有许多界限始终困扰着学者，难于划定。

关于"什么是比较文学"的定义，在欧美学界的界定除以梵·第根等人为代表的法国学者、以韦勒克等人为代表的美国学者外，还有以波斯奈特等人为代表的英国学者。

波斯奈特在1886年出版的《比较文学》一书里，把比较文学界定为"文学进化的一般理论，即文学要经过产生、衰亡这样一个进化的过程"。他认为比较文学研究的顺序是"采用逐步扩展的方法，从氏族到城市，从城市到国家，从以上两种到世界大同"①。与波斯奈特的观点相似的，还有19世纪德国的豪普特、俄国的维谢洛夫斯基、英国的西蒙兹和法国的勃吕纳狄尔等。但由于进化论根本无法真正解释文学的复杂

① 干永昌，等，编译. 比较文学研究译文集[M]. 上海：上海译文出版社，1985：384.

发展历程，因此这种以进化论为理论基础的比较文学观随着进化论的衰落必然走向消亡。

“比较文学不是文学比较”，比较文学只关注各国文学的“关系”，是法国学派对比较文学性质的界定，也是该学派学科理论基础的奠基石。

法国学派的奠基人梵·第根在论述比较文学的性质时指出：“真正的‘比较文学’的性质正如一切历史科学的性质一样，是把尽可能多的来源不同的事实采纳在一起，以便充分地把每一个事实加以解释；它是扩大认识的基础，以便找到尽可能多的种种结果的原因。总之，‘比较’两个字应该摆脱全部美学的含义，而取得一个科学的含义。”“比较文学的目的，主要是研究不同文学之间的相互联系”，而不注重关系的所谓“比较”是片面的、不足取的。梵·第根认为：“那‘比较’是在于把那些从各国不同的文学中取得的类似的书籍、典型人物、场面、文章等并列起来，从而证明它们的不同之处，相似之处，而除了得到一种好奇的兴味，美学上的满足，以及有时得到一种爱好上的批判以至于高下等级的分别之外，是没有其他目标的。这样地实行‘比较’，养成鉴赏力和思索力是很有兴味而又很有用的，但却一点也没有历史的含义：它并没有由它本身的力量使人们向文学史推进一步。”①

法国学派的主要理论家马·法·基亚（M. F. Guyard）进一步论述了比较文学其综合目的是研究各国文学在精神方面的关系，“比较文学的对象是本质地研究各国文学作品的相互联系”，“凡是不存在关系的地方，比较文学的领域也就停止了”。因此，比较文学的学科立足点不是“比较”，而是“关系”，他指出：“比较文学实际只是一种被误称了的科学方法，正确的定义应该是：国际文学关系史。”②

对此，美国学者并不认可，他们专门针对法国学派的观点，强调比较文学研究应当回归文学，以美学为中心。

美国学派对比较文学的定义大致包括两个方面的内容：一是“超国界”的文学研究；二是文学与其他学科的关系的研究。

雷马克认为：“比较文学是超越一国范围之外的文学研究，并且研究文学和其他知识领域及信仰领域之间的关系。包括艺术（如绘画、雕刻、建筑、音乐）、哲学、历史、社会科学（如政治、经济、社会学）、自然科学、宗教，等等。简言之，比较文学是一国文学与另一国或多国文学的比较，是文学与人类其他表现领域的比较。”③

韦勒克指出：“比较文学已经成为一个确认的术语，指的是超越国别文学局限的

---

① 提格亨（笔者注：现译为梵·第根）．比较文学论［M］．戴望舒，译．北京：商务印书馆，1937：17-18．

② 马·法·基亚．比较文学［M］．颜保，译．北京：北京大学出版社，1983：1．

③ 北京师范大学中文系比较文学研究组．比较文学资料［M］．北京：北京师范大学出版社，1986：1．

文学研究……就我个人来说，我希望干脆就称文学研究或文学学术研究。"[①]而韦斯坦因把文学分为国别文学（national literature）、世界文学（World literature）和比较文学（comparative literature）。在此意义上，他对比较文学的定义必须受到文学定义的约束做了进一步阐明，他认为凡是与文学有关的各方面都可列入讨论范围，可是与文学无关的科目则不应作为研究对象。奥尔德里奇认为，"比较文学"应当以不局限于一种国家文学的观点，或与他种或数种学科联合来研究文学现象。

我们可以从学者对比较文学定义的不同诠释概括出比较文学的根本属性：跨越性。法国学派重国别文学之间事实关系的跨越研究，美国学派提出对没有实际关系的国别文学文本也可以进行跨越性的文学研究，也就是所谓的平行研究，同时提出从文学和人类其他知识领域的跨越性研究也是比较文学不可缺少的一部分。不过由于西方中心主义的局限，一些美国学者拒绝将比较文学的跨越性研究拓展到异质性的东西文明之间的比较研究上面。

因此，当比较文学发展到第三阶段，法国学派、美国学派对比较文学定义的界定就显得不那么符合研究实践。于是，中国学派的学者们尝试着进一步深化对比较文学学科性质的认识。

由于跨越性是比较文学学科成立的核心属性之一，国内有影响的比较文学教材和最新研究论文都是根据"跨越性"特征来界定比较文学的，但对跨越的具体内容却各持己见。本教材在借鉴国内外学者研究成果的基础上，提出比较文学的定义：

> 比较文学是跨越不同国家、不同民族、不同文明和不同学科之间界限和视域的有关文学事实和理论的比较研究。它以实证影响研究、平行研究、文学变异研究为基本方法，主要考察和分析不同语境的文学现象之间的关联性、同源性、类同性或异质性和变异性。

需要说明的是，国内学者根据跨越性特征界定比较文学时，已有"跨国家、跨文化和跨学科"的提法，在此改用"跨文明"来代替跨文化，主要"因为只有'跨文明'才能真正彰显比较文学此次重大转折的基本特征，并且不至于与目前被滥用和乱用的'跨文化'一词相混淆"[②]。

"同源性"：是指法国学派强调的影响研究目标是通过梳理"影响"发生的"经过路线"：从放送者（起点）经传递者（媒介）再到接受者（到达点）的流传研究（形成流传学），从到达点出发向起点追根溯源的渊源研究（形成渊源学），以及流传影响的媒介

① 干永昌，等，编译．比较文学研究译文集[M]．上海：上海译文出版社，1985：130.

② 曹顺庆．跨文化比较诗学论稿[M]．桂林：广西师范大学出版社，2004：170.

研究(形成媒介学),都使得文学影响的过程保持其自身的同一性,也即影响的源头是相同的。法国学派理解的文学国际关系和相互影响就是某种实证关系、因果关系、求同关系。研究影响关系的同源性包括主题、形象和文类的同源性等。“同源性”是法国学派影响研究的可比性基础。

“类同性”:是指没有任何事实联系的不同国家的文学之间在风格、情节、技巧、手法、情调、流派、形象、主题、思潮乃至文学理论等方面表现出的相似或契合之处。类同性是美国学派平行研究的突出特征。

“异质性和变异性”:在本教材中异质性是指不同文明的本质差异性。跨文明研究是比较文学第三阶段的基本特征,而异质性则是跨文明研究的理论前提。忽略文明异质性的比较文学研究可能会落入简单的同中求异或异中求同的窠臼。变异性是指在国际文学关系和相互影响中,由于不同的文化、心理、意识形态、历史语境等因素,译介、流传和接受过程中存在着内容、形式等方面的变异。

“比较”作为一种研究方法,存在于一切学术领域之中。在比较哲学、比较史学、比较法学、比较文化等学科名称里,“比较”只是作为这些学科使用的一种方法,与这些学科本身是不能等同的。正如比较文学不等于用比较方法研究文学一样。比较文学作为一门学科,有自己的方法。

比较文学发展过程中的多次争论始终离不开方法论的争议。比较文学的研究方法最早是法国学派的“影响研究”,说得确切一点,是以法国为中心的整个欧洲的“影响研究”。

法国比较文学的奠基人巴登斯贝格深受19世纪实证主义和进化论的影响,崇尚考据和实证的研究方法。他认为:“仅仅对两个不同的对象同时看上一眼就作比较,仅仅靠记忆和印象的拼凑,靠一些主观臆想把可能游移不定的东西扯在一起来找类似点,这样的比较绝不可能产生论证的明晰性。”[①]可见他反对“主观臆断”,而主张比较文学要有“论证的明晰性”,强调在事实基础上进行比较论证。法国学派紧紧地抓住事实联系,把渊源、影响、媒介和名望等作为唯一的研究课题。此方法把文学作品看成是渊源和影响的总和,他们收集材料、分类鉴别,积累了大量的事实考据,如文学内部的关系、文学名誉的历史、不同国家文学之间的翻译者等;关注于文学事实的报道、翻译、考据和舆论等方面,把比较文学研究的根本对象——文学——抛到一边,忽视了文学作品是一个艺术整体而不是事实的拼凑。影响研究要求根据材料演绎或归纳出结论,论证过程严密,而忽视论证结论和内容的本质特征。

---

① 干永昌,等,编译.比较文学研究译文集[M].上海:上海译文出版社,1985:33.

这一学派的代表人物从梵·第根到卡雷都把比较文学看作文学史的一支，十分强调对历史脉络和事实联系的探索而排除文学的价值评论。巴登斯贝格曾猛烈地抨击价值评论："当这些作品结出丰硕果实的时候，他们又尖刻地将它们的价值进行比较，而这些价值往往又是无法估量的，他们这样做是为了证明什么？证明莎士比亚的成熟高于或低于高乃依；证明现代的古典主义是否是真正的古典主义；证明法兰西人绝不可能了解但丁。"[①]他极力批判美学的批评、心理分析批评，而坚持历史的观点。梵·第根在侧重于影响研究的同时也认为"接受到的和给予别人的那些'影响'的作用，是文学史的一个主要的因素"，可见他把影响研究归于历史范畴。梵·第根、卡雷和基亚等人都着重研究作家、作品、文体或一个国家的整个文学在外国产生的影响，强调"放送者/接受者"之间的相互影响。他们都忽视文学作品的内在结构和文学性，没有注意到文学艺术的独特内涵和性质，甚至还否定了结构主义和精神分析的研究方法，把影响研究局限于文学的事实、历史、源流及其与社会的关系中。因而比较文学陷入了文学事实比较的泥潭之中，在文学、社会学、历史学之间游走徘徊。

法国学派的这种种斤斤计较"文学外贸"的"研究"，不可避免地使比较文学领域成为"一潭死水"。

正是在此"岌岌可危"的处境中，1958 年，在美国举行的国际比较文学协会第二届年会上，一些美国学者对法国学派发起了大胆的挑战。美国学派针对"影响研究"提出了"平行研究"的方法。围绕这一方法的理论是由韦勒克、雷马克、马隆等人为核心的美国学者建立的。

平行研究在具体内容上反对法国学派重事实考据，因果解释的保守和狭隘，主张扩大研究范围，不囿于对影响的给予、接受、传播诸方面的事实考察，没有实际联系和影响的作家、作品均可在研究之列，甚至文学与别的学科之间的研究也可进行，从而探讨它们之间的类同和差异。平行研究破除了影响研究要求"事实联系"的界限，即便没有任何关联的各民族文学作品，也能进行平行的类同比较，意在探讨各自内在联系、规律和各民族文学的特质，正如雷马克所说的，"纯比较性的题目其实是一个不可穷尽的宝藏"，当然，这种比较要以有"可比性"和"文学性"作为前提，而非漫无边际地比较。

平行研究强调纯比较和大规模的综合，在方法上主要是美学的、批评的，而不是历史的、考据的。平行研究注意到比较文学研究的终极对象是文学，而不是一堆数字、符号，文学作品具有美学价值、人文特性，涉及人的美学判断和审美心理，它重视的是审

① 干永昌，等，编译. 比较文学研究译文集[M]. 上海：上海译文出版社，1985：131.

美价值的判断,而不是事实关系的考证。韦勒克大声疾呼反对以思想史的研究,或宗教和政治概念以及情感的研究来代替文学研究,强调文学艺术品本身作为一个整体的观念,尽管他并不否认产生文学作品的外部诸关系,但他不自觉地流露出更重视对文学"内在"研究的热情。

美国的平行研究和跨学科研究关注文学作品的文学性和其他学科的联系,注重作品的美学比较,在当时影响很大,把比较文学研究推向了一个新阶段。

在影响研究与平行研究两种方法的对立与争论中,不少学者看到了它们各自的偏颇与不足,力图采取调和折中的立场,如韦斯坦因。韦斯坦因力图取中间立场,弥补两派的不足,他表示:

> 我们愿意在自己限定的研究范围内取一条中间道路,即在法国学派的正统代表们(特别是梵·第根、卡雷、基亚)所持的相当狭隘的概念和所谓的美国学派的阐释者们所持的较为宽泛的观点之间取中。①

韦斯坦因主张融合法国学派、美国学派研究之长而避其短。他认为,依靠一种单一的方法研究文学作品或者从事比较文学研究,以及近年批评中出现的一元论都是错误的。这种比较文学"中道"蕴含着一种宝贵的文化相对主义立场,折射出其健康、公允、开放的思维方式,具有一定的学理价值。

当比较文学的新方法引起中国学界的关注之后,一些中国学者曾在上述两种方法之外提出了"阐发研究"的设想。古添洪在1978年所写的一篇文章中说:

> 利用西方有系统的文学批评来阐发中国文学及中国文学理论,我们可命之为"阐发法",这"阐发法"一直为中国比较学者所采用。②

1975年在台湾召开了第二届东西方文学关系的国际比较文学会议。会上,朱立民先生提出"运用西方的批评方法来研究中国古典和现代文学"的构想,但他的意见在讨论中遭到绝大多数与会者的反驳。③此后,"阐发研究"的方法虽在一些论文、教材中有所提及,也有一些学者在实践中运用,但并未有学者进行深入研究。"阐发研究"具有理论综合的意向,但理论在实践中仍然是分解运用,表现出方法机械化的单一操

---

① Ulrich Weisstein. *Comparative Literature and Literary Theory: Survey and Introduction.* Indiana University Press, Blooming & London, 1973:1.

② 古添洪.中西比较文学:范畴、方法、精神的初探[M]//比较文学论文选集.北京:中国社会科学院文学所,1982:43.

③ 李达三.比较文学研究之新方向[M].台北:台湾联经出版公司,1984:161-164.

作规范和程序。

2005 年,《比较文学学》[①]首次比较系统地提出将文学变异学作为比较文学研究的一个基本理论范畴,而文学变异研究作为一种研究方法是曹顺庆在其主编的《比较文学概论》[②]中提出来的。2006 年 1 月曹顺庆发表了《比较文学学科中的文学变异学研究》一文,阐释了文学变异学的实质内涵:"比较文学变异学将比较文学的跨越性和文学性作为自己的研究支点,它通过研究不同国家之间的文学现象交流的变异状态,以及研究没有事实关系的文学现象之间在同一范畴上存在着的文学表达上的异质性和变异性,从而探究文学现象差异与变异的内在规律性所在。"[③]该论文把文学变异学的研究对象归结为四个层面:语言层面变异学、民族国家形象变异学、文学文本变异学、文化变异学研究,这样就和法美学派的影响研究、平行研究有了鲜明界限,在跨异质文明比较文学研究过程中,对不同国家、文化、文明体系之间进行异同比较分析,从而总结出它们之间的"共同的诗心"。由于社会历史背景、审美习惯、文化传统等诸多方面的差异,必然导致一些全新的变异因素出现,这些往往就是文化和文学新质的最初萌芽,它最终必将推动不同文学和文化的发展进步,可以说,比较文学的跨异质文明研究方法在某种程度上有效地拓展了比较文学学科的研究领域。

【原典选读】

比较文学的定义与描述(节选)

◉克莱门茨

【导读】罗伯特·克莱门茨(Robert J. Clements, 1913—1993)是纽约大学比较文学系系主任,美国现代语言协会领军人物,主要从事比较文学理论研究和文艺复兴时期文学研究,著有《米开朗基罗艺术理论》(*Michelangelo's Theory of Art*)、《文艺复兴书信集:一个新世界的天启》(*Renaissance Letters: Revelations of a World Reborn*)、《中短篇小说解析》(*The Anatomy of the Novella*)等书。《比较文学学科》(*Comparative Literature As Academic Discipline: A Statement of Principles, Praxis, Standards*)是其研究比较文学的代表作品。《比较文学学科》全书共十五章,围绕着比较文学大学学科的建立和发展为中心,论述比较文学学科理论及大学比较文学学科的建设。在书中前五章,作者主要论述了比较文学学科的建立及课程的设置。从第六章开始,作者依次论述了比较文

① 曹顺庆. 比较文学学[M]. 成都:四川大学出版社,2005.

② 曹顺庆. 比较文学概论[M]. 北京:中国人民大学出版社,2011:6.

③ 曹顺庆. 比较文学学科中的文学变异学研究[J]. 复旦学报,2006(1):82.

学五种主要方法：文类与形式，时代、运动和影响，主题和神话，文学与其他艺术的相互关系研究，文学史和文学批评，并逐一探讨每一课题的课程安排。另外，除了比较文学学科书目和索引，本书还穿插了21个大学的比较文学程资料（如列表、摘要、教学大纲等），极具参考价值。本文节选自《比较文学学科》第一章“比较文学的定义与描述（Comparative Literature Defined and Described）”，主要对比较文学的定义作了详尽的阐述。文中，作者首先引用了基亚、科修斯、雷迈克和奥尔德里奇对比较文学的定义，然后对比较文学研究的三个主要范畴加以明确。同时，作者预示了今后比较文学的研究领域将超出这三个既有范畴，向其他被忽略的国家和民族的文学延伸开去。■

Comparative Literature Defined and Described

With some history behind us, we are able to address ourselves to a series of formal definitions of comparative literature articulated by some of its major proponents in America and Europe.

After the maturation of comparative literature during the first half of the present century, a new intensified effort was made to define in simple terms the nature and significance of our discipline. Some contemporary definitions of recent gestation follow from five works of wide circulation.

> Comparative Literature is the history of international literary relations. The comparatist stands at the frontiers, linguistic or national, and surveys the exchanges of themes, ideas, books, or feelings between two or several literatures. His working method will adapt itself to the diversity of his researches. A certain equipment is indispensable to him. He must be informed of the literatures of several countries. He must read several languages. He must know where to find the indispensable bibliographies.
>
> MARIUS-FRANÇOIS GUYARD, *La Littérature comparée*, pp. 12-13. (slightly condensed in translation)

> It is now generally agreed that comparative literature does not compare national literatures in the sense of setting one against the other. Instead, it provides a method of broadening one's perspective in the approach to single works of literature—a way of looking beyond the narrow boundaries of national frontiers in order to discern trends and movements in various national cultures and to see the relations between literature and other spheres of human activity.... Briefly defined, comparative literature can be considered the study of any literary phenomenon from the perspective of more than one national literature or in conjunction with another intellectual discipline or even several.
>
> A. OWEN ALDRIDGE, in *Comparative Literature: Matter and Method*, p. 1

> Comparative Literature is the study of literature beyond the confines of one particular country and the study of the relationships between literature on one hand and other areas of knowledge and belief, such as the (fine) arts, philosophy, history, the social sciences, the sciences, religion, etc. on the other. In brief it is the comparison of one literature with another or others, and the comparison of literature with other spheres of human expression.
>
> HENRY REMAK, in *Comparative Literature: Method and Perspective*, p. 1

> Western Literature forms a historical community of national literatures, which manifests itself in each of them. Each lyrical, epic, or dramatic text, no matter what its individual features, was drawn in part from common material, and in that way both confirms this community and perpetuates it. For the creator of works of literary art, literature from both the past and the present forms the main ideational and formal context within which he works. Literary movements and literary criticism also document this basic unity of Western Literature. Comparative Literature is based on this view of Western Literature. It is by viewing objects of literary research—texts, genres, movements, criticism—in their international perspectives that it contributes to the knowledge of literature.
>
> JAN BRANDT CORSTIUS, *Introduction to the Study of Literature*, p. V

Professors Pichois of Basel and Rousseau of Aix admit in *La Littérature comparée* a penchant, one toward philosophy and the other toward history, which infuses their definition "so lapidary as to figure in a repertory."

> Comparative literature: analytical description, methodic and differential comparison; synthetic interpretation of interlinguistic or intercultural literary phenomena, through history, criticism, and philosophy, in order to understand better literature as a specific function of the human spirit. (p. 197)

Not as a definition of comparative literature, but as an incremental view of the dual nature of literary study (viz., the work itself and the principles and criteria that envelop it), we add an often quoted passage from Wellek and Warren's *Theory of Literature*:

> Within our "proper study," the distinctions between literary theory, criticism, and history are clearly the most important. There is, first, the distinction between a view of literature which sees it primarily as a series of works arranged in chronological order and as integral parts of the historical process. There is, then, the further distinction between the study of the principles and criteria of literature and the study of the concrete literary works of art, whether we study them in isolation or in a chronological series. It seems best to draw attention to these distinctions by describing as "literary theory" the study of the principles of literature, its categories, criteria, and the like, and differentiating studies of concrete works of art as either "literary

criticism" (primarily static in approach) or "literary history."

These six recent quotations represent a whole catalog of similar statements concerning comparative literature as an art or a science. Although Guyard limits his remarks to the European heritage of literature, they tend to agree on the principles and methods of comparative literature and its involvement as a field of study and research with literary theory and criticism. There is little that anyone at this late date can contribute in the realm of definition.

I should like, however, to sum up and describe (not define) comparative literature as an academic discipline. Throughout the following pages this description will come into contact with definitions, of course, but the premises behind this volume must be stated in minimal form, to be explained and developed below. In the manner of the Renaissance philosophical tables, I shall describe the divisions and dimensions of our discipline—an area in which there is still something to contribute as more and more colleges and universities initiate comparative literature.

The basic premises of Guyard, Corstius, Remak, and Aldridge are all acceptable. Within these definitions five approaches to literature impose themselves: the study of (1) themes/myths, (2) genres/forms, (3) movements/eras, (4) interrelations of literature with other arts and disciplines, and (5) the involvement of literature as illustrative of evolving literary theory and criticism. The reading of literature must be in the original language, in conformity with, and to the extent of, the language requirement. A seminar on the nature and methods of comparative literature and another on the history of literary theory and criticism must be incorporated into the curriculum.

The three major dimensions of comparative literature as presently practiced must be firmly understood and will occupy Chapter ii. The narrowest dimension is the Western Heritage and its traditional minimal components French-English, German-French, Latin-English, etc. This narrowest dimension, when restricted to only two authors or literatures within the Western Heritage, is to be discouraged at the level of academic discipline. The second dimension is East-West, an area in which some exploration has been undertaken. The third dimension is World Literature, a much abused term in America. These three dimensions are not static terms, not passively conjoined, but they must, as fiefs of comparative literature, follow the methodology of Western Heritage comparative literature, utilizing the five approaches whenever possible to achieve meaningful comparison. It is of course logical to predict a future development of other dimensions than these three—conceivably Asian-African (Asian poets are now aware of the freedom movements in Africa, as demonstrated on p. 47), Western Heritage-African, or even an Eastern Heritage dimension within the vast continent of Asia itself, a development hindered by the particular language problems in Asia (see p. 33). As Pichois and Rousseau remind us, if our approaches and dimensions seem rigorously defined, our researches themselves offer great freedom.

All comparatists must surely be grateful to UNESCO for its effort to present a viable description of what goes on, or should go on, within comparative departments. Since UNESCO's *International Standard Classification of Education* (*ISCED*) (Paris, 1976) endeavors to summarize in three paragraphs the "Levels and Programs of Study" of our discipline—reducing the *Iliad ad nucem* as it were—it may be useful to quote them before embarking on a large and detailed volume on the subject. This statement in somewhat simplified form reads:

> Programs in comparative literature generally require as a minimum prerequisite a secondary-level education and lead to the following degrees: Bachelor of Arts, Master of Arts, and the doctorate, or their equivalents. Programs consist primarily of classroom sessions, seminar, or group discussions, and research.
>
> Programs that lead to a first university degree deal with the study of international literary and cultural relationships. Principal course content usually includes some of the following: the currency, reception, and influence of writers and their works in countries other than those of their origin; the transmission and evolution of international literary movements; the characteristics of and relationships between genres, themes, and motifs; folk literature and folklore; criticism; esthetics; intermediaries, and the relations between literatures, as well as those between literatures and the other disciplines. Background sources usually include history, the social and behavioral sciences, philosophy, religion and theology, and the natural sciences.
>
> Programs that lead to a postgraduate university degree deal with the advanced study of international and cultural relations. Emphasis is given to research work as substantiated by the presentation of a scholarly thesis or dissertation. Principal subject matter areas into which courses and research projects tend to fall include the origin and evolution of international literary movements, folk literature and folklore, criticism, esthetics, intermediaries, epics and sagas, tragedy, comedy, modern dramas, the contemporary novel, problems of comparative literature, the comparative method in literary studies, the forces in contemporary literature, and research techniques in comparative literature.

This composite description of comparative literature as an academic discipline will do very well as a start. Since it is applicable to Europe as well as America, one notes a few points on which American practice may differ. The basic foreign language requirements are bypassed. The early French, Dutch, and Finnish stress on folklore study is reflected. The various dimensions (Western Heritage, East-West, World) of comparative literature are not specified. The fairly common American honors thesis for the B. A. is not mentioned. Yet all these matters will be dealt with at length in the pages to follow.

The Names of Comparative Literature

The importance of Betz's bibliography of 1896-1897 was considerable, for it did much to establish the terminology of our discipline. Wellek's researches into the origins of this terminology have revealed the number of rival terms that persisted during the eighteenth and early nineteenth centuries: universal literature, international literature, general literature, world literature, comparative literature science, and so on. At least in French and English the term we use was eventually fixed once and for all. The European origins of comparative literature have been traced diligently by several European and American scholars, notably Baldensperger, Weisstein, and Wellek. The evolution toward a terminology satisfactory to all nationalities has understandably been a slow one.

As is further demonstrated in Chapter iii, the name of comparative literature has been elastic in its application. It is used for the study of one or more authors of one *sprachraum* with one or more authors of another speech area, or one national literature with another. It is used for the study of individuals or literatures within a more encompassing Western Heritage dimension. It is used for authors or literatures within the East-West or, finally, global dimension. Other dimensions, as yet largely unexploited, are mentioned in the following chapter. As we know from some commercial anthologies, these terms may be rendered static by the mere chronological juxtaposing of texts, making no commitment to method as comparative literature does. To be truly precise, one should in our profession refer to Comparative Western Literature, Comparative East-West Literature, and so on. However, in an academic context these terms in their simpler form imply a methodology and thus meet reservations of Bataillon, Frye, and others (see p. 13) about the exact meaning or *engagement* implied in the word "comparative."

(Robert J. Clements, *Comparative Literature as Academic Discipline.* The Modern Language Association of America, New York, 1978.)

比较文学概要(节选)

◉野上丰一郎

【导读】野上丰一郎(1883—1950),东京大学英文科博士,日本著名的外国文学研究者,能乐研究家。长期从事比较文学研究,著有《能乐研究的发现》《西洋纵览》《翻译论:翻译的理论与实际》等书。野上在1933发表的《比较文学论》中介绍了梵·第根的实证主义研究方法,这对法国学派的研究方法传入日本带来了积极的影响。《比较文学论要》一书是其有关比较文学思考的核心所在,书中分十二章分别讨论"比较文学产生的历史渊源""比较文学的方法论",以及"比较文学与国别文学、总体文学的关系"等相关问题。全书不仅跳出"欧美文学中心"的视角,将比较文学从西方扩大到东方,而且认为"文学的境界线"划分不仅要考虑国家的地理分界,还要考虑语际分界。此外,野上在该书第八章中提出"文学最重要的东西在表现",在此基础上他将文学的比较延展到文学表现的比较,并认为如果翻译者为了追求形式的一致而放弃原文的意涵,不如比较稳妥地保持意涵而舍弃与原文一致的形式。《比较文学概要》这本书写于1934年,被收进《岩波讲座·世界文学》系列丛书中。本文节选自原书的第四章、第五章,文中主要对比较文学的方法、类别及形式作一个介绍。■

比较文学的一般方法

比较文学是探讨什么问题的呢?

原则上说,比较文学的目的是研究各国文学作品的相互关系的学科。不待言,这包括西方与东方、古代与中世纪的、与现代的全部有价值的作品。现仅就西方世界来看:第一,古典文学之间的比较和研究。换句话说,希腊拉丁之间的关系,这里是后者接受前者的影响问题。其影响是单向的。其次,现代文学是受中世纪或者受古代,或者通过中世纪受古代的影响的研究。这也是一方负债的关系。最后是近代文学相互间的关系。例如,在英国文学与法国文学的关系中,英国文学有的地方来源于法国;同样,法国文学也有很多地方来源于英国。对于近代的各国的文学来说都有同样的现象。因此,这最后的问题是范围更加广泛,关系更加复杂了。

在"导言"中曾介绍我们的文学爱好者,偶然的机会沉溺于阅读《俄狄浦斯》,感受到对古典文学与近代文学的兴味。现在由于比较研究者的关心,将要解决各种各类的问题。但是,首先应该考虑的就是有关比较文学的一般方法问题。

首先是国界的问题,比较文学如前面所说,是一种国际文学的研究方法。它探究 A 国与 B 国文学的关系。假如研究者是 A 国人,当然他论及的是本国文学与外国文学的关系。多数情况下,即存在政治的国界也存在语言的国界。如英国与法国,或如法国和西班牙那样。然而,有时一个国家的语言可以越过国界被其他国家使用,这种情况产生的文学应归附到哪国去呢? 例如,据说德语被瑞士和奥地利使用,在德国,瑞士人鲍尔美尔(J. J. Bodmer)和哈莱尔(A. van Haller)、凯勒尔(G. Keller),以及奥地利人罗赛格尔(P. K. Rosegger)和盎森格鲁伯尔(L. Anzengruber)等归在本国(德国)的文学范围内。另外,在法国,日内瓦人卢梭(J. J. Rousseau)、沙伏阿伯爵、美斯特尔(Maistre)兄弟。其他瑞士人维奈(A. Vinet)、薛雷(E. Schérer)、洛德(E. Rod)、式尔布利(J. Cherbuliez)。另外,比利时人洛登巴克(G. Rodenbach)、维尔哈伦(E. Verhaeren)①都属于自己的文学伙伴。但是,也有相反的例子,英国人并不把使用同样语言的美国作家记载在他们的文学中。这个癖性,如使用苏格兰方言的彭斯(R. Burns)②被认为是引以自豪的诗人。③

根据这些例子,文学境界线的划分,大体上把国语的共同地带认为是同一圈内,但它是适用一切场合的。假如作更进一步历史性地考察,虽说有既定着的文学境界线的原则,

① 维尔哈伦(Emile, Verhaeren,1855—1916),比利时诗人,用法文写作,代表作长篇小说《贪婪的人》。

② 彭斯(Robert Burns,1759—1796),苏格兰诗人,主要用苏格兰方言写作,著名的抒情诗有《一朵红红的玫瑰》《往昔的时光》等。

③ 例外的一个例子是拉夫卡蒂奥・汉恩(Lafcadio Hearn)。虽然他属于日本国籍,但是,谁也没有看到他在日本文学中有所著述,由于用英语写作,属于英国文学。

却并非一成不变。它也是随着形势的转变而转变，它的转变方式也没有一定标准。

在这儿，作为比较文学的实际问题，无论在怎样的时期、被认为是怎样的文学境界线，A国的作品越过它的国境线移植到B国时，一定要经过作家的加工。这种移植的形式是作为书信的传达。假如A国的原作者或者原作品为“发信者”，而接收它的B国作者的作品为“收信者”，发信者与收信者之间应该要有担任中介工作的传达者。从中翻译、介绍、模仿等工作就是中介。往往是在收信者和发信者之间相互进行传达，传达者也像发信人一样选用受理。例如，在勒·都尔纳（Le Tourneur）[①]翻译了杨（Edward Young）的题为《哀怨》（*Night Thoughts*）的诗（1742年），生、死，对于不死的冥想的挽歌中，虽然没有那么深远的思想，但，一时在大陆也都宣传起来。由于原著没有直接移入，法语译Nuit（Le Tourneur）被看作原著。在意大利也好，或是西班牙也好，都传播开了。这样的例子还不少，传达者有时也是发信人及收信人，都受到同等的重视。

作为比较文学的实际问题，应该向着努力去发现移入的经过路线，有必要去研究原著。对影响的研究不应只局限于与原著的关系上，而应在同传达者的关系上。这意味着对首先移入的经过路线要作充分的探求。或者作品由A国移入B国当中往往被进行各种变更和修改，或者是由于时代的社会情况所致；或者是个人的、集团的、思想感情的原因。要想详细地调查，如果可能的话，希望把当时全部的定期刊物和个人日记、书简等类都收集起来，全部翻阅查对。

为了这个工作，比较文学家应该尽可能多的具备多国语言的知识。但也未必需要一定像语言学家、文法学家那样去掌握科学语法和惯用法等方面的问题。然而，假如我们用一种情况的例子来说明，把原作者讥讽的事物，却没有感觉到这种讥讽的尖锐，仅接受表面言词的意味，含糊、呆板、表面地解释，马马虎虎的语言是不行的。我们看到大量的像这样的翻译和介绍，我们也看见过，把那种阴郁而沉痛的调子，译得轻松而爽快来传播的例子。这种误谬比语法、文法的误谬还危险。这样说来，既不要犯文体上的误谬。当然也不可能要求达到完全标准。但至少说具备那种程度准确的语言知识对于比较文学家来说是必要的。比较文学家为了在比较上的需要，当然必须使用几国外国语。英国的研究者在调查法国的事情时，往往不能不接触西班牙的事情，也不能不读意大利语的书籍。另外，法国的研究者，对于德国的事情要做比较研究时，也会发现它与英国的事情有着联系，也与北欧的事情有着联系。就这样，特别是在近代由于这种关系是复杂的，所以，对研究家要求的语言学的负担并不一般。因为这种原因，在某种情况下分担进行研究是非常必要的。

所谓分担研究，不仅需要研究语言学方面的知识，而且也需要对世界文学史诸方面的

---

① 勒·都尔纳（Le Tourneur），法国18世纪英国文学介绍者。1769年不知是怎么译了杨（Young）的《哀怨》，把原作改得不成样子。译本在意大利和西班牙代替了原本，成了另外一部《哀怨》。

知识进行研究。例如,政治的、宗教的、哲学的、科学的、文学的等。要到所有的部门进行调查时,这种情况依靠一个人去完成终究是不可能的。而作为比较文学的研究方法,如前所述,和普通的文学史的研究方法一样,不仅取其一流的杰出的重要的作家,而且一直寻找和吸收二三流以及四五流的一群小作家来参加。因为,这些必须的研究资料,单单是作为统计的实际业务来看,也应迫切地有必要建立团体的调查机构。例如,戴克斯特的工作、巴登斯贝格的工作,无论谁都使用了很多助手。

其次,比较文学家应该具有关于文学传统的充分的知识,首先要观察现代欧洲文学的潮流的动向,认清其中什么是主流,什么是支流。特别是对那些具有代表性的作家,应该正确地捕捉它的思想表现的特点。

西方文化,溯其根源,是希腊和希伯来文化,是此二要素结合发展的结果,文学潮流也把此二要素作为源泉。按照阿诺鲁道(Matthew Arnold)的解释,支配希腊文化观念是意识的自然发生,希伯来则认为是严正的良心。①虽然是二要素,但是,用希伯来信徒的话来说,对于我们是把神的性质作为目的的②。然而,希腊是想依据理性来完成的,因而我们也要以其所有的原来的现象去看待。对于这些,希伯来则是以行为第一,要求我们去服从。前者使荷马的诗和雅典娜的悲剧开花,后者成了圣经中的结晶。现在的西方不仅仅文学,其他的艺术、哲学、科学、政治、法律等,一切都是从希腊精神发源的,也没有不是从希伯来的神话成长起来的。希腊精神与希伯来精神最初的结合是在亚利山大利亚大帝时代。当时希腊精神普及一切,开明国家,连最排外的希伯来民族也不能从那里免除。甚至巴勒斯坦的生活也已经希腊化了。与此同时,继巴勒斯坦以后,亚利山大利亚的都市成为犹太人生活的中心地。希腊精神、希伯来精神的第二次结合是在罗马帝国时进行的。使原来建立在传统希腊文化之上的罗马文化就更加希伯来化了。希腊文化具有看起来真实、爱美、喜爱单纯、喜欢新鲜等特长,而罗马人以他的适应性应用代替了希腊人的创造力。所以,在文学方面,即使罗马没受到希腊文化的影响,但却促进了罗马对国家法律、社会制度、家庭生活制度等这些方面的新生,形成了那样的新组织。现代文学的结构,提供了根深蒂固的值得吸收的各种要素。其后,形成了中世纪长时期内分散在各处的希腊、罗马精神与希伯来精神。通过文艺复兴的风潮刮到了一起,实现前所未见的紧密配合,这是第三个结合。就是从这次结合,开始了现代生活,产生了现代文学。

如果就人种观察这个变迁,最初登上舞台的是亚利安人种中的希腊民族和塞姆人种中的希伯来(犹太)民族。塞姆人种中的埃及民族、巴比伦民族、亚西利亚民族兴旺得很好,灭亡得也很早。其他民族,如阿拉伯民族对中世纪文学作出了贡献。亚利安人种、印度民族、西班牙民族与阿拉伯民族前后也对西方文学作出了贡献。同时亚利安人种克勒

---

① M. Arnold, Culture and Anachy.

② 《裴德罗后记》第1、4页。

特民族、斯拉夫(俄罗斯)民族、日耳曼民族等稍有落后。这些工作在中世纪阶段,其内部是混淆的。最后至文艺复兴的活跃时期才呈现出百花缭乱的局面。语言虽是这个民族的,但各自搬出各地的语法,使其改变、修正、翻译、模仿,结果其经过路线困难而复杂交错。……

比较文学的类别和形式

文学可分为内容和形式,对于比较文学来说,应该是对形式进行比较,或者是对内容进行比较。例如,英国的商籁诗(sonnet)的形式,能分为三种到四种。其中莎士比亚的商籁诗押韵形式(abab. cdcd. efef. gg)和弥尔顿的商籁诗的押韵形式(abba. abba. cde. cde)为什么有如此明显的不同呢?对于前者,使三个不同的四句诗的结尾添上联句,后者根据意大利的商籁体的正式的形式由前八句与后六句结合而成。此种诗形式的不同,认为其结果随着诗节的结构法、韵脚的运用法、主要音的反复法等不同带来的。在根本上是对诗人的韵律的感觉和韵律的效果的解释的不同。那么,莎士比亚的商籁诗与彼得拉克(Petrarca)①具有什么样的关系呢?法国文学史家认为商籁诗不是伯洛房斯地方产生的。今天都相信,这种诗体是从十三世纪的意大利挖掘出来的。福拉·古依道尼(Fra Guittone)被认为是诗形的创造者。另外成为西利亚的宫廷诗人的彼·德·维缪(Pier delle Vigne)也是有这样声誉的人。不管怎么说,商籁体诗是在意大利和法国形成和发展的。在英国它的诗的形式最流行的是十六世纪末期(1591—1597年)。最初是彼得拉克、龙沙·彼埃尔·德(Ronsard)②、杜·贝雷(Du Bellay)③等。由于已经被充分地介绍了,所以不受莎士比亚的影响。尽管这样,可是为什么离开莎士比亚的正式格式而采用自由格调呢?这样的问题也是比较文学研究的一个内容吧!

另外,关于对待内容方面,例如,在前章接触到的"浮士德"的主题。如全世界到手,而失去自己灵魂将会成了什么?像这类问题根据各个国家各个时代的诗人理解的不同去进行比较,这的确不失为一个好题目。再有,从浮士德的诱惑者靡非斯特与撒旦确立了怎样的关系来看,撒旦自《约伯记》④《历代志略》以来是对神的反抗者。在《马太传》中称呼贝尔支普(魔王),在《克林道附记》中嘲讽为贝里荷(卑怯的人),在《克兰》被取名为"撒

① 彼得拉克(Francesco Petrarca,1304—1374),是意大利文艺复兴的先驱之一,著名的抒情诗人。与但丁、薄伽丘并列,称为文艺复兴时期的三位"巨星"。

② 皮埃尔·德·龙沙(Ronsaed Pierre de,1524—1585),法国第一个近代诗人,被称为"法兰西的荷马","七星诗社"重要成员。

③ 杜·贝雷(Du Bellay,1522—1560),起草"七星诗社"宣言书《保卫和发扬法兰西语》(1540),"七星诗社"六个人文主义作家之一。

④ 《约伯记》,约伯,《约伯记》在《旧约》中。

旦”，琐罗阿斯德教（袄教、拜火教）的教义称代乌阿是阿里曼的代表者。但丁把他取名为鲁奇费洛，还有德第、倍支浓，描写着把他埋在地狱的最下层冰圈中。在他身旁出卖其恩惠的极恶的他的弟子们——伊斯卡里奥第的犹大，盖扎尔背叛的布尔刺斯、卡西乌斯之类受到永远的苛责。马洛用靡非斯特[①]的名字诱惑浮士德博士，莎士比亚以靡非斯特表现着他的罪恶灵魂[②]。在这以前英国的劝惩剧瓦依斯（不德）作为他（恶魔）的先锋很活跃。然而马洛的巴拉巴斯（《马尔他岛的犹太人》）与莎士比亚的夏洛克（《威尼斯商人》）一起大概以恶魔的成分来描写，对于莎士比亚的依阿古（《奥赛罗》）几乎是被人格化了的恶魔的上等成分。然而，弥尔顿（《失乐园》的撒旦）和歌德（《浮士德》的靡非斯特）对恶魔的目的却予以明确的性格。假如我们追溯到古代，罗马诗人也好、希腊诗人也好，看得出通过对各种恶魔的描写，会发现接受希伯莱思想洗礼后对恶的观念与希腊恶的观念有很多不同。另外，直到近代可见穿着黑衣服很多的恶魔跋扈于文学作品之中。把这等思想分类对照，也能见到对民族的、时代的影响的预料下的研究，成为研究的一个方法。

我们为了整理比较文学的研究范围，迫切需要谋求方法的统一。第一，必须决定的是文学有什么样的类别，有什么样的形式，在外国文学的影响下将可能发生怎样的变化。

文学的种类、产生、进化直到衰亡，某国产生的某种类的文学有被其他国家移植并在该处成长或者变种的情况。也有正在其他国家成长而在本国衰亡了的情况。在古代，非常繁盛的种类的文学也在继续变种，现在也有继续存在的。还有在比较近代的刚刚萌芽的东西，很快衰枯，今天已经看不到它的影子了。文学种类的兴衰变化与植物界或动物界的现象相似。在文学史家中如布伦第尔（Brunetiere）以进化论的理论应用于文学种类的进化的状态，进行了非常机械的说明[③]。因此，说到个人的才能，往往大部分被忽视了。也有反对的批评家，认为文学除了个人的才能的集合以外别的什么也没有。不管怎样，对于比较文学家来说，文学种类是非常重要的一个准则。对于这个准则，人类的思想不论是本能的采用，还是经过认真思考的选择，没有广泛的影响和联系铸成某种文体是不可能的。不能认为由某作家的天才造出一个文体。他只能是从各种各样的源泉中吸取材料，使他发挥自己的才能，这样作为一个改变了的文体才能被创造出来。若在变种的文体中照原样保持原型的东西，作家的人格与采用的文体的关系则形成一方面依据其他方面的东西进行说明倒是最方便最好的情况。采用原型的文体、刺激诱导作家，作家的思想、感情得到发展或者受到限制。因此，旧的传统形式与作家独创性之间屡屡发生冲突、引起斗争。特

---

① Mephistopheles 或者 Mephistophilis 或者 Mephostophilis（靡非斯特靡希斯）的确切的语源是不清楚的。或者意味着是希腊语 mephostophiles，解释为“不见阳光的人”；或者是法语 mephitis 后附加希腊语 philos，意味着“爱有害的散发物者”。至今还没有个正确的说法，希伯来语原是“破坏者”和“说谎者”两个语意的结合。

② Mephostophilus. of. The Merry Wives of Windsor, l. i.

③ Brunetiere, L' Evonlution des genres.

别是古典主义时代，这种现象最为多见。实际上，传统与个性的斗争被说成是为人类思想史提供的最动人情景的程度。这样的话、这样的传统就不一定是一国文学史上的传统，很多情形是属于国际的传统。如果我们不依据比较文学的研究方法，要想正确地解决这样的问题是不可能的。

文学的文体不仅仅只靠个人的才能的关系去考察，当然，这也能提供最好的文学作品的分类。特别是对于文化发展的初期，有着不能否认个人的人格在集成的作品中存在价值的原则。荷马的叙事诗是最显著的实例。例如，色诺芬（Xenophon）①所说《伊利亚特》（Ilias）与《奥德赛》（Odysseia）并非是荷马一个诗人创作。而是很多的吟咏诗人，由于口头吟咏没有记录下来。它的原型大概是继承伊俄尼亚民族，由埃俄利斯民族间简单形成，在继承中被集成统一的。第一，在奥林匹克时代，推断有几部被编成巨大的神话传说集的，一部分至今还保存着。当然与个人创作的东西不同，它是人们口耳相传和共同创作的形式。最初的个人创作存在形式已经消灭了。最初的一个人是荷马，还是最后一个集大成的诗人，今天都未能作出决定，主要是确定地承认了由荷马的名字传播的二个叙事诗，而不是某特定的个人的创作。

世界的时代也像人们幼年时代那样喜欢美好的话语，《伊利亚特》《奥德赛》和其他的许多个人的叙事诗的体裁就是在这种情况下产生的。故事、小说是它的近代形式。另外，也是像人类幼年那样，世界幼年也爱美好的歌，抒情诗也是在这种情况下形成的。它在近代的诗中又复活了。同样对于一切戏曲的种类、一切散文的种类也都适用。

在此对于一切文学种类的产生全部详述是不可能的。只叙述一下具有主要国际影响的文学类别。首先在神话故事的诗中，希腊、罗马的叙事诗，荷马、维吉尔——十六世纪给全欧洲带来了影响。因为叙事诗在希腊被吟咏是以民族的英雄事迹作为主题，构成一定的统一性。从这里可以看到叙述的事件和人物性格描写的进展。但未必是后人吟咏的条件，和其他种类的诗是相同的。然而，若是值得读的作品，对描写事件的情节和人物性格的发展的统一上会越来越紧密的。在中世纪，但丁的《神曲》中是显示得十分清楚的。十六世纪的叙事诗人达梭（Tasso）也是最突出的代表，特别是他给予法国和英国以很大的影响。

在抒情诗方面，像品达（Pindaros）②、施蒙尼迪（Simonides）③、斯泰希克洛

---

① 色诺芬（Xenophanes，公元前430？—前355？），希腊三位著名历史学家之一，他写过许多著作，代表作是《长征记》（又名《万人进军》）。

② 品达（Pindaros，公元前522？—前442，有的书上译平达，约公元前518—约前438），合唱琴歌最著名的抒情诗人。

③ 施蒙尼迪（Simonides，公元前556—前469），希腊抒情诗人。

(Stesichoros),会唱歌谣的作者如萨福(Sappho)①、阿那克瑞翁(Anakreon)②与歌唱个人情绪的作者们有区别,最初是伴着乐器演唱的。但是,在罗马诗人贺拉斯(Horatius)③的时代仍然还没能那样唱歌。这以后,随着诗的格调的旋律的变更,也传给了后代。作为抒情诗又分为挽歌、牧歌等派别。忒俄克里托斯(Theokritos)④创始的牧歌的诗格从维吉尔袭用而来,甚至对现代也给予强烈的刺激。

对于诗的现代种类的一种,实际并非是以演出作为目的。但是,往往部分地整理为戏曲形式。歌德的《浮士德》作为代表、拜伦(Byron)的《曼弗莱德》(Manfred)⑤,密茨凯维奇(Mickiewicz)的《祖先》(Aieux)⑥,缪塞(de Musset)的《酒杯和嘴唇》(*Coupe et les lévres*)⑦,爱斯泊龙赛达(Espronceda)的《恶魔世界》(Eldiablo mundo)等都可以称为对话诗,比依据简单的抒情诗更能表达作者的感情,得到更感人的效果。此种类诗的形式,对于今天的诗仍然有其影响。

戏曲的发源地希腊,公元前5世纪悲剧的形式与喜剧的形式一起完成了。狄俄尼索斯(Dionysos)⑧从祭礼的余兴开始。当悲剧由埃斯库罗斯、索福克勒斯、欧里庇得斯;还有喜剧由阿里斯托芬(Aristophanes)⑨以及稍后的米南德(Menandros)完成最终的形式时,宗教的仪礼的意义大体上已经全部失去了。用严肃的感情构成悲剧的基础,对于这人与命运对立的,都是以前者成为后者的牺牲品表现出来的,是根据这人类,特别是通过应该具有伟大性格而显露出来的。喜剧是以捉住现代人的弱点和缺点进行讽刺为目的,所以必须出现谐谑轻快的调子。在处理与人或与命运的对立中,常常是在人类没有被命运压倒方面具有特长。在罗马,作为悲剧诗人有塞内加(Seneca)⑩,喜剧诗人普拉图斯

---

① 萨福(Sappho,公元前612?—?),希腊琴歌最著名的作者。柏拉图称她为"第十位文艺女神"。

② 阿那克瑞翁(Anakreon,公元前550?—前465?又译为阿那克里翁),希腊著名琴歌作者。写了五卷诗,歌颂醇酒和爱情。后人多模仿他的诗体,称"阿那克瑞翁体"。

③ 贺拉斯(Quintus Horatius Flaccus,公元前65—前8),古罗马奥古斯都时代最主要的讽刺诗人、抒情诗人和文艺批评家。主要作品有《颂歌》四卷,《讽刺诗》两卷。代表作《诗艺》,对欧洲古典主义文艺理论影响很大。

④ 忒俄克里托斯(Thekritos,公元前310—前245?也有的书上认为:约公元前325—约前267),古希腊诗人,牧歌创始者。对欧洲文学中田园诗的发展有一定影响。

⑤ 《曼弗莱德》(*Manfred*,1817),拜伦的著名诗剧。贯穿《锡隆德囚犯》(*The prisoner of chillon*,1818)的悲哀的主题,剧中的主人公与浮士德相似。

⑥ 《祖先》(*Aienx*,又译《先人祭》),波兰诗人,革命家,于1823—1832年写成的诗剧。共分四部,揭露波兰被瓜分时期,沙俄对波兰人民的野蛮统治和对波兰爱国青年的残酷迫害。

⑦ 《酒杯与嘴唇》(*Coupe et les leures*),法国浪漫主义诗人德·缪塞(Alfred de Musset)的诗著。

⑧ 狄俄尼索斯(Dionysos,或译道尼苏斯),古希腊神话中的酒神。相传他首创葡萄酿酒……古希腊人在祭祀狄俄尼索斯时常表演。

⑨ 阿里斯托芬(Aristophanes,公元前446—前385),古希腊早期喜剧代表作家,恩格斯称其为"喜剧之父"。

⑩ 塞内加(Seneca Lucius Annaeas,公元前4?—65),是罗马最重要的悲剧作家,被称为"基督教的教父"。代表作是以亲血复仇为主题的《美狄亚》,描写强烈情欲的《费得尔》,反映妇女命运的《特洛亚妇女》等。

(Plautus)①、太伦斯(Terentius)②都是模仿希腊的原型写的。文艺复兴以后,得到近代欧洲直接影响的是罗马诗人们的作品,希腊的影响是间接的。在法国,高乃依(Corneille)③、拉辛(Racine)④、莫里哀(Molière)⑤;在西班牙,洛贝·德·维加(Lope de Vega)⑥、加尔德龙(Calderon);在英国,马洛(Marlowe)⑦、莎士比亚(Shakespeare)等。根据这些天才,在十七世纪创造了悲剧、喜剧、悲喜剧各种各样的形式,形成了国际的影响。法国的形式在英国、荷兰、波兰、意大利得到了研究。另外,英国的形式在法国、德国得到了研究,像这样的影响是交错复杂的。到了十八世纪到十九世纪,特别是莎士比亚的势力,单从国际影响这一点来考虑,至少在十九世纪后半期易卜生⑧的新的社会剧产生以前,它一直成为全世界占统治地位的伟大剧作。易卜生的社会剧是同以往的悲剧、喜剧、悲喜剧的形式完全脱离的剧种。他把诗从戏剧中驱逐出去,完成了拒绝在舞台上演出罗曼斯的革新,其影响速度之快,范围之大是史无前例的。

散文种类在近代发展了。由于古代,文学大体上都是韵文,没有韵文的东西主要是历史或是演说。作为历史家有希罗多德(Herodotos)、修昔底德(Thukydides)、泰西塔斯(Tacitus)、利威乌斯(Livius)等;作为雄辩家有像狄摩西尼(Demosthenes)、西赛罗(Cicero)等;此外,柏拉图(Platon)、亚里士多德(Aristoteles)、贺拉斯(Horatius)那样的哲学家、批评家;或以对话的形式,或以记录的形式,多半旨在事实的传达。这样,虽然得到了很大影响,但是像近代的随笔(essay)、小评论形式的在国际上还没有。完成作为文学的一个种类——随笔,最初的人是蒙田(Montaigne)⑨。他的有名的二卷《随笔》(Essais)于1580—1588年出版。在英国这种类的创始者培根(Bacon)⑩撰写的《随笔》(essays)在1597年出版。虽然比蒙田的翻译早数十年,但是,不能证明培根没接受蒙田的影响。不限于培根,

---

① 普拉图斯(Titus Maccius Plaotus,约公元前251—前184),古罗马喜剧作家。相传写过一百多部喜剧,代表作《一罐金子》《双生子》等。

② 太伦斯(Pulius Terentius Afer,约公元前190—前159),古罗马喜剧作家。对莫里哀的戏剧创作和18世纪欧洲喜剧作家有一定影响。

③ 高乃依(Pierre Corneille,1606—1684),法国作家,著有剧本三十余部。代表作《熙德》《贺拉斯》等,论文有《论悲剧》《论三一律》等。是法国古代主义戏剧的创始人。

④ 拉辛(Jean Baptiste Racine,1639—1699),法国剧作家。

⑤ 莫里哀(Moliere,1622—1673),法国喜剧作家、戏剧活动家,一生写成喜剧三十多部,对欧洲喜剧艺术的发展有深远影响。

⑥ 洛贝·德·维加(Lope Felix de Vega Carpio,1562—1635),西班牙戏剧家、作家。

⑦ 马洛(Christopher Marlowe,1564—1593),英国文艺复兴时期剧作家。

⑧ 易卜生(Henrik Johan Ibsen,1828—1905),挪威剧作家。问题剧的代表作家。共写剧本二十六部。代表作品《社会支柱》《玩偶之家》《群鬼》《国民公敌》等。其作品对近代戏剧的发展有广泛的影响。

⑨ 蒙田(Michel Eyquem de Montaigne,1533—1592),文艺复兴时期法兰西思想家和散文作家,主要著作有《散文集》。

⑩ 培根(Francis Bacon,1561—1626),英国哲学家、最重要的散文家。恩格斯称他为“英国唯物主义和整个现代实验科学的真正始祖”。主要著作《新工具》《科学进步论》。

英国的很多文人在法国的影响下写作随笔,逐渐形成英国固有的形式。可是之所以导致现在这个样子的形式,是因为英国取得了特殊的进展的缘故。可开列五六个杰出的名字:艾迪生(Addison)、斯蒂尔(Steele)、拉姆(Lamb)、赫胥黎(Huxley)、戴昆西(De Quincey)、利·罕特(Leigh Hunt)、海斯利特(Hazlitt)、斯蒂文生(R. L. Stevenson)①等都是具有独到见解的人。这里艾迪生和斯蒂尔在十八世纪初叶,在伦敦发行《闲话报》(*The Tatler*)和《旁观者》(*The Spectator*)刊载最初的道义性、政治性、文学性的论文。这以后的一个世纪里流行欧洲各国,波及的影响是无与伦比的。

作为散文的近代类别的一种,有虚构旅行故事,这也是十七世纪以后的产物。西哈诺·德·倍易合克(Cyrano de Bergerac)的《另一个世界》(*L'autre monde*)怎样影响着斯威夫特(Swift)②的《格列佛游记》(*Gulliver's Travels*)。另外,霍尔倍格(Holberg)的《尼尔·库里姆的地下旅行》(Niel Klim's Subterranean Journey)与《格列佛游记》一起,以后对伏尔泰的虚构旅行故事有什么影响;还有和以塞尔柯克(Selkirk)的经验为基础写成的,笛福的《鲁滨孙漂流记》(*Robinson Crusoe*)③一起,在后人的想象力刺激下,如何出现了许多模仿者,再有,这些由十九世纪的科学思想的进步所驱使或成为维尔涅(Jules Verne)的虚构旅行故事、地下游行故事、海底旅行故事,或者成为威尔斯(H. G. Wells)④的科学幻想小说。这种体裁是怎样发展到近代的呢?这些也就有资格成为比较文学研究的一个项目了。这些空想旅行的主题近来虽然面对着如何逐渐把我们的奇怪爱好合理地表现出来,但是,目前一个可行的方法是,建设一个在我们的世界之外的理想国。依据这些显示一种意向,以讽刺我们的世界组织的不完全。例如《格列佛游记》的第四篇,马的国的叙述,主要是对人类社会的谩骂、嘲笑,此外没有任何目的。假如回溯此类讽刺的体系,我们经过托马斯·莫尔(Thomes More)⑤的《乌托邦》(*Utopia*)和弗兰西斯·培根(Francis Bacon)的《新大西

---

① 艾迪生(Joseph Addison,1672—1719);斯蒂尔(Richard Steele,1672—1729)。在英国期刊事业前所未有的繁荣时期,他们合办了《旁观者》。发表介乎散文和小说体之间的作品。很有文学价值。戴昆西(De Quincey,1785—1859),英国作家。海斯利特(Hazlitt,1778—1830),英国批评家及散文家。斯蒂文生(R. L. Stevenson,1850—1894),苏格兰小说及散文作家。主要作品有《金银岛》《化身博士》《绑架》等。还著有游记和小品文。

② 斯威夫特(Swift Jonathan,1667—1745),英国讽刺作家。代表作长篇小说《格列佛游记》,全书分四卷,揭露英国社会的种种不合理现象,讽刺当时统治阶级的腐败。

③ 《鲁滨孙漂流记》(*Robinson Crusoe*)是英国小说家笛福的代表作。小说主要描写鲁滨逊在无人荒岛上28年的生活。它的价值在于我们从这部小说可以认识到资本主义原始积累时期新兴资产阶级的精神面貌。

④ 威尔斯(H. G. Wells,1866—1946),英国作家。以科学幻想小说较为出名。代表作《时间机器》(1805)、《隐形人》(1897)。小说以奇特的情节和夸张手法,讽刺资本主义社会的丑恶现象。

⑤ 莫尔(Thomas More,1478—1535),文艺复兴时期英国空想共产主义者,1516年用拉丁文写成《乌托邦》(意即"乌有之乡")一书。是一部对话形式的幻想小说。他从古希腊哲学家柏拉图手中借用本书这种结构主题,但又完全独出心裁地改造了这种形式。

岛》(*New Atlantis*)①到柏拉图(Platon)②的阿道兰特克斯(Atlantikos)的理想国的神话就可以看到了。③另外,再看看现代新发现的巴特勒·萨缪尔(Butlerv Samuel)④的《乌有乡游记》(*Erewhon*)和肖伯纳(Bernard Shaw)⑤的《回到马修斯拉时代》(*Back to Methuselah*)等。

散文最重要的种类是有着各种各样区别的小说。作为小说始祖的薄伽丘(Boccaccio)⑥在意大利起源,具有人情小说的传统,向着法国、西班牙、英国传播开来。在英国有了诗的形式,可是乔叟(Chaucer)⑦把它扩大了。从那里分出一派道义的小说,马尔孟岱尔(Marmontel)被称为是代表。另外短篇幻想志怪小说霍夫曼(Hoffmann)⑧和波(Poe)⑨最有名。再就是以司各特为中心的浪漫的历史小说;西班牙当地的作为被夸张的恶汉小说,十九世纪中叶在英国和法国流行的政治小说,这是十八世纪流行最多的形式。马里伏(Marlvaux)、理查逊(Richardson)⑩、卢梭(J. J. Rousseau)、歌德(Goethe)等都对当时给予很大影响。但是,对于小说最有研究意义的,是十九世纪后半期更为发展了的写实小说。所谓写实小说,或对心理进行观察,或进行性格描写,或者进行环境叙述,或者开展社会批评,重点偏重的不一样。可是,把人类生活作为社会结构的一个现象,努力欲将所见都表现出来,此乃是根本,也就是形成了最具有近代特色的文学种类。从英法发生的,然而俄国的天才对它的发展和完成贡献很大。所以,可以知道国际影响交错是越发复杂了。

其次就文学的形式可说是 Le style est de l'homme méme(样式是人本身)。那是它本身的东西,那是由于采用了本国语言的惯用表现法和一些不可分割的形式,与其他的文学成分比较,好多是非国际性的。换言之,形式给予外国的影响如果少,那么从外国接受的影

---

① 《新大西洋岛》(*New Atlantis*, 1627),英国散文作家培根写成的名作,描绘了一个理想国,在那里科学有很好的发展条件。

② 柏拉图(Plato,公元前427—前347),古希腊的客观唯心主义哲学家。在《理想国》中阐述了他的道德、政治等理论。

③ 参照《世界文学讲座》的《欧洲文学》(松浦路一)。

④ 巴特勒·萨缪尔(Butler Samuel,1835—1902),英国批判现实主义作家,代表作有《乌有乡游记》(1872)、《众生之路》(1903)。

⑤ 肖伯纳(George Bernard Shaw,1856—1950),英国剧作家、小说家及社会活动家。马修斯拉,据传享年963岁,创世纪五章二十七节记载,是年龄最高之一长老。

⑥ 薄伽丘(Giovanni Boccaccio,1313—1375),意大利文艺复兴时期作家,人文主义的重要代表。早期剧作多取材于古代传说,开辟了意大利歌文和小说创作的通路。代表作《十日谈》包括一百多则故事,他的作品对欧洲文学中短篇小说发展有较大影响。

⑦ 乔叟(Geoffrey Chaucer,约1343—1400),英国诗人。代表作《坎特伯雷故事集》《声誉之堂》等。他用伦敦方言进行创作,对英国民族语言的形成有较大影响。

⑧ 霍夫曼(E. T. A. Hoffman,1776—1832),德国作家。

⑨ 现译"坡",即埃德加·爱伦·坡(Edgar Allan Poe,1809—1849)。

⑩ 理查逊(Samuel Richardson,1689—1761),英国小说家,感伤主义早期的代表。

响也少,对于这些来说很明显的是翻译问题。斯莱格尔(W. von Schlegel)[①]的翻译无论怎样炫耀辞藻,也不能够写出莎士比亚的英语所具有的色彩和光泽。泰勒(Bayard Taylor)[②]翻译的《浮士德》,不管怎样忠实也未能完全嗅到从歌德那里散发的芳香。因为翻译,仅仅以正确的语言形式,却很难传播像文学写实那样的色彩光泽的。即使能够明白原作的形态和意向,作为对文学来说十分重要的如格调啦、形式啦,也很难从中体会到。因此,依靠翻译过来的作品,想去研究比较文学的人,首先不得不考虑到这个不方便的方面。

翻译只不过是一种情况,即我们欣赏外国文学,要想正确感受它的形式和格调,不知道用什么样的本国语言形式去表现。拘泥于词句则恐有失去原格调、注意形式严整又恐有牺牲原意的正确性。即使像英语与德语同属于一个语系尚且如此,若在语系不同的场合可以预见到会更加困难了。

假如像这样,语言越过国境想要波及形式也是必然的。使作品形式发生变化,其原因能够考虑到的大致有三点。以梵·第根为例,一,个人的影响。二,民族的传统。三,外国影响的兴起。在这里对于个人的影响和民族的传统没有必要重新说明。作为外国文学对形式上的一个起很大作用的例子,可以看出表现在爱情的题材上。一般说来,像恋爱诗这样丰富地积累爱情的语汇的例子是很少的。往往是,发现新的表现形式就马上模仿,然后很快又陈旧了。再考虑出新的表现形式、再陈旧。例如彼得拉克,以表现美丽的新鲜的恋爱形式而超越国界,急速传播。不论是西班牙、法国、英国都被迎接。西班牙、法国、英国采用了像意大利一样的表现形式。彼得拉克的十四行诗不仅在外国开始形成诗的新的种类,也开始用新的形式开始创作了。这样的例子于近代特别多。不仅仅是在欧洲诸国之间,今天,对容纳于世界的大部分有巨大影响的国家都是适合的。我们的文学表现,不言而喻,就以日常生活的表现形式,像西方那样激烈地使其受到影响。我们经常浸于其中。由于正在出现着连续的变化,对这种情况并非那样明显地感觉到。假如隔一段时间回顾起来看,那么,对它就有明确的认识了。

(刘介民.比较文学译文选[M].刘介民,译.长沙:湖南人民出版社,1984:17-115.)

【延伸阅读】

1. Yves Chevrel. *Comparative Literature Today: Methods and Perspectives*[M]. Kirksville: Thomas Jefferson University Press, 1995.

伊夫·谢弗勒被视为基亚的接班人,但在比较文学学科建设和理论建设方面,他

① 斯莱格尔(Wilhelm Von Schlegel,1767—1845),德国批评家及诗人,因译莎士比亚作品为德文而享盛名。

② 泰勒(Bayard Taylor,1825—1878),美国作家。

却比前辈走得更远，其主要成就就体现在这本书中。在书里，作者跳脱出“西方中心主义”的视阈，有意识地对被长期遮蔽的东方文化给予关注。他认为，当前比较文学界处在一种不合时宜的批评框架（分类因素）（classificateurs）中，也就是套用西方的批评模式对东方资源进行分析，这很容易陷入对他者异质性的片面关注。因此，作者颇具学术胸怀地提出“世界文学不应只归结为远东/西方这个轴心”这个概念，将东方资源纳入“诗学”范畴，显然给比较文学界带来了新的活力。

2. Gayatri C. Spivak. *Death of a Discipline* [M]. New York: Columbia University Press, 2003.

这篇文章是斯皮瓦克在韦勒克图书馆的演讲。作者试图站在后殖民主义和解构主义的角度来质疑比较文学学科中由来已久的“西方中心论”，并进而指出学科近来意识到的“全球化”问题实际上是“西方中心主义”的变相形式。比较文学学科中惯常出现的“狂热的宗主国意识（metropolitan enthusiasm）”，使得西方比较文学尊崇西方主流文化，忽视边缘文化的多样性和独特性。文章建议：比较文学应与区域研究相联系，利用区域研究的资源，摆脱对他者“想象物”的局限。其次，要用“星球化（planetarity）”取代“全球化”，为比较文学带来全新的思考方式。

第二章　影响研究与国际文学关系

影响研究作为理论的兴起与初步形成是在19世纪初期至20世纪初期，这也是法国学派形成并在国际上确立中心地位的时期。法国学派将影响研究厚实的理论奠定于各国文学相互交流的史实与实践，考本溯源，沿波追流，爬梳史料，细心求证，从而迈开了比较文学学科建设关键的第一步。20世纪50年代末，也就是比较文学的第一阶段，影响研究展示了法国学派从发展过渡到成熟的辉煌历程。

第一节　国际文学关系视域下的影响研究

作为比较文学最传统研究范式的影响研究，它探究的是文学传播者与接受者之间影响与被影响的关系。影响研究在早期，以法国学派的巴登斯贝格、梵·第根、卡雷、基亚等人为代表，形成了一套经典的比较文学实证关系的研究范式，并逐步确立了流传学、渊源学、媒介学等研究方法，它注重的是被比较对象之间的实证性和同源性的关系因素。随着学科的发展，影响研究已不再是单纯的实证性的国际文学关系史研究，而开始关注文学影响中的美学因素和心理学因素，法国学派的一些研究者也开始反思影响研究的方式。

什么是“影响”呢？“影响”就是“存在于作品中的某种东西，这种东西如果作者不曾读过某个以前的作家的作品就不会存在”[艾尔德里奇(Aldridge)]。但影响并不止于模仿，它“不能限于两个对象相似的一瞥，回忆、印象所产生的联系，飘浮的观点，脑中的奇想都是不可靠的”[巴尔邓斯柏耶(Baldensperger)]。“影响”是一种艺术所呈现出来的渗透，一种有机的掺入，它必须“表明被影响的作家所产生的作品本质上是属于他自己的”[弗伦兹(Frenz)]。因此，也可以说，“影响”是某种文学现象的“创造性变形”。两个民族之间的交往通常是沿着“翻译—改编—模仿—影响”这样一条途径来实现的，而“影响”是这一过程的最高阶段。

约瑟夫·T. 肖认为：“一位作家和他的艺术作品，如果显示出某种外来的效果，而这种效果又是他的本国文学传统和他本人的发展无法解释的，那么，我们可以说这位作家受到了外国作家的影响(influence)。影响与模仿不同，被影响的作家的作品基本上是他本人的，影响并不局限于具体的细节、意象、借用，甚或出源——当然，这些都包括在内——而是一种渗透在艺术作品之中，成为艺术作品有机的部分，并通过艺术作品再现出来的东西。……一个作家所受的文学影响，最终将渗透到他的文学作品之中，成为作品的有机部分，从而决定他们的作品的基本灵感和艺术表现，如果没有这种影响，这种灵感和艺术表现就不会以这样的形式出现，或者不会在作家的这个发展阶段上出现。”他认为：“有意义的影响必须以内在的形式在文学作品中表现出来，它可以表现在文体、意象、人物形象、主题或独特的手法风格上，它也可以表现在具体作品所反映出的内容、思想、意念或总的世界观上。”①

一国文学的活动家与别国文学的事实和现象产生这种不同的关系，是由许多原因造成的，如作者的不同阶级立场，世界观的差别，创作个性和生活经验的特点。文学联系按其内容和性质来说不仅可以是相去悬殊，而且在每一种文学里可以产生极其不同的后果。引力与拒力的复杂结合正构成了各种文学相互关系的实质。

影响研究要求研究两国或者两国以上的文学交流中已经存在着的客观联系，整理并分析发现有着客观联系的材料，从文学流传的起点寻找达到终点的迹象和媒介。因此，法国学派要求一个比较文学家首先是一个历史学家，至少是文学史家、文学关系史家；必须熟悉一种乃至多种外语；一国、一时、一地的影响和作用不能靠别人的译著而从事研究，必须自己进入原文，在交流史中发现材料并展开研究。

国际文学关系研究的对象是国家和国家之间，即跨国家的文学关系。它既包含不同国家、不同文学体系之间实证性的影响关系，也包含对不同国家跨越异质文明中不同文学体系之间变异性的关系。它既具实证性的一面，也具非实证性即变异性的一面。因此，实证性的文学关系与变异性的文学关系构成了国际文学关系研究的两大支柱。

国际文学关系研究是对各国文学之间关系的研究，传统的文学研究只限于某一国文学的研究，而比较文学要求从国际的角度出发，打破时空的界限，研究不同民族、不同语言、不同文化之间的文学交流与关联。虽然各国利益和意识形态不尽相同，但文学艺术的交流是人类思想的交流、灵魂的碰撞，应当永远进行下去。各国作家都承载着历史的责任，有义务推进各国文学领域的交流。

国际文学关系研究绝非单纯的史学研究，而是综合性的各个层次的研究。它所关注的是文学交流中产生的种种跨文化、跨语言的现象事实，因此属于影响研究的范畴，除了回答“是什么”“怎么样”以外，还必须探讨分析“为什么”的问题，也就是说，研究国际文学交流现象事实是缘何及如何在文学场的合力作用下生发、演变、成形的。探讨这些现象事实产生的内在逻辑，不仅要研究文学史实的外部联系（即这些史实现象与社会文化语境的关系），还必须涉及无“事实联系”的类比研究，才能把“关系”缘何产生分析清楚。这样的研究势必要导向文学内部关系的思考，终究要揭示出人类在文学方面交流、对话、互视互补的内在逻辑与规律，反过来更为积极地促进各国文学的交流。

---

① 约瑟夫·T.肖.文学借鉴与比较文学研究[M]//比较文学译文集.北京：北京大学出版社，1982：38-39.

在两国文学的界限确定之后,紧接着的就是着手研究在文学领域中从这一边移到那一边而发生作用的一切因素或现象。这些作用的性质,往往很不相同,或是因为知识的获得带来的心智的发达;或是由于艺术手段的模仿带来的技巧的改善;或是因为感觉的相似带来的感觉的同情以及那些丰富的反感与反响。如果把这一大群的现象加以整理,最终便可划分出比较文学的领域。

首先是去考察穿过文学界限的路线的起点——作家、著作、思想,这就是所谓的"放送者"。其次是到达点——某一作家、某一作品或某一页、某一思想或某一情感,这就是所谓的"接受者"。"放送者"和"接受者"之间,往往需要媒介的沟通。充当这一角色的,包括个人或集团、原文的翻译或模仿,这就是所谓的"传递者"。一个国家的"接受者"对另一个来说往往担当着"传递者"的任务。

文学的国际影响通过的途径,主要有下述情况:某一作家对他国某一作家的影响,也有对他国很多作家的影响,还有某一个流派的运动对其他流派的影响,或者这个流派对其他某一作家或很多作家的影响。这些影响有直接的,也有间接的。另外,影响或源自作品本身,或来自作品以外。

有意义的影响必须以内在的形式在文学作品中表现出来。它可以表现在文体、意象、人物形象、主题或独特的手法风格上,也可表现在具体作品所反映的内容、思想、意念或总的世界观上。为了说明被影响的作家可能受产生影响的作家的影响,完全有必要列出作品之外的令人信服的证据。因此,各种文献记载、引语、日记、同代人的见证和作者的阅读书目等都必须加以运用。可是,最基本的证明又必须在作品的本身。具体的借用是否表现为影响,取决于它们在新作中的作用和重要程度。考察一位作家的发展过程时,影响研究显得格外重要。

文学在创作上相互影响的具体形式和艺术本身一样,都是无限多样化的,并处于历史变化之中,其特有的不同表现的可能性无穷无尽。文学创作上的相互影响表现:类似的和不同的文学流派之间能够发生相互影响;在思想和美学原则上接近,或者差距很大的各个艺术家也会发生相互影响。相互影响有助于任何民族文学体裁的出现、发展与变化,可以促进新的艺术形式的发展和旧的艺术形式臻于完美,也可以影响个别语言艺术大师的语言风格。文学的相互影响可以直接(通过原著或翻译)实现,也可以通过其他意识形态,如通过美学思想来实现。它还可以在其他艺术的协助下得到加强。相互影响也时常表现为一个大艺术家的作品或整个流派的文学有意识地放弃自己所具有的思想和美学的原则。各种文学之间的相互影响可以是同步的,也可以是非同步的,或者是几种文学同时起主要作用,这都要视这些文学在文学史发展的总过程中具有怎样的意义而定。

比较文学的影响研究基本上涉及文学的文化因素、内部构成、社会效果等方面，其意图是想从两国或两国以上的文学交流和影响的角度揭示出文学存在的另外一面，即一国文学与另外一国文学的客观联系。在实际研究中，影响研究往往涉及文化的各方面，这不是因为别的，而是因为两国间的文学交流影响从来都与文化各个方面具有联系，文学创作本身与之密不可分。乐黛云曾说："任何文化的发展都不能脱离其他文化的影响，任何文化都是世界文化的一部分来发展的。历史事实说明，许多灿烂辉煌的文化都是在外来文化的影响和刺激下形成起来。例如，盛唐文化的繁荣离不开印度佛教的传入，俄国19世纪文学的兴旺也离不开法国文化的多方面影响，中国现代文学的诞生更是和20世纪以来世界文化的发展密切相关。因此，如果没有一种世界性的比较眼光就很难教好一国文学史。我认为所谓比较文学的根本原则就是把某国文学放在是世界文学的宏观发展中来加以考察。"①影响研究可以丰富世界文化的研究。如果借用世界文化的力量进行影响研究，可以为文化交流影响史提供更多的材料和线索。从这个意义上说，比较文学的影响研究即为文化交流史的一部分。从事影响研究的比较文学者，必须站在文化交流史和对所涉论题的材料十分熟悉的情况下，才能予以研究。

影响研究注重作品形象和技巧的比较。这样可以使这一研究更加具体化，从文化交流深入文学作品之中，使影响比较更加文学化。影响是多方面的：有总体的影响，也有个别的影响；有题材方面的影响，也有技巧方面的影响；有环境的影响，也有集团的影响；有成功的影响，也有非成功的影响，或者说，有积极的影响，也有负面的影响。

外国文学给予本国文学的影响往往有三种方式：第一，作家的人格影响。具体地说，包括作家的理智和道义的人格，作家创作的想象或写实的性格，作家才智特异性的影响。第二，艺术手法所涉及的影响。这不仅是来自作家自己的态度或者人格，而且来自作品或技巧。第三，为外国的模仿者提供了素材和主题。

比较文学的研究由于从影响的结果出发，所以，研究者应该居于接受者的侧位。这样就可以探讨某作家从哪里获得这样的思想，取得这样的体裁，以及是怎样受到这种倾向影响的。如此就获得研究的出发点，即是对源泉的搜索和对原典的探究，包括探讨文学影响的渊源、作品的题材、思想倾向，还有一些事件等，这也可以进入接受美学。

严格地说，中西文学的相互影响，从全部历史传统上来说，幅度并不太大。由于近代交通工具的发达，缩小了人们的生活领域，使东方人和西方人的生活关系日益密切，

---

① 乐黛云. 比较文学与现代文学[M]. 北京：北京大学出版社，1987：44-45.

不再像以前有那么多隔阂。故东西文学在极为自然的情况下，渐渐起了较大幅度的影响。西洋近代文学对中国新文学创作的影响固然明显，但是中国古代文学的研究与介绍也在影响着西洋，使它有更新的开拓。所以在研讨中西文学的相互影响时，应先有一个整体的观念，亦即从一种历史的角度来透视此一题目，而不宜局限于短暂的片段。应该针对中国传统文学的特点和西方文学的不同，提纲挈领地作一简要说明，同时展望中西文学的未来。例如，东方新文学的创作，以世界的眼光来看，还是离不开对古典传统的认识。即使是最传统的实证性的影响研究，至今也仍未过时。对于现今中国学界来说，这种实证精神，这种踏踏实实的学风，尤其重要。而且，许许多多的领域还有待于我们运用传统的影响研究方法去开掘。

没有具体事实联系为依据的研究不能算影响研究。影响研究特别地注重史料，不允许任何没有直接或间接联系的材料的人空口说白话。它抉幽择微，细密翔实。随着接受美学的发展，影响比较研究还会有新的转机；随着东西方政治和文化关系的改善，文学的渗透力和影响力还会强大，影响研究仍将会深入持久地发展下去。但是，由于影响研究过分拘泥于直接交流的材料之中，考证、训诂、渊源学、媒介学的烦琐阻碍了它的发展，尤其是在遭到美国比较文学理论家韦勒克等人的质疑和批评后，已不如20世纪那么兴盛；而且，20世纪文化科学的精神有了新的发展，整个文化氛围也不允许影响研究单一的发展。但是，作为比较文学的一种研究方法，影响研究特别是实证方法依然可以长期生存下去。

影响研究注重的是文学之间影响的“实证性”关系，主要包括流传学、渊源学、媒介学的研究。流传学是给予影响的放送者为起点，去探讨一国文学或文学流派、文学思潮，或作家及作品在他国的命运与成就，或遭遇之影响以及接受的历史境况之研究。还包括鉴定资料来源和鉴定借取成分的研究。渊源学是以接受者为基点对某一作家及文学作品的主题、题材、思想、人物、情节、风格、形式等来源的研究。也包括文学作品的际遇的探讨与判断。媒介学是对不同民族文学之间产生影响事实的途径、方法、手段及其因果关系的研究。媒介学研究的对象是有助于国与国之间或文学与文学之间了解的人或典籍，包括：①语言知识或语言学家；②翻译作品或译者；③评论文献与报章杂志；④旅游与观光客；⑤一种因为地理与文化的特殊情况所造成的国际公民。

传统的影响研究在20世纪50年代受到后起的美国学派的质疑与批评，70年代随着接受理论的兴起，又再度受到冲击。然而，影响研究学者不断克服自身的保守主义和狭隘观点，发展更新自己的理论，特别是在接受理论对影响研究作了全面的刷新之后，影响研究不仅仅是研究一民族文学如何影响另一民族文学，更重要的是要研究一民族文学是如何接受另一民族文学的影响。这样，过去强调的单向影响的过程变成了双向的过程,从而为影响研究领域开辟出许多新的层面,使更多影响现象得到更加合理的解释及更加深刻的研究。

【原典选读】

比较文学论(节选)

◉梵·第根

【导读】比较文学学科在20世纪初诞生不久,就遭到来自多方面的批评。以意大利美学家克罗齐为代表,在各种场合以各种不同方式否定比较文学。然而,比较文学却在一片诘难声中依然保持了迅猛的发展势头,并形成比较文学史上第一个学派——法国学派。法国学派提倡以事实联系为基础的影响研究,因此也被称为"影响研究学派"。深受实证主义哲学的影响,法国学派崇尚文献考据,表现出严谨的学术风格。但其不足之处也很明显,即研究往往局限在欧洲文化系统内部,研究对象囿于有实际联系的两个国家的作家作品。早期法国学派的杰出代表是梵·第根(Paul Van Tiegehm,1871—1948),他的经典论著《比较文学论》全面阐述了法国学派的观点:"比较文学的对象是本质地研究各国文学作品的相互关系","真正的'比较文学'的特质,正如一切历史科学的特质一样,是把尽可能多的来源不同的事实采纳在一起,以便充分地把每一个事实加以解释;是扩大认识的基础,以便找到尽可能多的种种结果的原因。总之,'比较'这两个字应该摆脱全部美学的含义,而取得一个科学的含义。"梵·第根还为两国之间文学作品的相互关系设计了一个"经过路线",其起点是作家、著作、思想,即"放送者";终点是另一国家的某一作家作品或某一页,某一思想或某一情感,即"接受者";"经过路线往往是由一个媒介者勾通的:个人或集团,原文的翻译或模仿。这便是人们所谓'传递者'"。整个比较文学的目的在于刻画出"经过路线",有时考虑路线本身,有时考虑路线是如何发生的。■

可是有一点还没有充分说明白。前面我们说起过那些接受到的或给予别人的影响;我们的意思是指源流以及主题、思想或形式的借用。在一国的文学之中,这种影响已经可能成为重要,值得详细研究了。在《思想集》中,巴斯加显得是饱读蒙田的,他追随蒙田,却同时又和他背道而驰。伏尔泰以及法国十八世纪其他悲剧家都是以拉辛为模范的;显然地,丹纳是季若的弟子,蒲尔惹是司汤达的门徒,瓦雷里是马拉美的后辈。可是,在同一种族同一语言的作家们之间,模仿并不是很丰富的。这种模仿也许只是一种一般的影响,一种因对于取为模范的先进者的研究和钦佩而起的潜在的性癖之觉醒;它也许一点不能摆脱窠臼,而一无独特见长之处。然而即在后面这一种情形之下,模仿也绝不会十分明显的。

反之,如果我们在涉猎法国文学的时候,把我们的注意力集中于它和别国文学的接触,那时我们便会立刻见到这些接触的频繁以及重要了。那如我们上文所叙述的文学史,必须不断地专注于那些影响、模仿和假借。不能研究“七星诗社”而不说龙沙、都·伯莱,以及其他诗人之得力于希腊、罗马、意大利诸诗人之处。如果碰到蒙田,那时便当说他是熟读古人之书,饱学深思,得益于普鲁塔克和塞内加。在文艺复兴时代以及其后的两个古典的世纪,法国的全部诗歌和一部分散文,都是浸润于希腊、罗马的古色古香之中的。高乃依从西班牙采取了《熙德》,莫里哀从那里借来了《唐·璜》,勒萨日又从那里提取了《吉尔·布拉斯》。孟德斯鸠、伏尔泰、狄德罗、卢梭都得益于英国甚多;法国的诸多浪漫诗人都颇有赖于各国的文学,丹纳很借重英国和德国,而勒南得益于德国之处尤多。这种例子我们当然还可以成倍地增加,并延续下来,一直至于今日。

当一位法国文学的史家,来到了他的探讨的这一点上,而又碰到了这对于他所研究的作家们起作用的诸势力的几乎无限制的网线的时候,那么他便怎样办呢?在他只需致力于法国文学内部的活动的时候,他还应付裕如,如果莫里哀的某一个剧本是模仿斯加龙的一篇短篇小说的,某一个剧本是模仿贝尔易合克的一部喜剧或模仿中世纪的一部趣剧的,那么文学史家还可以在同一个书库里找到那些原来的范本;这些原文是他随手可得而且充分理解的。可是如果他要知道在《冒失鬼》《唐·璜》或《悭吝人》诸剧中,莫里哀的独创之处,那么他便不得不先知道莫里哀在倍尔特拉麦、莫利拿,或西高尼尼、柏鲁特等外国作家中所获得的是什么,并贴近地研究他们的类似之处和不同之处。夏多勃里昂是受着《圣经》、荷马、莪相、塔索、弥尔顿的支配的;他同时也受着基督教英国诸护教论者的支配。有几位法国作家,如果我们对于他们的作品之源流作一点小小的研究,那时我们便会被牵引开去,去经历一个非常广大而又不大有人开拓的土地,法国文学的史家那时怎么办呢?

我们应当分别出两种情形。最简单的是模仿古代文学的那个情形:希腊的、拉丁的、希伯莱的(在法国,希伯莱文学主要是由于《圣经》的拉丁文译文或由于其他法文译本而被人认识)。

这些原文,那些深通古文字的古典学者是直接地理解的;那些与时俱增的其余的人们,便可以很容易找到一些完善的译本了;这是他们的独一无二的资料,和原本相比,颇有逊色,而又有许多不妥之处。

可是说到近代作家和近代外国作家的接触,问题就格外复杂了。当一位法国作家单靠了译本而认识外国作品的时候(这情形是很多的),那么只要单参考这个译本去作一切必要的探讨就够了。卢梭是靠了泊莱服和于伯尔的法译本而模仿理查逊并爱好格斯纳的,因为他既不懂英文又不懂德文。可是伏尔泰、狄德罗、夏多勃里昂、维尼却都深通英文,而法国十七世纪的古典作家又都懂得意大利文和西班牙文的。在这种情形之下,那便要一直追溯到原文了。再则，在那些使法国作家受影响的许多外国作品之中，有一些是从来也没有译成法文的。因此法国文学史家便应该深通许多种外国语言文字：因为单单认识那些有关系的原文是不够的，还得把那些原文安置在他所从属的整体之中。法国文学史家因此就可以看出他的任务是无限地增大了。

如果他克尽厥职，把他所研究的法国作家，不视为各种潮流或影响的终点，却视为通过边疆、通过系代而流出去的水流的出发点，那会怎样呢？对于拉辛、卢梭、左拉的完备的研究，不仅应该包含他们的作品在法国的生存和影响，还应该包含它们在外国的际遇。为了要稍稍画这样一幅草图，那是必须要有对于各国文学的广博的知识的。那一般地研究这些作家以及其他许许多多作家的文学史家，很可以互通声气并陈述那最专门的探讨者所能获得的结果；除了他最熟悉的几点之外，他不能自己一个人发现它们。

一直到现在为止，我们故意只单就法国文学讲，可是同样的推论是可以适用于任何别国文学的，在意大利，在英国，在德国，在俄国，外国影响所起的作用至少是和在法国同样重要。在这些国家的每一个国家中(特别是关于范围不广的几国的文学，例如荷兰、丹麦、瑞典、匈牙利、波兰等国文学)，本国文学的专家如何能够懂得那么许多语言和外国文学；去发现并就近研究那些他所研究的作家所受到的许许多多影响，以及他们所假借的形式内容呢？的确，这些学者们之中有许多人比他们的法国同志更擅长于外国语言。然而我们却不能勉强要求他们对于他们所研究的每一位作家都有种种确切的知识，因为这是超越他们所能从事的力量和时间了。

现在只有一个方法来解决这个困难：那便是分工从事。既然那组成对于一件作品或一位作家的完全研究之各部分，可以单凭本国文学史着手，而不及于那接受到或给予别人的诸影响之探讨和分析的，那么就让这种探讨自立门户，具有它的确切的目标，它的专家，它的方法，这想来也并无不合吧。它可以在各方面延长一个国家的文学史所获得的结果，将这些结果和别的诸国家的文学史家们所获得的结果联在一起，于是这各种影响的复杂的网线，便组成了一个独立的领域，它绝对不想去代替各种本国的文学史：它只补充那些本国的文学史并把它们联合在一起。同时，它在它们之间以及它们之上，纺织一个更普遍的文学史的网。这个门类是存在的；它是这部书的研究对象；它名为“比较文学”。

(于永昌，廖鸿钧，倪蕊琴. 比较文学研究译文集[M]. 上海：上海译文出版社，1985：51-55.)

《比较文学》初版序言（节选）

◉伽列

【导读】1951 年基亚出版《比较文学》给比较文学下的定义是：“比较文学就是国际文

学的关系史。比较文学工作者站在语言的或民族的边缘，注视着两种或多种文学之间在题材、思想、书籍或感想方面的彼此渗透。”同年，基亚的老师伽列为《比较文学》一书的初版作了序言，他提出：“比较文学是文学史的一个分支；它在研究拜伦与普希金，歌德与卡莱尔，瓦尔特·司各特与维尼之间，是属于一种以上文学背景的不同作品、不同构思以至不同作家的生平之间所曾存在过的跨国度的精神交往（des relations spirituelles internationales）与实际联系（des rapports de fait）。”“比较文学不是文学的比较。问题并不在于将高乃依与拉辛、伏尔泰与卢梭等人的旧辞藻之间的平行现象简单地搬到外国文学的领域中去。我们不大喜欢不厌其烦地探讨丁尼生与缪塞、狄更斯与都德等之间有什么相似与相异之处。”伽列把研究国际文学上事实联系作为比较文学研究的目标，重视不同民族作家之间的精神联系。他强调研究的“事实联系”具有鲜明的实证倾向，但又拘于史而忽视论，烦琐考证胜于美学把握。伽列上述观点虽然有些褊狭，但却划定了比较文学最为坚实的一个领域，也是比较文学成果最重要的一个领域，即实证性的影响研究。■

在当今的法国，比较文学的发展既令人鼓舞又使人担忧。（自从“解放”[①]以来，在索尔本学院[②]注册的学位论文已逾两百份。）这种热衷的情形已经达到如此令人振奋的程度，以致可能导致无政府的混乱状态。为此应当感谢基亚先生将它加以澄清。他的明白晓畅的阐述，足以醒耳目、正视听。

有鉴于此，比较文学的定义有必要再一次加以廓清。（第一次全面论述是由我们的大师巴登斯贝格于一九二一年在《比较文学杂志》第一期上作出的。也可参见梵·第根所著《比较文学》一书，该书初版于一九三一年。）并非随便什么事物、随便什么时间地点都可以拿来比较。

比较文学不是文学的比较。问题并不在于将高乃依[③]与拉辛[④]、伏尔泰[⑤]与卢梭[⑥]等人的旧辞藻之间的平行现象简单地搬到外国文学的领域中去。我们不大喜欢不厌其烦地探

---

① 指1944—1945年间法国从德国法西斯的占领下解放出来。

② 索尔本学院系巴黎历史悠久的高等学府，初建于13世纪，组织机构几经变迁。这里指巴黎高等研究院文学系。

③ 高乃依（P. Corncille，1606—1684），法国古典主义悲剧作家。

④ 拉辛（J. Racine，1639—1699），法国古典主义悲剧作家。

⑤ 伏尔泰（F. M. A. Voltaire，1694—1778），法国启蒙时代思想家、作家。

⑥ 卢梭（J. J. Rousseau，1712—1778），法国启蒙时代思想家、作家。

讨丁尼生[①]与缪塞[②]、狄更斯[③]与都德[④]等之间有什么相似与相异之处。

比较文学是文学史的一个分支;它研究在拜伦[⑤]与普希金[⑥]、歌德[⑦]与卡莱尔[⑧]、瓦尔特·司各特[⑨]与维尼[⑩]之间,在属于一种以上文学背景的不同作品、不同构思以至不同作家的生平之间所曾存在过的跨国度的精神交往(des relations spirituelles internationales)与实际联系(des rapports de fait)。

比较文学主要不是评定作品的原有价值,而是侧重于每个民族、每个作家所借鉴的那种种发展演变。一提到影响,往往便意味着解释、反馈、抗力、搏斗。瓦雷利[⑪]说:"用别人充实自己;没有比这更本分、更合于自我的了。但是必须将别人消化掉。一只狮子就是由许多被同化了的绵羊构成的。"

此外,人们或许又过分专注于影响研究(les études d'influence)了。这种研究做起来是十分困难的,而且经常是靠不住的。在这种研究中,人们往往试图将一些不可称量的因素加以称量。相比之下,更为可靠的则是由作品的成就、某位作家的境遇、某位大人物的命运、不同民族之间的相互理解以及旅行和见闻等所构成的历史。例如英国人与法国人、法国人与德国人等之间彼此如何看法。

最后,比较文学并不是总体文学(lalittérature générale)(它只在美国被作为研究目标)。比较文学可以导致总体文学:在有些情况下甚至是一种必然趋势。但是,诸如人文主义、古典主义、浪漫主义、现实主义、象征主义这样一些大的平行性(同时也是同步性)的领域,往往会有失于刻板,在时间与空间上都过于空泛,以致有可能导致抽象,而且带有随意性和空洞性。运动是在发展中证实自身的。问题在于不应漫无边际地发展,而应限定我们的进程。基亚先生的这本书将会为我们廓清道路。

(北京师范大学中文系比较文学研究组.比较文学研究资料[M].北京:北京大学出版社,1986:42-44.)

① 丁尼生(A. Tennyson,1809—1892),浪漫主义时代英国诗人。
② 缪塞(A. de Musset,1810—1859),法国浪漫派诗人。
③ 狄更斯(Ch. Dickens,1812—1870),英国批判现实主义小说家。
④ 都德(A. Daudet,1840—1897),法国小说家,曾被誉为"法国的狄更斯"。
⑤ 拜伦(G. G. Byron,1788—1824),英国著名浪漫派诗人。
⑥ 普希金(A. C. Пушкин,1799—1837),著名俄国诗人。
⑦ 歌德(J. W. von Goethe, 1749—1832),著名德国作家。
⑧ 卡莱尔(Th. Carlyle,1795—1881),英国作家。
⑨ 瓦尔特·司各特(Walter Scott, 1771—1832),苏格兰诗人和小说家。
⑩ 维尼(A. de Vigny, 1797—1863),法国浪漫派作家。
⑪ 瓦雷利(P. Valéry,1871—1945),法国作家。

【延伸阅读】

1. 艾田蒲. 从纪君祥到伏尔泰・中国之欧洲[M]. 桂林:广西师大出版社,2008.

纪君祥的《赵氏孤儿》由传教士马约瑟神甫于1731年译成法文并在次年传入法国,法国启蒙思想家、文学家伏尔泰据此写成五幕悲剧《中国孤儿》于1755年搬上舞台公演。纪君祥的《赵氏孤儿》以怎样富有哲思的题材引起伏尔泰的兴趣,后者所创作的《中国孤儿》又是怎样的一部剧作?艾田蒲对这一古老的课题进行了跨文化的哲学审视和美学思考。在这个过程中,他严格遵循影响研究的历史考察的原则,注意事实的联系与梳理,显示了法国学派影响研究特有的严谨、深度和魅力。

2. 叶维廉. 比较诗学[M]. 台北:东大图书有限公司,1983.

叶维廉作为比较诗学中国学派的开创者,在《比较诗学》一书中除了对西方文学理论应用到中国文学研究的可行性及危机作出思考外,针对当时国人过分单方面依赖西方文学批评的模子,而造成对传统美学歪曲的现象,提出了"同异全识并用"的观念,从新的角度肯定和发挥了传统中国美学的含义,并通过"语法与表现""语言与真实世界""媒体与超媒体"等理论架构的比较和对比,寻求更合理的共同文学规律与美学观念。"文化模子"理论作为其开展中西比较诗学理论研究的一个支点,给中外的跨文化诗学研究提供了可行的范式。

第二节　流传学

流传学(Doxologie)一词源于在宗教仪式上赞美上帝荣耀的颂歌,也称为誉舆学。法国比较文学理论家梵・第根将这一宗教述语引入比较文学研究,形成了比较文学影响研究的重要理论模式。流传学是指从给予影响的放送者出发,去研究作为终点的接受者的情况,即作家、作品、文学流派和文艺思潮在他国的际遇、影响和接受情况。

流传学是在实证主义哲学影响下形成的研究模式。以法国哲学家孔德为代表的实证主义哲学认为一切事物的本质都源于"实证(positive)",将自然科学的研究方法引入人文社会科学的研究之中。实证主义哲学尊重事实和擅长运用比较为流传学奠定的理论基础，在实证主义哲学影响下形成了流传学研究事实、崇尚实证的研究方法，“实证性”也成为影响研究的本质特征。

在流传学萌芽时期，始终伴随着欧洲文化优越感，欧洲中心主义思想已见端倪。早期流传学研究者普遍认为欧洲文学是最优秀的，其他地区的文学不能与欧洲文学相提并论。不仅如此，欧洲文学对其他地区还有当然的影响和辐射作用，在影响和辐射过程中，被影响和辐射地区的文学水平永远低于欧洲文学所达到的水平。因此，流传学一开始就抹上了欧洲文化优越感的民族沙文主义色彩，表面上是客观的“实证研究”，实际上受到主观的“目的论”的操控，成为证明欧洲文学影响世界文学的有力证据。

随着流传学的发展，许多学者意识到单向地研究欧洲文学对其他文学的影响，既违背了世界相互影响、共同促进的实际情况，又锁定了学科的研究视野，对学科的发展极为不利。因此，越来越多的学者关注世界不同民族、不同国度、不同文明之间的相互影响，通过跨文明、跨民族、跨国度的互识、互证、互补来建构更加广阔、更符合文学发展实际的流传学研究体系。

流传学的研究对象是文学关系。梵·第根将这种关系限定在两国文学间的相互关系上，而实际上，文学在流传过程中的影响远远超越“两国”关系，呈现出“多元”的流传态势，尤其是在文化全球化的今天，国与国、民族与民族、文化与文化、文明与文明之间的相互流传、相互影响更是司空见惯。因此，文学在流传过程中形成的关系也就异常纷繁复杂，文学关系的确认也就更需要耐心细致的深入研究。

流传学的研究对象决定了其研究方法必定以实证性研究为根基。某种文学关系的确认只能建立在“事实”基础上，没有可靠的“事实”为基础，文学之间的“关系”就成为无源之水、无本之木，其“文学关系”就必定会受到质疑。因此，遵循严格实证研究路径是流传学得以成立的必要条件。实证研究以事实为依据，就必然强调历史意识，这也是早期的比较文学被视为文学史的分支学科的原因。流传学的实证研究既要关注文学形象、文学观念、文学思潮、文学流派、文学作品的纵向发展、流变，又要厘清传承、流变过程中的各种横向关系。

总体而言，流传学研究过程中形成四种流传、影响关系。第一，个体对个体的影响研究，如托尔斯泰对茅盾的影响；第二，个体对群体的影响研究，如西班牙流浪汉小说对欧洲长篇小说的影响；第三，群体对个体的影响研究，如果戈里、契诃夫为代表的俄罗斯批判现实主义对鲁迅的影响；第四，群体对群体的影响研究，如西方批判现实主义文学对中国“五四”新文学的影响。

【原典选读】

比较文学（节选）

◉基亚

【导读】“比较文学”作为一门学科一开始就受到质疑和挑战。其理由主要是认为“比较”只是一种研究方法，而不是一门独立学科的基石，意大利著名美学家克罗齐指出，比较方法“只是历史研究的一种简单的考察性方法”，是任何学科都可以使用的一种方法。克罗齐对比较文学学科的非难，引起欧洲比较文学学者对比较文学学科理论的反思。

法国比较文学著名学者马·法·基亚在《比较文学》一书中正面回应了克罗齐等人的质疑和非难。基亚以“比较文学并非比较，比较文学实际只是一种被误称了的科学方法，正确的定义应该是，国际文学关系史”来回击学界对比较文学学科的挑战。既然比较文学并非简单的文学比较，不是将简单比较方法运用于文学研究，那么别人也就很难通过“比较”来做文章，挡住了外界对比较文学作为一门学科的合法性的攻击。

然而，“比较文学并非比较”仅仅成为挡住别人攻击的盾牌，并非因为有此盾牌就可以忽略比较文学学科理论的建构。基亚的《比较文学》试图从“关系”的角度来重新定位比较文学，“比较文学就是国际文学的关系史。比较文学工作者站在语言的或民族的边缘，注视着两种或多种文学之间在题材、思想、书籍或感情方面的彼此渗透”。基亚的研究方法注重依靠文学关系中的事实，因此在其论述不同民族文学在流传和影响的过程时非常重视文献依据，甚至将民间传说、旅行见闻、文坛趣事、文学评论等都视为文学“关系”的支撑材料。基亚的《比较文学》初步建立起了比较文学影响研究的基本范式。■

比较文学并非比较。比较文学实际只是一种被误称了的科学方法，正确的定义应该是：国际文学关系史。

关系，这个词在“世界”方面划出了一条界线。人们曾想，现在也还在想把比较文学发展成为一种“总体文学”来研究；找出“多种文学的共同点”（梵・第根），来看看它们之间存在的是主从关系抑或仅只是一种偶合。为了纪念“世界文学”这个词的发明者——歌德，人们还想撰写一部“世界文学”，目的是要说明“人们共同喜爱的作品的主体”（盖拉尔）。1951 年时，无论是前一种还是后一种打算，对大部分法国比较文学工作者来说，都是些形而上学的或无益的工作。我的老师伽雷（Carré）继 P. 阿扎尔（P. Hazard）和巴登斯贝格(F. Baldensperger)之后,认为什么地方的"联系"消失了——某人与某篇文章,某部作品与某个环境,某个国家与某个旅游者等,那么那里的比较工作也就不存在了,取而代之的如果不是修辞学,那就是批评领域的开始。(前言 pp. 1-2)

比较文学是由于世界主义文学的觉醒而产生的,它兼有历史地研究世界主义文学的意愿。中世纪的欧洲是属于世界主义的,它被基督教和拉丁文化统一起来;文艺复兴时期,共同的人文主义则把欧洲的作家们结合起来,到了十八世纪,欧洲竟然法国化、哲学化了。(p. 1)

比较文学就是国际文学的关系史。比较文学工作者站在语言的或民族的边缘,注视着两种或多种文学之间在题材、思想、书籍或感情方面的彼此渗透。(p. 4)

伏尔泰、雨果、克洛代尔(Claudel)①、布莱希特(Brecht)②都曾怀着不同的意图去从莎士比亚戏剧理论那里获得启发,这是直接借鉴。对这种借鉴也需要估计它的影响范围。伏尔泰、雨果、克洛代尔或布莱希特也去启发自己的竞争者。某些竞争者在某些时候只能从其启发者那里接受莎士比亚的戏剧理论,这就是间接借鉴。离开第一个借鉴者越远,问题就越不易得到证实。(p. 11)

我们需要把"传播""模仿""成功"与"影响"都仔细地区别开来。一本"畅销"书是一本成功的书,但它的文学影响却可能等于零。马拉美(Mallarmé)③的诗传播的范围并不广,但它启发了相当多的外国作家。研究一部作品的传播、模仿和成功情况是一件需要耐性和方法的工作,识别一种影响更是一件细致的工作。首先,因为存在许多种影响:

个人方面的:对卢梭生前和死后的崇拜。

技术方面的:莎士比亚剧作在法国浪漫主义时期的威望。

精神方面的:伏尔泰思想的传播。

题材或背景方面的:我们十七世纪的戏剧理论家借用了西班牙戏剧的一些题材、浪漫主义时期奥西昂式风景画的兴时等。(pp. 13-14)

我们不像梵·第根过去在阐明自己的"总体文学"研究方法时那样富有野心,那类综合性的工作只有在一位学者已经广泛阅读作品之后才能进行。即便如此,要认为肯定会有收获也还未免有点自负呢。在这里,更具有危险性的是误把巧合当作了影响。不过,巧合还是具有教益的,它能给每一种文学的历史增添一点它单独存在时缺少的相对

① 克洛代尔(1868—1955),法国作家和外交家。著有《人质》等。

② 布莱希特(1898—1956),现代德国著名戏剧家和诗人,创立了"史诗剧"的理论和表演体系。

③ 马拉美(1842—1898),法国诗人。象征主义理论家,认为诗歌应当表现"理想世界"。

感。(p. 15)

每个民族都能以自己的性格为别的民族提供一种比较持久的模式,而且传说往往比实事更起作用。一位拙劣的作曲家倒可能获得声望,正如每个法国人都知道"葡萄牙人是快活的人"这首歌一样。还有一些更深刻的原因,如法国人不像德国人那么能够欣赏和理解英国人民族性格中的同一个特点。而在塑造这些民族典型的过程中,文学、旅游故事、小说、戏剧都起着决定性的作用。试问,能有多少人愿意费神去找机会来验证莫洛亚(Maurois)①有关英国的一些说法,或史达尔夫人有关德国的说法呢?比较文学的任务就是要研究对某个国家的种种阐述的产生及发展情况。(p. 16)

英国在我们19世纪文学中的情况:有哪些法国人曾向自己的同胞提供过英国的情况?英国人有哪些偏见、哪些知识?他们来过法国吗?他们看到了些什么?一些小说、戏剧中提到过英国人物吗?如果有,又赋予他们些什么特点?为什么会这样?这不属于影响问题而是有关阐明的问题。对这些问题的研究会使我们懂得我们是怎样看待英国人的,以及为什么是这样看待的。这种工作要求人们在仔细阅读法文作品的同时,对英国还要有亲身的体验。在这方面,比较文学可以帮助两国进行某种民族的心理分析——在了解了存在于彼此之间的那些成见的来源之后,双方也会各自加深对自己的了解,而对某些相同的先入之见也就更能谅解了。(p. 16)

对译作的研究看来似乎是徒劳无功的工作,但还是值得去做的,因为它可以使我们了解译者的情况。水平最差的译者也能反映一个集团或一个时代的审美观;最忠实的译者则可以为人们了解外国文化的情况作出贡献;而那些真正的创造者则在移植和改写他们认为需要的作品。(p. 20)

在可以作为各民族文学媒介的书籍中,比较文学工作者也把旅游故事算在内了。阅读外国的原著,一般来说还是比较少的,连专业作家也是如此,能读到一些译作和旅游笔记也就感到满足了。如对纪德来说,英国就是一些小说家和诗人,然而对伏尔泰和他的同时代人来说,英国则是一种生活方式和某种政治体制——舒适的生活和议院。比较文学的任务就是要让人们知道旅游者们是如何表现外国人民的,因为通过他们的故事,一些题材才蔓延到他们本国的文学中,如英国人的宽容、德国人的道德、斯拉夫族的神秘主义等。(p. 22)

很久以来,抒情诗、史诗都有固定的框框,这是从古代希腊、罗马继承下来的。如哀

① 莫洛亚(1885—1967),法国现代作家,写过许多有关英国的作品。

歌、颂歌、多段歌曲等。也有这样的情况,即某种形式是从欧洲某种文学中借鉴来的,如十四行诗诗体是从意大利移植来的;歌曲是由德国移植来的;基督教史诗是从塔索[①](Tasso)那儿借鉴来的。这类借鉴的历史即属于比较文学的一部分,它已多少被全面地研究过了。梵・第根曾研究过该斯那(Gessner)的田园诗在欧洲的命运,他不仅指出田园诗题材的成功情况,同时也指出了该类诗歌形式的成功情况。(p. 37)

不仅要研究一个作家而且还要研究一种文学类型的影响的重要性。司各特给我们提供了什么呢?很少是思想方面的,主要是创作技巧。由于作家们不能适应这种创作技巧,所以许多与司各特一样有才华的作家恰恰就在他成功的地方摔倒了。这些作家,每一个都缺少某种才能,这些才能加在一起便形成了司各特的成就:维尼不懂得或不大懂得要使必不可少的群众活跃起来,以便使过去的情景活生生地再现;巴尔扎克选择的题材太近,使读者感到很不自在;梅里美的人物缺少感情;雨果作品中过多的美景使美景的本身被窒息了,使生命缺少了生机。司各特不如雨果那样有神韵;不如梅里美那样才华横溢;不如巴尔扎克那样酋劲;不如维尼那样隽永,但司各特却在他们所欠缺的方面成功了——阴谋和历史、美景和生活、主角和群众,没有一个因素是被忽略掉的。(p. 40)

同德国和英国的伟大先驱者们相比,我们的浪漫主义显得那样迟缓和畏缩不前,以至只能在国境内发出一些光亮。在研究了19世纪开头数十年的情况以后,比较文学工作者们比较容易,也比较乐意来证实我们作家所接受的外国来源和"指导",而不愿指出这些作家对英国或德国的影响,这是正常的现象。无论是拉马丁、维尼、雨果或缪塞,都不能像《歌德在法国》(*Goethe en France*)那样给人们提供丰富而有意义的研究资料。(pp. 53-54)

对有关影响问题的研究是很广泛的、多式多样的,而且在不同的时期、不同的国度,情况也是不均衡的。因此,如果不观察两例早已被几乎全面研究过的例子——莎士比亚和歌德这样在欧洲具有巨大影响的人物,那么人们对这领域里比较工作的活动余地就难免要产生某些不太正确的看法了。把比较文学工作者们对这两个人物所进行的研究工作做一次粗略的统计,就可以看出在这种超越国界的情况下,是多么需要细心地分辨什么是影响和传播,什么是荣誉和成就了。用这两个外国人做例子,比用一个法国作家做例子对我们的意图更有用,因为如果要刻画出其特点时,会有许多人的名字可以供我们选择,当然对我们的文学来说这还是一种特殊待遇呢。对英国人或德国人就不同了,他们没有犹豫的余地,因为毫无疑问,莎士比亚和歌德是他们的状元:研究他俩的命运,也就等于发扬光大了英国人的天才、德国人的天才。(p. 65)

---

① 塔索(1544—1595),是史诗《被解放的耶路撒冷》(1575)的作者。

在法国，十八世纪时莎士比亚几乎是无人不知的。如果说是伏尔泰把莎士比亚介绍到法国这种说法不确切的话，那起码也可以说是他使莎氏传播开来的。大家都很熟悉这个惯用语："一个天才的野蛮人。"这个评语占据了光明时代为这位戏剧理论家组织的辩论的整个过程。所有的人都接受了这个定论：不过有的人，像伏尔泰在流亡归国后那样，只把重点放在"天才"这个字眼上，另外，像伏尔泰在1760年以后那样，又只把重点放在"野蛮"上。（p.66）

我们可以为歌德在英国和法国的截然不同的命运下一个相同的结论：他的绝大部分作品还没有被人认识或了解。而当人们从对少年《维特》的同一种迷恋中看到英国和法国的解释的分歧时——一方是朝伦理方面走去，另一方则朝纯艺术方面走去，谁又能不对歌德作品中所表现出来的巨大民族差异而表示敬意呢？再者，对作品在两个国家里的命运的调查，还可以突出一些具有"代表性"的人物，如卡莱尔或席勒、泰恩或巴莱斯（Barrès）等。

莎士比亚和歌德这两个例子奇迹般地显示出比较文学在民族思想史和文学史处在面临抉择的关头时所能起的作用。研究莎士比亚和歌德在法国的命运，可促使我们更加了解自己的文学，使我们能更明确地指出我们的特征，同时也可以分辨清楚欧洲空前伟大的两部作品的主要意义和它们的演变情况。（p.71）

（马·法·基亚.比较文学[M].颜保，译.北京：北京大学出版社，1983.）

【研究范例】

《罗摩衍那》在中国（节选）

◉季羡林

【导读】季羡林先生是我国东方文学学科和东方比较文学学科的奠基者。东方比较文学观念是季先生晚年学术思想的重要结晶，而在他的东方比较文学研究中，中印文化、文学比较研究所取得的成就尤其突出。

季羡林先生在翻译印度史诗《罗摩衍那》时，"读了大量的书籍，思考了一些问题，逐渐对《罗摩衍那》有关的一些问题形成了自己的一些看法"。季先生特别关注《罗摩衍那》与中国的关系，梳理了汉译佛经中与《罗摩衍那》相关的内容，并以此来说明这部史诗通过佛经在中国可能产生的影响。

季先生在《罗摩衍那》的翻译和研究中发现《罗摩衍罗》中的神猴哈奴曼与《西游记》中的孙悟空有很强的相似度和相关度，通过大量的中印文献资料的梳理，得出哈奴曼是孙悟空的原型的结论。《〈罗摩衍罗〉在中国》一文，系统论及了《罗摩衍罗》与

《西游记》之间存在的联系,哈奴曼与孙悟空之间存在的联系。同时季先生还论及了《罗摩衍那》对我国少数民族地区文化和文学的影响,其中包括云南的傣族地区、西藏地区和内蒙地区的影响,分析了在交通、通信不发达的情况下文学在迁徙过程中一些独特而有趣的现象,也通过这一现象展开了流传学和变异学理论问题的探讨。■

我在这里想顺便谈一谈《西游记》中的主角孙悟空。这个猴子至少有一部分有《罗摩衍那》中神猴哈奴曼的影子,无论如何标新立异,这一点也是否认不掉的。如果正视事实的话,我们只能承认《罗摩衍那》在这方面也影响了中国文学的创作。这个问题我在这里不细谈。

我只谈一下孙悟空与福建泉州的关系。这一点过去知道的人是非常少的。最近日本学者中野美代子教授送给我一篇《福建省与〈西游记〉》。我觉得这是一篇有独到见解的文章。我在这里简略地加以介绍。

在泉州开元寺,南宋嘉熙元年(公元 1237 年)修建的西塔第四层壁面上有一个猴子浮雕,戴着金箍,脖子上挂着念珠,腰上挂着一卷佛经,右肩上有一个小小的和尚像。这和尚是否就是玄奘?这不敢说。在西塔第四层其他壁上有玄奘的像。另外在泉州的一座婆罗门教寺院里,大柱子上有一个猴子浮雕,尾巴拖得很长很长,手里拿着像草似的东西。这让人自然而然地想到《罗摩衍那》中的哈奴曼。他曾用尾巴带火烧毁楞伽城,并手托大山,带来仙草,救了罗摩和罗什曼那的性命。

这明确地说明了,南宋时期《西游记》的故事还不像以后这样完备,只能算是一个滥觞。中野美代子研究猴行者的来源,说是在宋代《罗摩衍那》经过南海传到泉州。泉州当时是中国最大的港口,与阿拉伯和印度等地海上来往极其频繁。说猴行者不是直接从印度传过来而是通过南海的媒介,是顺理成章的。我推测,在这之前关于神猴的故事,一方面中国有巫支祁这个基础,再加上印度哈奴曼的成分,早已在一些地方流行。泉州的猴行者并不是最早传入的。在八九世纪以后,《罗摩衍那》已逐渐传入斯里兰卡、缅甸、泰国、老挝、柬埔寨、马来西亚等地。从这一带再传入中国,是比较方便的。

福建泉州发现了孙悟空,这一件事实虽简单,我觉得却给我们提出了非常值得考虑的问题:研究中印文化交流的学者,不管是中国的,还是外国的,大都认为中印文化交流渠道只有西域一条,时间都比较早,也就是说在唐宋以前;现在看来,这种想法必须加以纠正:中印文化交流从时间上来说,宋以后仍然有比较重要的交流。从空间上来说,海路宋代才大为畅通。此外,还有一个川滇缅印通道,也往往为学者所忽略。

我国云南的傣族,由于与缅甸接壤,而缅甸受印度文化影响较早;又因为傣语与泰语同系,泰国也早已受到印度的影响,近水楼台先得月,因而比较早地接受了印度的文学、宗教等。印度《罗摩衍那》虽然没有全部传至中国内地,却传到了傣族地区,在这地区的民间流行极广。根据现在的调查,至少有这样一些不同的本子,首先有大小《兰嘎》,即《兰嘎竜》和《兰嘎囡》之分,在大《兰嘎》中又分为《兰嘎西贺》与《兰嘎双贺》。在中国傣族地区,罗摩故事译本极多,这里无法详细列举。大概每一个罗摩故事的民间演唱者,都根据当时当地的情况而随时有所增删,以适应听者。这充分显示了傣族艺人的才能,但也产生了另一结果:异本蜂起,头绪纷繁。

总起来看,这故事大大地傣族化了,也就是中国化了。好多印度地名都换成了中国地名,也就是云南本地的地名。比如阿努曼丢下来的仙草山,就落在云南傣族地区。此外,还有不少的本地民间故事串入整个故事之中。这些都是难以避免的,也是合乎规律的。第五部分,召朗玛与勐哥孙之间爆发战争,故事就发生在傣族地区,这已不仅是中国化,而是中国的创造了。

我国西藏地区,由于同印度接壤,在文化交流方面,有特别有利的条件。根据王辅仁的《西藏佛教史略》,佛教入藏在公元5世纪。但是大规模的传入恐怕是在公元7世纪松赞干布时期。在这个时期,一方面印度的宗教、哲学、文学、艺术、医学、天文历算等直接传入,另一方面又从汉族传入一些佛教典籍,而文成公主入藏,又带去了汉族的文化,再加上西藏人民的创造与发展,结果是藏、汉、印三方面智慧汇流,形成了保留在西藏典籍中的伟大的文化宝库。

在文学方面,许多梵文古典文学也传入西藏,比如迦梨陀娑的《云使》就有藏文译本。《罗摩衍那》也传入西藏。时间估计当在佛教传入之后,也就是在7世纪以后。

在西藏,从今天已经发现的本子来看,一方面有根据梵文或其他印度语言的本子翻译加创造的《罗摩衍那》,比如在敦煌石窟就发现了有五个编号的《罗摩衍那》故事,这样的故事在新疆也发现过;另一方面又有自己的创造,比如1980年四川民族出版社出版的雄巴·曲旺扎巴(1404—1469)所著的《罗摩衍那颂赞》就是在印度传统的基础上自己创作的。

总起来看,蒙古文罗摩故事,与中国其他地区相同,是宣传佛教的。整个的Jīvaka故事是一个本生故事,故事中的罗摩就是释迦牟尼本人,而且有两处提到除邪信佛。在过去世中,Jīvaka王曾在海岛上遇到除邪信佛。在Jīvaka(等于十车王)故事中,罗摩当了国王以后,又请除邪信佛来传经说法。佛教色彩应说是非常浓的。

罗摩故事也传入蒙古民间传说与信仰中去。蒙古是没有猴子的,但却有猴子崇拜,甚至有专门的讲祭祀猴子的书,讲到如何上供、求财、满足愿望。在流传于藏、蒙地区北方的商跋尔(Shambal)国王的传说中,哈奴曼变成了商跋尔国王的参谋。

(季羡林. 季羡林学术精粹(第四卷)·《罗摩衍那》在中国[M]. 济南:山东友谊出版社,2006.)

【延伸阅读】

1. 钱林森. 法国作家与中国[M]. 福州:福建教育出版社,1995.

作者穿越浩瀚的文化时空,借助东方之光的朗照,一路巡游,给我们展示了启蒙主义作家作品,19 世纪浪漫主义、批判现实主义、自然主义、象征主义作家作品,20 世纪法国作家作品在中国传播,以及在这种传播的过程中,中法两种文明由陌生、误解,直至会通乃至互补、交融的图景。但由于其立足点是法国作家的汉语翻译和中国批评,所选取的大多是法国名家,几乎没有关注到中国作家的接受和创作事实。

2. 陈铨. 中德文学研究[M]. 沈阳:辽宁教育出版社,1997.

本书从中国作品在德国的翻译入手,全面、详尽地讨论了中国纯文学对德国文学的影响,文章又按照外来文学发生影响一般可经过翻译、仿作、创造三个阶段的理论来衡量这一时期的中德文学关系,指出德国人对中国文学的接受始终没有超过翻译阶段,并指出德国大诗人歌德和海涅实际上是最早对中国文学的价值有一定了解的德国学者。这部著作虽不深入,但材料丰富、论述全面,至今仍是人们研究中德文学关系的一本不可多得的著作。

第三节　渊源学

渊源学(Chronology),又称"源流学""源泉学",是影响研究的另一重要范畴。梵·第根认为:"思想、主题和艺术形式之从一国文学到另一国文学的经过,是照着种种形态而通过去的。这一次,我们已不复置身于出发点上,却置身于到达点上。这时所提出的问题便是如此,探讨某一作家的这个思想、这个主题、这个作风、这个艺术形式的来源,我们给这个研究定名为'渊源学'。"[①]因此,与流传学站在"放送者"的立场或角度研究一部作品、一个作家、一国文学或某种文学潮流对"接受者"的"影响"不

① 梵·第根. 比较文学论[M]. 戴望舒,译. 北京:商务印书馆,1937:170.

同,渊源学则站在“接受者”的立场或角度,探讨一部作品、一个作家、一国文学或某种文法学潮流所接受的“放送者”的“影响”。

何之谓“影响”?在法国的《小罗伯尔》辞典以及《法语大拉罗斯》词典中,“影响”的原本意义是神秘的“主宰人类命运的天体之力”,后转义为“主宰他者的精神的理智的力”,而这正是“法国文艺对外国的‘影响’”这样的文艺批评所采用的“影响”的内涵。英国的《简明牛津词典》则强调“影响”的效果或结果,认为“影响”只有在其效果或结果中被察觉。日本的《日本国语大辞典》既强调“影响”如影随形的密切、迅速的相关系,又认为“影响”是“波及他者,使之产生反应和变化”,大塚幸男更欣赏后一种释义。法、英、日三国词典义的考察中,我们看到“影响”一词的内涵,逐渐从“放送者”强调的“影响力”转移到了“接受者”所产生的“效果”“反应”和“变化”。

关于“影响”的类型,朗松的《文学与社会学》将影响分为两类:一是因某一外国政治的、军事的威慑而接受他民族的文学影响,一是因一国文学不能满足大多数人或少数人的精神需求而失却生命活力之际,便会迎合外国文学潮流。大塚幸男补充了大量史实,进一步证明“影响”的两种类型或两条原则。

朗松的《从法国文学的发达看外国文学的影响作用》认为影响有两种主要作用:一是外国的影响能振奋国民精神,培育并促使它发展;二是外国的影响,每每可以起到“解放的作用”,如英国的浪漫主义就从程式化的古典主义中解放了法国文学。朗松特别强调“接受者”接受“影响”的主体性。他指出:“我们到外国文学中去寻找‘理想’,其实正是为了实现本国‘理想’的文学。”因此,对外国文学理解正确与否无关紧要,因为“我们不是去索求外国文学的价值,而是为了求得我们自身文学的价值。我们是‘为了更好地表现自己’,而向外国文学学习的”。

真正的、特定含义的“影响”。朗松在《十七世纪法国文学同西班牙文学的关系》中认为,真正的“影响”,是“当一国文学中的突变,无以用该国以往的文学传统和各个作家的独创性来加以解释时在该国文学中所呈现出来的那种情状——究其实质,真正的影响,较之于题材选择而言,更是一种精神存在”①。进而,大塚幸男认为,特定含义上的“影响”是一种“创造的刺激”,是“得以意会而无可实指的”。影响的研究,“必须从可视之处着手而后导致不可视的世界之中,并以发现和把握潜藏于对象深处的本质为其目的”。

渊源学研究中还包含着对跨学科的影响以及对文学接受过程中异质性、变异性与

① 朗松. 试论“影响”的概念[M]//大塚幸男. 比较文学原理. 西安:陕西人民出版社,1985:32.

创新性的考察。我们从陈寅恪《西游记玄奘弟子故事之演变》这一范例即不难发现上述特性的精彩呈现。

无论是流传学还是渊源学,学界更多关注的是跨越国界的文学、文论的影响,至于跨学科影响研究,一直为中外比较文学研究所忽略。但陈寅恪《西游记玄奘弟子故事之演变》不仅为我们展示了跨国界影响研究或渊源学的范例,同时也提出了跨学科的影响研究或渊源学问题。佛经故事的变异,不仅证明了佛教流传过程或影响研究流传学的变异,而且为跨学科渊源学的变异创造了范例,为佛经故事变异为文学故事奠定了基础。

更准确地说,《西游记》中玄奘三大弟子都有佛经的渊源,而只有孙悟空、猪八戒有外国(印度)的渊源。《慈恩法师传》为惠立所撰。惠立俗姓赵,天水(今属甘肃)人,唐代高僧,慈恩寺翻译大德。源于《慈恩法师传》的沙和尚及流沙河的故事,不能说有外国(印度)的渊源。《慈恩法师传》既可视为传记文学,又可视为佛教经典——收入佛教典藏《大正藏 · 史传部》中。

如同陈寅恪所说,以故事阐释经义,“实印度人解释佛典之正宗”。佛经中顶生王的故事,其核心要旨在于阐明佛教三毒之一的“贪”的极度恐惧性。顶生王“统领四域,四十亿岁,七日雨宝,及在二天”,但其仍不满足,意欲加害帝释,独霸天地。而当其“恶心已生,寻即堕落。当本殿前,委顿欲死”。佛教以极端之故事阐释“贪”的极端之危害,教人去“贪”。

《佛制苾刍发不应长因缘》中牛卧比丘的故事,旨在说明佛教律法,收录在《大正藏 · 律法部》中。牛卧比丘须发蓬长、衣裙破垢的窘困外形,被佛主斥责为“非法恶形状”。告诫诸比丘,留长发者才有这样的祸害,并制定了不剃发者犯“越法罪”的规定。至于《慈恩法师传》中玄奘诵《般若经》退恶鬼的故事,则旨在宣传《般若经》的无上法力。

显然,作为佛经故事,其核心功能在于阐释佛旨、弘扬佛法、宣传佛经。与玄奘三大弟子及其故事,本非一族。小说从艺术审美的目标出发,其情节人物必然发生变异。如同陈寅恪所指出的:“夫说经多引故事,而故事一经演讲,不得不随其说者听者本身之程度及环境而生变易。”因为故事是工具而非目的。于是“有原为一故事,而歧为二者,亦有原为二故事,而混为一者。又在同一事之中,亦可以甲人代乙人,或在同一人之身,亦可易丙事为丁事”。

总而言之,当我们对一部作品进行寻本追源的考证时,一定要注意多向度、全方位地考察,不要放过任何蛛丝马迹。

【原典选读】

“影响”及诸问题（节选）

◉大塚幸男

【导读】日本比较文学家大塚幸男的《“影响”及诸问题》，主要从“何之谓‘影响’”以及如何捕捉“影响”两个方面，探讨了渊源学的理论内涵。文中主要介绍了法国学者朗松对于影响研究的见解。继而，大塚幸男从六个方面指出了捕捉“影响”的途径：①熟读作品。②检索作家日记、创作手记和备忘录等第一手资料。③研究作家一生中所阅读的书目。④研究作家的朋友、社交关系，给亲朋知己的信件。⑤作家出国旅行及游记。⑥作家生活时代进口的外国原版文学书籍。本文存在的不足在于：①忽略了跨学科的“影响”。如中国园林艺术对欧洲浪漫主义的影响，印度佛教对中国诗歌、散文及小说的影响等。②忽略了文学影响的“异质性”。朗松对“影响”的论述，局限在西方文学传统之内，尚未触及东西方文学的“异质性”问题。大塚幸男虽然看到了东西文学的影响，但也忽略了东西文学的异质性。③忽略了文学影响过程中的“变异性”。朗松及大塚幸男都将“影响”视为一种“精神存在”，一种“创造的刺激物”，这对于校正法国学派或影响研究过分注重“实证性”的缺陷无疑具有重要的意义。但是，无论是朗松还是大塚幸男，都未曾看到影响过程中的变异性。■

Felix qui potuit rerum cognoscere causas. 能把握事物神秘之因者，不是个幸运儿吗？

（维吉尔）

迄今为止，我们常用“影响”一词。比较文学，尤其是法国比较文学学派所标榜的“研究两国以上的文学影响关系”，最终总要归结到阐明某一作家接受了怎样的外来影响这一点上来。可是，何之谓“影响”，它又如何为我们所捕捉呢？

根据《小罗伯尔》辞典以及《法语大拉罗斯》辞书所释，具有影响含义的英语和法语 influence（德语是 Influenz）一词，是由中世纪拉丁语 influentia 衍化而来的，因而在原本意义上，它包含有“主宰人类命运的天体之力”的意思。这种“力”，具有“神秘”的本质。而且，这一名词是由古典拉丁语中的动词 influere（流向、流出的意思）演变而成的，后转义为“主宰他者的精神的·理智的力”，被“法国文艺对外国的影响（influence）”这样的文艺批评所采用。……同样，对“影响（influence）”一词，在《简明牛津词典》中下了这样的定义：“Action of person or thing on or upon another, perceptible only in its effects.”所谓只有在其结果（效果）之中被觉察，不是极妙地道出了“影响”一词的特质了吗？对于我们来说，重要的是如何觉察它。

日语中“影响”一词，据《日本国语大辞典》所释具有以下几种含义：(1)映象同反响。人影及人声。(2)具有影从形、响随音那样密切、迅速的相应关系。(3)波及他者，使之产生反应和变化，并照此行动。哲学词汇“Consequence：干系·结果·余波·影响。Influence：感化·风动·权威·影响”。

……朗松清楚地意识到外国以及外国文学的影响对于一国文学发展的重大意义并对此深加探究。也正因如此，所以他在著述文学史的时候，理应不可避免地遇到了文学的“影响”问题。

以下，姑且来看看朗松的影响论吧。首先，是国与国之间的影响：

> 外国诸影响的原则——有两种情况，可实际上，这两种情况是相互渗透的，人们难以把两者区分得一清二楚。
>
> (1)因执着于某一外国政治的、军事的威慑而推及该国在文明上通常亦呈优越，从而接受他民族的文学影响。其他各个民族并不考虑自身的欲求、能力、传统和生活条件，盲目地从在大民族中所见到的一切——风俗、习惯、艺术、文学，都生吞活剥地照搬到自己国内。在这种场合，可以看到文学同社会关系的暂时间离。这类如法炮制的毫无生气的作品，本身是当时的一个事实，即无非是一民族对他民族影响力的表现。例如十七、十八世纪德国对法国文学的模仿。
>
> (2)因种种缘由，当一国文学不能满足大多数人或少数人的精神需求时，即当一国文学或因烦琐，或因涸竭，或因贫乏，或因停滞，或因僵化而失却生命活力之际，便会迎合外国文学潮流。此时，政治的、军事的威慑则退居第二位，战胜国往往从战败国文学那里获取借鉴，如同贺拉斯所说的“被征服的希腊人的文化震慑了强悍的罗马征服者”[Graecia capta ferum victorem cepit.（Horatius，Epistolae，Ⅱ，1，156）]那样，意大利发现查理八世时代的法国人发现意大利文学也是一例。
>
> 外国作品对一国文化的影响具有三重职能，即：确认探求新事物的正当性；为所求者提供范例而使其新的理想明朗化；使人们得到本国文学所无法给予的理知的、美的满足(见前所列举的《方法·批评·文学史论集》中《文学与社会学》一文)。

有关第一条原则须待补充的是——十七世纪的德国，无论在其风俗、语言或是文学上，始终与意大利、西班牙，尤其同法国亦步亦趋。唯独只有西利西亚派起而反对这一潮流而企求民族文学的更生，其代表人物便是被誉之为“德国的马雷伯”的诗人、批评家奥皮茨。十八世纪，德国再度为鼎盛的法国文化所折服。对此，给我留下深刻影响的，是在游览慕尼黑城堡的时候。这座城堡是巴伐利亚王路德维希一世执政时建造的，它无非是对法国凡尔赛宫的一种仿造——虽则规模甚小。更不用说普鲁士国王弗利德里希二世仿照凡尔赛宫建造的波茨坦宫——用法语把它命名为“无忧宫(Sans-Souci)”,并邀请伏尔泰在这里用法语著写诗文。许多法语词汇之所以原封不动地被吸收到德语词汇之中,也正是基于这一历史根由。在日本,与十七、十八世纪德国相当的,该是鹿鸣馆时代吧。这使人回想起开设“明六社”、致力于启蒙西方思想,甚至主张把英语作为日本国国语的森有礼君。此外,作为醉心于别国语言的一例,尚须提及沙皇帝政时代的俄国。屠格涅夫、陀思妥耶夫斯基、列夫·托尔斯泰等人小说中经常出现法语一事清晰地表明,当时的俄国贵族完全置于法国文化影响之下。

其次,关于第二条原则附带要说的是,实际上,战胜国为战败国文化所折服的例子也是屡见不鲜的。查理八世(在位1483—1498年)的那波利远征,以及十六世纪弗朗索瓦一世发动的侵意(大利)战争——其结局总是法国取胜——可促使法国发现了意大利文艺,并成为掀起法国文艺复兴运动的一大契机。作为近代显著一例的,可以列举出日俄战争后战败国俄国文学源源不绝地传入战胜国日本。第二次世界大战后的美国(基恩、赛德斯蒂克等人)和西欧各国对日本文学的研究日趋兴盛一事,也是一例。战争是该受诅咒的,可具有讽刺意义的是,它却促进了当事国间的文化交流,这是必须承认的事实。……

再者,朗松著有题为《从法国文学的发达看外国文学的影响作用》一文(初载于《两个世界评论》一九一七年二月十五日号,后收录在《方法·批评·文学史论集》一书),其主要内容如下:

(1)有人对法国文学接受外来影响持偏激态度,并以个人好恶而妄加断决,如勒美特尔、拉塞尔、路易·莱伊诺以及其他民族主义的批评家们。可是,我们不该诅咒外国影响,对于法国来说,它正是一种“获得物(conquête)”。在这一方面,杜·倍雷的主张是正确的。

(2)外国的影响具有两种作用:

a. 这种影响力能振奋国民精神,培育并促使它发展。由于影响所给予的刺激,致使接受国(现今称之为接受因素)超越给予国(即所谓传播因素),而且它能引发出一国文学的“潜在力”。

b. 外国的影响,每每可以起到“解放的作用”——例如,拉丁语语法从意大利语语法之中解放了法国文学(文艺复兴、十七世纪的古典主义)。再如,英文学首创的浪漫主义,从希腊浪漫蒂克的陈腐旧俗(程式化的古典主义)之中解放了法国文学。

我们到外国文学中去寻求“理想”,其实正是为了实现本国“理想”的文学。一国文学为表现新时代的“感情”和“流派”,就要借助于外国文学,即外国的影响可使我们的文学增辉添色。

模仿是自我解放的一种手段——例如,牺牲古典主义传统的浪漫主义,如同我们所看到的那样,不是给法国文学带来结构不完整、富有异国色彩和怪诞之类的影响吗？而实际上，正是浪漫主义打破了陈腐程式，铸直了凝化了的国语（法语），并促使法国文学得以适应新时代法国人的生活。

有人说我们法国人不能理解外国文学，例如，英国人嗤笑法国人对莎士比亚的模仿，拉腊嘲讽《欧那尼》中的西班牙。然而就我们来说，重要的不是原模原样地照搬外国文学及其思想，而只是汲取于我们有用之处。至于我们对外国文学的理解正确与否，这是无关紧要的。我们只是为我所用。我们不是去索求外国文学的价值，而是为了求得我们文学自身的价值。我们是"为了更好地表现自己"而向外国文学学习的。

诚然，不是没有"机械的""隶属的"模仿。可是，今日之失败，孕育着明日之胜利。那种对国外文学顶礼膜拜的民族，原本就是毫无创建的民族。法兰西民族对于外国文学的好奇心及其强大的同化力，是同法国文学的显著特性——人性及其普遍性密切相关的。我们文学的膨胀力，来自于它的吸收性。

大凡说到底，人是无以自足的。不借取他者来充实自己，就不能使自己变得丰满、深邃、高大和得到发展，不，尚且不能得以自立。从他者摄取养分，对于肉体和精神说来同样都是不可欠缺的。可是，我们每每忘却这一事实。

由此可知，"所谓特定含义上的'影响'，我们可以下这样的定义，即为：一部作品所具有的由它而产生出另一部作品的那种微妙、神秘的过程"（Pichois et Rousseau, op. cit., P.75）。一言以蔽之，所谓特定含义上——严格意义上的"影响"，便是一种"创造的刺激"。

朗松对于确定"影响"的含义，一向是慎之又慎的，可也得出了同样的结论。他在《试论"影响"的概念》一文中（收入《方法·批评·文学史论集》一书，原题为《十七世纪法国文学同西班牙文学的关系》，刊载于《法国文学史评论》一九〇一年第八期）认为：

外国影响有以下四种：

（1）法国人接受外国的观念。

a. 对时事政治的关心。

b. 因对古代政治的关心所产生的称之为"遗传"的感情。

c. 社会的、商业的、社交的关系。

d. 对法国民众的历史知识的影响。

e. 有关该国的文学知识（但处在实际上尚未阅读文学作品的阶段）。

（2）因外国书籍的实际普及而获得的知识——然而，知识未必就意味着影响。

（3）从外国文学中获得灵感，对外国文学的改写和模仿——这仍然不能称之为"影响"，我们即便借取某种外国文学题材，却无以把握其精髓。在决定"影响"上有着深刻意义并成为决定“影响”标志的，只是在此种借取为数众多而又构成连续性的场合。

（4）假若如此，那么何谓真正的“影响”呢？真正的影响，是当一国文学中的突变，无以用该国以往的文学传统和各个作家的独创性来加以解释时在该国文学中所呈现出来的那种情状——究其实质，真正的影响，较之于题材选择而言，更是一种精神存在。而且，这种真正的影响，与其是靠具体的有形之物（matérialité）的借取，不如是凭借某些国家文学精髓（Pénétration des génies）的渗透，即谓之“作品的色调和构思的恰当”而加以显现，真正的影响理应是得以意会而无可实指的。

特定含义上的“影响”，如上所述，是一种“创造的刺激”，“是得以意会而无可实指的”。“影响的研究，必须从可视之处着手而后导致不可视的世界之中，并以发现和把握潜藏于对象深处的本质为其目的”（矢野峰人：《新文学概论》，大明堂一九六一年版，第193页）。

虽说如此，但我们不能把作为研究准备的对可视事实的探究当作徒劳之举。成为我们研究提供线索的这种准备工作，大致有以下几个方面：

（1）作品——熟读作品，不用说这是至关重要的。

（2）检索作家日记、创作手记和备忘录等第一手资料——尤其是一个作家的“读书历”往往因参见日记而愈显明晰。例如永井荷风的《断肠亭日乘》，现选取一节聊以作证——“今天读了皮埃罗切《墓诣》（*Fantôme d' Orient*）一书，这回该是第三次拜读了。如果第一次是从在纽约时阅读此书算起，第二次则是在三十余年前读到的法文版原文。首次拜读莫泊桑的水上游记”（一九三九年四月八日）。

（3）“读书历”（德语：Belesenhcit）——把作家在他一生中所阅读的书目（尤其是外国作品，不管是原版还是译本）制列成表并加以研究。这正如（2）中所述的那样，也可从作家的日记之中窥见一斑。在我国近来出版的个人全集中，也有附作家藏书书目的（如筑摩书房出版的《藤村全集》别卷）。河盛好藏先生在其《书橱回顾》（新潮社一九七六年版）一书中，根据藤村的藏书目录，著有题为“藤村的学习”这别开生面的一章。这一藏书目录，也使我在执笔著写《桃李花丛中——伦理学家岛崎藤村》（新潮社一九七二年版）时得益匪浅。另外，在岩波书店出版的夏目漱石全集第十六卷里，也收录有《藏书补白短评并杂感》。此类记载，由于如实地记述了作家接受外国文学影响的过程，因而是比较研究的一份珍贵资料（参照拙著《法国文学随缘录》中收录的《夏目漱石论法国作家》一文）。

（4）作家的朋友、社交关系，给亲朋知己的信件——作家对外国文学的了解，不能只局限于阅读著述，我们也不能忽视他同友人交往（口耳之学）的重要性。例如，人称“文学之鬼”、以“阅读了大量译作、对翻译（和杰出的翻译家）备为推崇”（河盛好藏语）而称雄文坛的宇野浩二——并常使人们想起逢人便始终话不离文学的宇野浩二同其亲友广津和郎谈话时的情景——在作家同朋友的谈吐中，不光能接受外国文学的影响，而且在话兴由至之时，尚可泄露出意想不到的秘密。下面引用的，仍然是河盛好藏相传的有关他俩的一段逸话：

> ……广津只清楚地记得，在初次见面的寒暄之后，宇野便对我说道，新潮流社的维特丛书[大正末期至昭和初期(1924—1925 年前后)，一种广受男女青年文学爱好者欢迎的黄褐色封面的小型翻译丛书。出版的第一部译作，是秦丰吉翻译的《少年维特之烦恼》(1924)，因而该丛书便称为维特丛书]中刊载的先生的译作《曼侬·雷斯戈》，实际上是我翻译的。因为我确实翻译过《曼侬·雷斯戈》一书(岩波文库)，所以他才作这样的申述。宇野所指的是自己的英译本吧，它虽是一种原作的改译本，可由于他第一次把该书介绍到日本，在我把原作译成日文时，曾作过许多参考。尽管如此，宇野先生最初涉足文坛是翻译《曼侬·雷斯戈》的这一事实，也是耐人寻味的。(《书橱回想》第 44-45 页)

因而，我们必须到同时代的，尤其是与作家关系至为密切的同时代人的回忆及研究著述之中，去追寻作家谈话的踪迹。然而作家自己的亲笔书信，不用说是最为确凿的实证。西欧作家都写有大量的信件，而且几乎都完整无缺地被保存下来作为“书简集”加以出版。伏尔泰、卢梭、巴尔扎克、乔治·桑、福楼拜、波德莱尔等文豪都是如此。更有甚者，他们还保存着许多对方的来信，而汇编成“往来书简集”。此种情况也非属罕见，如罗曼·罗兰书简集。罗兰即便在他的《战时日记》(*Journal des années de guerre*, 1914—1919)(Albin Michel, 1962)中，也一一收集了亲朋来信及自己的回函，最近出版的《志贺直哉全集》(岩波版)，收录了志贺先生的两卷书信，并且还把收藏的友人知己写给志贺先生的信件编就“致志贺直哉书简集”，作为别卷出版。这对于我国作家的个人全集来说，是一件具有划时期意义的大事。

(5)作家出国旅行及游记(参照第七章)。

(6)作家生活时代进口的外国原版文学书籍。当代介绍、翻译及备受读者欢迎的外国作家及作品。对于原版书的翻译，重要的是要区别它是直接翻译原文呢还是转译。例如，我国明治时代至大正时代初期(1886—1911 年前后)，几乎是通过英译本来阅读法国文学的；对于俄国文学，也通常是阅读原著的英译本(主要由加尼特翻译)(参见第八章)。而这种读书的影响，在我们青少年时代具有强大的吸引力，因此我们有必要尽可能详尽地探究作家年轻时期即学生时代的阅读书目。

(大塚幸男. 比较文学原理[M]. 陈秋峰，杨国华，译. 西安：陕西人民出版社，1985.)

【研究范例】

西游记玄奘弟子故事之演变

◉陈寅恪

【导读】如何进行渊源学的研究？陈寅恪的《西游记玄奘弟子故事之演变》为我们提供了一个可资借鉴的范例。

玄奘三大弟子——孙悟空、猪八戒和沙和尚可以说妇孺皆知。但是，他们是吴承恩依据中国文化、文学传统的独创，还是受到了印度佛教或佛教故事的影响？如果是前者，则属于传统文学的研究范畴，如果是后者，则属于比较文学影响研究渊源学的范畴。陈寅恪在《西游记玄奘弟子故事之演变》一文中，为我们捕捉了玄奘三大弟子的佛经渊源，并总结了佛经故事演变为小说内容的公例，启发我们去思考渊源学研究中的跨学科性、异质性、变异性和创新性。

1. 玄奘三大弟子的佛经渊源

(1)孙悟空的形象及大闹天宫故事的渊源。佛经中顶生王升天争帝释之位的故事，与印度史诗《罗摩衍那》第六篇(《战斗篇》)中工巧神猴“Nala”助罗摩造桥渡海故事的结合，构成了《西游记》中孙悟空的形象及大闹天宫故事之渊源。

(2)猪八戒形象及高家庄招亲故事的渊源。佛经《佛制苾刍发不应长因缘》中在猪坎窟中修行的牛卧苾刍(比丘)，因其须发蓬长，衣裙破垢，惊犯宫女，出光王愤怒，吩咐大臣以蚂蚁填窟中以蛰螫比丘。天神慈悲，化猪从窟中出，出光王乘马持剑，逐猪而去，牛卧比丘趁机逃走。此故事经后来讲说演变而成为猪八戒形象及高家庄招亲故事之渊源。

(3)沙和尚形象及流沙河故事之渊源。《慈恩法师传》中玄奘西行取经，至流沙河，为奇形怪状恶鬼所困，因诵《般若经》而得解的故事，乃是沙和尚形象及流沙河故事之渊源。

2. 佛经故事演变为小说故事的公例

(1)纵贯式之一：以一简单故事为基础，稍加变易后再略为附会，如沙和尚流沙河的故事。

(2)纵贯式之二：仍以一较为复杂故事为基础，将故事中有关的多人多事融合为一人一事，如猪八戒高家庄招亲的故事。

(3)横通式：将两个来源不同，毫无关联之故事融合为一人一事，如将顶生王升天争帝释之位的故事与工巧猿助罗摩造桥渡海的故事合二为一，便构成了孙悟空大闹天宫的故事。

进而,陈寅恪探讨了取材范围的广狭与人物形象性格的关系,得出了“玄奘弟子三人,其法宝神通各有阶级。其高下之分别,乃其故事构成时取材范围广狭所使然”的结论。

如果说佛经故事旨在阐释佛旨、弘扬佛法、宣传佛经,那么文学故事则旨在塑造个性与普遍性统一的形象,反映时代生活,创造美。因此,作为小说的《西游记》,尽管有着佛经的跨学科渊源,从佛经故事到小说故事,其变异或变易不仅是必然的而且是必需的。而变异或变易的基本途径,则是以文学的规则改变佛经故事。至于陈寅恪总结的演变公例,仅仅是变易的具体方法而已。由此看来,如果把影响仅仅视为“创造的刺激物”“较之于题材选择而言,更是一种精神存在”,恐有以偏概全之失。■

印度人为最富于玄想之民族,世界之神话故事多起源于天竺,今日治民俗学者皆知之矣。自佛教流传中土后,印度神话故事亦随之输入,观近年发现之敦煌卷子中如《维摩诘经文殊问疾品演义》诸书,益知宋代说经与近世弹词章回体小说等多出于一源,而佛教经典之体裁与后来小说文学盖有直接关系,此为昔日吾国之治文学史者所未尝留意者也。

僧祐《出三藏记集》卷九《贤愚经记》云:

> “河西沙门释昙学威德等凡有八僧,结志游方,远寻经典,于于阗大寺遇般遮于瑟之会。般遮于瑟者汉言五年一切大众集也,三藏诸学各弘法宝,说经讲律,依业而教。学等八僧随缘分听,于是竞习胡言,折以汉义。精思通译,各书所闻。还至高昌,乃集为一部。”

据此,则《贤愚经》者本当时昙学等八僧听讲之笔记也。今检其内容,乃一杂集印度故事之书。以此推之,可知当日中央亚细亚说经例引故事以阐经义,此风盖导源于天竺,后渐及于东方。故今大藏中《法句譬喻经》等之体制,实印度人解释佛典之正宗,此土释经著述如天台诸祖之书则已支那化,固与印度释经之著作有异也。夫说经多引故事,而故事一经演讲,不得不随其说者听者本身之程度及环境而生变易,故有原为一故事,而歧为二者,亦有原为二故事,而混为一者。又在同一事之中,亦可以甲人代乙人,或在同一人之身,亦可易丙事为丁事。若能溯其本源,析其成分,则可以窥见时代之风气,批评作者之技能,于治小说文学史者傥亦一助欤?

鸠摩罗什译《大庄严经论》卷三第十五故事,难陀王说偈言:

> “昔者顶生王。将从诸军众。并象马七宝。悉到于天上。罗摩造草桥。得至楞伽城。吾今欲升天。无有诸梯隥。次诣楞伽城。又复无津梁。”

案此所言乃二故事，一为顶生王升天因缘，一为罗摩造草桥因缘。顶生王因缘见于康僧会译《六度集经》卷四第四十故事，《涅槃经·圣行品》，《中阿含经》卷十一《王相应品四洲经》，元魏吉迦夜昙曜共译之《付法藏因缘传》卷一，鸠摩罗什译《仁王般若波罗蜜经》下卷，不空译《仁王护国般若波罗蜜经护国品》，法炬译《顶生王故事经》，昙无谶译《文陀竭王经》，施护译《顶生王因缘经》及《贤愚经》卷十三等。梵文 Divyāvadāna 第十七篇亦载之，盖印度最流行故事之一也。兹节录《贤愚经》卷十三《顶生王缘品》第六十四之文如下：

“(顶生王)意中复念，欲生忉利，即与群众蹈虚登上。时有五百仙人住在须弥山腹，王之象马屎尿落汙仙人身。诸仙相问：何缘有此？中有智者告众人言：吾闻顶生欲上三十三天，必是象马失此不净。仙人忿恨，便结神咒，令顶生王及其人众悉住不转。王复知之，即立誓愿，若我有福，斯诸仙人悉皆当来，承供所为。王德弘博，能有感致，五百仙人尽到王边，扶轮御马，共至天上。未至之顷，遥睹天城，名曰快见，其色皦白，高显特殊。此快见城有千二百门，诸天惶怖，悉闭诸门，著三重铁门。顶生王兵众直趣不疑，王即取贝吹之，张弓扣弹，千二百门一时皆开。帝释寻出，与共相见，因请入宫，与共分坐。天帝人王貌类一种，其初见者不能分别，唯以眼眴迟疾知其异耳。王于天上受五欲乐，尽三十六帝，末后帝释是大迦叶。时阿修罗王兴军上天，与帝释斗，帝释不如。顶生复出，吹贝扣弓，阿修罗王即时崩坠。顶生自念，我力如是，无有等者，今与帝释共坐何为，不如害之，独霸为快。恶心已生，寻即堕落。当本殿前，委顿欲死。诸人来问：若后世人间顶生王云何命终，何以报之？王对之曰：若有此问，便可答之，顶生王者由贪而死，统领四域，四十亿岁，七日雨宝，及在二天，而无厌足，故致坠落。”

此闹天宫之故事也。

又印度最著名之纪事诗《罗摩延传》第六编工巧猿名 Nala 者造桥渡海，直抵楞伽，此猿猴故事也。

盖此二故事本不相关涉，殆因讲说《大庄严经论》时，此二故事适相连接，讲说者有意或无意之间，并合闹天宫故事与猿猴故事为一，遂成猿猴闹天宫故事。其实印度猿猴之故事虽多，猿猴而闹天宫则未之闻。支那亦有猿猴故事。然以吾国昔时社会心理，君臣之伦，神兽之界，分别至严，若绝无依藉，恐未必能联想及之。此《西游记》孙行者大闹天宫故事之起源也。

又义净译《根本说一切有部毗奈耶杂事》卷三《佛制苾刍发不应长因缘》略云：

“时具寿牛卧在憍闪毗国住水林山住光王园内猪坎窟中。后于异时，其出光王于春阳月，林木皆茂，鹅雁鸳鸯舍利孔雀诸鸟，在处哀鸣，遍诸林苑。出光王命掌园人曰:汝今可于水林山处,周遍芳园,皆可修治,除众瓦砾。多安净水,置守卫人,我欲暂住园中游戏。彼人敬诺,一依王教。既修营已,还白王知。时彼王即便将诸内官以为侍从,往诣芳园,游戏既疲,偃卧而睡。时彼内人,性爱花果,于芳园里随处追求。时牛卧苾刍须发皆长,上衣破碎,下裙垢恶,于一树下跏趺而坐。宫人遥见,并各惊惶,唱言:有鬼!有鬼!苾刍即往坎窟中,王闻声已,即便睡觉,拔剑走趁。问宫人曰:鬼在何处?答曰:走入猪坎窟中。时王闻已,行至窟所,执剑而问:汝是何物?答曰:大王!我是沙门。王曰:是何沙门?答曰:释迦子。问曰:汝得阿罗汉果耶?答曰:不得。汝得不还,一来,预流果耶?答言不得。且置是事,汝得初定乃至四定?答并不得。王闻是已,转更瞋怒,告大臣曰:此是凡人,犯我宫女,可将大蚁填满窟中,蜇螫其身。时有旧住天神近窟边者,闻斯语已,便作是念:此善沙门来依附我,实无所犯,少欲自居,非法恶王横加伤害,今宜可作救济缘。即自变身为一大猪,从窟走出。王见猪已,告大臣曰,可将马来,并持弓箭。臣即授与,其猪遂走,急出花园,王随后逐。时彼苾刍急持衣钵,疾行而去。"

《西游记》猪八戒高家庄招亲故事必非全出中国人臆撰,而印度又无猪豕招亲之故事,观此上述故事,则知居猪坎窟中,须发蓬长,衣裙破垢,惊犯宫女者牛卧苾刍也。变为大猪,从窟走出,代受伤害者,则窟边旧住之天神也。牛卧苾刍虽非猪身,而居猪坎窟中,天神又变为猪以代之,出光王因持弓乘马以逐之,可知此故事中之出光王,即以牛卧苾刍为猪。此故事复经后来之讲说,憍闪毗国之憍以音相同之故,变为高。惊犯宫女以事相类之故,变为招亲。辗转代易,宾主淆混,指牛卧为猪精,尤觉可笑。然故事文学之演变,其意义往往由严正而趋于滑稽,由教训而变为讥讽,故观其与前此原文之相异,即知其为后来作者之改良,此《西游记》猪八戒高家庄招亲故事之起源也。

又《慈恩法师传》卷一云:

"后度莫贺延碛长八百余里,古曰沙河。上无飞鸟,下无走兽,复无水草。是时顾影,唯一心念观音菩萨及《般若经》。初法师在蜀,见一病人身疮臭秽,衣服破污,愍将向寺,施与衣服饮食之直。病者惭愧,乃授法师此经,因常诵习。至沙河,逢诸恶鬼,奇状异类,绕人前后。虽念观音,不能全去,及诵此经,发声皆散。在危获济,实所凭焉。"

此传所载、世人习知(胡适教授《西游记考证》亦引之),即《西游记》流沙河沙僧故事之起源也。

据此三者之起源,可以推得故事演变之公例焉。一曰:仅就一故事之内容而稍变易之,其事实成分殊简单,其演变程序为纵贯式。如原有玄奘度流沙河逢诸恶鬼之旧说,略加附会，遂成流沙河沙僧故事之例是也。二曰：虽仅就一故事之内容而变易之，而其事实成分不似前者之简单，但其演变程序尚为纵贯式。如牛卧苾刍之惊犯宫女，天神之化为大猪，此二人二事虽互有关系，然其人其事固有分别，乃接合之，使为一人一事，遂成猪八戒招亲故事之例是也。三曰：有二故事，其内容本绝无关涉，以偶然之机会混合为一，其事实成分因之而复杂，其演变程序则为横通式。如顶生王升天争帝释之位，与工巧猿助罗摩造桥渡海，本为各自分别之二故事，而混合为一。遂成孙行者大闹天宫故事之例是也。

又就故事中主人之构造成分言之，第三例之范围不限于一故事，故其取用材料至广。第二例之范围虽限于一故事，但在一故事中之材料，其本属于甲者，犹可取而附诸乙，故其取材尚不甚狭。第一例之范围则甚小，其取材亦因而限制，此故事中原有之此人此事，虽稍加变易，仍演为此人此事。今《西游记》中玄奘弟子三人，其法宝神通各有阶级。其高下之分别，乃其故事构成时取材范围之广狭所使然。观于上述三故事之起源，可以为证也。

予讲授佛教翻译文学，以《西游记》玄奘弟子三人其故事适各为一类，可以阐发演变之公例，因考其起原，并略究其流别，以求教于世之治民俗学者。

（陈寅恪先生论集.台湾中央研究院历史语言研究所，1971.）

【延伸阅读】

1. 季羡林.《西游记》里面的印度成分[M]//季羡林.比较文学与民间文学.北京：北京大学出版社，1991.

在这篇论文中，季羡林认为，否认孙悟空与《罗摩衍那》的那罗与哈奴曼等猴子的关系是徒劳的，但同时也不能否认中国作者在孙悟空身上有所发展，有所创新。把印度神猴与中国的无支祁结合起来，再加以幻想润饰，塑造成了孙悟空这样为广大人民所喜爱的艺术形象。此外，季羡林先生还有一段富有深意的话，那便是："也许有人会说，《罗摩衍那》没有汉文译本，无从借起。这是一种误会。比较文学史已经用无数的事例证明了，一个国家的人民口头创作，不必等到写成定本，有了翻译，才能向外国传播。人民口头创作，也口头传播，国界在这里是难以起到阻拦作用的。故事的流传是不管什么海关的。"比较文学研究中，文字的证据固然极其重要，但一切必待文字证据而后方予采信，似乎是不必要的。

2. 洛夫乔伊.浪漫主义的中国起源[C]//洛夫乔伊.观念史论文集.吴湘，译.南京：南京教育出版社，2005.

洛夫乔伊（Arthur Oncken Lovejoy，1873—1962），美国哲学家、批判实在论的重要代表、美国观念史研究的主要倡导者。《观念史论文集》是洛夫乔伊的代表作之一，这部文集涉及思想史、哲学史、文学、历史乃至造园艺术等诸多领域,论题广泛,征引繁复,充分体现了作者以尖锐的批判精神,在多元世界探索“可理解性”的学术特色。《浪漫主义的中国起源》为该书第七章的内容,考察浪漫主义在中国的缘起。

3. 钱林森. 巴尔扎克与中国作家[J]. 首都师范大学学报:社科版,1993(5).

作为西方现实主义大师的巴尔扎克对我国文学究竟有着怎样的影响?我国新文学作者对巴尔扎克和《人间喜剧》有着怎样的观照?钱林森指出,巴尔扎克是西方现实主义大师,在中国新旧文学交替的时代,他的《人间喜剧》传进中国,对我国现实主义文学产生了深远的影响。鲁迅惊服巴尔扎克小说写对话的巧妙。他们在塑造人物、提炼典型上有相似的追求、相同的手法和相通的感受。茅盾则不仅在创作方法上,而且在创作主旨和总体风格上都和巴尔扎克有相通的地方。他们的创作都具浓厚的历史趣味和历史意识,重视社会全貌和历史全景的再现,都以经济为切入点来深刻解剖社会。巴尔扎克的现实主义艺术还深深感染了路翎、胡风、端木蕻良、周立波、王蒙等一代代中国作家。

第四节 媒介学

异质文化之间文学的相互交流和汇通是世界文化史中非常普遍的现象,但是放送者和接收者之间的交流由于地理环境、文化传统、语言习惯、民族习俗、政治体制等诸方面存在的隔阂和阻塞,往往不能畅通进行,特别是语言之间的巨大差异,更使得异质文化之间交流的可能性和有效性受到极大影响。而为了使不同文化之间的文学文化交流得以顺利展开,在输送者和接收者之间便会存在一个使二者顺利接通的中介和桥梁,这个中介和桥梁就是媒介。比较文学范畴上的媒介和一般语言学概念的媒介既有共性又有区别,它除了承担一般中介的基本功能外,还有复杂的文化内涵。比较文学领域的媒介具体指的是把一国文学介绍传播到另一国,使彼此间发生文学交流及影响作用的流传途径与方式,即重点研究交流和汇通得以展开的“经过路线”,其理论源流主要来自于法国学派。法国学派的代表人物梵·第根认为,在两种或两种以上文学发生相互关系的“经过路线”中,从“放送者”到“接收者”,往往是由媒介来沟通的,媒介在文学交流和传递中扮演着重要角色，比如个人、朋友集团、文学社团、沙龙、宫廷等是典型的人物媒介；而评论、报章译本则是重要的物质媒介。为此，法国学者伊夫·谢弗勒精确指出：“‘媒介’这个用语在此包括一切作用于文化传播的东西，既指其物质载体，也指人物行动。”①

对连接放送者和接收者的经过路线，即中介和桥梁的研究在比较文学研究领域就形成了媒介学。具体而言，媒介学(mesologie)属于比较文学影响研究的范畴，是法国学派影响研究的一个重要组成部分，因此对媒介学进行相关定义和作出独特贡献的是法国学派的研究者们，如早期的巴登斯贝格、梵·第根，后期的卡雷、基亚等人。法国学派将自然科学的研究方法引入比较文学领域，研究不同国家之间的文学影响、流传模式、接受事实等。他们认为不同国家间的文学影响是实证的存在，无论影响行为直接与否，都存在一个中间的“媒介”。这一媒介在发生影响力的文学关系中具有“工具”和“史料”的双重价值，如果“媒介”存在于正发生影响的文学关系中，它体现的是工具价值；而当媒介是作为已发生过影响的文学关系的见证物，它则体现的是史料价值。从科学与历史角度研究媒介，无疑起到强化史料研究作为比较文学学科拓展的中介方式的作用。法国学派恪守比较文学的实证研究，注重考据和材料的真实性，他们在研究媒介学的同时一般都将其和渊源学和流传学进行组合研究，探波求源，综合考量。他们研究不同文化体系的语言文学之间产生影响联系的具体途径、方法手段及原因与规律，对不同民族文学之间产生影响这一事实的途径、方法、手段及其因果关系进行实证研究。按照梵·第根的观点，在两种民族文学发生相互关系的“经过路线”中，从“放送者”到“接收者”，“那经过路线往往是由一个媒介者来沟通的”。这媒介者即是“传递者”，他可以是人，也可以是物，梵·第根把比较文学的媒介分为个人媒介、社会环境媒介、批评；报章和杂志、译本和翻译者四种类型，既有物质媒介，又有人物媒介。由此可见，媒介学研究的对象是有助于国与国之间或文学与文学之间了解的人或典籍，包括：①语言知识或语言学家；②翻译作品或翻译者；③评论文献与报章杂志；④旅游与观光客；⑤一种因为地理与文化的特殊情况所造成的国际公民等。

在具体的比较文学研究实践中，媒介类型主要有个人媒介、团体媒介、书刊资料的媒介等。其中起作用最大的是个人媒介，特别是翻译者，众多翻译者共同组成了一个庞大的中介和桥梁，使得文化传递和交融得以顺利实现。从比较文学发展的理论和实践来看，主要有以下几种媒介类型。

---

①　伊夫·谢弗勒．比较文学[M]．王炳东，译．北京：商务印书馆，2007：81．

一、个人媒介

个人媒介是指将一国文学或他国文学介绍、传播到另一国文学中去的译者、作家或其他人员，也可以是"接收者"国家中的个人媒介者。根据出发点不同，个人媒介又可分为以下几种类型：一是接收者国家的个人媒介，即将域外文学和文化介绍到本国来的人员，如《圣经·旧约》的70子译本和拉丁文译本、玄奘翻译的印度佛经、五四时期翻译大量外国理论和文学作品的学者等都是个人媒介的典型代表。二是放送者国家的个人媒介，即将自己国家的文学介绍给外国的人员，如杨宪益将《红楼梦》翻译成英文介绍给西方，明清时期的西方传教士翻译的西方文献等。三是第三国的个人媒介，既非放送者国家也非接收者国家的人员，他们是以世界公民的身份来促进各国文学交流的，如勃兰兑斯(被尼采称为欧洲好人)于1842年出生于丹麦哥本哈根的一个犹太人家庭，在哥本哈根讲学期间写了《十九世纪文学主流》，概述了19世纪初叶以来欧洲几个主要国家的文学发展状况，着重分析了这几个国家的浪漫主义的盛衰消长过程，以及现实主义相继而起的历史必然性。个人媒介在文化交流中起的作用最为重大。例如，意大利人马可·波罗，13世纪来到中国，写了《马可·波罗游记》，描写了中国元朝大都的繁华景象，在欧洲人心中种下了一个"中国梦"，直接刺激了哥伦布的航海热情。又如利玛窦、汤若望、南怀仁等西方传教士，他们在中国待了很多年，学到了当时西方人几乎一无所知的中国语言、文化知识，也传播了很多西方的东西，有效促进了中西方文化和文学的交流。

二、团体媒介

团体媒介指由社会、集团充当介绍和传播文化和文学的媒介。这种媒介超越了个人由团体或环境、场所构成。主要有文学社团或文学派别的媒介、"沙龙"客厅或文学集会的媒介等。其中文学社团、文学派别在这方面具有重要作用，因为人物众多，实力强劲，有利于文化和文学的大面积快速传播。如现代文学史上由沈雁冰、郑振铎、周作人、叶圣陶等作家在北京发起建立的"文学研究会"，就是以"研究世界文学、整理中国旧文学、创造新文学"为宗旨的，他们在引进和传播外国文学方面作出了较大的贡献；创造社的作家在引进和介绍日本文学方面也功不可没；而在十八十九世纪的西方贵族的客厅、文化沙龙等也是文化传播的有效方式，在这些沙龙和客厅里，聚集着很多文人，他们之间由于见解相似和互相欣赏就成为某一个文学社团，这些都是传播文化的交流文学的重要媒介。新闻机构在传播外来文化上具有得天独厚的优势，其影响之广、速度之快是其他社团无法与之相比的，但由于新闻受意识形态控制较严，因此我们在接受时要警惕新闻的妖魔化倾向。其三是国际性学术会议，这是文化交流和传播的一种直接手段，各种民族的声音和各种文化理念，都可以在这里汇集、交锋，并通过会议代表带回各地。此外，团体媒介还包括民间流传、旅行、迁徙的过程，实际上也是一个文化传播和融合的过程。

三、环境媒介

环境媒介是指特殊的地理位置所形成的沟通渠道充当了媒介的功能。例如，举世闻名的“丝绸之路”就是中国与阿拉伯民族乃至西方文化的交往之道；敦煌则是中华文明、印度文明、伊斯兰文明，乃至基督教文明这四大文明的聚汇地。通过这条丝绸之路，中国的丝绸、刺绣、陶瓷和其他绚丽多彩的工艺产品被运往中亚乃至欧洲，而异域的核桃、蚕豆、胡萝卜、葡萄酒和多姿多彩的音乐、舞蹈、绘画也在汉唐社会产生了广泛的影响。特别是印度佛教的传入，大大改变了中国原有的哲学、文学和艺术的风貌；而中国四大发明传入阿拉伯和欧洲，也使整个人类文明发生了深刻的变化。另外，处于政治文化中心的城市也具有影响和交流的性质。例如，埃及的亚历山大利亚城、盛唐时期的长安、现在的北京、美国的纽约、法国的巴黎、瑞士的日内瓦，这些城市都是政治文化的中心，它们不仅为文化和文学的交流提供了场所，而且本身就处于交流之中。

四、文字媒介

古语云，言之无文，行而不远。文字是保存人类文献的重要载体，也是后世一切研究的根据和逻辑起点。比较文学媒介学的文字媒介主要是译本、批评文字，也包括报章和杂志等其他文字资料，还有作家的游记，介绍外国文化和文学的刊物等。在文学和文化交流中，不是每个人都能识读外国或外民族语言，这就需要专业人士把外来文学转化成母语，如果阅读难度较大，还必须借助专业人士的批评和评论进行面上推广，以加快传播的进程。在具体的文化交流过程中，文字媒介和个人媒介、社会环境等并不是割裂的，而是综合起来共同成为连接起放送者和接收者之间的有效桥梁，从而使文化和文学交流得以高效推进。

人类历史的发展充分证明，一种文化只有不断吸收外来文化，补充新型的文化血液，文化才会推陈出新，不断往前发展推进；如果一个国家和民族采取封闭的发展模式，则再强势的文化都会走向衰落，中国文化史就充分证明了这一点，如唐代的开放和清朝的闭关，直接导致汉文化发展的两种截然不同的结果。文化交流的重要性由此可见一斑。而跨文化交流过程是否能都实现，取决于交流者之间的媒介是否通畅无阻。比较文学研究的历史充分证明，文学的交流伴随着文化交流的深度推进而产生，这中间的桥梁作用是十分重要的，如果没有汉唐时代的佛经翻译家，则中国和印度文化就不可能产生共鸣，如果没有希腊化时期的桥梁，则圣经就难以在西方世界取得压倒性的统治地位。从这个中间环节出发，可以有效探求源头，也能有效追溯结果，去发现源头文化的特征，也可理顺受影响文化的变异。因此，作为研究比较文学的重要环节，媒介学就具有十分重要的理论价值和实践意义，媒介学的特性要求研究者进行实实在在的资料整理，要下考证之功，一旦找到事实支撑，研究就有价值，结论就能服众，对于文学的基础研究、比较文学史的更新意义重大，正如张隆溪所言："法国式的影响研究当然自有其价值，在研究文学史、研究重要作品在不同文化和社会环境中的接受，以及研究介绍者、翻译者和出版者的作用等方面，法国式的影响研究都作出了很大的贡献。"①影响研究永远不会过时，媒介学作为中间环节必将受到文化多元化时代文学研究之重视，我们应该高度重视这一中间环节，从而有效开展比较文学的研究。

【原典选读】

比较文学论（节选）

◉梵·第根

【导读】法国学者梵·第根的《比较文学论》是比较文学研究入门必读的经典之一。全书分为导言"文学批评、文学史和比较文学""比较文学之形成与发展""比较文学之方法与成就""总体文学"四个部分。梵·第根以开阔的学术眼光，翔实而令人信服的材料，系统梳理了比较文学近百年的发展历史，阐明了法国学派的理论，从理论范式上奠定了比较文学法国学派的研究根基。在法国学派理论范式中，比较文学研究的三要素为输出者、接收者、媒介者，相应的研究方法有流传学、渊源学、媒介学，研究的目的在于描绘出传播的路线。对于媒介学部分也是如此，梵·第根通过翔实的例子，有效论述了媒介的类型、作用等，是比较文学媒介学的经典文献，法国学派讲究实实在在的资料整理、考证功夫，一旦找到事实支撑，研究就有价值，结论就能服众，对于文学的基础研究、比较文学史的更新意义重大。梵·第根把文学和文化交流中的媒介分为个人媒介、社会媒介、批评报章和杂志、译本翻译者四个类型，并以具体的史实和例证分析这几种类型在欧洲文学交流中的实际情况，最为梵·第根所重的是个人媒介、译本翻译者。其中个人媒介可以是接收者一端的介绍外国文学的本国人，即"属于接收

---

① 张隆溪.比较文学研究入门[M].上海:复旦大学出版社,2006:11.

者国家中的那些人"；这种情形最多；也可以是处于放送者一端的中介，这样的中介较少；也可以是第三国的翻译者，即"属于一个第三者国家的"。社会环境的媒介包括朋友集团、文学会社、沙龙、客厅等，此外还有译本、批评报章和杂志等文字媒介。梵·第根的著作全面建构了媒介学的理论路数，基本上涵盖了文化交流中媒介的类型，在今天的比较文学研究中，仍然具有较大的理论意义和参考价值。■

【个人】——在两国文学交换之形态间，我们应该让一个地位——而且是一个重要的地位——给促进一种外国文学所有的著作、思想和形式在一个国家中的传播，以及它们被一国文学采纳的那些"媒介者"。我们可以称这类研究为"仲介学"（语源出自希腊文 MEOOS，译为居间者）。这些媒介者的种类是各相殊异的。

第一是那些"个人"。在第一个场合中，那是关于属于"接收者"国家中的那些人的。这些人或者由于他们生活中的偶然，或者由于决然的意志，认识了那些外国的作品，并将它们传播到自己的国中。在十八世纪，法国有拉勃朗教士（Abbé Beblanc）、泊莱服教士（Abbé Lrévost）、拉·柏拉斯（La Place）、须阿尔（Suard）、勒·都尔纳（Le Tourneur）相继地做着英国文学的传令使；对于德国文学有力波（Liebault）、鲍纳维尔（Bonnevilie），对于西班牙文学有兰该（Linguet）等，担任着同样的任务；都尔各（Turgot）早就第一个发现了莪相和格斯奈尔。在同一个时代，阿尔加洛谛（Algarotti）和倍尔多拉（Bertola）一个将牛顿的哲学，一个将德国的诗歌，介绍到意大利去。俄罗斯人加拉姆新（Karamzine）做了卢骚的使徒。瑞典人乔尔威尔（Giörwell）呈现出这类各外国文学的热忱者的一个完备的典型：他的好奇心特别侧重于英国的新奇事物。德国人鲍德（Bode），英国人太劳（Taylor）和克拉勃·鲁宾生（Crabb Robinson），都是德国文学和英国文学的重要的媒介者。在十九世纪的初叶，那完全归化于德国的哲学和文学的流寓德国的法国人查理·德·维莱（Charles de Villers），竭其全力把德国的文学和哲学介绍给他的祖国；丹麦人奥兰式莱格尔（Oehlensehlaeger）在把德国的浪漫主义介绍到斯干第拿维亚去的时候担任着一个重要的角色〔这是哲学家兼博物学家斯代芬思（Stèffens）在一次十六小时的长谈话中解释给他听的〕。以后（单就法国说）蒙德居（Montégut）使法国更认识英国文学，而那北方诸国的大旅行家克沙维艾·马密尔（Xavier Marmier）又使法国知道了斯干第拿维亚文学。

相反的场合是比较少一点。那些定居在一个外国或至少长期寄寓在外国的人们，很少有把他们自己国中的文学介绍到那些外国去的。在这些"放送者"国家的文士们之间，我们并没有见到十六世纪的路易季·阿拉马尼（Luigi Alamanni）或斯加里吉尔（Scaliger），十七世纪的汉米尔顿（Hamilton），十八世纪的加里修里（Caraccioli）、加里阿尼（Galiani）、霍拉斯·华尔浦尔（Horace Walpole），或美尔丘尔·格里姆（Melchor Grimm），十九世纪的海涅、彭恩（Borne）或杜格涅夫，曾把意大利、英国、德国或俄国的文学，大大地介绍到法国去。只有在路易十三世时代的意大利人马里尼却在巴黎大大地介绍——马里尼主义。

在这些人物以及其余类似的人物间，没有几个人本身是重要的作家；他们之所以见重者，是为了他们的促成某一些外国作品在他们本国之传播或成功这任务。可是我们也应得把有几位第一流作者放在一边说，因为他们在一生中有一个时候也曾出色地担任过这种任务。伏尔泰和斯达尔夫人便是如此的。前者用了他的《哲学通信》在一七三五年光景把英国启示给法国，而在这启示中，文学是演着一个重要的角色的；后者由于她的《德国论》在八十年之后起了一种更决然的作用——虽则其启示是比较不完全新得多。文学在它的这部书中占着一个极大的位置，人们称这部书为“浪漫主义者的圣经”，因为许多法国作家是通过了这部书去认识、欣赏并甚至模仿德国文学的。

我们还常常碰到这样的事：便是有一些特别有效能的媒介者既不属于放送者国家，又不属于接收者国家，却是属于一个第三者国家的；他们以他们本身的资格演着“传递者”的角色。这些人大都是属于介乎两国之间的国家，用两种语言的国家，或智识力量不广大的国家的。这些人往往因为天性生成或因长久寄寓在外国的缘故，而具有无国境论的气质。那生于荷兰的爱拉思麦（Erasme）尽了许多力把西欧思想界的精粹移到人文主义的共同领域中；在两世纪以后，他的同国人房・爱芬（Van Effen）把英国的“旁观者”的道德随笔移植到法国语言中去。在这一方面，瑞典是特别人才辈出：在十八世纪初叶有《论英国人与法国人书》的作者倍尔诺阿・缪拉尔（Bernois Muralt）；稍迟一点有自左里克（Zurich）教德国人模仿英国诗的鲍德美尔（Bodmer）和勃莱丁格尔（Breitinger）；在一七五六年有把斯干第拿维亚古代的宗教和诗歌启示给欧洲的，定居于柯本哈格的日内瓦人马莱（Mallet）；在十九世纪初叶有久居在高倍别墅斯达尔夫人家中，在法国人和德国人之间调和文学上的分歧的伏县人本约明・龚斯当（Benjamin Constant）和倍尔纳人彭斯德丹（Bonstetten）。这些媒介者大部分都做过一些有用的专论的对象。

【社会环境】——另一种媒介是由团体或“社会环境”组成的。文学史应该注意这些活跃而繁殖的细胞；朋友的集团，文学会社，“沙龙”，宫廷，这些有时都助长移植或推行某一些外国作品。我们看到那些趣味之相投和倾向之相合所联合成的集团，而不是真正的文学会社。一五三〇年光景，西班牙的加尔西拉梭・德・拉・维加（Garcilaso de la Vega）和他的朋友鲍思冈（Boscún），便是这样地顺利地模仿着意大利诗的；在一五四五年光景，法国的里昂派便是这样地热烈地模仿着贝特拉尔格的；在一五九二年光景，英国的潘勃洛克（Pembroke）伯爵夫人便是这样地把那些竭力模仿洛贝尔・加尔尼艾（Robert Garnier）写悲剧，而反抗莎士比亚前期的自由剧的诗人们集合在她周围的；在一八二五年光景，巴黎的斯当达尔、昂拜尔（Ampére）、约克蒙（Jacquemont）、梅里美、梭德莱（Sautelet）也是这样地结为朋友，聚集在德莱格吕思（Delécluze）周围诵读并欣赏莪相和莎士比亚的。

……

我们还碰到其他的一些宜于移植外国的思想和作品的更广阔的环境。这些环境往往是王侯的“宫廷”，如丹麦弗莱德里克五世的，普鲁士弗莱德里克二世的，十八世纪之凯瑟琳二世的，巴尔麦诸大公的宫廷。这些环境也是一些“都市”，如里昂之在十六世纪——意大利趣味入法国之第一程；如日内瓦之在接连许多时代；如那真正的国际文学中心沮里克；如弗兰克福(Francfort-sur-main)(人们证明了十八世纪在那里有一种重要的法国教化)，如王政复古时期的巴黎及其和英国人的社交关系。

【批评；报章和杂志】——另一些媒介不复是人或人的团体，却是那排列在书架上的书籍了。这是一些使得一位作家传播到外国去的文字。有两个主要的分类：批评文字和译本。

比较文学者的注意最先被那些研究外国作家的书籍、小册子和其他“单独的出版物”所吸引。如斯达尔夫人的《德国论》，卡莱尔的《席勒传》，雨果的《威廉·莎士比亚》或勒惠思(Lewes)等一类典型的重要著作，在十九世纪之前是很稀少；十九世纪以来就增多起来了。在这些著作之间，我们应该辨别出哪几部是在把一个外国作家介绍到接收者国家来作移植之预备的；哪几部是特别表现这些书的作者的个人的意见的；哪几部是在外国作品逐渐传播开去之后长久巩固那传播的成绩，并指出那些作品出来的时候明眼的批评家的一遍意见是什么的。在十九世纪以前，我们见到最多的是译本的序文(我们以后当再谈)、小册子或其他的短文章；这便是当一位外国作家引起了笔战的时候的事，如一七七六年法英的莎士比亚伏尔泰“事件”，如以后一八二二年至一八二七年巴黎的拉西纳莎士比亚论争。

可是比较文学家所参考的，特别是那些“定期刊物”、报章或杂志。有些刊物是以把一个或许多个国家的文学富源之认识散播到国中为唯一之任务的。这种专门的刊物在十八世纪之前是没有的。从十八世纪起，各国出了许许多多的文学报、周刊、半月刊、月刊都有。这些刊物的“编者”(主干者)好好歹歹用一些翻译或外国作品之叙述去充篇幅。可是没有一个刊物是长寿的。在这一方面，法国是特别丰富：在这些短命的刊物之中，我们可以列举出那停刊改变过许多次的《外国报》，继它而起的《欧罗巴文学报》《英国报》等。在十九世纪，出来了《欧罗巴文学杂志》《不列颠评论》，第二帝国时代的最初的《德国评论》，以及其他等。可是我相信我们现在已找不到和这些专谈外国文学的杂志同等的杂志了。那些取着类似的名称《德国评论》《英美评论》《意大利公报》等的杂志，都是具有学术性质刊载研究文学的刊物，它们并不着眼于把外国文学作品加以翻译式叙述给大众阅读，就是偶然这样做了也是例外的。十八世纪和十九世纪的那些文学杂志的任务，现在倒是由一些并非专门于外国文学的一般杂志担任着，为法国的《两世界评论》《巴黎评论》《法国水星》以及许多其他的杂志。在那里,非专门的读者才找到了那大众可读的翻译、梗概、批评的和历史的研究。

(梵・第根. 比较文学论[M]. 戴望舒,译. 北京:商务印书馆,1937.)

【研究范例】

明清之际的中国文人与传教士(节选)

◉张西平

【导读】《明清之际的中国文人与传教士》是北京外国语大学张西平教授的专著《跟随利玛窦到中国》的其中一部分。该文较为清晰地梳理了明清时期外国传教士在中国所进行的传教活动及其取得成功的策略。可谓是媒介学研究实践的典范之作。明清之际,中西文化交流虽然已经比较常见,但是没有全面铺开,因此,研究起来也相对较难。《明清之际的中国文人与传教士》共有利玛窦与《交友论》、因求异而交往、因信仰而交往三个部分。论证了利玛窦、汤若望等西方传教士作为传播天主教的使者,他们从中国的现实情况出发,认真学习中国文化和礼仪,采用了迎合儒家思想以接近明清时期的要人和知识分子的方式,走上层传教路线,在中国取得了初步成功。在双方互动中,西方传教士以过人的学识、坚强的心智,特别是西方先进的科技发明和天文历法,吸引了明清时期很多知识分子和士大夫,结识的都是上层官吏和文人士绅,如徐光启、李之藻、李贽、李日华、丁耀亢、方以智、黄宗羲、陆陇其等精英,而这些人都对传教士表现出莫大的兴趣和好感,如徐光启、李之藻等人还皈依了天主教,由此开启了早期西学东渐的大门。

文章认为,利玛窦、汤若望、南怀仁等人的策略之所以成功,根本原因是明末清初西学传入中国时,正是中国传统思想发生重大转变之际,此时外来文化相对容易产生影响。而重要原因有二:一方面在于中国士大夫的猎奇心态,对于传教士手里的物件感到好奇。"他们献上表和几只三角形玻璃镜,镜中的物品映出五颜六色。在中国人看来,这是新鲜玩意儿,长期以来他们认为玻璃是一种极为宝贵的宝石。"士大夫们由于好奇而和他们交往,在交往过程中逐渐接受天主教的一些东西;传教士身上体现出很多优秀的素质和过人的科学知识,这和明清之际光死读书的士大夫相比,多了几分实在。二是传教士们在传教过程中,天主教的教义有很多在儒家思想中是没有的,在士大夫看来是合理的,出于文化互补的目的,很多士大夫也皈依天主教。但是他们信奉天主教的目的还是为儒家文化寻找辅助元素,以完善儒家传统的不足之处。整个论述逻辑清晰,材料翔实,语言朴实中透出一定的穿透性,研究以翔实的资料,深入浅出的分析,成为媒介学研究方面不可多得的范文。■

罗明坚和利玛窦1582年入住肇庆时，身着僧服，自称为"西僧"。后来利玛窦的中国朋友瞿太素告诉他，和尚历来为中国文人所鄙视，如果以僧为名会引起文人们的误会。于是，利玛窦开始考虑脱掉袈裟，换上儒服。1594年经耶稣会在东方的负责人范利安同意后，利玛窦和他的同事们开始正式留须留发，戴儒冠，着童生服，见客时行秀才礼。"合儒易佛"的路线确立以后，结交中国传统士大大就成为耶稣会士最重要的任务之一。

利玛窦第一次去见明朝宗室建安王时，见面礼就是他的新著《交友论》。此时利玛窦在中国已经生活了十几年，深知中国文人对友道的重视，所以闭口不谈宗教，滔滔不绝地大讲了一番西方的交友之道。他在《交友论》中说："吾友非他，即我之半，乃第二我也，故当视友如己焉。"

利玛窦的这种交友态度，赢得了中国文人的普遍好感。冯应京（1555—1606）对其高度赞扬，说："西泰子间关八万里，东游中国，为交友业。其悟交之道也深，故其相求也切，相与也笃，而论交道独详……视西泰子迢遥山海，以交友为务，殊有余愧。"连冯应京这样的大儒都被利玛窦所倾倒，可见其影响之大，以致当时"四方人士无不知有利先生者，诸博雅名流亦无不延颈愿望见焉"。

在与传教士的交往中，明清之际的文人表现出了多重而复杂的心态。我们大体可以将这些文人分为两类：因求异而交往、因信仰而交往。

……

对现实不满，期望一个理想的世界，由此而接受天主教，这方面徐光启十分典型。1596年在广州韶州时，徐光启就认识了意大利传教士郭居静（Lazare Cattaneo，1560—1640），1600年在南京第一次结识了利玛窦，利玛窦送他一本《天主实义》和《天主教要》。三年后，徐光启又来到南京，利氏此时已到北京，他向罗如望（Jean de Rocha，1566—1623）神父提出要加入天主教。在接受了8天的天主教神学知识教育以后，正式受洗，教名"保禄"（Paul）。徐光启加入天主教绝非一时冲动，而是有着深入的思考。万历四十四年（1616）发生"南京教案"，他在为传教士辩护而写的奏疏中，公开说明了自己信仰天主教的理由：第一，仅靠伦理的约束不能解决人生的全部问题。徐光启说这个问题早在司马迁（公元前145？—前87？）时就已经提出，为什么颜回有德而早逝，盗跖有罪而长寿？后世想通过立法来解决这一问题，但结果更糟，历代统治者"空有愿治之心，恨无必治之术"。正是在此种背景下，佛教才传入中国，但世道人心并未因此有任何进步。第二，他认为传教士所介绍的天主教是一种理想的宗教，这一宗教在西方实行了上千年，人们"大小相恤，上下相安，路不拾遗，夜不闭关，其长治久安如此"。所以，他认为耶稣会"所传天学之事，真可以补益王化，左右儒术，救正佛法者也"。

实际上，当时西方的问题绝不比中国少，但徐光启是一个理想主义者，他又无法去欧洲实地考察，所以传教士所介绍的西方成了他心中的乌托邦。

徐光启对自己的信仰非常自信。他在给皇帝的奏疏中说，有三个办法可以验证他的说法，其一，让传教士把西学的书翻译出来，然后请天下的儒生来研究，如果这些书是旁门左道，自己甘愿受罚；其二，让传教士和中国寺院的大师、道观的天师们论战，如果传教士"言无可采，理屈词穷"，立即将他们赶走，自己也情愿受罚；其三，在信天主教的地方作一个调查，三年中看犯罪的人里有没有教徒，这样就可知天主教究竟是好是坏。

在徐光启的全部言论和著作中，我们可以看到他对本土文化的热爱和对外来文化的开放心态。自明以来，在中国思想史上，像徐光启这样融融大度、涵养开明，既立足本土文化，又很好地吸收外来文化的人实属罕见。

"儒耶相融"的天学理论，是儒生们和传教士接触的思想基础。即便是徐光启那样坚定信奉传教士学术者，也并非被动地接受天主教的理论，他对天主教的理解是建立在"补儒易佛"的基础上的。他在文章中说，利玛窦等人所讲的道理"百千万言中，求一语不合忠孝大旨，求一语无益于人心世道者，竟不可得"。这说明，他自信天主教是完全符合儒家伦理道德的，并且弥补了儒家之不足。

（张西平. 跟随利玛窦去中国[M]. 北京：五洲传播出版社，2006：37-48.）

【延伸阅读】

1. 伊夫·谢弗勒. 比较文学[M]. 王炳东，译. 北京：商务印书馆，2007.

世界闻名的《我知道什么？》丛书是法国大学出版社 1941 年开始编纂出版的一套普及性百科知识丛书。作为丛书之一的《比较文学》清晰地介绍了比较文学这个学科的新老研究方法和取得的成就，内容包括比较文学的定义、外国作品、比较文学的著述、文学神话、艺术形式、文学的疆界等。

2. 李奭学. 中国晚明与欧洲文学：明末耶稣会古典型证道故事考诠[M]. 台北：中研院，联经图书公司，2005.

近代对明末以来到中国传教的耶稣会教士的研究，多聚焦在交流史、科技史或传教史上，而本书研究的重点则在于明末传入中国的天主教西洋古典证道故事，除《圣经》之外，耶稣会传教士极好地使用欧洲神话、动物寓言、传奇和历史逸事证道，这是最早传入中国的欧洲文学。作者分别就文学、哲学、修辞学和传教学考察他们训练的谱系及实践，不仅钩稽其源流，且着重文本分析，填补了 17 世纪中、欧文化交流研究工作的重要空白，是这方面的开山之作。

3. 谢天振. 译介学[M]. 上海:上海外语教育出版社,1999.

译介学,从宽泛意义上来讲,就是指从文化层面上对翻译,尤其对文学翻译所进行的一种跨文化研究。谢天振的《译介学》作为中国第一部这方面的理论著作,通过大量例证具体讨论翻译过程中出现的文化信息的失落与变形、"创造性叛逆"、翻译文学的承认以及翻译与政治意识形态之关系等译介学问题。《译介学》的出版,揭开了从比较文学和比较文化角度研究翻译的新层面,开拓了国内翻译研究的新领域。

第三章　平行研究与文学类型研究

历时地看，“平行研究（Parallel Study）”本是世界比较文学史上的第二个学派——“美国学派”的学科理论与研究方法。但是，共性地看，它更应该理解为世界比较文学一种可以超越时代与学派的理论视野与研究范式。它以“跨越性”（跨语言、跨国家、跨民族、跨学科、跨文化/文明）为首要特征，以全球一体的世界性胸怀来考察、分析与研究不同语言、国家、民族与文明体系中文学的同与异，在很大程度上代表了“比较文学”这一独特人文领域的学科气质与基本属性。

第一节　平行研究

奠定“平行研究”这一比较文学研究范式的学者是被称为“美国学派”的比较文学家，其代表学者是雷纳·韦勒克（René Wellek，1903—1995）、亨利·雷马克（Henry H. H. Remak，1916—2009）、哈利·列文（Harry Levin，1912—1994）、A. O. 奥尔德里奇（Alfrod Owen Aldriage，1915—2005）、W. P. 弗里德里希（Werner Paul Friederich，1905—1983）等。就“平行研究”这一学科理论的建构而言，贡献最大的是韦勒克、雷马克和列文。

韦勒克、雷马克、列文等美国学派代表人物不仅揭示了法国影响学派“国际文学关系史研究”因尽量缩小比较文学研究领域而形成的“危机”，而且还从理论上建构学科理论并在实践上成功拓展了比较文学的研究范围，从而为世界比较文学贡献了以跨国家和跨学科为特征的新研究范式——“平行研究”。“平行研究”重新规划了比较文学的研究领域、研究方法和研究目的。我们可以从三个方面对“平行研究”的理论内涵与方法论特征进行较全面的归纳与呈现。

一、“跨国家与跨学科”：平行研究的研究领域

从研究对象看，“平行研究”将超越事实性影响关系的文学类同性与差异性现象作为研究目标，形成了以跨语言、跨民族、跨国家、跨学科等跨越性为基本特征的另一种研究范式。在世界比较文学史上，“平行研究”长期以来都与“国际文学关系”双峰并置，成为比较文学最成熟的两大研究形态。

我们知道，法国学派将比较文学的研究对象限制为两国文学之间的事实性影响关系。这就为比较文学套上了一个沉重的枷锁。“影响性的文学关系研究”，一方面反对无事实性相互影响关系的比较，另一方面又反对文学与其他艺术门类或文化形态的比较。

“平行研究”则与此不同，它从上述两个方面突破了“影响研究”对比较文学研究对象与领域的限制。其中，雷马克对“平行研究”研究对象与领域的表述最为经典。

"比较文学是超出一国范围之外的文学研究,并且研究文学与其他知识和信仰领域之间的关系,包括艺术(如绘画、雕刻、建筑、音乐)、哲学、历史、社会科学(如政治、经济、社会学),自然科学、宗教等。简言之,比较文学是一国文学与另一国或多国的文学的比较,是文学与人类其他表现领域的比较。"①在这个著名的定义中,雷马克将比较文学"平行研究"概括为两方面的研究内容,其一是一国或几国的文学比较,其二是文学与其他艺术门类或知识形态的比较。许多学者都持同样的观点,但雷马克的上述定义最为精练,从而得到了学术界的认可,最终成为阐述"平行研究"学科方法引用频率最高的定义。

首先,"平行研究"表现在跨越国界的文学平行比较上。法国学派"影响研究"区别了"总体文学""比较文学"和"国别文学"三个不同的研究领域或层次,其目的是将比较文学限制在两国文学的二元关系之内。而"平行研究"却从根本上取消了这一制约,所谓总体文学与比较文学的区分不复存在。美国学派的比较文学家们可以将欧洲各国文学当作一个整体来加以研究,既可以局限于两国之间,更多的则是进行多国平行比较。这样,法国学派的"三元区分"被彻底打破。韦勒克率先批评了法国学派,认为法国学派在"比较文学"与"总体文学"之间所作的划分是毫无道理的,将比较文学限制在两国文学的二元关系之间只会使比较文学成为文学"外贸"研究。韦勒克指出,"在比较文学和总体文学之间构筑一道人造的藩篱,是绝对行不通的,因为文学史和文学研究只有一个对象,就是文学。把'比较文学'局限于研究二国文学之间的'贸易交往'这一愿望,使比较文学变得仅仅注意研究外部情况,研究二流作家,研究翻译、游记和'媒介物'。一言以蔽之,它使'比较文学'成了只不过是研究国外渊源和作家声誉的附属学科而已"②。雷马克则借用一个比喻形象地说,法国学派的民族文学是在墙里研究文学,比较文学跨过墙去,而总体文学则高于墙之上。但是他认为法国学派的这种区分逻辑上并不连贯。他的看法是,"在研究民族文学、比较文学和总体文学的学者之间进行刻板的分析既不实际,又无必要"③。

"平行研究"不仅突破了比较文学的二元关系论,而且进一步突破了影响研究对比较文学研究以影响和事实联系为基础的理论限制。他们认为,人类不同国度和民族都有相似的社会历史发展阶段、类似的思想情感和心理特征,也有类似的文学表现手法和类型。这就使国别文学之间尽管毫无事实性联系,但仍存在着十分相同或类似的现象。对这些相似点的比较研究和整体研究,可以得出真正文学的规律和性质。韦勒

① 雷马克.比较文学的定义和功用[M]//张隆溪.比较文学译文集.北京:北京大学出版社,1982:1.

② 韦勒克.比较文学的危机[M]//干永昌,等.比较文学研究译文集.上海:上海译文出版社,1985:124.

③ 雷马克.比较文学的定义和功用[M]//张隆溪.比较文学译文集.北京:北京大学出版社,1982:18.

克一生坚持世界文学的“一元论”和“总体论”，坚决反对过分强调国别文学之间的语言差异，一贯认为世界文学是一个整体，比较文学就是从国际的角度，超越语言和民族的界线，将它作为一个整体加以研究。他的八卷本《近代文学批评史》纵论整个西方世界（包括欧洲、北美和俄罗斯等地区和国家从1750—1950年两百年间的文学批评、思想和观念），给人以恢宏的历史感和整体感。他关于文学史分期、文学史上的潮流的单篇论文同样如此。他在阐述“古典主义”“巴洛克”“浪漫主义”“现实主义”“象征主义”等文学批评史上的关键性概念时，同样超越语言和民族的界线，从极其宽广的视野将世界文学史当作一个整体来加以研究，显示了比较文学在文学研究上的巨大潜力。与韦勒克一样，雷马克也反对法国学派仅将比较文学局限在事实联系上。他在著名的《比较文学的定义和功用》一文中强调美国学派必须比较互相并没有影响的作家和作品，认为“纯比较文学的题目其实是一个不可穷尽的宝藏”。在另一篇论文中，雷马克再次指出，美国学派的“目的主要在于显示一部文学作品的艺术特征，被比较的作品之间就不一定要有遗传关系”，因为“它可能显示某种关系性，但这种关系性可能与作者A在写作品C时是否认识外国作家B这一问题毫无关系”①。

其次，在跨学科问题上，“平行研究”同样取得了重大的突破。雷马克高度重视这一突破，他甚至认为这是美国学派与法国学派的根本分歧。他说，在文学与其他学科领域之间的关系问题上，“我们遇到的不是强调重点的不同，而是‘美国学派’与‘法国学派’之间阵线分明的根本分歧”②。的确，法国学派根本不将文学与其他艺术和文化形态的相互比较纳入比较文学之中。在法国学派代表理论家梵·第根和基亚的著作和巴登斯贝格主编的《比较文学评论》杂志中，根本就不包括这一研究领域。在这个领域中，美国学派把比较文学扩大到文学与其他艺术，以及文学与其他文化形态的比较中。文学与绘画、雕塑、建筑、音乐、戏剧、电影等的相互关系，文学与哲学、历史、宗教、心理学、政治、经济等的相互关系，对这些关系的研究统统都可以纳入比较文学。

这样，“平行研究”彻底突破了比较文学“文学关系学”的研究对象和领域，将没有事实性的影响与被影响关系的相同、相似、相异的文学现象作为研究对象，从而获得了一种超越时代、国家、民族、学科与文明的全球一体的大眼光与大视野。

二、“审美主义”：平行研究的研究方法

在研究方法上，“平行研究”将“审美主义（aestheticism）”作为基本方法。“平行研

① 雷马克．比较文学的法国学派与美国学派[M]//比较文学研究资料．北京：北京师范大学出版社，1986：71．

② 雷马克．比较文学的定义和功用[M]//张隆溪．比较文学译文集．北京：北京大学出版社，1982：4．

究”反对“影响研究”的“实证主义”方法，倡导用文学批评和分析美学的方法来分析“文学性”问题。

韦勒克为突破法国学派的实证主义方法论作出了巨大贡献。在韦勒克看来，如果把比较文学局限于对文学相互影响的外部事实的研究，只会使比较文学研究成为研究民族社会、交往和文化相互关系的研究。韦勒克指出：“很多在文学研究方面，特别是比较文学研究方面的著名人物，根本不是真正对文学感兴趣，而是热衷于研究公众舆论史、旅游报道和民族特点的见解。总之，对一般文化史感兴趣。文学研究这个概念被他们扩大到竟与整个人类史等同起来了。就方法论而言，文学研究如不决心将文学作为有别于人类其他活动及产物的学科来研究，就不可能有什么进展。为此我们必须正视‘文学性（literariness）’这个问题，它是美学的中心问题，是文学和艺术的本质。”[①]在韦勒克看来，比较文学就是从国际角度将世界文学作为一个整体加以研究，其目的是揭示文学的审美特征。韦勒克在他与沃伦合著的《文学理论》中，从文学作品的存在方式研究出发，将文学研究区分为“内部研究”和“外部研究”两个部分。“外部研究”就是一种“因果关系”的实证主义研究法，致力于考察文学作品产生原因和背景，但它无法完成分析和评价文学作品的根本任务。而“内部研究”则是“以文学为中心”的研究，注重研究文学作品从声音层面、意义单元层面、世界层面到“形而上学”层面的所有内在因素及其审美特征。“内部研究”把艺术品看成“是一个为某种特别的审美目的服务的完整的符号体系或者符号结构”[②]。根据这一文学本体论，韦勒克认为法国学派的比较文学研究只不过是一种实证主义的研究，是一种对文学的“外部研究”，而“平行研究”要做的是突破“影响研究”的这一限制，将审美分析引入比较文学。正如韦勒克所说，“真正的文学研究所关心的不是毫无生气的事实，而是标准和质量”[③]。比较文学既然是超语言、国别、民族的文学研究，也就应该关注的是对文学内在审美“结构”的研究。韦勒克由此指出，比较文学只要超越民族文学界线，就一定会走向世界文学一体化的美学批评。对于这样的比较文学概念，他说：“这样一种全球性的文学理论，即诗学，将无可避免地导向美学标准。”[④]（Such a universal theory of literature, poetics, will inevitably appeal to aesthetic criteria.）

雷马克深刻地分析了法国学派寻求“科学性”，忠实于19世纪实证主义学术研究

---

① 韦勒克.比较文学的危机[M]//干永昌,等.比较文学研究译文集.上海:上海译文出版社,1985:133.

② 韦勒克,沃伦.文学理论[M]//刘象愚,等,译.北京:三联书店,1984:147.

③ 韦勒克.比较文学的危机[M]//干永昌,等,编译.比较文学研究译文集.上海:上海译文出版社,1985:131.

④ René Wellek: *Criticism as Evaluation*, *The Attack on Literature and Other Essays*, The University of North Carolina Press, 1982:57.

的原因本质。他分析说:"法国比较文学否定'纯粹'的比较,它忠实于19世纪实证主义学术研究的传统,即实证主义所坚持并热切期望的文学研究的'科学性'。按照这种观点,纯粹的类比不会得出任何结论,尤其是不能得出有更大意义的、系统的、概括性的结论。……既然值得尊重的科学必须致力于因果关系的探索,而比较文学必须具有科学性,因此,比较文学应该研究因果关系,即影响、交流、变更等。"①雷马克的这一段话切中了法国学派的要害。它深刻地分析出了法国学派在进行比较文学学科建设中所走过的心路历程,也客观呈现了"平行研究"与"影响研究"在比较文学研究方法性气质上的不同之处。

三、"世界主义":平行研究的研究目标

在研究目标方面,"平行研究"反对民族主义而提倡"世界主义(Cosmopolitanism)"。正如韦勒克和雷马克等美国学派学者所揭示的,法国学派在比较文学研究问题上,长期困扰于民族主义危机之中。韦勒克尖锐指责他们的比较文学是"外贸"研究,只会在两国文学与文化关系上"计算财富"。雷马克则形象地比喻说,法国学派将本国文学领会为一棵独立存在的树木,从不顾及它周围其他树木和整个树林。雷马克说:"法国比较文学是以进一步扩展法国文学研究为起点的。过去,它主要研究法国文学在国外的影响和外国文学对法国文学的贡献,现在仍然如此。"②这种民族主义的倾向是法国学派限定比较文学研究目的和根本任务的必然结果。

韦勒克一生坚持世界文学的"整体论"观点。对他而言,比较文学的特殊性在于它的角度和精神气质——国际性。比较也不能仅仅局限在事实性联系上,毫无历史关系的语言现象或类型也能进行平行比较。有时,韦勒克甚至将比较文学平行研究的范围扩大东方国家,从而显示出他的世界主义视野。他在《比较文学的名称和实质》一文中提到:"对中国、朝鲜、缅甸和波斯叙述方法或者抒情形式的研究同伏尔泰的《中国孤儿》这类同东方偶然接触之后产生的作品的影响研究同样重要。"③在《今日比较文学》一文中,他也提出要"研究各国文学及其共同倾向",甚至"比较研究包括远东文学在内的一切文学"④。倡导"平行研究"的其他学者同样坚持超国家和文化的"世界主义"视野。雷马克论述比较文学研究可以研究某个历史阶段并无事实性联系的国别文学时,提到过可以"对古希腊和古印度,中世纪日本和中世纪欧洲的比较",认为

---

① 雷马克.比较文学的法国学派与美国学派[M]//比较文学研究资料.北京:北京师范大学出版社,1986:67-68.

② 雷马克.比较文学的法国学派与美国学派[M]//比较文学研究资料.北京:北京师范大学出版社,1986:74.

③ 韦勒克.比较文学的名称和实质[M]//比较文学研究资料.北京:北京师范大学出版社,1986:29.

④ 韦勒克.今日之比较文学[M]//干永昌,等.比较文学研究译文集.上海:上海译文出版社,1985:165.

这样"比较文学有可能通过审慎的比较进一步修正我们对亚洲文学在理解上的严重缺陷"①。

当然,作为比较文学一种重要研究范式,"平行研究"在理论特征与最终成效上同样存在着一些不足与局限。限于篇幅,此处不再赘述。有兴趣进一步了解的读者,可以查阅《比较文学学科史》一书的相关内容。

【原典选读】

比较文学的危机(节选)

◉韦勒克

【导读】雷纳·韦勒克(René Wellek)的《比较文学的危机》(*The Crisis of Comparative Literature*)是比较文学"美国学派"与"平行研究"兴起的标志性作品。20世纪上半叶,比较文学研究的主导倾向是法国学派确立的"影响研究"。在它所确立的"国际文学关系"视角下,比较文学出现了越来越多的"危机"。这一危机终于由世界著名文学批评家、比较文学家雷纳·韦勒克在1958年9月国际比较文学协会第二次大会(因会议在美国北卡罗莱大学所在地教堂山举行,故此次大会史称"教堂山会议")上明确揭示出来了。在这届年会上,韦勒克作了题为《比较文学的危机》的挑战性发言,对当时一统天下的法国学派进行了猛烈批判,宣告了比较文学美国学派和"平行研究"范式的诞生。

在这篇比较文学经典文献中,韦勒克一开篇就将当时"影响研究"笼罩下比较文学的研究局面概括为"持久的危机状态"。紧接着,他从三个方面全面、深刻地揭示了法国学派"影响研究"学科范式给比较文学所带来的"危机"。韦勒克说:"我认为,内容和方法之间的人为界线,渊源和影响的机械主义概念,以及尽管是十分慷慨的但仍属文化民族主义的动机,是比较文学研究中持久危机的症状。"②这句话可以看作整篇文章承上启下的关键性语句。

在文章后半部分,韦勒克针对"影响研究"三大缺陷,在渊博的比较文学学识和坚实的文学理论基础上明确界定了"平行研究"范式在跨越国界/民族界线的总体文学性研究对象、美学分析的研究方法和世界主义研究目标三个方面所体现出来的基本理论特征。

韦勒克对比较文学学科理论第二次危机的揭示和对法国学派比较文学学科理论

---

① 雷马克.比较文学的法国学派与美国学派[M]//比较文学研究资料.北京:北京师范大学出版社,1986:71.

② 韦勒克.比较文学的危机[M]//干永昌,等.比较文学研究译文集.上海:上海译文出版社,1985:130.

的挑战其实并不始于也不仅见于他的上述《比较文学的危机》一文。按他自己的说法:"早在国际比协成立之前,多年来我就已在各种场合批评过比较文学的方法论。"①韦勒克在《文学史理论》《比较文学的概念》《文学理论》,以及《比较文学的名称与性质》《今日之比较文学》等论文中,分别多次对法国学派的比较文学学科理论提出过挑战。要更加全面和深入理解《比较文学的危机》这篇著名论文以及比较"平行研究"范式的理论内涵,我们还需要将这篇文章与韦勒克的其他论著关联起来阅读。■

An artificial demarcation of subject matter and methodology, a mechanistic concept of sources and influences, a motivation by cultural nationalism, however generous—these seem to me the symptoms of the long-drawn-out crisis of comparative literature.

A thorough reorientation is needed in all these three directions. The artificial demarcation between "comparative" and "general" literature should be abandoned. "Comparative" literature has become an established term for any study of literature transcending the limits of one national literature. There is little use in deploring the grammar of the term and to insist that it should be called "the comparative study of literature," since everybody understands the elliptic usage. "General" literature has not caught on, at least in English, possibly because it has still its old connotation of referring to poetics and theory. Personally I wish we could simply speak of the study of literature or of literary scholarship and that there were, as Albert Thibaudet proposed, professors of literature just as there are professors of philosophy and of history and not professors of the history of English philosophy even though the individual may very well specialize in this or that particular period or country or even in a particular author. Fortunately, we still have no professors of English eighteenth-century literature or of Goethe philology. But the naming of our subject is an institutional matter of academic interest in the most literal sense. What matters is the concept of literary scholarship as a unified discipline unhampered by linguistic restrictions. I cannot thus agree with Friederich's view that comparatists "cannot and dare not encroach upon other territories," i. e. those of the students of English, French, German, and other national literatures. Nor can I see how it is even possible to follow his advice not to "poach in each other's territory."② There are no proprietary rights and no recognized "vested interests" in literary scholarship. Everybody has the right to study any question even if it is confined to a single work in a single language and everybody has the right to study even history or philosophy of any other topic. He runs of course the risk of criticism by the specialists, but it is a risk he has to take. We comparatists surely would not want to prevent English professors from studying the French sources of Chaucer, or French professors from studying the Spanish sources of Corneille, etc., since we comparatists would not want to be forbidden to publish on topics confined to specific

① 韦勒克.今日之比较文学[M]//干永昌,等.比较文学研究译文集.上海:上海译文出版社,1985:160.

② *Yearbook of Comparative and General Literature*, 4(1955), 57.

national literatures. Far too much has been made of the "authority" of the specialist who often may have only the bibliographical knowledge or the external information without necessarily having the taste, the sensibility, and the range of the nonspecialist whose wider perspective and keener insight may well make up for years of intense application. There is nothing presumptuous or arrogant in advocating a greater mobility and ideal universality in our studies. The whole conception of fenced-off reservations with signs of "no trespassing" must be distasteful to a free mind. It can arise only within the limits of the obsolete methodology preached and practiced by the standard theorists of comparative literature who assume that "facts" are to be discovered like nuggets of gold for which we can stake out prospectors' claims.

But true literary scholarship is not concerned with inert facts, but with values and qualities. That is why there is no distinction between literary history and criticism. Even the simplest problem of literary history requires an act of judgment. Even such a statement that Racine influenced Voltaire, or Herder influenced Goethe requires, to be meaningful, a knowledge of the characteristics of Racine and Voltaire. Herder and Goethe, and hence a knowledge of the context of their traditions, an unremitting activity of weighing, comparing, analysing, and diseriminating which is essenitially critical. No literary history has ever been written without some principle of selection and some attempt at characterization and evaluation. Literary historians who deny the importance of criticism are themselves unconscious critics, usually derivative critics who have merely taken over traditional standards and accepted conventional reputations. A work of art cannot be analyzed, characterized, and evaluated without recourse to critical principles, however unconsciously held and obscurely formulated. Norman Foerster in a still pertinent booklet, *The American Scholar*, said very cogently that the literary historian ①"must be a critic *in order* to be a historian." In literary scholarship theory, criticism, and history collaborate to achieve its central task: the description, interpretation, and evaluation of a work of art or any group of works of art. Comparative literature which, at least with its official theorists has shunned this collaboration and has clung to "factual relations," sources and influences, intermediaries and reputations as its only topics, will have to find its way back into the great stream of contemporary literary scholarship and criticism. In its methods and methodological reflections comparative literature has become, to put it bluntly, a stagnant backwater. We can think of many scholarly and critical movements and groupings during this century quite diverse in their aims and methods—Croce and his followers in Italy, Russian formalism and its offshoots and developments in Poland and Czechoslovakia, German *Geistesgeschichte* and stylistics which have found such an echo in the Spanish-speaking countries, French and German existentialist criticism, the American "New Criticism," the myth criticism inspired by Jung's archetypal patterns, and even Freudian psychoanalysis or Marxism: all these are, whatever their limitations and demerits, united in a common reaction against the external factualism and atomism which is still lettering the study of comparative literature.

① Chapell Hill, 1929:36.

Literary scholarship today needs primarily a realization of the need to define its subject matter and focus. It must be distinguished from the study of the history of ideas, or religious and political concepts and sentiments which are often suggested as alternatives to literary studies. Many eminent men in literary scholarship and particularly in comparative literature are not really interested in literature at all but in the history of public opinion, the reports of travelers, the ideas about national character—in short, in general cultural history. The concept of literary study is broadened by them so radically that it becomes identical with the whole history of humanity. But literary scholarship will not make any progress, methodologically, unless it determines to study literature as a subject distinct from other activities and products of man. Hence we must face the problem of "literariness," the central issue of aesthetics, the nature of art and literature.

In such a conception of literary scholarship the literary work of art itself will be the necessary focus and we will recognize that we study different problems when we examine the relations of a work of art to the psychology of the author or to the sociology of his society. The work of art, I have argued, can be conceived as a stratified structure of signs and meanings which is totally distinct from the mental processes of the author at the time of composition and hence of the influences which may have formed his mind. There is what has been rightly called an "ontological gap" between the psychology of the author and a work of art, between life and society on the one hand and the aesthetic object. I have called the study of the work of art "intrinsic" and that of its relations to the mind of the author, to society, etc., "extrinsic." Still, this distinction cannot mean that genetic relations should be ignored or even despised or that intrinsic study is mere formalism or irrelevant aestheticism. Precisely the carefully worked out concept of a stratified structure of signs and meanings attempts to overcome the old dichotomy of content and form. What is usually called "content" or "idea" in a work of art is incorporated into the structure of the work of art as part of its "world" of projected meanings. Nothing would be further from my mind than to deny the human relevance of art or to erect a barrier between history and formal study. While I have learned from the Russian formalists and German *Stilforscher*, I would not want to confine the study of literature either to the study of sound, verse and compositional devices or to elements of diction and syntax; nor would I want to equate literature with language. In my conception these linguistic elements form, so to say, the two bottom strata: the sound stratum and that of the units of meaning. But from them there emerges a "world" of situations, characters, and events which cannot be identified with any single linguistic element or, least of all, with any element of external ornamental form. The only right conception seems to me a resolutely "holistic" one which sees the work of art as a diversified totality, as a structure of signs which, however, imply and require meanings and values. Both a relativistic antiquarianism and an external formalism are mistaken attempts to dehumanize literary study. Criticism cannot and must not be expelled from literary scholarship.

(René Wellek: *The Crisis of Comparative Literature*, from René Wellek: *Concepts of Criticism*, New Haven and London: Yale University Press, 1963:290-294.)

比较文学的定义与功能(节选)

◉雷马克

【导读】世界比较文学学者对雷马克(Henry H. H. Remak)的《比较文学的定义与功能》(*Comparative Literature, Its Definition and Function*)一文的引证非常频繁。其原因在于,雷马克在这篇论文中不仅开宗明义地提出了"美国学派"所具有的"平行研究"特征,而且还明确将"法国学派"与"美国学派"对立起来进行论述,以一种明晰的理论方式将两种学派及其所代表的两种范式确立为比较文学最有代表性的方法论体系。

雷马克从两个方面来表述比较文学美国学派"平行研究"的特征:一是超事实性影响关系的不同国家之间的文学比较,二是跨学科的文化与其他知识领域的系统性比较。"比较文学是超出一国范围之外的文学研究,并且研究文学与其他知识和信仰领域之间的关系,包括艺术(如绘画、雕刻、建筑、音乐)、哲学、历史、社会科学(如政治、经济、社会学)、自然科学、宗教等。简言之,比较文学是一国文学与另一国或多国的文学的比较,是文学与人类其他表现领域的比较。"这样简洁而明确的定义获得了绝大多数比较文学学者的认可,影响十分深远。

文章批评法国学派"实证主义"研究方法,认为影响研究把"文学批评排斥在比较文学领域之外",这种局限于史实与材料的学科理论过于"保守"。雷马克指出:"影响研究如果主要限于找出和证明某种影响的存在,却忽略更重要的艺术理解和评价的问题,那么对于阐明文学作品的实质所作的贡献,就可能不及比较互相并没有影响或重点不在于指出这种影响的各种对作家、作品、文体、倾向性、文学传统等的研究。"在这方面,雷马克与韦勒克是一致的,目的都在强调"平行研究"需要摆脱"影响研究"的实证主义倾向,将"文学性"与审美特征当作比较文学的关注重心。

在论文的第二大部分,雷马克还对"民族文学""比较文学""世界文学"和"总体文学"等术语的内涵与外延进行了分析与界定。比如,尽管语言、国家与民族之间的界线在历史时空中常常变动不居,形成了相互交织难以区分的复杂状态,但是雷马克指出"大多数比较学者都承认这些问题的复杂和互相混淆,但又一致认为这类难题毕竟是不常见的,也没有严重到足以混淆民族文学研究和超出民族文学界限的研究"。这里,我们选读的内容是这篇文章最为精彩的第一部分,即关于美国学派"平行研究"范式进行详细阐释的文字。其中,删除了雷马克原文对跨学科研究的论述,这部分文字将移入本章第五节再深入阅读。■

COMPARATIVE literature is the study of literature beyond the confines of one particular country, and the study of the relationships between literature on the one hand and other areas of knowledge and belief, such as the arts (e. g., painting, sculpture, architecture, music), philosophy, history, the social sciences (e. g., politics, economics, sociology), the sciences, religion, etc., on the other. In brief, it is the comparison of one literature with another or others, and the comparison of literature with other spheres of human expression.

This definition is probably acceptable to most students of comparative literature in this country, but would be subject to considerable argument among an important segment of comparatists which we shall, for brevity's sake, call the "French school." For the purpose of clarifying these differences of opinion, some rather basic, others more of emphasis, it may be wise to take up the first part of our definition before dealing with the second.

While the American and the French "schools" will both subscribe to this portion of our definition, viz. comparative literature as the study of literature beyond national boundaries, there are important variations of relative stress in its practical application. The French are inclined to favor questions which can be solved on the basis of factual evidence (often involving personal documents). They tend to exclude literary criticism from the domain of comparative literature. They look askance at studies which "merely" compare, which "merely" point out analogies and contrasts. Carré and Guyard even warn against influence studies as being too hazy, too uncertain, and would have us concentrate on questions of reception, intermediaries, foreign travel, and attitudes toward a given country in the literature of another country during a certain period. Unlike Van Tieghem, these two scholars are also chary of vast syntheses of European literature as courting superficiality, dangerous simplifications and slippery metaphysics.

The positivistic roots of these reservations are clearly discernible. In our opinion, the French desire for literary "sécurité" is unfortunate at a time which cries, as Peyre has pointed out, for more (not less) imagination. To be sure, the problem of influences is a very delicate one and requires of its devotee more encyclopedic knowledge and more finesse than has been exhibited in some past endeavors of this kind. In a good many influence studies, the location of sources has been given too much attention, rather than such questions as: what was *retained* and what was *rejected*, and *why*, and *how* was the material absorbed and integrated, and with *what success*? If conducted in this fashion, influence studies contribute not only to our knowledge of literary history but to our understanding of the creative process and of the literary work of art.

To the extent that the preoccupation with locating and proving an influence may overshadow more crucial questions of artistic interpretation and evaluation, influence studies may contribute less to the elucidation of the essence of a literary work than studies comparing authors, works, styles, tendencies and literatures in which no influence can or is intended to be shown. Purely comparative subjects constitute an inexhaustible reservoir hardly tapped by contemporary scholars who seem to have forgotten that the name of our discipline is "comparative literature," not "influential literature." Herder and Diderot, Novalis and Chateaubriand, Musset and Heine, Balzac and Dickens, *Moby Dick* and

Faust, Hawthorne *Roger Malvin's Burial* and Droste-Hülshoff *Judenbuche*, Hardy and Hauptmann, Azorín and Anatole France, Baroja and Stendhal, Hamsun and Giono, Thomas Mann and Gide are eminently comparable regardless of whether or how much the one influenced the other.

Carré's and Guyard's disinclination toward large-scale syntheses in comparative literature strikes us likewise as excessively cautious. We *must* have syntheses unless the study of literature wants to condemn itself to eternal fragmentation and isolation. If we have any ambitions of participating in the intellectual and emotional life of the world, we must, now and then, pull together the insights and results achieved by research in literature and make available meaningful conclusions to other disciplines, to the nation and to the world at large. The dangers of hurried generalizations, real as they are, are too often advanced as a shield covering up the all too human temptation of playing it safe. "We must wait till all the data are in." But all the data will never be in, and we know it. Even if a single generation succeeded in assembling all the data on a given author or topic, the same "facts" will and should always be subject to different interpretations by different generations. Scholarship must take reasonable precautions, but it should not be paralyzed by illusory perfectionism.

Fortunately, the French have been far less timid and doctrinaire in actual practice than in theory. To French and French-trained scholars, comparative literature owes a large, probably the largest share of important comparative scholarship. Texte *Rousseau and the Origins of Literary Cosmopolitanism*, Baldensperger *Goethe in France* and *The Circulation of Ideas in the French Emigration*, *Carré Goethe in England*, Hazard's admirable panorama of the Enlightenment throughout Europe are only a few among French syntheses distinguished by a dexterous and sensitive handling of comparisons and influences, by a subtle awareness of literary values and of the fine shadings of the uniquely individual as well as an uncanny ability to direct a myriad of observations into lucid patterns of overall developments. Van Tieghem's and Guyard's French introductions to comparative literature are themselves syntheses of substantial usefulness. American scholars, in their turn, must guard against dismissing lightly certain topics (studies of reception, attitudes, intermediaries, travelers, *Belesenheit*) merely because the French seem to have favored them to the exclusion or neglect of other comparative subjects.

...

With this caveat in mind, our preference goes nevertheless to the more inclusive "American" concept of comparative literature. We must, to be sure, strive to achieve and maintain a minimum set of criteria marking off our chosen field; but we must not be so concerned with its theoretical unity as to forget the perhaps more important *functional* aspect of comparative literature. We conceive of comparative literature less as an independent subject which must at all costs set up its own inflexible laws, than as a badly needed auxiliary discipline, a link between smaller segments of parochial literature, a bridge between organically related but physically separated areas of human creativeness. Whatever the disagreements on the theoretical aspects of comparative literature be, there is agreement on its task: to give scholars, teachers, students and last but not least readers a better, more comprehensive understanding of literature as a whole rather than of a departmental fragment or several isolated departmental fragments of literature. It can do so best by not only relating several literatures to each other but by relating literature to other fields of human knowledge and activity, especially artistic and ideological fields; that is, by extending the investigation of literature both geographically and generically.

(Henry H. H. Remak: Comparative Literature: Its Definition and Function. From *Comparative Literatreu*: *Method and Perspective*, Edited By Newton P. Stallknecht and Horst Frenz, Southern Illinois University Press, 1961:3-10.)

【延伸阅读】

1. 韦勒克. 今日之比较文学[M]//干永昌,等. 比较文学研究译文集. 上海:上海译文出版社,1985.

本文发表于1965年,是韦勒克在美国比较文学学会大会上所作的报告,距他在1958年发表那篇宣告美国学派及平行研究诞生的论文已经过了七年时间。韦勒克在文章中较详细地回顾了自己的学术经历,不仅对《比较文学的危机》一文所产生的学术背景进行了较详细的介绍,而且对比较文学的现状与趋向进行了较深入的分析,有利于我们更深入地理解平行研究三大理论内涵与方法论特征。

2. 雷马克. 十字路口的比较文学:诊断、治疗与处方(中文节译为《比较文学的美国学派与法国学派》)[M]//北京师范大学中文系比较文学研究组. 比较文学研究资料. 北京:北京师范大学出版社,1986.

作为美国学派平行研究范式的主要发言人之一,雷马克在此文中对比较文学的两个学派与两种学科理论进行了更加详细的阐述。雷马克虽然承认法国学派的比较文学观并不是"铁板一块",但仍然认为,在坚持实用主义研究方法方面法国学派各学者仍然体现了"明显的内部一致性"。就美国学派,此文提出"美国比较文学实质性的主张在于:使文学研究得以合理存在的主要依据是文学作品","新批评派"对平行研究的影响"显而易见",这对我们深入理解平行研究的理论内涵及其与"英美新批评派"文学理论的关系具有重要的参考价值。

3. 勃洛克. 比较文学的新动向[M]//干永昌,等. 比较文学研究译文集. 上海:上海译文出版社,1985.

美国纽约市立大学教授勃洛克(Haskell M. Block)在本文中对法国学派与美国学派的理论论争进行了较为详细的评述。通过文章可以看出,比较文学在勃洛克写作此文的年代(1969)已经"被看作人文科学中最具活力、最能引起人们兴趣的科目之一"了。针对韦勒克的《比较文学的危机》,勃洛克表示,比较文学遇到"危机并不是一件坏事"。文章一方面称《比较文学的危机》一文是对实证主义的比较文学研究"最有力、最富论战性的表现”，另一方面，也批评韦勒克“稍嫌过火”地否认了法国学派所“做出的积极建树”，并对法国学派的学术贡献进行了中肯的评价。文章批评了那种在法国学派与美国学派之间进行“肤浅的”对立的做法，有利于我们超越影响研究与平行研究的二元对立。

第二节　主题学

翻开近30年来中国大陆任何一本比较文学概论性质的著作，几乎都能找到“主题学”章节，加之数量可观的期刊论文，有关“主题学”的理论探讨可谓层出不穷。由于不同的学科立场以及相同学科在观念与架构上的差异，论者对“主题学”的性质、内容与方法作出了各有侧重甚至彼此反对的描述与阐释。

就学科立场而言，有民俗（故事）主题学、文学主题学、文化主题学、比较文学主题学等。单从比较文学的立场来看，有以基亚为代表的影响研究视域中的主题学，有以哈利·列文、乌尔利希·韦斯坦因为代表的注重美学阐释与社会分析相结合的主题学，当然也有以费尔南德·巴登斯贝格、保尔·梵·第根、克罗齐、韦勒克等为代表的反对或拒斥主题学的观点。

就我国而言，鲁迅的《摩罗诗力说》、顾颉刚的《孟姜女故事研究集》、茅盾的《神话研究》、朱光潜的《中西诗在情趣上的比较》、钱南扬的《祝英台故事叙论》、陈寅恪的《〈西游记〉玄奘弟子故事的演变》、钱锺书的《一节历史掌故、一个宗教寓言、一篇历史小说》、季羡林的《罗摩衍那在中国》、钟敬文的《中国的天鹅处女型故事》、戴不凡的《试论〈白蛇传〉故事》、罗永麟的《试论〈牛郎织女〉》、丁乃通的《中西叙事文学比较研究》、马幼垣的《三现身故事与清风闸》、钱理群的《丰富的痛苦：“堂吉诃德”与“哈姆雷特”的东移》、陈鹏翔的《中英古典诗歌里的秋天：主题学研究》、林文月的《源氏物语桐壶与长恨歌》、田毓英的《西班牙骑士与中国侠》、何新的《诸神的起源》、叶舒宪的《英雄与太阳》和《高唐神女与维纳斯：中西文化中的爱与美主题》、龚鹏程的《大侠》、刘守华的《比较故事学》、王立的《中国文学主题学》和《中国古代文学复仇主题》、段宝林的《“狼外婆”故事比较初探》等一系列论著展示了百余年主题学研究所取得的突出成就。但就从这些被普遍公认的主题学成果来看，它们的学科属性显然难以确定，比较恰当的看法是：主题学是一门具有交叉或边缘性质的学科。这虽然会给比较文学主题学的理论研究带来诸多困惑，但从另一方面看，它也相当程度地与比较文学跨学科的特质相契合。

前文已经指出，近 30 年来我国比较文学界有关主题学的理论探讨十分活跃。不过，众多论述尽管表面看来似乎是在各抒己见，但骨子里的学理依据却无一例外地来自西方，由此便形成了以下几个方面的"共识"。

第一，"主题学"起源于德国民俗学，更具体地说就是 19 世纪初期《格林童话》的作者格林兄弟在采撷加工民间童话的时候，发现不同地域流传有诸多颇为类似的故事与传说，由此开始追寻它们的演变历程与相互关系，这大概还属于德文 Stoffgeschichte（主题史、题材史）的研究范畴；当这一研究进而发展成探讨相同或相似的神话故事、民间传说在不同时代、不同地域、不同作家那里所存在的种种差异及其原因时，就被德国学者称之为 Motivgeschichite（动机史）的研究；但当其进一步扩大到对其他被看作适当的主题的事物，如时间、空间、海洋、山脉、黑夜、动物、英雄、牧童、死亡、牺牲、离别、宿命以及如雄伟的、美丽的、原始的、进步的等知性观念的研究时，就和比较文学学科联系了起来，而这时已经到了 20 世纪的中叶。在这一过程中，主题学受到人类学、民俗学、心理学、原型批评等多学科、多方位的影响与洗礼，开始突破 Stoffgeschichte、Motivgeschichite 的范畴，希求新的命名与内涵。而与德国的 Stoffgeschichte、Motivgeschichite 相类似的术语，"法国学称为主题学（thé matologie），在英语国家中学者们却以妥协的方式使用 Stoffgeschichte，至少在哈利·列文创造的'主题学（thematology）'这一新的术语尚未被多数人采用之前是如此"①。

第二，美国的哈利·列文（Harry Levin）是比较文学学科中"主题学（thematics/thematology）"一词的创造者。1968 年，哈利·列文的论文《主题学与文学批评》（Thematics and Criticism）被收入 Peter Demetz，Thomas Greene，Lowry Nelson 合编由耶鲁大学出版社出版的 *The Disciplines of Criticism* 一书中。这篇文章后来又成为哈利·列文 *Grounds for Comparison*：*Essays in Literary Theory*，*Interpretation*，*and History* 的一个部分，该书 1972 年由哈佛大学出版社出版。在这一篇幅不长的文章中，哈利·列文通过考察"主题"含义的演变，"渐渐地、小心翼翼地"接近"主题学"领域，并颇为辩证地指出："如果说曾经有过这样一个词，它的被提出是为了被否定的话，那么，它一定是那个迄今为止没有一部字典有足够大的气量予以承认的、可怕的词。但这可能也预

① 乌尔利希·韦斯坦因．比较文学与文学理论［M］．刘象愚，译．沈阳：辽宁人民出版社，1987：122.

示着主题科学的来临，尽管甚至某些热衷此道的先驱者或许也会对把自己说成是主题学研究者和参加一个主题学研讨会而犹疑不决。”①当然，这篇被视为探讨比较文学主题学里程碑式的文章的主要贡献，是较为细致地梳理了此一领域的重要研究成果，初步建立起一个包括学者、作家、艺术家乃至于心理学家在内的阵容可观的主题学研究队伍，并且还对容易产生混淆的主题、母题、象征等范畴进行了大致的辨析。此外，还有一点值得注意的是，除了 thematology 之外，哈利·列文在该文中还创造并使用“thematics”来指称这门新领域。对此，台湾学者陈鹏翔有这样的阐释：“勒文在创造 thematics 这个名词时就曾提到，其形容词 thematic 恰好与‘主题（theme）’变成形容词时，字母完全一样；主题研究（thematic studies）一般侧重在探讨作品的意义，而主题学研究则是探究同一主题在不同时代不同作家的处理，其侧重点是技巧的。……勒文虽知道 thematics 与 thematic 会造成困扰，但是，他在文章里却是 thematics 与 thematology 相互应用，或许是拟使二词共存。”②

第三，主题学与主题研究的区别。作出这种区分的原因，应该是由“主题”的复杂含义以及众多貌同心异的“主题学”研究实践所引起的困惑。既然“主题学”被视为比较文学学科的一个重要分支，它就应该具备比较文学的属性，也就是跨语言、跨民族—国家、跨学科、跨文化（跨文明）等。但实际上很多自称是主题学或者被划归于主题学的研究成果，并不具有上述这些比较文学的属性，比如顾颉刚的文章《孟姜女故事的转变》，甚或是王立的被冠之于《中国文学主题学》的一系列成果，都不是有意识地从比较文学学科视角所展开的研究，其比较文学的性质并不鲜明。但另一方面，由于中国文学与文化中较早地融入了外来的佛教文化，所以探讨那些与印度佛教有关的中国文学主题的论著，也就可以划归到比较文学的领域，比如陈寅恪的《〈西游记〉玄奘弟子故事的演变》、季羡林的《“猫名”寓言的演变》就是这样的论文。

为了能够更好地判定这些不同种类的主题学研究，陈鹏翔较早地对“主题学和一般主题研究作出区分与说明”：“主题学是比较文学中的一个部门（a field of study），而普通一般主题研究（thematic studies）则是任何文学作品许多层面中一个层面的研究；主题学探索的是相同主题（包含套语、意象和母题等）在不同时代以及不同的作家手中的处理，据以了解时代的特征和作家的‘用意（intention）’，而一般的主题研究探讨的是个别主题的呈现。最重要的是，主题学溯自 19 世纪德国民俗学的开拓，而主题研

① 哈利·列文. 主题学与文学批评[M]//廖世奇，译. 乐黛云. 比较文学原理·附录三. 长沙：湖南文艺出版社，1988：263.

② 陈鹏翔. 主题学研究与中国文学[M]//陈鹏翔. 主题学研究论文集. 台北：台湾东大图书股份有限公司，1983：2 页注释②.

究应可溯自柏拉图的‘文以载道’观和儒家的诗教观。假使我们接受汤姆森(Stith Thompason)把民间故事分成类型和母题(type and motif)的做法以及他给构成母题(constituent motifs)所下的定义,则主题学应侧重在母题的研究,而普通主题研究要探索的是作家的理念或用意的表现。早期主题史研究侧重在探索同一母题的演变,鲜少有挖掘不同作者应用同一母题的意欲;现在主题学的发展(其实顾颉刚五十五年前早已做到),上面已提及,则有这种趋向。也就是说,批评家可经由剖析分解故事的途径,进而来揣测作者的用意。如果我们就这个角度来看,则主题学研究显然有借助于普通主题研究的地方。”[①]这段较长且稍嫌缠夹的引文涉及多个范畴,其观点也不一定能够获得普遍认可,但其对大陆比较文学主题学的理论启示不可小觑。1988 年出版的乐黛云主编的《中西比较文学教程》,也做了类似的区分:“主题研究探求某一作品或某一个人物典型所表现的思想,重点在于研究对象的内涵;主题学研究讨论的是不同作家对同一主题、题材、情节、人物典型的不同处理,重点在于研究对象的外部——手段和形式。形象地说,前者着眼于一个点,而后者着眼于一条线,甚至一个面。”[②]由此我们可以看到陈鹏翔与乐黛云之间的联系与区别,不过将主题研究、母题研究视为主题学的一部分,则是大陆比较文学界较为普遍的认识。

第四,主题学的研究范围。自从哈利·列文、乌尔利希·韦斯坦因的专论发表之后,主题学的研究范围被大体勾勒了出来,除了主题、母题之外,题材、意象、情景、典型、文学惯用语等也被视为比较文学主题学的对象。但这些方面在中国学者的论著中,被给予了不同的取舍与组合。由于受到民俗学、原型批评等的影响,加之中国文学中的母题、意象、情景、典型、惯用语等更多地体现在神话尤其是民间传说以及元明之后的戏剧、小说之中,所以就实践层面而言,我国主题学的对象集中在叙事文学上,而且时至今日这一领域的研究尤其是从比较文学学科入手的研究还有较大的拓展空间。比如顾颉刚早在 1928 年为《孟姜女故事研究集》第一册所作的序文中就曾写道:“像观音、关帝、龙王、八仙、祝英台、诸葛亮等大故事,若去收集起来,真不知有多少的新发现……这类故事如果都有人去专门研究,分工合作,就可画出许多图表,勘定故事的流通区域,指出故事的演变法则,成就故事的大系统。我的孟姜女研究既供给了别的故事研究者以形式和比较材料,而别的故事研究者也同样地供给我,许多不能单独解决的问题都有解决之望,岂非大快!”[③]但直到 50 年之后的 1978 年,马幼垣在《三现身故

---

① 陈鹏翔. 主题学研究与中国文学[M]//陈鹏翔. 主题学研究论文集. 台北:台湾大东图书股份有限公司,1983:15-16.

② 乐黛云. 中西比较文学教程[M]. 北京:高等教育出版社,1988:185.

③ 陈鹏翔. 主题学研究与中国文学[M]//陈鹏翔. 主题学研究论文集. 台北:台湾大东图书股份有限公司:11-12.

事与清风闸》一文中仍然指出："近年来比较文学兴盛，大家开始在'主题研究(Thematic studies)'上下功夫。在中国文学内，此种课题甚多，包公自然是其中显著之例，其他如孟姜女、王昭君、董永、八仙、目连、刘知远、杨家将、呼家将、狄青、岳飞、白蛇等，都是极繁绕的问题，牵涉长时期的演化和好几种不同的文体，而且往往还需借重西方学者对西方同类文学作品的研究，以资启发参证。由于此等问题的异常复杂，对研究者来说，挑衅性也增加。"①今天距马幼垣此文又过去快40年了，这一领域的研究似乎仍未达到顾颉刚当年的期望。

第五，主题与母题之关系。这是从哈利·列文、乌尔利希·韦斯坦因之后一直在讨论的问题，中国学者也发表了较多的见解，但不少都是对列文、韦斯坦因系列观点的引申。列文在梳理伊丽莎白·弗兰采尔、欧文·帕诺夫斯基、恩斯特·罗伯特·柯蒂斯等人的见解之后，讲过以下一些话："如果说主题是与人物相联系的，那么，母题则是情节的片段。有关罗密欧与朱丽叶的故事是一个主题，而有关皮刺摩斯与提斯柏的故事则是另一个主题，但二者都有一个共同的母题，即在墓穴里的幽会，这和特里斯坦与绮索尔德的故事又有某些联系。……主题，和象征一样，是多义的，也就是说，在不同的场合里，可以赋予它们以不同的意义。这就使得对主题的流变的考察成为对思想史的探索。……和生物体一样，主题似乎也有自己的周期……但母题似乎是用之不竭的。"②而韦斯坦因也对雷蒙·图松、弗兰采尔、列文等有关主题、母题的见解进行了点评，同时也发表了自己的看法，其中给中国学者较多启发的有这样一些："母题与形势(situations)有关，而主题与人物有关。主题是通过人物具体化的，而母题是从形势中来的……形势是个人的观点、感情或者行为方式的组合……毋庸置疑，母题永远上升不到抽象的层面上，即属于问题或思想的层面上……我们可以把母题和形势的固定搭配叫作'程式(formulae)'。""世界上的作家们可以利用的整个母题库相对来说是小的。保尔·梅克尔估计总数大约为一百个。但主题实际上却是无限的。从数学上说，在两个、三个、四个或四个以上的母题组合中，各种可能的主题组合的和是容易计算的。此外，由于时间和地点不同，还会出现无数的主题变体，而在历史的、神话的、传说的或幻想的各种花絮和彩饰中也可能包裹着主题。"③

这些论述涉及主题与母题的层级、数量以及发生关联的中介问题。列文与韦斯坦因都认为主题与人物、故事有关，"母题"是构成主题的要素，主题可以上升到抽象的

---

① 陈鹏翔. 主题学研究与中国文学[M]//陈鹏翔. 主题学研究论文集. 台北：台湾大东图书股份有限公司：255.

② 哈利·列文. 主题学与文学批评[M]//乐黛云. 比较文学原理·附录三. 长沙：湖南文艺出版社，1988：283-284.

③ 乌尔利希·韦斯坦因. 比较文学与文学理论[M]. 刘象愚，译. 沈阳：辽宁人民出版社，1987：137.

层面，主题学能够成为思想史、精神史，但就数量来看，列文认为主题有可能衰落甚至处于枯竭状态，而母题却是用之不竭的，韦斯坦因则说母题有限而主题可以是无限的。韦斯坦因不仅在母题与主题之间加上了“典型”这个环节，而且还在图松的启示下提出了“形势”概念，尽管他认为“形势”只具备较小的主题学意义，但以下的看法却能给我们带来不小的启示：“从主题学上来看，形势构成了母题和行动之间的一个环节……”

【原典选读】

主题学（节选）

◉韦斯坦因

【导读】乌尔利希·韦斯坦因(Ulrich Weisstein, 1925—　)，德裔美籍学者，曾任美国印第安那大学日耳曼学和比较文学教授、国际比较文学学会秘书长等职务。他的英文版《比较文学与文学理论》(*Comparative Literature and Literary theory*, 1973)是根据德文版《比较文学导论》(1968)修订而成的。全书正文共七章，“主题学(Comparative Literature and Literary: Survey and Introduction)”排在第六，题为“Thematology (Stoffgeschichte)”，是目录中同时标出德文名称的唯一一章①，由此可以发现韦斯坦因对主题学之德国起源与内涵的看重，也许对“thematology”的命名还存有一丝戒心。不过从内容上看，韦斯坦因还是借鉴、引证了 thematology 一词的创造者哈利·列文(Harry Levin)的不少观点，并称赞他为比较文学主题学的复兴所作出的贡献。在“主题学”一章中，韦斯坦因完成了三方面的任务，一是梳理主题学的发展历程，二是探讨主题学的方法学问题，三是简略地讨论最小的主题性单位(the smallest thematic units)：特性(trait, Zug)、意象(image)、惯用语(topos)等。《比较文学与文学理论》自 1987 年由刘象愚翻译成中文出版以来，对我国比较文学界产生过重大影响，而且这种影响还将持续下去。■

For the sake of clarity and consistency, it would be useful, in principle, if we could replace the German word *Stoff* by "theme"; for the German *Thema* and the French *theme* obviously have the same root as their English cognate, whereas the German *Stoff* corresponds more closely to the English "subject matter" and the French *matière*. But the problem is complicated by the fact that theme or *Thema* point towards the History of Ideas

① 当然韦斯坦因也指出，在 thematology 被创造出来之前，德国学者使用的 Stoffgeschichte 也被英语国家的学者以妥协的方式使用。

and seem to imply an abstraction from *Stoff* (as in the German phrase "Eräussert sich zum Thema" [he comments on the subject]). Moreover, as Levin points out, in both English and French the word has a distinctly rhetorical-pedagogical ring:

> Our keyword *theme* may sound somewhat jejune, particularly to those who associate it with required compositions for Freshman English. The original Greco-Latin *thema* simply denoted a rhetorical proposition, the argument of a discourse, what in Jamesian parlance we now like to term the *donnée*. It could be the topic chosen by the orator or assigned to the schoolboy; through the pedagogical influence of the Jesuits the term became equated with an academic exercise; ane the French soon specialized it to mean a translation of a given passage into another language. (*The Disciplines of Criticism*, p. 128)

Van Tieghem further adds to the confusion by designating as themes precisely those phenomena which I prefer to call *motifs*, namely, "the impersonal situations, the traditional motifs, he subjects, places, settings, usages, etc." while labeling *légendes* those "events or groups of events whose protagonists are mythic, legendary, or historical heroes" (Van Tieghem, p. 90). For our present purpose, then, the word "theme" would seem to be less suitable than *Stoff*. However, in order to honor usage, I shall, in the remainder of this chapter, use *Stoff* in the singular but themes (instead of the awkward *Stoffe*) in the plural.

In this context, musical terminology could give rise to further confusion between *Stoff* and theme. Since the socalled "absolute" music has no content properly speaking, the thematic material here takes the place of the subject matter. The musical theme, however, as the starting point of an instrumental composition or as a basis for variations, is the member of a series which extends from the individual note over the motive to melody. Since the difference is largely quantitative, it is not always possible to distinguish between a long motive and a short theme, or between a long theme and a short melody.

What, then, is the relation between motif and theme in literature? For an answer to that important question we turn first to Frenzel and Trousson. In the opinion of the German scholar,

> the word "motif" designates a smaller thematic (*stofflich*) unit, which does not yet encompass an entire plot or story line but in itself constitutes an element pertaining to content and situation. In literary works whose content is relatively simple, it may be rendered in condensed form through the central motif [*Kernmotiv*]; generally, however, in the pragmatic literary genres, several motifs are required to make up the content. In lyric poetry, which has no actual content and, thus, no subject matter in the sense here intended, one or several motifs constitute the sole thematic substance. (p. 26)

Trousson parallels this view:

> What is a motif? We have chosen to use this term for designating a setting or large concept denoting either a certain attitude—e. g. rebellion—or a basic impersonal situation in which the actors are not yet individualized—for example, the situation of a man between two women, of the strife between two friends or between a father and his son, of the abandoned woman, etc. (Trousson, p. 12)

What is striking in Trousson's treatment is the fact that the Frenchman, who calls the theme (*thème*) "a specific expression of a motif, its individualization or, if you wish, the result of a passage from the general to the particular" (ibid., p. 13), regards literary motifs as part of the *Rohstoff*. This view, however, is unique in literary scholarship.

From the two above definitions it follows that, generally, motifs relate to situations, and themes to characters. Themes are concretized through characters,① whereas motifs are derived from situations, for "we grasp them only when we abstract them from their specific embodiments."②(Situations, by the way, are groupings of human views, feelings, or modes of behavior, which give rise to, or result from, actions in which several individuals participate.) Decidedly, motifs never reach the level of abstraction proper to problems or ideas; and Trousson errs when listing as motifs "the idea of happiness or progress" (p. 13). Using the terminology adopted by Robert Petsch, one may, moreover, speak of stereotyped combinations of motifs and situations as *formulae*. Such formulae are, naturally, often found in Jolles' simple forms—like fairy tales, fables, folk tales, and legends.

The total store of motifs available to writers throughout the world is relatively small—Paul Merker estimates their number as amounting to about one hundred③—that of themes, on the other hand, is practically unlimited. Mathematically, the sum of possible thematic combinations among motifs in groups of two, three, four, or more, is easy enough to calculate. In addition, there are the endless variants governed by time and place and in the historical, mythological, legendary, or fantastic trappings in which a theme may be clothed. The total number of available situations, of course, is even smaller than that of possible motifs, as there are relatively few characteristic modes of human behavior capable of producing and sustaining action. (Semantically, the possibility of theatrical realization is clearly inherent in the concept of situation.) Thus Georges Polit, emulating Carlo Gozzi, sought to define pragmatically the *Thirty-Six Dramatic Situations*, convinced as he was that their number could not be increased. ④

(节选自 Ulrich Weisstein. *Comparative Literature and Literary: Survey and Introduction*, translated by William Riggan in collaboration with the author, Indiana University Press, 1973:137-140.)

【研究范例】

中西诗在情趣上的比较（节选）

◉朱光潜

【导读】我们知道"情趣"与"意象"是朱光潜论诗的两个核心范畴，他曾在《诗论》中指

① In the order of magnitude, motifs are the smaller units, and themes the larger. Trousson muddles the issue when he calls the Hundred Years War a motif but the Joan of Arc *Stoff* a theme (p. 15, note).

② Kayser, *Das sprachliche Kunstwerk*, p. 62.

③ *Reallexikon*, *Ⅲ* (1928/29), p. 303.

④ I have consulted the English version by Lucille Ray (Boston, 1916). The second edition of the original French text appeared in Paris (Mercure de France, 1912).

出:“每个诗的境界都必须有‘情趣(feeling)’和‘意象’两个要素”,“诗的理想是情趣与意象的忻合无间。”[1]或许正是基于这样的认识,朱光潜才专门撰写了《中西诗在情趣上的比较》[2]一文。文章近8 000字,主要从“人伦”“自然”“宗教和哲学”三个层面论述中西诗在情趣上的种种差异及其文化内涵。我们从文章的开头部分,就能看出朱光潜具有自觉的中西“参观互较”以见出异同的比较诗学意识。在“先说人伦”“次说自然”两个部分中,中西比较的特色表现得非常鲜明,第三部分可能是因为涉及的内容较为复杂,他将笔墨主要放在中国哲学、宗教与诗歌的关系上,对西方的情况仅仅是点到为止,但也明确地指出:“我爱中国诗,我觉得在神韵微妙格调高雅方面往往非西诗所能及,但是说到深广伟大,我终于无法为它护短。”

诗的情趣随时随地而异,各民族各时代的诗都各有它的特色。拿它们来参观互较是一种很有趣味的研究。我们姑且拿中国诗和西方诗来说,它们在情趣上就有许多有趣的同点和异点。西方诗和中国诗的情趣都集中于几种普泛的题材,其中最重要者有人伦、自然、宗教和哲学几种。我们现在就依着这个层次来说:

1. 先说人伦。西方关于人伦的诗大半以恋爱为中心。中国诗言爱情的虽然很多,但是没有让爱情把其他人伦抹煞。朋友的交情和君臣的恩谊在西方诗中不甚重要,而在中国诗中则几与爱情占同等位置。把屈原、杜甫、陆游诸人的忠君爱国爱民的情感拿去,他们诗的精华便已剥丧大半。从前注诗注词的人往往在爱情诗上贴上忠君爱国的徽帜,例如毛苌注《诗经》把许多男女相悦的诗看成讽刺时事的。张惠言说温飞卿的《菩萨蛮》十四章为“感力相遇之作”。这种办法固然有些牵强附会。近来人却又另走极端,把真正忠君爱国的诗也贴上爱情的徽帜,例如《离骚》《远游》一类的著作竟有人认为是爱情诗。我以为这也未免失之牵强附会。看过西方诗的学者见到爱情在西方诗中那样重要,以为它在中国诗中也应该很重要。他们不知道中西社会情形和伦理思想本来不同,恋爱在从前的中国实在没有现代中国人所想的那样重要。中国叙人伦的诗,通盘计算,关于友朋交谊的比关于男女恋爱的还要多,在许多诗人的集中,赠答酬唱的作品,往往占其大半。苏李、建安七子、李杜、韩孟、苏黄、纳兰成德与顾贞观诸人的交谊古今传为美谈,在西方诗人中为哥德和席勒、华滋华斯与柯勒律治、济慈和雪莱、魏尔伦与冉波诸人虽亦以交谊著称,而他们的集中叙友朋乐趣的诗却极少。

恋爱在中国诗中不如在西方诗中重要,有几层原因。第一,西方社会表面上虽以国家

① 1933年秋,36岁的朱光潜回国任教于北京大学西语系,受胡适邀请在中文系讲过《诗论》一年,同一时期,朱自清也邀请他在清华大学研究班讲授过此课。

② 最初发表于《申报月刊》1934年版第3卷第1号,1943年重庆国民图书出版社印行《诗论》时,该文附于第三章的后面。

为基础，骨子里却侧重个人主义。爱情在个人生命中最关痛痒，所以尽量发展，以至掩盖其他人与人的关系。说尽一个诗人的恋爱史往往就已说尽他的生命史，在近代尤其如此。中国社会表面上虽以家庭为基础，骨子里却侧重兼善主义。文人往往费大半生的光阴于仕宦羁旅，“老妻寄异县”是常事。他们朝夕所接触的不是妇女而是同僚与文字友。

第二，西方受中世纪骑士风的影响，女子地位较高，教育也比较完善，在学问和情趣上往往可以与男子欣合，在中国得于友朋的乐趣，在西方往往可以得之于妇人女子。中国受儒家思想的影响，女子的地位较低。夫妇恩爱常起于伦理观念，在实际上志同道合的乐趣颇不易得。加以中国社会理想侧重功名事业，“随着四婆裙”在儒家看是一件耻事。

第三，东西恋爱观相差也甚远。西方人重视恋爱，有“恋爱最上”的标语。中国人重视婚姻而轻视恋爱，真正的恋爱往往见于“桑间濮上”。潦倒无聊、悲观厌世的人才肯公然寄情于声色，像隋炀帝、李后主几位风流天子都为世所诟病。我们可以说，西方诗人要在恋爱中实现人生，中国诗人往往只求在恋爱中消遣人生。中国诗人脚踏实地，爱情只是爱情；西方诗人比较能高瞻远瞩，爱情之中都有几分人生哲学和宗教情操。

这并非说中国诗人不能深于情。西方爱情诗大半写于婚媾之前，所以称赞容貌诉申爱慕者最多；中国爱情诗大半写于婚媾之后，所以最佳者往往是惜别悼亡。西方爱情诗最长于“慕”，莎士比亚的十四行体诗，雪莱和白朗宁诸人的短诗是“慕”的胜境；中国爱情诗最善于“怨”，《卷耳》《柏舟》《迢迢牵牛星》，曹丕的《燕歌行》，梁玄帝的《荡妇秋思赋》以及李白的《长相思》《怨情》《春思》诸作是“怨”的胜境。纵观全体，我们可以说，西诗以直率胜，中诗以委婉胜；西诗以深刻胜，中诗以微妙胜；西诗以铺陈胜，中诗以简隽胜。

2. 次说自然。在中国和在西方一样，诗人对于自然的爱好都比较晚起。最初的诗都偏重人事，纵使偶尔涉及自然，也不过如最初的画家用山水为人物画的背景，兴趣中心却不在自然本身。《诗经》是最好的例子。“关关雎鸠，在河之洲”只是作“窈窕淑女，君子好逑”的陪衬。“蒹葭苍苍，白露为霜”只是作“所谓伊人，在水一方”的陪衬。自然比较人事广大，兴趣由人也因之得到较深广的意蕴。所以自然情趣的兴起是诗的发达史中一件大事。这件大事在中国起于晋宋之交约当公历纪元后五世纪左右；在西方则起于浪漫运动的初期，在公历纪元后十八世纪左右。所以中国自然诗的发生比西方的要早一千三百年的光景。一般说诗的人颇鄙视六朝，我以为这是一个最大的误解。六朝是中国自然诗发轫的时期，也是中国诗脱离音乐而在文字本身求音乐的时期。从六朝起，中国诗才有音律的专门研究，才创新形式，才寻新情趣，才有较精妍的意象，才吸收哲理来扩大诗的内容。就这几层说，六朝可以说是中国诗的浪漫时期，它对于中国诗的重要亦正不让于浪漫运动之于西方诗。

中国自然诗和西方自然诗相比，也像爱情诗一样，一个以委婉、微妙、简隽胜，一个以直率、深刻、铺陈胜。本来自然美有两种，一种是刚性美，一种是柔性美。刚性美如高山、大海、狂风、暴雨、沉寂的夜和无垠的沙漠；柔性美如清风皓月、暗香、疏影、青螺似的山光和媚眼似的湖水。昔人诗有“骏马秋风冀北，杏花春雨江南”两句可以包括这两种美的胜境。艺术美也有刚柔的分别，姚鼐《复鲁絜非书》已详论过。诗如李杜，词如苏辛，是刚性美的代表；诗如王孟，词如温李，是柔性美的代表。中国诗自身已有刚柔的分别，但是如果拿它来比较西方诗，则又西诗偏于刚，而中诗偏于柔。西方诗人所爱好的自然是大海，是狂风暴雨，是峭崖荒谷，是日景；中国诗人所爱好的自然是明溪疏柳，是微风细雨，是湖光山色，是月景。这当然只就其大概说。西方未尝没有柔性美的诗，中国也未尝没有刚性美的诗，但西方诗的柔和中国诗的刚都不是它们的本色特长。

诗人对于自然的爱好可分三种。最粗浅的是“感官主义”，爱微风以其凉爽，爱花以其气香色美，爱鸟声泉水声以其对于听官愉快，爱青天碧水以其对于视官愉快。这是健全人所本有的倾向，凡是诗人都不免带有几分“感官主义”。近代西方有一派诗人，叫做“颓废派”的，专重这种感官主义，在诗中尽量铺陈声色臭味。这种嗜好往往出于个人的怪癖，不能算诗的上乘。诗人对于自然爱好的第二种起于情趣的默契欣合。“相看两不厌，惟有敬亭山”，“平畴交远风，良苗亦怀新”，“万物静观皆自得，四时佳兴与人同”诸诗所表现的态度都属于这一类。这是多数中国诗人对于自然的态度。第三种是泛神主义，把大自然全体看作神灵的表现，在其中看出不可思议的妙谛，觉到超于人而时时在支配人的力量。自然的崇拜于是成为一种宗教，它含有极原始的迷信和极神秘的哲学。这是多数西方诗人对于自然的态度，中国诗人很少有达到这种境界的。陶潜和华滋华斯都是著名的自然诗人，他们的诗有许多相类似。我们拿他们两人来比较，就可以见出中西诗人对于自然的态度大有分别。我们姑拿陶诗《归园田居》为例：

> 采菊东篱下，悠然见南山。山气日夕佳，飞鸟相与还。此中有真意，欲辩已忘言。

由此可知他对于自然，还是取“好读书不求甚解”的态度。他不喜“久在樊笼里”，喜“园林无俗情”，所以居在“方宅十馀亩，草屋八九间”的宇宙里，也觉得“称心而言，人亦易足”。他的胸襟这样豁达闲适，所以在“缅然睇曾邱”之际常“欣然有会意”。但是他不“欲辨”，这就是他和华滋华斯及一般西方诗人的最大异点。华滋华斯也讨厌“俗情”，“爱邱山”，也能乐天知足，但是他是一个沉思者，是一个富于宗教情感者。他自述经验说：“一朵极平凡的随风荡漾的花，对于我可以引起不能用泪表现得出来的那么深的思想。”他在《听滩寺》诗里又说他觉得有“一种精灵在驱遣一切深思者和一切思想对象，并且在一切事物中运旋”。这种彻悟和这种神秘主义和中国诗人与自然默契相安的态度显然不同。中国诗人在自然中只能听见到自然，西方诗人在自然中往往能见出一种神秘的巨大的力量。

（朱光潜. 诗论[M]. 北京：三联书店，1984：71-76. 据安徽教育出版社 1997 年 2 月版《诗论》校改部分文字及标点）

【延伸阅读】

1. 哈利·列文（Harry Levin）：《主题学与文学批评》（*Thematics and Criticism*）

该文最初发表于 1968 年，用他自己的话说：This article was written as a tribute to appear in the *Festschrift* for René Wellek, *The Disciplines of Criticism: Essays in Literary Theory, Interpretation, and History*, edited by Peter Demetz, Thomas Greene, Lowry Nelson, Jr. (New Haven, 1968). It is a kind of prospectus for a fairly new method, which I myself have tried to utilize in *The Power of Blackness and The Myth of the Golden Age in the Renaissance*-and which has something in common with what is called structuralism, though it has a more historical orientation. I have since undertaken a more precise and systematic treatment of the same approach in connection with an article on Motif, which is scheduled for publication in the forthcoming *Dictionary of the History of Ideas*.[①]本文由廖世奇译为中文，附录在乐黛云的《比较文学原理》（湖南文艺出版社，1988 年 8 月）。

2. 陈鹏翔. 主题学研究论文集[M]. 台北：台湾东大图书股份有限公司，1983.

该文集是“比较文学丛书”（叶维廉主编）中的一种，除了陈鹏翔撰写的相当于导论性质的《主题学研究与中国文学》之外，还选录了 20 篇论文，作者包括顾颉刚、林文月、钱南扬、杨牧、曾永义、马幼垣、张静二等。编者在《前言》中说：“收集在这本论文集里的主要文章，是从比较文学的角度探讨的，在精神上和叶维廉教授所提供的架构有着一定的呼应；但为了使主题学的某些层面更加透彻，这里也收了一些不尽是从比较文学立场出发的文章，作为一种印证与延伸，有些甚至只可视为主题史的研究；但是，它们在考证某一个主题的源流或在立说上颇为可取，可为真正的主题学研究奠基。”

① Harry Levin, *Grounds for Comparison*, Harvard University Press, Massachusetts, 1972:91.

第三节 文类学

“文类学”是一门探讨文学类型和体裁的学科，是文学研究的一项基本内容，在比较文学研究中更有着重要的意义。世界各国的文类学无不诞生于文学批评发展史的初始阶段，而且一直为历代学者所关注。文类学包括文类的总体研究、文体的分类学研究、文体的形态学研究、文体发生流变的历史学研究等内容。

一、文类学的术语

文类学的研究有两个层面：文类和体裁。在目前的研究中，由于没有很好地辨析这两个概念和术语的真正含义，常常发生一些绞缠不清的现象。

西方普遍使用的“genre(文类)”一词系法文，源自拉丁文“genus”。它本来是指事物的品种或种类，在文学理论中，一般指文学作品的种类或类型，也就是说，它可视为“文学类型(literary genre)”的简称。但它具体运用时往往不分主次，不辨等级，或者指较大的主要类型，如戏剧、史诗、小说，或者指较细小类型，如十四行诗、民谣。除此而外，还有一些术语，如“form(形式)”“kind(种类)”“type(类型)”等，经常和“genre(文类)”互换混用。

术语运用的混乱现象也见之于我国的传统文类学。现代所谓的“文类”，在古代一般称作“体”或“文体”。魏晋时期“体”这一术语已经成了核心概念，而“体”的含义在具体指代时也是不确定的。如曹丕的《典论·论文》，“体”用了三次：“文非一体，鲜能备善。”“唯通才能备其体。”“文以气为主，气之清浊有体。”“体”字根据上下文可知，在第一、第二句中的“体”，指文章的“体制”(体裁)和文章的“体貌”(风格)。在第三句中，“体”字则指的是文章创作者的精神气质特征。同时，在基本术语“体”的运用中不重视分辨类型主次或等级的做法，与西方基本是相同的。在我国文体分类发展史上，从《文选》到《文苑英华》《文体明辨》等众多文集的编次可见一斑。明代徐师曾所编的《文体明辨》，选文名目多达 127 类，清代吴曾祺的《古今文钞》分文体 213 类，而张相《古今文综》将文体分为 400 多种，基本都是平行排列。

既然中西文类概念不尽相同，那么，在两者及其相关术语对译时，就必然产生新的混乱。“genre”译为文类、文体、体裁、样式、类型；“genology”译为文类学、文体学、体裁学、样式学；“style”译为风格、文体；“stylistics”译为风格学、文体学、修辞学。在此，“文类”“文类学”“文体”和“文体学”四个译名出现了交叉使用的情况。因此，为了避免混淆起见，最好给这几个术语的翻译确定各自的疆域。根据它们各自的含义，“genre”译为文类，“style”译为风格，把由这两个词派生而来的“Genology”和“stylisyics”分别译为文类学和风格学较为妥当。法国比较文学先驱梵·第根用的是法文“genologie”，就是专指文类史研究。

文类和体裁是两个不同层面的概念，常常混用的结果是文类学研究状况驳杂混乱，因此，区分这两个概念术语的内涵和外延很有必要。俄罗斯学者瓦·叶·哈利泽夫认为，文学类别就是指语言艺术作品通常被归并的三大类：叙事类、戏剧类、抒情类。而文学体裁是在文学类别框架内所划分出来的作品类群。[①]这种辨析很好地区分了文类和体裁，为文类学的研究提供了理论的基石。

文学类别这一概念，在西方古希腊的思想家的论述中就形成了。柏拉图在《理想国》中，已经做了为文学作品进行分类的尝试；而亚里士多德的《诗学》则是按照模仿方式即非个人性叙述、戏剧化表现和直接叙说，把作品分作史诗、戏剧和抒情诗。在文艺复兴时期，明托诺在《诗艺》中，从语言艺术中划分出史诗（叙事类）、抒情诗（抒情类）、舞台诗（戏剧类）。到了18—19世纪，叙事类、抒情类、戏剧类三分法的概念基本上得以确立，成为具有普适意义文学类别形式的概念。浪漫主义作家认为文学类型限制着感情的自由抒发，起而反对世代相沿的文类规则。尤其是后来的意大利美学家克罗齐因承浪漫主义的余绪，把文学类型斥之为“虚假的区分”。但是其他学派的许多学者，如巴赫金、赫什（E. D. Hirsch）、姚斯（Hans R. Jauss）、阿利斯泰尔·福勒（Alistair Fowler）等，都在文类学理论和实践上有所建树。

文学体裁是产生在一定的文化土壤之上的，许多都源于民间文学，是在各自的文学经验的基础上形成的，鲜明地体现了一个民族一种文化的个性。由于不同文化不同民族在历史的发展中产生了非常多的体裁种类，诸体裁中的每一种都具有特定的、由稳定的特性所合成的特征结。体裁与文学类别不同，是很难置于超时代的和全世界的背景中根据某一种理论进行系统化分类的。其原因，一是体裁的数量太多，二是体裁有各自不同的历史范围，有些是跨历史的，有些是一定历史阶段的产物，具有历史的局部性。所以，我们只能是历史地去看待，研究某个时期某种文化的文学体裁的分类状

① 瓦·叶·哈利泽夫. 文学学导论[M]. 周启朝，等，译. 北京：北京大学出版社，2006：360.

况和方法。

据此，比较文学中的文类学研究就可以从两个层面入手：一是从文学类别上进行文类的总体研究；二是从文学体裁上进行文体的分类学比较研究、文体的形态学比较研究、文体的发生流变的历史学比较研究，还有不同文化中体裁的缺类现象的研究。

二、文类的总体研究

从宏观上看，文学类别的叙事类、戏剧类、抒情类都有自己的特征。黑格尔借助于"客观"和"主观"这一对范畴来界说叙事、抒情、戏剧的基本特征：叙事诗具有客观性，抒情诗具有主观性，戏剧诗则是这两种元素相结合。在20世纪，西方试图从心理学的角度把它们概括为回忆、表象、紧张；从语言学的角度概括为第一、第二、第三人称；从时间的范畴概括为过去、现在、将来。尤为突出的是，德国语言学家K. 比勒在20世纪30年代创建了言语理论。他认为言语行为包括三个方面：描叙传达、表现、呈诉。以这种理论区分了三种类别的特征：抒情类体现的是言语的表现力，戏剧类强调的是呈诉性，而叙事类则是对言语对象的描述传达和呈诉的结合。除了言语结构的这些特征外，文学类别在时空组织方式，人在作品中表现特色，作者的出场方式，文本呈诉和读者的关系诸方面存在着明显的差异。换言之，文学类别中的每一种都具有特殊的、其自身固有的特征结。各种文类的特征往往通过具体的某一种体裁表现出来，但是某一种体裁并不一定完全和某一类文类相对应，如叙事类特征既体现在神话和史诗中，也体现在小说中。

大体明确了文学类别的基本特征后，我们就可以展开比较文学文类的总体研究。如中西叙事类的作品，从叙事学的角度看，可以从叙事的结构、叙事的视角、叙事的节奏、叙事的话语、叙事的精神等方面去辨析比较。我们可以发现中西叙事类作品有许多相似或相同之处。但是，由于中西文化背景的不同，在叙事理论和方法上也存在着诸多的差异。观照中西神话，可以看到，中国神话缺少故事性，重视空间的展现，呈现给读者的是一幅幅图景。正如美国学者浦安迪在《中国叙事学》中所说："希腊神话以时间为轴心，故重过程而善于讲故事；中国神话以空间为宗旨，故重本体而善于画图案。"①

三、文体的分类学比较研究

文学类别的概念相对比较抽象，大体是可以系统化的，而文学体裁古今中外种类繁多、变动不居，却难以建立一个跨时空的分类系统。正如米哈伊·格洛文斯基所言：

---

① 浦安迪. 中国叙事学[M]. 北京：北京大学出版社，1996：56.

“人们很快明白，号称放之四海而皆准的文类学显然是不可能。即使勉为其难人为地建立一种雄心勃勃的文类学，其结果必然空泛、概念化，难以具体谈论体裁、体裁的特性及其运作机制。”①因此，众多的学者对这种追求系统化的努力都表示怀疑。但是，从文学的实践看，文体的分类又是必需的，这关乎文学的学习欣赏和创作的规范。因为如果没有文体分类，人们在日常阅读、评论、教学和创作中，就无法组织和从事具有意义的文学活动。

从历史看中外的学者都在不断尝试着做文体分类工作。中国古代不同时代的批评家们面对众多的作品努力区分出不同的体裁，清理它们的关系，寻找它们的区别与联系。魏晋南北朝时期，曹丕《典论·论文》把当时较为流行的文体分为八类，归纳为四科，就是“四科八体之说”。陆机《文赋》分出了诗、赋、碑、诔、铭、箴、颂、论、奏、说十体。梁代萧统的《昭明文选》列出的诗文有39类。刘勰的《文心雕龙》用了近一半的篇幅来论说文体。国外的一些学者也很重视文体分类问题。乌尔利希·韦斯坦因的《比较文学与文学理论》，诺思罗普·弗莱的《批评的剖析》等著作都高度重视文体分类问题。

对文学分类进行的研究虽然已有几千年的历史，但直到目前为止各国学者仍然未能有一致的意见。不仅如此，在分类问题上至今还存在着一定程度的混乱现象。大体上有三种情况，一是根据体制规模、结构样式、语言特点等来加以区分，如小说、诗歌、散文、戏剧等；二是根据情调态度、表现手段、功能取向等来加以区分，如戏剧可以分为悲剧、喜剧、悲喜剧，诗歌可以分为抒情诗、叙事诗、赞美诗、讽刺诗等；三是根据对象和题材来加以区分，如我国古代就有田园诗、山水诗、边塞诗、玄言诗、宫体诗等。第一种的分类标准偏于形式，第二种开始从形式转向内容，第三种则主要偏于内容了。

文体分类学比较不是追求一个跨时空的文体分类体系，而是去比较各个文化在历史发展中是如何为文体分类，以什么样的标准为文体分类，进而探讨它的历史价值和现实意义，从而窥见文学观念的变迁，了解他们对文学本质的认识。

四、文体的形态比较研究

一种文学体裁不是某些文本的简单组合，它有自身相对固定的特征。一方面体现在一些内涵上、实质性的品质上，更重要的是体现在体裁的形式方面，比如布局谋篇的方法、言语结构的组织原则等，从而形成一种文体的风格。从历史上看，有的文学体裁

---

① 马克·昂热诺，让·贝西埃，杜沃·佛克马，伊娃·库什纳．问题与观点——20世纪文艺理论综述[M]．史忠义，田庆生，译．长沙：百花文艺出版社，2000：98．

是跨时代的，而有的是阶段性的；有的比较稳定变化较小，而有的是灵活的不断变化的。

世界各个文化在历史上产生难以统计的众多的文学体裁样式。如果我们用比较文学世界的眼光去看，不同文化有许多相同或相似的体裁，我们在比较中就会发现它们的差异，进而领略到不同的风格。以中西常见的小说、诗歌、戏剧为例，中西小说在艺术结构上就有三点区别：一是中国小说往往首尾呼应，结构完整，而西方小说往往是一种横截面式的、片段式的；二是中国古典小说的代表体式是章回体，往往是单线式的发展线索，是一种标准的线性结构，西方小说往往是复线性的，并且是相互交织，形成一种蛛网式的密集结构；三是中国小说往往有一种大故事中套小故事的艺术格局，西方小说往往在时序上有倒叙、插叙和交叉叙述，有的小说在时间上的先后不是很明显。中西诗歌的差别也是多方面的。中国诗歌善于写景抒情，以写景烘托气氛或造出意境，而西方诗歌则注重描写景物在人们心里唤起的反应，以此来表达自己的主观意识。正像朱光潜先生所说："西诗以直率胜，中诗以委婉胜；西诗以深刻胜，中诗以微妙胜；西诗以铺陈胜，中诗以简隽胜。"可谓准确道出了中西诗歌形态风格上的差异。中西戏剧从戏剧结构上看，中国戏曲多是线状结构，线索简单，以抒情演唱为主，节奏必然进行缓慢；西方戏剧多是网状结构，一开始就集中了很多矛盾，相互交织，在冲突中展开戏剧活动，形成高潮。以上只是从中西小说、诗歌、戏剧的某个方面做了简单的比较，我们就可以看出文学体裁形态的比较确实是一个广阔的值得开发的领地。

五、文体发生流变的比较研究

各种文学体裁总是产生在特定的历史时期和一定文化背景中，从历史角度观察文体的发生、发展、变异和消亡，是文类学研究的另一个较大的范畴。如中外学者探讨小说的源头，都追溯"小说"一词来源。美国著名的汉学家倪豪士（William H. Nienhauser, Jr.）在《中国小说的起源》①中，考察中国"小说"一词出现在先秦，当时它的含义并不明确，既可以指关于哲理、政事的辩说，又可以指朝官所记的用以劝诫、娱乐的街谈巷议。而虚构的著作，却远在它出现之前就已经有了。《庄子》《孟子》《战国策》《国语》等著作，包含着后来小说家采用的叙事技巧，《山海经》《穆天子传》《楚辞》等作品，为后代小说提供了素材。他继而解释说，英文"虚构"（亦即"小说"）是"fiction"，它来自拉丁文"fingere"，本义是"造作"；而中文"造""作"亦与虚构有关。由此，他认为：可以利用周代典籍来探讨中国小说的起源和发展，早期包含小说因素的作品，应该分作传记和历史著作、游说辞以及志怪述异三种类型。这种从文体发生学

① 载于《华裔学志》第38卷（1988—1989）。

的角度研究小说起源，为我们打开了新的视野。

我们从事比较文类学的研究要特别关注的一个现象是，一种文体跨越国界流传出现的变异。可以从传播学的角度去认识，会有许多惊人的发现。总之，文类学的研究既要追溯渊源，有历史眼光，同时也应该注重横向考察并存文体间的借鉴关系。换句话说，就是历时研究与共时研究的结合。

六、文体缺类现象研究

缺类现象指的是一种文体在某国或某民族文学中存在但在其他国家和民族的文学中却没有。或者即使有这种文体的形式，而其实质或表现形式又相差甚远等。对这一现象的思考为文类学研究开辟了一个新的领域。比如中国有没有悲剧？中国有没有史诗？朱光潜先生在《悲剧心理学》中说："事实上，戏剧在中国几乎都是喜剧的同义词……仅仅元代（即不到一百年的时间）就有五百多部剧作，但其中没有一部可以真正算得悲剧。"对这类问题，我们应该怎样去看待是值得思考的。中国早期汉民族的史诗出现在周文王时代，"文王史诗"这种中国式的史诗是不同于西方史诗的。如果从中华民族大视野看，我们少数民族基本上都有自己的史诗，其中最著名的三大史诗即为：藏族民间说唱体长篇英雄史诗《格萨尔》，蒙古族英雄史诗《江格尔》和柯尔克孜族传记性史诗《玛纳斯》。至于中国有无悲剧的问题，我们要思考有没有依照西方界定悲剧的来框定中国的戏曲，这都是要涉及的内容。

【原典选读】

文学体裁（节选）

◉韦斯坦因

【导读】韦斯坦因（Ulrich Weisstein），美国著名比较文学家。1925 年 11 月 14 日出生于德国。1951 年赴布鲁明顿的印第安纳大学攻读比较文学、德国文学和文学批评，1954 年获得博士头衔。1959 年入美国国籍并执教于印第安纳大学。1966 年任该校日耳曼学和比较文学教授，正式步入国际比较文学界，声名渐起。除在美国本土多所大学作短期讲学外，他不断应邀外出访问讲学，为促进世界比较文学的交流和发展做了有益的工作。韦斯坦因主要从事比较文学的历史和理论研究，所著《比较文学与文学理论》和《比较文学——第一个报告：1968—1977》两书是他治学成就的集中反映。

在《比较文学与文学理论》这本书中，作者较为系统地讲述了比较文学的内容和方法，即什么是比较文学和如何进行比较文学研究的问题。全书共分七章，它们分别是:定义;影响和模仿;接受和效果;时代、时期、代和运动;体裁;主题学;各种艺术的相互阐发。此外,书后有两个附录(历史和书目问题)。该书从定义入手,再论各主要问题,层层深入,对各章所论题目都进行了历史和材料的发掘,且在附录部分运用较大篇幅进行说明。作者以比较文学家的眼光看待文学现象,从文学理论(文学批评、文学史)的学术资源,结合比较文学发展实际,梳理出比较文学之道。

在"文学体裁(The Study of Literary Genres)"这一章中,作者回顾了文学体裁划分的历史和方法,探讨了一些概念的内涵,指出了文学体裁划分的历史相对性,研究者要采取一种灵活而不是机械的态度。首先,韦斯坦因认为,在普遍性的文学体裁之中,人们对戏剧的研究最充分,而对长篇小说(或整个小说类)以及抒情诗则还未做过全面的考察。问题的症结在于文学类型的分类标准不尽统一。例如,源自古希腊的三分法(即史诗、抒情诗、戏剧三种类型)。这种观点尽管在理论上是成立的,实际上却做不到;再如出自歌德的三种自然形式(即清晰的叙述式、热情的激动式和个人的行动式)。作者在大体论及了一般的文学种类之后,接着讨论了实际存在的体裁,以及确定它们在美学领域中的地位。作者认为,必须以系统的方式来确定不同体裁各自的位置,因为仅仅把数量众多的文学现象加以罗列,非但不会在文类学上给人以启迪,反而会造成混乱。最后,作者讨论了文学分类的各种原则,从比较的视角对体裁作出历史——批评的研究确立价值。作者在章末指出,从历史的角度进行文类学的研究,很难建立一个把各种体裁和类型都安置其上的参照框架。所以对于体裁研究而言,"解开一些棘手的乱麻团,指出一些时代错误以及修正一些文学史上长期未决的混淆",便是最大的成就了。■

In his inaugural lecture at St. Petersburg, Alexander Veselovsky, harking back to A. W. Schlegel, championed the theory of an inevitable step-by-step progression of the three major literary "kinds". In his opinion, the successive flowering of epic poetry (Homer), lyric poetry(Pindar), and drama(Aeschylus), in the early stages of Greek literary history was the necessary correlate of a historical movement leading from the objective to the subjective, and from there to a fusion of the two modes in a state perhaps most aptly described as that of reflection. Thus, in the Russian scholar's view, "what we might call the epic, lyric and dramatic world view actually had to occur in the particular succession indicated, determined by the ever greater development of individualism." This is a theory not unparalleled in the age of positivism; for it finds its more strictly sociological analogue in Posnett's book *Comparative Literature*(1886) and—with greater literary sophistication—in the writings of Brunetière. However, contemporary scholarship justly rejects such simplistic—evolutionary or teleological—schemes of historical progression.

If, continuing to treat our problem historically, we consult the Greeks themselves, we find that, for them, a tripartite division of the major kinds was theoretically possible but practically unfeasible. Thus, for Aristotle, the epic and the drama were the only two "kinds" identifiable as such, while—for reasons still to be accounted for—lyric poetry remained amorphous and therefore hard to classify. When the Stagirite posed the question as to the superiority of one kind over the other, the choice was only between tragedy and the epic. Aristotle opted for the former by arguing:

> And superior it is because it has all the epic elements... with the music and scenic effects as important accessories; and these afford the most vivid combination of pleasures. Further, it has vividness of impression in reading as well as in representation. Moreover, the art attains its end within narrower limits; for the concentrated effect is more pleasurable than one which is spread over a long time and so diluted.

...

A manner of classification particularly congenial to the student of the arts and their interrelationship is the division according to what Aristotle calls the *means* of imitation. This criterion is used in the opening passage of the *Poetics*, where literature is confronted with those other arts with which it shares one or several of these means. Indeed, no genological study would be complete without a reference to music—not because language, too, makes use of sounds, but primarily because music (literally, the art inspired by the Muses) was originally wedded to the verbal arts. I specifically exclude epic poetry, although the bards or minstrels recited the verses to [their own?] musical accompaniment; for even in Antiquity this practice has a bearing only on the actual presentation, since no music was specifically composed to go with the poetry. For this reason Aristotle justly includes the epic among the strictly literary "kinds," since it is one of the arts which "imitate by means of language alone, and that either in prose or verse—which verse, again, may either combine different meters or consist of but one kind."

...

Having so far primarily concerned myself with the literary "kinds," I now turn to the actual genres and the various ways of fixing them in an aesthetic cosmos. For it is understood that some such systematic arrangement must be attempted, since a mere cataloguing of the diverse phenomena, whose number is legion, would yield no genological insight but would amount to acquiescence in chaos. The need for clarification is underscored by the lists furnished by Goethe and Kayser. In his Notes to *Der WestÖstliche Divan*, Goethe alphabetically (in the German order) enumerates "allegory, ballad, cantata, drama, elegy, epigram, epistle, epic, novella (*Erzählung*), fable, heroid, idyl, didactic poem (*Lehrgedicht*), ode, parody, novel (*Roman*), romance, satire," whereas Kayser places his entries in the more hierarchic order "novel, epistolary novel, *Dialogroman*, picaresque novel, historical novel; ode, elegy, sonnet, *alba* (dawn song); auto, vaudeville, tragedy, comedy, Greek tragedy, melodrama."

...

One would think that purely statistical criteria of genre classification require no comment, insofar as they are quantitative. Thus there is no problem in grouping plays according to the number of acts into which they are divided (but where would we place

Greek tragedy?) and in arranging various kinds of narrative according to their length (such as 50,000 words constitute a minimum for the novel, 10,000 words a maximum for the novella, with the short novel, the novelette, and the long novella falling in between, and the anecdote and short story occupying the lowest rungs of the arithmetical ladder). Although such divisions would seem to be altogether mechanical, quantitative criteria—like the annalistic labels attached to period styles—may sometimes acquire a qualitative flavor. This is certainly true of such lyric genres as the sonnet in general and the Petrarchan sonnet in particular, and although like Aristotle I would reject the *ars metrica* in principle, I grant that on occasion the specialist may well associate distinct generic properties with specific metrical patterns, as in the case of the *endecasillabo*, the *terza rima*, the *Alexandrine*, and the *Schüttelreim* (poetic spoonerism). The same applies, with even greater force, to lyrical poetry, as Paul Valéry demonstrates in his persuasive essay on "*Le Cimetière Marin.*"

I started out by saying that, given the enormous range and complexity of the literary phenomena known variously as kinds, types, genres, and classes, the historiographer among the students of genology as a branch of Comparative Literature will find it next to impossible to fashion a frame of reference in which a distinct place is assigned to each of these. The best he can hope for is to disentangle some of the knottiest problems, reveal anachronisms and shed light on a few of the many errors perpetrated in the course of literary history. In addition to handling the various approaches to genre definition in as deft and flexible a manner as the circumstances may require, he must also see to it that generic qualities are separated from those relating primarily to technique (as in satire) and from those infringing on thematic categories (as in Northrop Frye's *modes*). Thus, while in our post-Romantic age it would be vain to insist, with Horace, that "each particular genre should keep the place allotted to it," we should nevertheless endeavor to draw lines of demarcation where conditions are suitable and make sure that our terminology is as consistent as is humanly possible, and as is compatible with the historical context.

(节选自 Ulrich Weisstein. *Comparative Literature and Literary: Survey and Introduction*, translated by William Riggan in collaboration with the author, Indiana University Press, 1973.)

【研究范例】

李渔论戏剧结构（节选）

◉杨绛

【导读】杨绛，原名杨季康，生于1911年7月17日，祖籍江苏无锡，1932年毕业于苏州东吴大学。1935—1938年留学英法，回国后曾在上海震旦女子文理学院、清华大学任教。1949年后，在中国社会科学院文学研究所、外国文学研究所工作。杨绛先生是著名作家、翻译家、外国文学研究家。著有剧本《称心如意》《弄真成假》《风絮》等，翻译了《一九三九年以来英国散文作品》、西班牙著名的流浪汉小说《小癞子》、法国勒萨日的长篇小说《吉尔·布拉斯》,文学理论方面著有论集《春泥集》《关于小说》。

《李渔论戏剧结构》这篇文章就出自论集《春泥集》。这本小小的文集共包括六篇文章:关于西班牙文学名著《堂吉诃德》的有两篇;关于英国19世纪现实主义名著《名利场》和18世纪小说家菲尔丁的各一篇;此外还有两篇是关于《红楼梦》的艺术处理和李渔的戏剧结构论。

在《李渔论戏剧结构》这篇文章中,杨绛用大部分篇幅评述了李渔和亚里士多德在戏剧结构上存在着的表面上相似而实际却有着巨大差异的现象。首先,杨绛从两个方面总结了李渔的戏剧思想,即作为中国的戏曲结构要集中整一,也要首尾呼应,情节连贯统一。在这一问题上李渔同亚里士多德是相似的,亚里士多德在他的《诗学》中对情节的整一性有深刻的论述,同时也强调戏剧的完整性。在文章中,杨绛指出无论中国的戏曲,还是西方的戏剧都要做到将纷繁复杂的故事情节锤炼成一个完整的行动,使戏剧做到事件相互关联、相互推进,与此事件无关的部分将被删去。其次,杨绛指出,戏剧结构是剧作家对戏剧的一种时空排序,中西戏剧在结构上的最大差异是对戏剧时间的处理,由于中国戏曲结构大多是按照时间发展的顺序来处理戏剧的发生、发展、高潮、结尾,因而称之为"开放式戏剧结构",这种结构也决定了中国戏曲在时间、地点上的宽松。之所以产生这种结构,究其原因是由于中国戏曲对虚实艺术手法的处理等都建立在中国戏曲写意性的基础之上,它使得中国戏曲在表演中不拘泥具体的、现实的生活场景的束缚,能够充分传达剧作家的意图和思想。而西方戏剧从古希腊开始所认同的美学思想就是文学反映自然,积极倡导摹仿说。这使得一些剧作家通过有限的时间和空间,把自己要表述的故事表现出来,所以西方戏剧大都从故事的腰部或尾部开始,因而被称为"锁闭式戏剧结构"。

杨绛先生对中西戏剧在戏剧结构问题上的真知灼见,对我们更加深入地认识中国戏曲和西方戏剧存在的差异性具有重要的学术意义。■

李渔的理论和西方戏剧理论相似或相同的地方,不必一一列举。我们从这些例子,无非看到在若干一般适用的文艺原则上,我国和西方理论家所见略同。本文不想探讨那些东西,而想指出我国和西方在理论上很相似而实践上大不相同的一点——戏剧结构。

……

亚里士多德也是说:悲剧演一个人的一桩事,不是演一个人一生的事;这桩事件像完整的有机体,开头、中段和结尾前后承接,各部分有当然或必然的关系,结局是以前种种情节造成的后果。李渔对于戏剧结构的要求,跟《诗学》所论悲剧结构的整一性几乎相同,只是没提到《诗学》所说的广度。《诗学》说，戏剧所演的一桩事件需有相当广度。“只要显然是一个整体，故事就越长越美。一般说来，故事只要容许主角按当然或必然的程序，由逆境转入顺境，或从顺境转入逆境，就是长短合度”①。不过李渔虽然没有提到这一点，他的理论和这点并无抵触。因为按他的主张，绝不容许故事在半途中收场，也不会要求一个戏由悲而欢、由离而合之后，再来一番离合悲欢。他主张一本戏演一个故事，不是半个故事或两个故事。所以单从理论的表面看来，李渔论戏剧结构时提出的各点，正就是亚里士多德论戏剧结构时所提出的故事整一性。

可是实际上李渔讲究的戏剧结构的整一，并不是亚里士多德《诗学》讲究的戏剧结构的整一。一个是根据我国的戏剧传统总结经验，一个是根据古希腊的戏剧传统总结经验。表面上看似相同的理论，所讲的却是性质不同的两种结构。

希腊悲剧不分幕，悲剧里的合唱队从戏开场到收场一直站在戏台上。因此，戏里的地点就是不变的，戏里所表示的时间也不宜太长，而一个戏台所代表的地域也不能太广。希腊悲剧除了个别例外，一般说来，地点都不变，时间都很短。亚里士多德在区分史诗和悲剧时指出，悲剧的时间只在一天以内。② 时间和地点的集中，把故事约束得非常紧凑。戏台上表演的只是一桩事件的一个方面——就是在戏台所代表的那一个地点上所发生的事情。至于这件事情的其他方面，就好比一幅画的背面，不能反过来看。那些方面，只好由剧中人（包括合唱队）对话里叙述。例如《普罗米修斯被囚缚》一剧，台上演出的是普罗米修斯被钉在石壁上受罪，至于天上的宙斯怎么和他作对，都是叙述，不是排演出来的。又例如以结构完美著称的《俄狄浦斯王》一剧，戏台上表演的只是宫殿门前发生的事，宫殿里面的事以及使者在别处干的事，都是叙述出来的。

……

我国传统戏剧里的叙述，不是向观众叙述戏台以外所发生的事，而是剧中人向其他不知情的角色叙述台上已经演过的事。例如《西厢记》卷五第三折红娘对郑恒叙张生下书解围的事；《琵琶记》三十八出张公向李旺叙赵五娘吃糠、剪发、筑坟的事；《窦娥冤》第四折窦娥的鬼魂向窦天章叙她受屈的始末。莎士比亚《哈姆莱特》剧中鬼魂向哈姆莱特叙述的，是戏开场以前的往事，窦娥叙述的却是第一、二、三折的全部情节。假如仿照希腊悲剧的结构，这许多重复叙述的情节也许都该划在整一的故事之外，成为追叙的往事。可是在我国传统的戏剧里，并没有必要把戏的起点挨近结局，因而把许多情节挤到戏剧故事以外，成为叙述的部分。我国传统戏剧里时间的长短，只凭故事需要，并没有规定的限度。例如《西厢记》的时间比较紧凑。张生和莺莺从相遇到幽会，不过三四天的事。张生中举

---

① 《诗学》7,1451a。

② 《诗学》5,1449b。

荣归和莺莺成婚，也不过是半年以后的事。《琵琶记》的时间就宽绰得多。戏开场时蔡伯喈还在家乡，不肯应举。他进京赴试，中状元，做官六七载，才和赵五娘重逢。然后又庐墓三年，到合家旌表后才收场。又如《窦娥冤》只是短短四折的杂剧，在楔子里窦娥才七岁，戏到窦娥死后四年才结束。因为没有时间的限制，故事不必挤在一个点上，幅度不妨宽阔，步骤就从容不迫，绰有余地穿插一些较长的情节。

李渔说，“戏之好者必长”，[①]又怕贵人没闲暇从开场看到终场，就想出个“缩长为短”的办法，去掉几折，上下加几语叙述。[②] 按亚里士多德的理论，这些可去的情节就不是整体中的有机部分；结构整一的戏剧里容纳不下这些无关紧要的情节。我们现在又往往提出一折作为“折子戏”，可见这些情节有相当的长度。有相当长度的情节，《诗学》所讲究的戏剧结构里也是容纳不下的。

法国古典派理论家在解释《诗学》所论戏剧故事的整一性时指出，故事到收场，就不容穿插任何情节。因为观者很着急，凡是不直接关涉主题的事都无暇留连。这是古典派理论家一致承认的规则。[③] 可是在我国传统的戏剧里，故事收场时并不急转直下，还有余闲添些转折，李渔所谓求“团圆之趣”该有“临去秋波那一转”：

> 水穷山尽之处，偏宜突起波澜，或先惊而后喜，或始疑而终信，或喜极、信极而反致惊疑，务使一折之中，七情俱备……
>
> 收场一出，即勾魂摄魄之具，使人看过数日而犹觉声音在耳、情形在目者，全亏此出撒娇，作临去秋波那一转也。[④]

《西厢记》结尾，张生报捷，莺莺寄汗衫，两人马上就要团圆，可是第五卷的第三折还来个郑恒求配的转折。《琵琶记》结尾蔡伯喈和两个妻子已经团聚，第三十九出牛丞相还要阻挠女儿随婿还乡。李渔所著十种曲，每本收场都有一番波折。例如《巧团圆》第三十二出一家骨肉已经团聚，第三十四出又来个义父、亲父抢夺儿子。《慎莺交》结局时有情人将成眷属，第三十四出还要来一番定计试探。《怜香伴》第三十五出一男二女已奉旨完婚，可是第三十六出还要来个丈人作梗。这类穿插，西洋史诗的结构可以容许，西洋戏剧的结构就容纳不下。

以上种种，都证明我国传统戏剧的结构，不符合亚里士多德所谓戏剧的结构，而接近于他所谓史诗的结构。李渔关于戏剧结构的理论，表面上或脱离了他自己的戏剧实践看来，尽管和《诗学》所说相似相同，实质上他所讲的戏剧结构，不同于西洋传统的戏剧结构，

---

① 《中国古典戏曲论著集成》第7册77页。
② 《中国古典戏曲论著集成》第7册77页。
③ 《法国古典主义的形成》250页。
④ 《中国古典戏曲论著集成》第7册69页。

而是史诗的结构——所谓比较差的结构。他这套理论适用于我国传统戏剧,如果全部移用于承袭西方传统的话剧,就有问题,因为史诗结构不是戏剧结构,一部史诗不能改编为一个悲剧,一本我国传统的戏也不能不经裁剪而改编为一个话剧。由此也可见,如果脱离了具体作品而孤立地单看理论,就容易迷误混淆。

(杨绛. 春泥集[M]. 上海:上海文艺出版社,1979.)

【延伸阅读】

1. 饶芃子,等. 中西小说比较[M]. 合肥:安徽教育出版社,1997.

本书是在吸收前人成果的基础上,从宏观角度对中西小说比较做了研究,形成自己的框架和体系。全书从七个方面展开分析:中西小说渊源、形成过程比较;中西小说观念比较;中西小说题材比较;中西小说主题比较;中西小说人物形象与表现方法比较;中西小说结构叙述模式比较;中西小说创作方法比较。对我们开展文类学的比较研究有启发意义。

2. 褚斌杰. 中国古代文体概论[M]. 北京:北京大学出版社,1990.

本书初版于 1984 年,后来增订做了较大增补。全书通论中国古代文学体裁,共分绪论、原始型二言、四言诗、楚辞、赋体、乐府体诗、古体诗、骈体文、近体律诗、其他诗歌、曲、文章各体 12 章。对我们认识中国古代文体形态有很大帮助。

3. 瓦·叶·哈利泽夫. 文学学导论[M]. 周启朝,等,译. 北京:北京大学出版社,2006.

本书作者系莫斯科大学文学理论教研室资深教授。全书由导言与六章组成,分别论"艺术本质""作为一门艺术的文学""文学的功能""文学作品""文学类别与文学体裁""文学发展的规律性"。其中"文学类别与文学体裁"一章对我们研究文类学颇有理论价值。

第四节 比较诗学

作为比较文学一个重要的研究领域和分支,"比较诗学(Comparative Poetics)"由比较文学"美国学派"的倡导而正式诞生,最终成为"平行研究"学科理论与研究范式大厦的四大支柱之一。从学术视野与研究气质看,“比较诗学”最能够代表比较文学不断冲破国家、民族、语言和文明体系等形形色色外在束缚的超越性、开放性与前沿性。随着比较文学不断走向“全球化时代”,“比较诗学”不仅在中国比较文学界取得了一系列重大成就,而且还将引起世界比较文学界越来越多的关注。

一、比较诗学的内涵与产生

正如比较文学美国学派韦勒克和雷马克等学者所言,比较文学一旦从影响研究范式中挣脱出来,超越流传与渊源等影响性事实关系的形象分析、母题研究、体裁对比、风格分析等审美分析和文学批评问题必然成为比较文学研究的核心关切。关于这些问题,古往今来各国的诗学话语和文学理论最早已经积累了大量的学术成果和理论资源。从诗学术语、美学命题到理论体系,无论是西方还是东方,这些理论资源对于比较文学家从事不同国家文学形态与风格的比较具有重要的学术价值。不同国家、民族、语言与文明体系诗学、文论与美学之间的跨超性比较必然发展为比较文学“平行研究”中一个重要的研究领域与分支学科。法国比较文学家艾金伯勒(Rene Etiemble)对此的预见具有前瞻性:“历史的探寻和批判的或美学的沉思,这两种方法以为它们自己是势不两立的对头,而事实上,必须互相补充;如果能将两者结合起来,比较文学便会不可违拗地导向比较诗学。”①

“比较诗学”中的“诗学(Poetics)”不能从字面上将其理解为“关于诗歌的学问或研究”。事实上,我们必须将其看成一个源自西方的文学研究术语。在西方语境中,“诗学”事实上是“文学理论”的同义语。从亚里士多德著《诗学》开始,“诗学”就成为西方语文中深入研究文学创造这一人类独特文化活动的专用术语。在《诗学》这一奠定西方语文 Poetics 语义的著作中,亚里士多德研究的对象虽然主要是悲剧这一文学形式,但他仍然综合了史诗、喜剧、神话、抒情诗等文学体裁的诸多特征,对作为“摹仿”的文学创造、作为“卡塔西斯”的文学功能等一系列文学理论重大问题进行了系统的论述。根据“诗学”这一基础性意义,“比较诗学”指的是超越国家、民族、语言和文化界线的文学理论术语、命题与理论体系的比较研究。

自产生以来,比较诗学在西方与东方的发展并不平衡。在西方,法国学派将关注重心集中在国际文学关系上,本来就缺少理论兴趣,比较诗学在影响研究主导时期,基

① 艾金伯勒.比较文学的目的、方法、规划》[M]//干永昌,等.比较文学研究译文集.上海:上海译文出版社,1985:116.

本没有重视，更谈不上得到什么发展。比较文学法国学派代表人物之一的梵·第根明确要求将“美学”关切排除在“比较文学”之外。“‘比较’这两个字应该摆脱全部美学的含义，而取得一个科学的含义。而那对于用不相同的语言文字写的两种或许多种书籍、场面、主题或文章等所有的同点和异点的考察，只是那使我们可以发现一种影响，一种假借，以及其他等，并因而使我们可以局部地用一个作品解释另一个作品的必然的出发点而已。”①只有到了美国学派崛起之后，“比较诗学”才取得了长足的进展。以韦勒克为例，他的主要学术成果都集中在比较诗学领域，他的八卷本《近代文学批评史》详尽考辨200年间英、美、法、德、意、俄罗斯等西方各国的文学批评与理论，本身就是一部“比较诗学”或“比较文论史”。但是，限于时代的制约，绝大多数美国学派的学者并未能真正突破东西方诗学之间的语言与文化障碍，这导致他们的比较诗学基本局限在西方文化单一文明体系当中，远未达到他们所倡导的“世界主义”目标。

相反，中国比较文学却在“比较诗学”领域取得了大量的学术成果。中国比较诗学以中国古典文论与美学修养为基础，擅长对东西方文学思想进行跨文化思考，从而将比较诗学推向了一个新的发展阶段。

二、中国比较诗学的发展阶段

中国比较诗学可以分为两大阶段：前学科时期（1919—1988）和学科成熟时期（1988年以后）。

在前学科时期，中国比较文学的溯源至少可以上溯到20世纪初期。王国维的《红楼梦评论》（1904）和《人间词话》（1908）以及鲁迅的《摩罗诗力说》（1908）开创了中国比较文学学者开始从世界诗学视野来从事比较诗学研究的全新局面。此后，中国比较文学界出现了以钱锺书、朱光潜、宗白华等学贯中西的比较诗学大家。朱光潜（1897—1986）于1931年前写成《诗论》一书，出版以后成为中国著名的诗论著作，可以看成中国比较诗学前学科时期的代表性著作之一。《诗论》一书的突出特点是突破中国传统诗话、诗评的书写方式，自觉运用西方诗学来解释中国古典文学观念与诗歌现象。朱光潜曾自述：“在我过去的写作中，如果说还有点什么自己独立的东西，那还是《诗论》。《诗论》对中国诗的音律，为什么中国诗后来走上律诗的道路，作了一些科学的分析。”其实，除了以西方理性思维方式来解析中国诗歌的节奏、声韵、格律等特

---

① 梵·第根. 比较文学论[M]//干永昌，等. 比较文学研究译文集. 上海：上海译文出版社，1985：57.

征,《诗论》最为突出的贡献是援用克罗齐表现主义美学的"直觉"观来揭示中国诗学的"意境"与"意象"等的理论内涵。钱锺书的《谈艺录》(1948)在形式与体例上沿用中国传统"诗话",但内容上则将古今中外文学理论现象、术语与命题熔于一炉,成为世界文学界一部独特的比较诗学著作。20 世纪 50 至 70 年代,中国比较诗学前学科时期的成就主要体现为中国港台和美国华人学者的著述。其中,刘若愚的《中国文学理论》、叶维廉的《比较诗学》等可以作为代表。

中国大陆比较诗学学科复兴的标志性事件是钱锺书《管锥编》1979 年在中华书局正式出版。从整体上看,《管锥编》并不仅仅是一部比较诗学著作,而是一部包括比较诗学在内的人文学术思想巨著。该书以《周易正义》《毛诗正义》《左传正义》《史记会注考证》《列子张湛注》《焦氏易林》《老子王弼注》《楚辞洪兴祖补注》《太平广记》《全上古三代秦汉三国六朝文》十种中国文化经典著作为研究对象,采用"中西互证""以小见大"的研究方式,以全球化的文化眼光与学术修养探讨那些"隐于针锋粟颗,放而成山河大地"的世界性人文现象和文艺规律。在中国古典学术方面,钱锺书博学强记,出入经史子集,体现了中国传统学人文史不分、经史皆通的学术理想;在西方学术资源方面,他广泛引证英、法、德、西、拉丁等多种语言数千余种文献,充分展示了中国融入世界文化潮流之后新一代学者的宽广学术视野。从比较诗学角度看,《管锥编》一书中既有对中西文论比较异同的内部研究,也有从大文化范畴来解析诗学与美学问题的外在研究。无论从多么小的细节入手,钱锺书都能够在世界文明的总体背景之下来审视诗学问题,这种原创性思路与海纳百川的世界眼光及其广征博引的文献材料使其成为享誉全球比较诗学界的经典著作。在钱锺书《管锥编》一书出版之后,王元化的《文心雕龙创作论》(1979 年,上海古籍出版社),宗白华的《美学散步》(1981 年,上海人民出版社)以及杨周翰的《攻玉集》(1983 年,北京大学出版社)等一起预示了中国比较诗学学科化时代的到来。

20 世纪 80 年代中后期以来,以四川、北京、上海、广东等地高等院校学者为主体的比较诗学群体正式开启了中国比较诗学的学科化时代。特别是曹顺庆的《中西比较诗学》(1988 年在北京出版社出版),可以当作中国比较诗学科化时代的开端。紧接着,刘小枫的《拯救与逍遥》(上海人民出版社,1988 年第一版),黄药眠、童庆炳主编的《中西比较诗学体系》(人民文学出版社,1991 年第一版),张法的《中西美学与文化精神》(北京大学出版社,1994 年第一版),乐黛云、叶朗、倪培耕主编的《世界诗学大辞典》(春风文艺出版社,1993 年第一版),余虹的《中国文论与西方诗学》(三联书店出版社,1999 年第一版)等先后出版,成为中国比较诗学学科化时期很有影响的学术著作。中国比较诗学在 20 世纪 80 年代复兴之初,钱锺书曾经指出:"文艺理论的比较研究即所谓比较诗学(comparative poetics)是一个重要而且大有可为的领域”。① 事实证明,比较诗学确已成为中国比较文学最引人瞩目的研究领域。

三、比较诗学的研究范式

学科化之后,比较诗学主要有以下五种研究范式。

其一是“术语范畴命题比较型”。这以曹顺庆《中西比较诗学》为代表。这种形态的比较诗学范式从中西诗学中选取一对相似的术语、范畴或命题从同与异两个方面进行平行比较,从而揭示出中西文论对同一理论问题的相似看法与不同见解。本节原典选读部分还会对此书进行详细介绍。

其二是“价值观念比较型”。这种比较诗学的代表之作是刘小枫的《拯救与逍遥》。刘小枫从基督教神学的超验性立场出发,将西方文化与诗学的价值观念归纳为“拯救”,与此相对,又将中国文化与诗学的价值观念归纳为“逍遥”。从这样的差异性角度,刘小枫对中西文学进行了富有激情的比较研究,在20世纪80年代后期及90年代的汉语学界产生了很大影响。

其三是张法《中西美学与文化精神》所体现的“文化精神比较型”。张法在《中西美学与文化精神》中从“有与无”“形式与整体”“明晰与模糊”等角度来比较中西美学不同的“文化范式”与文化精神。在基础上,该书进一步对“和谐”“悲剧”“崇高”“荒诞与逍遥”“文与形式”“典型与意境”等中西美学的基本概念,以及世界诗学理论中的“创作理论”“灵感理论”“灵感的主体构成”和“审美具体方式”等重大问题进行了全新的阐述。

其四是“异质维度比较型”。这一类型的比较诗学深度关注不同诗学理论的内在差异,在充分体认西方诗学与中国文化的“不可通约性”基础上运用“现象学还原”方法来重新探寻比较诗学的新支点。余虹的《中国文论与西方诗学》是这一类型比较诗学的代表之作。作者不同意“比较诗学”这一理论术语,认为它以西方诗学中心主义来审视中国传统文论思想,从而不经意之间通过所谓“平行研究”抹杀了中国传统文论的理论异质性。在此基础上,作者进而将“中国文论”细分为“道家超越文论”“儒家正统文论”“儒家异端文论”“儒家道学文论”,将西方诗学细分为“前柏拉图诗学”“古典主义诗学”“浪漫主义诗学”和“教条主义诗学”等不同的话语体系,进而在相应的理论维度上进行文化异质性诗学体系的平行比较。

其五是“历史人物著述比较型”。这一类型的比较诗学以历史发展为纲,对中外

① 张隆溪.钱锺书谈比较文学与“文学比较”[M].上海:生活、读书、新知三联书店,1981:135.

最重要的文学理论家及其著作进行横向的平行比较。曹顺庆《中外比较文论史·上古时期》(山东教育出版社,1998 年第一版)是这一类型比较诗学开风气之作。最近出版的四卷本《中外文论史》(曹顺庆主编,巴蜀书社,2012 年第一版)则是这种形态比较诗学的集大成之作。这部宏大的比较诗学著作采用以纪年为主,以各文化圈大致相似的文论史发展阶段为辅的分期方法,将中外文论的发展历程分为七个不同的大阶段进行横向比较。第一大阶段是公元前 2 世纪以前,主题是中外文论的滥觞与奠基;第二大阶段包括中国两汉、古罗马与印度孔雀王朝及贵霜帝国时期文论;第三大阶段包括公元 3 世纪至 6 世纪的中外文论;第四大阶段为公元 7 世纪至 9 世纪的中外文论;第五大阶段包括公元 10 世纪至 13 世纪的中外文论;第六大阶段论述公元 14 世纪至 16 世纪的中外文论;最后第七大阶段比较公元 17 世纪至 19 世纪之间的中外文论。本书以"总体文学理论"为远大的学术目标,时间跨度长达 2000 余年,对中国文化、西方文化、印度文化、日本文化、阿拉伯文化等世界主要文化体系的文学理论进行了全方位的比较,不仅向读者展示一个全面、系统的世界诗学发展全貌,还在平行比较中对不同文化体系各国文论的理论特征与独特贡献进行了深入的论述。

【原典选读】

比较诗学(节选)

◉厄尔·迈纳

【导读】厄尔·迈纳(Earl Roy Mine,1927—2004),中文名孟而康,生前为普林斯顿大学比较文学与日本文学教授。在求学阶段,他在明尼苏达大学先后获得日本研究(日本文学)学士学位、硕士学位和英语博士学位,曾任美国弥尔顿学会、美国十八世纪研究学会、国际比较文学学会会长,在弥尔顿研究、日本文学(尤其日本诗歌)和比较诗学研究领域具有世界性影响。在中西比较文学界,厄尔·迈纳的贡献还在于他与其他美国学者一起打开了中美比较文学研究的通道。1983 年,他与刘若愚一起率领美国比较文学十人代表团访问北京,与钱锺书、杨周翰等中国同事一起召开了"首界中美比较文学双边会议"。此后,"中美比较文学双边会议"成为中美比较文学研究学者定期会晤的常设性学术交流活动。

《比较诗学:文学理论的跨文化研究札记》(*Comparative Poetics: An intercultural Essay on Theories of Literature*)出版于 1990 年,共分为五章。在第一章"比较诗学"中,厄尔·迈纳令人耳目一新地提出了一种超越"西方中心主义"的比较诗学观。第二章、第三章、第四章在上述比较诗学观念的指导下分别对戏剧、抒情诗和叙事文学这三种重要的文学类型及其文学观念进行了比较研究。第五章对比较文学研究中的文化“相对主义”问题进行了深入研究,其主旨仍然意在倡导东方与西方文学与文化的平等对话。

“比较诗学”这一章分“诗学”“文学要素”“比较”“文学特征”和“比较诗学简论”五个小节,对比较诗学的主要内涵与要素进行了深入讨论,对“西方中心主义”倾向及其产生原因进行了非常具有启发性的讨论。厄尔·迈纳通过“基础文类(Foundation Genre)”与“原创诗学(Originative Poetics)”两个重要概念来解构“本质主义”与“中心主义”的比较诗学观。在他看来,世界各国所有具有“原创性”的诗学理论或文论体系都必须建在某种“基础文类”之上。基于不同的“基础文类”,各种“原创诗学”具有全然不同的关注对象和理论特征,这就内在地决定了其理论体系的理论优势与学术盲点。就“原创诗学”的产生,厄尔·迈纳是这样分析的:“当某个天才的批评家从被认为是当时最有影响的文类出发去解释文学概念时,这个文化体系中系统、明确而具有创造性的诗学就应运而生了。”现行比较诗学研究受到西方“摹访诗学(Mimetic Poetics)”制约,而这一“原创诗学”建立在“戏剧”这一西方文学史的“基础文类”之上。厄尔·迈纳认为,中国和日本产生了另外一种“原创诗学”,他称为“情感—表现的诗学(Affective-expressive Poetics)”,其“基础文类”是抒情诗。通过这样的分析,比较诗学研究显然必须重视“基础文类”的问题,不能将“原创诗学”作为放诸四海而皆准的诗学来审视和判断其他的诗学形态,因为“没有任何一种诗学可以包容一切”。这样,比较诗学必须要进入“跨文化视野”当中,必须关注并分析不同文化体系的“基础文类”,并由此确定其“原创诗学”可以阐释与无法阐释的对象及其边界。■

……我认为,一种原创性诗学不是在某一特定文化体系发轫之初就出现了,而是出现于紧随其后的某个时期,在诗人由无名氏变成公认的作者、诗被赋予独立性存在之后。亚里士多德《诗学》的两个显著特征必须引起我们的注意。其一是,虽然希腊文学中最伟大的名字——荷马——是与叙事诗和史诗联系在一起的,但亚里士多德的诗学却是基于戏剧的。其二是,亚里士多德必须为自己的理论在传统中找到一个强有力的思想后盾,于是为了完成他的诗学,他不得不沿用柏拉图的摹仿概念,这表明他与他老师对抗的终结。从这两个重要事实之中可以形成这样的论点:当某个天才的批评家从被认为是当时最有影响的文类出发去解释文学概念时,这个文化体系中系统、明确而具有创造性的诗学就应运而生了。

接下来的一步是证明这个论点。对于中国的情形来说这个论点是成立的,因为中国的诗学是在《诗大序》的基础上产生的。(序之“大”是按规格和层次而言的,其篇幅实际上远比“小序”的要少)。对日本来说它也是成立的,因为日本诗学是在纪贯之的《古今集》日文序的基础上产生的。中国的(朝鲜和日本也一样)“文学”这个范畴是由一个叫作“文”的符号来表示的(韩语音作“mun”,日语音作“bun”“fumi”)。围绕着抒情诗这个中心,这个文学范畴还附带一些多少带点传奇性的基本历史内容。历史的介入极为重要,正如亚里士多德提到荷马时的情形一样。但是这些地区的原创性诗学却是在抒情诗的直接背景中产生的。

既然该论点对于东亚以及早期欧洲诗学来说都是成立的,那么探讨欧洲传统之外的其他文学传统就很有价值。这意味着必须向那些精通我所不熟悉的文学的人们讨教。其结果令人吃惊。据称,除了一个例外(复杂的印度文化),这些文化体系中的诗学都是通过对抒情作品的分析而产生的(通常是以一种隐含的方式)。这是对下面两种说法的另一种表述:似乎没有哪个原创性诗学是基于叙事文类而产生的;西方诗学是从戏剧中产生出来的唯一例子。虽然实际情况非常复杂,但这两个基本事实却颇具启发意义。

亚里士多德的诗学是一种摹仿诗学,这不足为奇,因为它建立在戏剧的基础上,而戏剧是一种再现(representing)的文类。欧洲中心主义观念使得我们把别的诗学——世界上其他地区诗学——称为非摹仿的(nonmimetic)诗学,假如果真存在这种诗学的话,西方诗学倒成为真正非实体性(nonentity)的了。因此提出另一种命名法便势在必行了。我把基于抒情作品的不同种类的诗学统称为“情感—表现的”(affectisive-expressive)诗学,因为这种诗学认为,诗人受到经验或外物的触发,用语言把自己的情感表达出来就是诗,而且正是这种表现感染着读者或听众。虽然我们必须考虑到每种文学中产生的诗学后来各自的相应发展,但引人注目的是,“情感—表现诗学”和“摹仿诗学”确实都有着也许可以被称为“首要前提”(prior presumption)这种共同的东西。传统上两者都坚持唯物的哲学观点,认为世界是真实可知的。只有基于这种观点,诗人才可能被感动,才可能找到合适的词来表现内心的情感;也只有基于这种观点,诗人才可能去摹仿世界上人性的特征。这种没有明确表达出来的前提假设也许可以使我们对这些生成性诗学(generative poetics)长盛不衰的魅力作出解释。许多现代西方文学打破了这种前提假设,并因此也打破了摹仿的原则。那种所谓的“反摹仿”(antimimesis)必须与“情感—表现”说的“非摹仿”(unmimesis)区别开来。由于西方读者熟悉了西方反摹仿的作品,因而向其传授基于“情感—表现”传统的作品(不管是东亚的还是伊斯兰地区的)反而更加容易。这真是一个善意的讽刺。同样应该指出的是,在今天,日本也有些作品否定现实主义的前提观念,但是——这一点非常重要——这样做并未导致形成反摹仿的理论,而是形成了一种“反表现”(antiexpressivist)的诗学。

欧洲诗学以及亚洲诗学发展的一些特征将有助于我们理解它们之间的差异。亚里士多德强调悲剧所激起的怜悯和恐惧,并且曾经(对此我们依然没有把握)提到了“katharsis”(净化)。这显然暗示着一种从情感的角度讨论文学以及把读者这一方面包含在其诗学体系之中的观念。然而，亚里士多德在雅典学院的地位使其不可能把情感设立为诗学的一个独立分支。哲学家们，尤其是亚里士多德的老师，认为哲学比诗学更具感染力（也理该如此），因此才产生了柏拉图对“古老的哲学与诗学之争”的评论（《理想国》：10，607）。参与这场争论的还有第三个团体，即智者学派（the Sophists）。柏拉图在《斐德若》（Phaedrus）篇里以圆熟的技巧再现了这场辩论。因受到这种观念的制约，亚里士多德无法正确地讨论我们前面提出的五要素中的两个：读者与读者之诗。

贺拉斯在《诗艺》中弥补了这一缺陷。贺拉斯对亚里士多德《诗学》的了解似乎来源于亚历山大，虽然这一点还不敢肯定，有待进一步的分析（见第五章）。但是，我们既不能就此宣称他从亚里士多德那里吸收了很多东西，也不能认为亚里士多德是贺拉斯诗学产生的原动力。从严格的意义上说（在贺拉斯的时代），首创（某种诗学理论）已为时过晚，但是应该承认，他可以对亚氏的诗学理论作一些校正。贺拉斯凭借作为一名抒情诗人、讽刺诗人和书信体诗人（大约三分之一是讽刺诗）的实践经验做到了这一点。他的理论主要是基于抒情性文类（虽然他的确也经常论及戏剧和绘画）。令人惊异的是，其结果竟然与情感—表现诗学相似。他最著名的观点是：诗能感动我们。可以这么说，在接下来的几个世纪中，西方人对于诗的目的的看法一直是贺拉斯的“寓教于乐”，而达此目的的方式则一直是亚里士多德的摹仿。对于贺拉斯来说，“读者”乃诗学不折不扣的组成部分。“读者之诗”同样如此，因为贺拉斯像中国和日本人一样注重字斟句酌，虽然这个事实很少被人论及。为了做到这一点，贺拉斯似乎究分利用了拉丁语言宝库中丰富的语词表达法，包括那个彻头彻尾的贺拉斯式表达法：norma loquendi（《诗艺》，1.72，说话的规则、模式和样式）。

关注语言表明其文学观念是基于抒情作品的，正如关注再现表明其文学观念是基于戏剧作品一样。这一点无论怎么强调也不过分。

值得再次回顾一下比较诗学的中心问题：西方诗学与世界上其他地方的诗学之间存在的显著差异。从历史上看，贺拉斯之后的西方诗学可以说是摹仿的和情感的，或者甚至是摹仿的、情感的和表现的。以后我们会有理由去考虑不同时代所发生的许多情况的复杂性。当然这样做违反了逻辑的以及（确实是）比较的原则。因为一种思想观念的重要特征当然在于它的独特本性——也就是说，是什么使之与同类中别的东西区别开来。西方诗学的区别性特征正在于由摹仿衍生出来的一系列观念。

今天，大多数具有理论头脑的西方学者会否认他们是摹仿说的继承者，否认他们的思想受到了摹仿说的支配。不过，有许多符号（正如符号学家所说，这些符号是武断的）却揭穿了他们的老底。他们并非中立的。你只需像一个对口令非常敏感的哨兵那样念一念或听一听这些符号就明白了。只要一听到“再现”“虚构”“来源”“创造性”“文学性”“整一性”“情节”或“人物”这些词，你就知道谈论的是摹仿。（Representation，représentation 和 Darstellung 这三个词特别富于启发性。）也许有人会反驳说这些术语并非摹仿说所独有，它们只不过是人人都在使用的普通词汇。没有什么比这更富于欧洲中心主义色彩的了！这些术语并不是人人都使用的普通词汇，而是那些有着根深蒂固的摹仿观念的人们一直使用着的术语。也许有人会提出另一种反驳意见：某作家或者某批评家曾公开地反对摹仿说。但是只要这些关键术语已经被假定出来这个事实存在，它们是否受人青睐或是否引起争论并不重要。反摹仿说只不过是根植于它所攻击的对象之内的摹仿说的变体而已。

对历史的兴趣会导致对这个问题的进一步探讨。我们也许会仔细考虑用前后并不一致的标准来评判是道德教谕还是娱人心志更为重要这一争论，也许会注意摹仿说的主要原则在浪漫主义者那里发生的变化，例如柯勒律治接受了摹仿的观念（mimesis）却反对依样画葫芦式的机械模拟（imitation）。我们也许会关注小说发展的黄金时期，关注这个时期对摹仿及其前提假设二者的同时强调。但是，还是让一切成规都成为过去吧。

一个更好的论题需要对各种不同的情感论（affectivisms）作出细微的区分。与东亚的诗学相比，贺拉斯的情感论更加关心读者而较少关注诗人。这似乎是亚里士多德摹仿说遗产的一部分。在情感方面，亚氏仅仅关心读者或戏剧的观众（正如我们所见，对于情感的关注在逻辑上并不构成单独的文学类型）。作为世界的再现者，摹仿诗人被赋予摹仿力而不是感染力。我们还可以作进一步的区分。就读者而言，中国的情感论包含教化和娱乐，这一点与贺拉斯的相似。中国官方的倾向很明显：恪守儒家“教重于乐”的观念。（当然存在也许可以说是比较温和的道家思想，这种思想使“红楼幽梦”之类的意境得以滋生。）日本与中国有着同一种前提，即认为诗人乃有感而发，但道德教化观念在日本却很难找到。除了早期有少数（但很重要）的几个例外，儒家学说，或者更准确地说是新儒家学说，直到大约公元1600年，才因德川幕府把它采纳为官方意识形态而获得发展的动力。但即使是到了这时，作家们大都还是持抵制态度。因此，我们或许可以说，中国的情感论正好处于日本与贺拉斯二者之间。

（厄尔·迈纳.比较诗学：文学理论的跨文化研究札记[M].王宇根，等，译.北京：中央编译出版社，1998：32-36.）

【研究范例】

意境与典型（节选）

◉曹顺庆

【导读】曹顺庆（1954—　），四川大学文学与新闻学院教授、院长，1987年获四川大学中国文学批评史专业博士学位，现任中国比较文学学会会长、中国中外文化学会副会长、中国古代文学理论学会副会长。曹顺庆长期从事比较文学研究，在中西比较诗学、中外文学比较发展史、比较文学学科理论等领域取得大量突出的研究成果。其《中西比较诗学》(1988)、《中外比较文论史:上古时期》(1998)、《中西比较诗学史》(2008)和《中外文论史》(四卷,2012)在世界比较文学界都有着深远的影响。

曹顺庆的《中西比较诗学》出版于1988年,是中国大陆学者第一部以《比较诗学》为题名出版的著作,是中国"比较诗学"学科化时期的代表性著作,确立了中西比较诗学最基本的一种研究范式——"术语范畴命题比较"。全书分为六章,第一章绪论三个小节分别从地理环境、经济形态、政治特征等社会因素和宗教、科学、伦理等文化因素,以及思维方式、语言特征等文艺因素三个层面来总论中西诗学不同理论特色的产生原因。全书的主体部分从第二章到第六章展开。在这部分,该书以"本质论""起源论""思维论""风格论""鉴赏论"五大理论为比较框架,分别从中西诗学中选择数对关键性概念、范畴或术语进行平行比较,既阐释二者相同之外,也分析其相异之处。这样的理论路数奠定了中国比较诗学一种最基本的写作方式。全书通篇贯穿中西文化对话的"平等意识",力图从"总体诗学观念"看待中国古典文论并通过比较来阐释其现代价值。

在艺术本质论问题上,中西诗学美学都提出过一系列重要的概念、范畴或术语。其中,中国诗学的"意境"和西方诗学的"典型"都很精彩地揭示了文学艺术从个别见一般、从偶然见出必然的艺术感染力。与此同时,它们又充分体现了东方与西方两种不同文学体系的审美特征。在艺术本质论这一章,曹顺庆一共选择了三对概念"意境与典型""和谐与文采""美本身与大音大象"来进行比较。在"意境与典型"的比较中,《中西比较诗学》从主观与客观、人物与景物、共性个性与虚实形神、求真与求美、酝酿感悟与分析综合五个层面来分析"意境"与"典型"这一对概念在美学内涵上的同与异。就同的方面而言,中国诗学的"意境"与西方诗学的"典型"都具有"以少总多,寓无限于有限"的特点。就异的方面而言,二者的审美感受不同:"艺术典型令人难忘,艺术意境则耐人咀嚼。"紧接着,作者深入分析了"意境"与"典型"不同美感产生的原因,提出不同之处在于二者对生活所用的"概括方法"不同。西方诗学的"典型"观念受到"摹仿说"和"一般与个别关系之论争"的影响,按必然律或可然律来概括人物的本质特征,而中国诗学"意境"的概括方法则是"虚实相生"和"形神兼备"。■

既然典型论与意境说都是对于艺术美之奥秘——把深广的社会生活内容和具体生动鲜明的形象结合起来,集中提炼到最高度和谐统一——的探索之结晶,那么它们就具有着这样的共同性:即要能以少总多,寓无限于有限。所以巴尔扎克说:"艺术作品就是用最小的面积惊人地集中了最大量的思想"(见《古典文艺理论译丛》10辑101页)。典型就是"在这个人物身上包括着所有那些在某种程度上跟它相似的人们的最鲜明的性格待征”（同上书137页）。故司马迁称赞屈原的作品“称文小而其指极大，举类迩而见义远”（《史记·屈原贾生列传》）。刘勰主张“以少总多”。司空图主张意境要能“万取一收”（《二十四诗品》）。在这一点上，典型论与意境说虽有相同之处，但也呈现出不同的特色。当你欣赏一个艺术典型与品味一件有意境的作品之时，其滋味是很不相同的。一般说来，艺术典型令人难忘，艺术意境则耐人咀嚼，这是两种不同的审美感受。但凡成功的艺术典型，总是令人难以忘怀的，唐·吉诃德、奥赛罗、答尔丢夫、奥勃洛摩夫、哈姆雷特……这些典型人物形象，似乎已经铭刻在人们的心中了。典型人物的这种永恒的艺术生命来自何处呢？正在于它以鲜明的个性特征反映出了生活的必然本质。当我们欣赏艺术典型时，可以发现两个有趣的现象，其一是许多人在欣赏之时，发现作者是在写自己，有的人甚至疑神疑鬼，怀疑作者是在揭自己的隐私。所以有的作家只好声明：“不要把书中某些情景误解为影射某人。……我写这样一个可怜虫，并不是要使一小撮凡夫俗子见了就认出是他们的某某熟人，而是给千万个藏在密室里的人照一面镜子，使他们能够端详一下自己的丑态，好努力克服”（菲尔丁《约瑟夫·安德路斯》卷三，见《文艺理论译丛》1辑204-205页）。其二是成功的艺术典型的名字成为了一个共名，流行在生活中。正如别林斯基所说：“典型是一类人的代表，是很多对象的普通名词，却以专有名词表现出来。举例说，奥赛罗是属于莎士比亚所描写的一个人物的专有名词，然而当我们看到了一个人嫉妒心发作时，就会叫他奥赛罗。……我的天！如果你留意的话，伊凡·阿列克山德罗维奇·赫列斯塔科夫这一个值得传扬的名字是贴切地适用于多少人啊”（《别林斯基论文学》1958年版120页）。今天，我们在生活中还经常说某某是唐·吉诃德，某某是答尔丢夫，葛朗台，……，虽然产生这些典型的时代已经过去，但是这些典型形象仍然活着，并且将具有着“永久的魅力”。典型形象的生命力就在于此。与典型一样，意境也是对生活的高度概括，寓无限于有限。但是欣赏艺术意境与欣赏典型形象的审美感受是大不一样的。读一首诗，看一幅画，要想体会其中的意境，需要反复吟咏，反复赏鉴，方能品出其中的滋味来，才能深得其中三味，才能吟出“韵外之致”，见出“象外之象”来，例如我们欣赏汉乐府民歌《江南》时，初看是没有什么味道的。“河南可采莲，莲叶何田田！鱼戏莲叶间。魚戏莲叶东，鱼戏莲叶西。鱼戏莲叶南，鱼戏莲叶北”。颠来倒去就那么几句，似乎很简单，但如果我们仔细领略一番，“处身于境”，就会不知不觉地捕捉和体会到其中蕴藏着无比活泼的情趣；荷叶挺出水面，饱满劲秀，鱼儿在莲叶间穿来穿去，好像在游戏作乐。在充满青春活力的池塘里，荡漾着姑娘们的歌声。（余冠英说：“鱼戏莲叶东，以下可能是和声，相和歌本是一人唱，多人和的。”）她们此唱彼和，歌唱她们的劳动，歌唱她们对美好生活的向往，一派蓬勃的生机溢于言表，一幅充满诗意的天然图画“超以象外”！真能使人味之无极，一唱三叹。故况周颐说：“读词之法。取前人名句意境绝佳者，将此意境缔构于吾想望中。然后澄思渺虑，以吾身入乎其中而涵咏玩索之，性灵相与而俱化，乃真实为吾有而外物不能夺(《蕙风词话》)。”魏泰《临汉隐居诗话》说：“凡诗须使挹之而源不穷，咀之而味愈长。”贺贻孙说得更有意思，读诗须“反复朗诵至数十百过，口颔涎流，滋味无穷，咀嚼不尽。乃至自少至老，诵之不辍，其境愈熟，其味愈长”(《诗筏》)。所以我们说艺术典型令人难忘，而艺术意境则耐人咀嚼。谈到这里，或许有人要问，典型与意境都是对于现实生活的集中概栝，以少总多，寓无限于有限。但是为什么同是对生活的概括，却呈现出了不同的审美色彩呢？笔者认为，这主要是由于它们所用的概括方法不同。

在西方以描写人物为主的叙事文学传统的基础上产生出来的典型论，既受亚里士多德“摹仿说”的影响，又受亚里士多德与柏拉图在美学问题上一般与个别之论争的影响。这就形成了它概括生活的特殊方式。叙事文学传统要求以写人物为主，“摹仿说”要求按必然律或可然律来摹仿人物；美学上一般与个别的论争，结果是要求作家从个别中反映出一般，从个性中体现出共性。这几点，经西方从古到今的理论家们不断发展完善，日趋成熟，形成了典型概括生活的特征，即从具体、鲜明、生动、独特的个性中，反映出最大量的共性；从个别人物形象上，体现出广阔的社会生活的必然的本质内容。简言之，即在某一人物形象上寓共性于个性，寓必然于偶然。在这种寓无限于有限的人物形象上，体现了人类与社会的某些共性与本质。因而许多读者能从典型形象中发现一些自己的特征。典型人物形象的名字能够成为某类人物的代名词，正如别林斯基所说：“把现实理想化，意味着通过个别的，有限的现象来表现普遍的，无限的事物，不是从现实中摹写某些偶然现象，而是创造典型的形象”(《别林斯基选集》卷 2、102-103 页)。这样的典型形象，魅力无穷，“他们的面貌、声音、举止和思想方式一一完全呈现在你的面前，他们永远不可磨灭地印在你的记忆中，使你任何时候都不会忘记他们”(《别林斯基论文学》新文艺出版社 1958 年版 4-5 页)。人物形象的概括力越大，包含的社会生活必然的本质内容越多，那么它的典型性就越强，揭示生活的本质就越深刻，自然，它的生命力就越强，就越令人难忘。这是典型论的最突出的特征之一。

从中国表现情感为主的抒情文学传统的基础上产生出来的意境说，既受儒家“物感说”的影响，又受道家言意形神之辩的影响。这就形成了它概括生活的特殊方式：抒情文学传统与“物感说”要求要情物相观，以境寓情。言意形神之辩，追求言外之意，以形求神。这几点，经中国理论家的不断发展，意境说终于形成了情境交融，虚实相生，形神兼备的独特的审美持征，衡量一件作品有无意境以及意境的深与浅，以什么为标准呢？那就是看该作品能否通过具体、鲜明、生动的境，传达出作者无穷无尽的情思，勾引起无数形象在读者的想象中诞生，体会出作者的真情实感，品味出事物的神采丰韵……总之，看它在有限的形象中，包蕴了多少生活的内容。所以王国维说：“文学之工不工，亦视其意境之有无，与深浅而已”(《人间词话附录》)。那么,怎样才能叫有意境呢?王国维评姜白石曰:“古今词人格调之高,无如白石,惜不于意境上用力,故觉无言外之味,弦外之响”(《人间词话》)。可见,王国维认为,有意境的作品,应当是有言外之味,弦外之响的。言外之意越多,则意境越深,言外之意越少,则意境越浅。故王国维说:“至于国朝而纳兰侍卫以天赋之才,崛起于方兴之族。其所为词,悲凉、顽艳,独有得意境之深,……至乾嘉以降,审乎体格韵律之间者愈微,而意味之溢于字句之表者愈浅(《人间词话附录》)。”这一点,正是意境说的重要特征。所以司空图说:“长于思与境偕乃诗家之所尚”(《与王驾评诗书》)“象外之象,景外之景,岂容易可谭哉”(《与极浦书》)?那么,要怎样才能使作品具有言外之意,象外之象,从而形成以少总多的艺术意境呢?中国的理论家们用的是虚实相生、形神兼备的方法来概括生活,寓无限于有限,做到“万取一收”的。虚实相生,则可以少总多;形神兼备,则可用具体的形象表现事物丰富的内在本质。老庄讲言不尽意,是一个很有意思的问题。一般说来,语言不能完全达意,是个缺点,但在某种意义上讲,这也是个优点。因为它能充分运用语言的暗示性,唤起读者的联想,让读者自己去体会那“象外之象”,去咀嚼品味那字句之外隽永深长的情思和意趣,以达到“言有尽而意无穷”“不着一字,尽得风流”的效果。无论中国的诗、画、书法、音乐、戏剧乃至一些小说,都善于运用这种虚实相生,形神兼备的求得意境的方法。

着力提倡意境的司空图就十分重视艺术的高度概括性。“犹矿出金。如铅出银”(《洗炼》),“浅深聚散,万取一收”(《含蓄》)。然而怎样来概栝呢?司空图认为,其一是虚实相生。即诗要能味在“咸酸之外”,要有“象外之象,景外之景。”其二是形神兼备,在描写“风云变态,花草精神”之时,要能“离形得似。”即以形求神(《形容》)。故严沧浪说:“语忌直,意忌浅,脉忌露,味忌短”(《沧浪诗话·诗法》)。笪重光论画曰:“空本难图,实景清而空景现。神无可绘,真境逼而神境生。位置相戾,有画处多属赘疣;虚实相生,无画处皆成妙境”(《画筌》)。这段话相当清楚地说明了虚实相生,形神兼备与艺术意境之关系。(正是这种虚实相生,形神兼备的概括方法,形成了艺术意境耐人咀嚼的特色。因为作者只写了“实”,留下了许多“虚”;只是将富于暗示性的言与象呈现出来,却留下了许多空白与余地,让读者去体会其形中之神,言外之意,去品味那些不好说,也不用说的“韵外之致”,去捕捉那些如“蓝田日暖,良玉生烟,可望而不可置于眉睫之前”的“象外之象,景外之景”。这种艺术意境,的确耐人咀嚼,令人味之无极,一唱三叹,拍案叫绝!意境越深,包蕴的东西就越多,概括力就越强,就越能引起读者丰富的联想,给人的审美感受就越多。自然,它的生命力就越强,越令人咀嚼。这是艺术意境的最突出的特征之一。)

(曹顺庆.中西比较诗学[M].北京:北京出版社,1988:50-55.)

【延伸阅读】

1. Stephen Owen: *Readings in Chinese Literary Thought*. (Cambridge, Mass.: Council on East Asian Studies Distributed by Harvard University Press, Harvard-Yenching Institute Monograph Series, 1992.)

Stephen Owen,中文名宇文所安,美国汉学家、哈佛大学东亚系教授,长期致力于中国古典文学研究,著有《初唐诗》《盛唐诗》《追忆:中国古典文学中的往事再现》《迷楼:诗与欲望的迷宫》《晚唐:九世纪中叶的中国诗歌(827—860)》等著作。在比较诗学领域,宇文所安这本书由王柏华、陶庆梅译为《中国文论:英译与评论》(上海社会科学院出版社,2002)。全书精选翻译(节译或全译)从孔子《论语》到叶燮《原诗》(包括《诗大序》《典论·论文》《二十四诗品》《沧浪诗话》等)大量中国古典文论经典。虽非比较诗学专题著作,但除翻译之外,该书大量导言、评述、阐释、术语阐释等文字蕴含着丰富的比较诗学观念,对我们从事中西诗学比较具有重要的启发。

2. 乐黛云,叶朗,倪培耕. 世界诗学大辞典[M]. 北京:春风文艺出版社,1993.

本辞典采用"总体诗学"的时空视野,在中国文论界第一次从古到今地把中、西、印、日、阿拉伯等世界国的诗学人物、著作、概念、术语、观念和命题融为一体,为中西比较诗学研究提供了超越西方诗学视野的丰富的理论资源,值得参考。

3. 曹顺庆. 中西比较诗学史[M]. 成都:巴蜀书店,2008.

该书共分七个章节,以时间发展为纵向线索,在时空两个层面上全面和系统地回顾了中西比较诗学从 1840 到 2000 年 160 余年的发展历程。在学科发展史的时间层面上,该书将中西比较诗学划分为萌芽时期(1840—1919)、前学科时期(1919—1987)和学科化时期(1988—2000)三大阶段。在空间上,还对台港中西比较诗学、海外汉学界的中西比较诗学、诗学话语的论争与中西比较诗学的拓展以及全球化语境中比较诗学等问题进行了专题研究。举凡中西比较诗学的名家学者、重要著作、基本概念以及焦点问题都在本书得到了学科史的定位与讨论,很有参考价值。

第五节　跨学科研究

“跨学科研究(Cross-disciplinary Study)”在比较文学“平行研究”学科范式中占有重要地位。它不仅突破了“影响研究”将比较文学研究领域限定在“文学关系史”上的局限,而且进一步将“平行研究”推进到“超文学研究”更加宽广的学科领域。在这个意义上,比较文学“跨学科研究”充分地体现了比较文学这门人文学科所固有的“开放性”学科特征。

一、“跨学科研究”的理论内涵与产生原因

在比较文学界,“跨学科研究”也可以称为“超文学研究”“科际研究”或“科际整合研究”。在比较文学美国学派的倡导之下,“跨学科研究”以文学为中心,通过文学与其他知识形态和学科领域的系统比较反过来加深对文学本质与特征的认识。

根据雷马克从平行研究角度提出来的界定,“跨学科研究”主要“研究文学与其他知识和信仰领域之间的关系,包括艺术(如绘画、雕刻、建筑、音乐)、哲学、历史、社会科学(如政治、经济、社会学),自然科学、宗教等”。也就是说,“跨学科研究”将比较文学领入了涵盖人类所有知识领域与文化形态的学科空间。

从比较文学学科理论发展角度看,“跨学科研究”的产生是比较文学从“影响研究”向“平行研究”拓展的必然结果。关于这一点,雷马克有过非常准确的分析。雷马克将比较文学看作“连接人类创造事业中实质上有机联系着而形体上分离着的各领域的桥梁”。文学批评在很大程度上演示了一个文学与其他知识领域“合—分—合”的关系史。在人类文化早期,文学与神话、宗教、哲学、科学、音乐、舞蹈等文化形态是一种水乳交融的关系。正是基于这一点,不同文明体系早期的文学研究都走过一段学科融合的发展阶段。只是到了现代知识分化时期,随着“知—情—意”思想框架的形成与“自然科学—人文社会科学”的独立,文学研究才逐渐演化为以“文学性”和“审美性”为内在属性的人文学科。雷马克认为,“平行研究”不仅要将比较文学的研究视野从“国际文学关系史”的实证主义局限中解放出来,而且还应该从更广阔的研究空间

来将世界各国的文学当作一个整体。“做到这一点的最好方法,就是不仅把几种文学相互联系起来,而且把文学与人类知识与活动的其他领域联系起来,特别是艺术和思想领域;也就是说,不仅从地理的方面,而且从不同领域的方面扩大文学研究的范围。”[①]这样,“跨学科研究”将一度被排斥在文学批评之外的其他知识类型又一次纳入到文学研究的领域当中,从而成为比较文学美国学派“平行研究”理论建构的关键性环节。

二、“跨学科研究”的研究形态

从研究对象来分,比较文学“跨学科研究”主要可以分为三大形态。

其一,文学与其他艺术的比较研究。“艺术”这个术语,其内涵与外延都非常复杂。在实际运用中,“艺术”至少可以区分为狭义、中义和广义三个层次。狭义的“艺术”专指美术或造型艺术(绘画、雕塑、建筑、摄影等),中间意义层次上的“艺术”将外延扩展到视觉艺术(绘画、雕塑、摄影、书法、舞蹈等)、听觉艺术(音乐)与综合艺术(戏剧、电影、电视等)门类,但并不包括作为语言艺术的文学。广义“艺术”则指包括文学在内的所有艺术形式。“跨学科研究”所说的“文学与其他艺术的比较”,采用的是“艺术”的广义概念。正是因为文学本是广义的“艺术”之一种,我们才将第一种形态的比较文学“跨学科研究”称为“文学与其他艺术的比较研究”。“文学与其他艺术的比较研究”在比较文学“跨学科研究”中占有优先位置。这主要是因为文学与美术、音乐、舞蹈、戏剧、影视等其他艺术门类同属以想象性、情感性和审美性为特性的文化类型。通过文学与这些艺术门类的比较,最容易探得文学作为语言艺术不同于其他艺术门类的独特性质,也最容易探得文学与其他艺术一同分享的美学特征和共同规律。

其二,文学与社会科学的比较研究。文学不仅是一种以语言为媒介进行形象创造的艺术,而且是人类最古老的文化形式。它以一种综合性的方式来体现人在信仰、道德、阶级、种族、法律、经济等人类活动领域中的状态与情形。在这些类型中,哲学、历史、宗教、社会学、法学和经济学等社会科学已经分门别类地积累了大量的理论资源。由于共同植根于形形色色的人类活动本身,文学与社会科学具有了可资比较的前提。比较文学“跨学科研究”在这个领域分别形成了“文学与哲学的比较研究”“文学与历史的比较研究”“文学与宗教的比较研究”“文学与心理学的比较研究”等具体的研究类型。

其三,文学与自然科学的比较研究。从基本气质看,文学与自然科学分属于两个

---

① 雷马克.比较文学的定义和功用[M]//张隆溪.比较文学译文集.北京:北京大学出版社,1982:7.

全然不同的情感光谱与知识板块当中。但是，在从事比较文学“跨学科研究”的学者眼中，文学与数学、医学、物理学、生物学、地理学等自然科学仍然存在着密切的，甚至是许多深刻而有趣的关联。文学具有很强的认知意义和教育作用，这一点很早就为思想家们所承认。即使是从伦理教化角度出发的儒家，其“诗教”观也承认这一点。比如，孔子就强调过《诗经》具有除政治伦理功能之外的认识功能：“《诗》，可以兴，可以观，可以群，可以怨。迩之事父，远之事君，多识于鸟兽草木之名。”（《论语·阳货》）从人类文化史上看，自然科学与文学也多有交集。既有张衡、歌德这样跨界的科学家与文学家，也有自然主义文学、精神分析文学和科幻文学等自觉运用遗传学、心理学和现代科学技术而形成的文学思潮。

当然，“跨学科研究”的作用与形态在比较文学学科理论界还存在着一些争议。即使大力倡导“平行研究”的美国学派内部也存在着不同看法。雷马克明确将文学与其他知识领域的比较纳入比较文学“平行研究”范式，但韦勒克则并不认同。韦勒克强调比较文学和一切文学研究都应以文学文本的“文学性”研究为立足点。在著名的《文学理论》中，韦勒克将文学研究分为“内部研究”和“外部研究”两大部分。在他看来，文学作品是“一个为某种特别的审美目的服务的完整的符号体系或者符号结构”①。而这一语言符号结构又是一个多层结构，它具有“声音、意义和世界”等多个层次。根据这个标准，韦勒克提出文学“内部研究”的对象是谐音、节奏、意象、象征和叙述手法等文学文本的语言结构。与此相对，“外部研究”则包括所有文学与作家生平、传记、文学与心理学、文学与思想、文学与社会、文学与其他艺术相互关系的研究。非常明显，雷马克大力倡导的比较文学“跨学科研究”，在韦勒克那里，最多只能称得上是文学的“外部研究”。

三、“跨学科研究”的争论与未来发展

近年来，“跨学科研究”引起了越来越大的争议。这主要体现为愈演愈烈的比较文学“无边论”倾向。美国文学理论家米勒认为：“自 1979 年以来，文学研究的兴趣中心已发生大规模的转移：从对文学作修辞学式的‘内部’研究，转为研究文学的‘外部’联系，确定它在心理学、历史或社会学背景中的位置。换言之，文学研究的兴趣已从解读（即集中注意研究语言本身及其性质和能力）转移到各种形式的阐释学解释上（即注意语言同上帝、自然、社会、历史等被看作语言之外的事物的关系）。”②特别是近年

---

① 韦勒克，沃伦. 文学理论[M]. 刘象愚，等，译. 北京：三联书店，1984：147.

② 米勒. 文学理论在今天的功能[M]//拉尔夫·科恩. 文学理论的未来. 程锡麟，等，译. 北京：中国社会科学出版社，1993：121.

“文化研究”兴起以后,比较文学进一步向“跨学科研究”方向倾斜。畅销书、商业电影、流行音乐、商业设计等大众文化大量进入比较文学研究领域,性别、种族、阶级等社会问题成为比较文学研究的热门主题。传统比较文学研究的“文学性”“审美性”和“生存诗性”等问题在大多数学者的视野中逐渐消隐。在这样的背景之下,无论是文学与其他艺术、文学与社会科学,还是文学与自然科学,无论什么形态的“跨学科研究”都被视为比较文学在“文化研究”转向过程中被逐渐消融的始作俑者。

因此,“跨学科研究”要归属于成功的“平行研究”,必须要树立“文学文本中心”意识。即是说,无论我们是将文学与自然科学、社会科学还是其他艺术门类进行平行研究,都要有意识地以文学文本为中心。只有紧紧抓住语言文本这一独特的符号表意体系,我们才能守住文学研究的底线,才能充分发挥比较文学研究的真正优势,才不至于沉入泛文化研究和社会批评的汪洋大海而泯灭了比较文学的学科界线和独特的学术个性。

【原典选读】

比较文学的定义与功能(节选)

◉雷马克

【导读】作为比较文学学科理论史上的经典文献,雷马克的《比较文学的定义与功能》一文对美国学派的平行研究进行了非常准确而具有概括性的阐释。它不仅从超出一个国别文学界线和非事实性影响这个角度来界定比较文学的“平行研究”范式,而且还将文学与其他艺术、社会科学和自然科学之间的比较明确纳入比较文学学科领域,从而确立了“跨学科研究”在比较文学学科理论上的合法性。

本节选自雷马克(Henry H. H. Remak)《比较文学的定义与功能》(*Comparative Literature, Its Definition and Function*)一文关于“跨学科研究”部分。在雷马克看来,文学与其他学科领域之间的比较研究是“美国学派”与“法国学派”的“根本分歧”。文章举出许多例子来论证巴登斯贝格、梵·第根、基亚等法国学派的代表人物对“跨学科研究”的忽视甚至排斥。雷马克一直坚持这个论点,在后来写成的《十字路口的比较文学:诊断、治疗与处方》一文中,雷马克同样将“跨学科研究”的有无当作“美国学派”与“法国学派”的一个重要区别。

毫无疑问,“跨学科研究”成功拓展了法国学派“影响研究”对比较文学研究领域所做的人为限制,但同时,也为比较文学学科边界的消解打开了通道。毕竟,随着文学与哲学、历史、宗教、社会学、经济学、心理学、数学、物理学之间比较研究的过多涌入,比较文学的确很容易变得过于“宽泛无边”。在这个问题上,我们需要特别注意的是雷马克对“跨学科研究”所进行的限制。雷马克的原话是:“假如的确存在某一题目的‘比较性’难以确定的过渡区域,那么我们将来必须更加严格,不要随便把这种题目算做比较文学的范围。我们必须弄确实,文学和文学以外的一个领域的比较,只有是系统性的时候,只有在把文学以外的领域作为确实独立连贯的学科来加以研究的时候,才能算是‘比较文学’。”这反映出,雷马克对后来比较文学因跨学科研究而越来越“无边化”的倾向已经有所预见并进行了防范。但是,雷马克对跨科研究所提出的“系统性”限定有没有说服力呢?

应该说,从雷马克所举的四个例子看,跨学科研究究竟怎样进行“系统性”的比较仍然不甚明确。历史现象、经济现象、宗教现象和心理活动,本是文学创作最重要的素材与内容。事实上,传统文学批评一直都在研究文学作品中的历史因素、经济因素、宗教因素与心理因素。难道通过所谓的“系统性”研究,这些传统的研究方法就能够摇身一变而成为“比较文学”?关键是,我们也许需要对作为题材的文学内容与作为研究方法的“比较文学”作出一个区分。究竟对文学作品所反映的社会现象与生活内容的研究与比较文学“跨学科研究”有什么区别?这是我们在阅读这个原典时需要深入思考的问题。

In examining the second part of our definition, viz. the relationship between literature and other fields, we come up against a difference not of emphasis but of basic distinction between the "American" and "French" schools. In the only contemporary surveys of the field of comparative literature written to date in book form, Van Tieghem and Guyard do not discuss or even list the relationship between literature and other areas (art, music, philosophy, politics, etc.). During the many years that the *Revue de littérature comparée* was directed by Baldensperger and Hazard, its quarterly bibliographies did not recognize this category of topics at all. This policy has remained unchanged under succeeding editors. In contrast, American comparative-literature curricula and publications (including bibliographies) generally take in this realm.

The French are certainly interested in such topics as the comparative arts, but they do not think of them as being within the jurisdiction of comparative literature. There are historical reasons for this attitude. Despite the rigidities of academic compartmentalization, comparative literature has been able, for more than half a century, to occupy a distinct and distinguished niche in French universities precisely because it combined a wider coverage *of* literature with a prudent restriction *to* literature. The student and teacher of literature who venture beyond national frontiers already assume an extra burden. The French seem to fear that taking on, in addition, the systematic study of the relationship between literature and any other area of human endeavor invites the accusation of charlatanism and would, at any rate, be detrimental to the acceptance of comparative literature as a respectable and respected academic domain.

A related, more fundamental objection should also be taken into consideration: the lack of logical coherence between comparative literature as the study of literature beyond national boundaries and comparative literature as the study of the ramifications of literature beyond its own boundaries. Furthermore, while the geographical connotations of the term comparative literature are fairly concrete, the generic ramifications implied in the American concept raise serious problems of demarcation which American scholars have not been willing to face squarely.

It is difficult to find firm criteria for selection when one scans the mass of titles in Baldensperger-Friederich *Bibliography of Comparative Literature*, especially in those portions of Book One covering "*Generalities*" "*Thematology*" and "*Literary Genres*" and in the chapter on "*Literary Cur-rents*" in Book Three. We are speaking here only of entries which are, neither by title nor (upon examination) by contents comparative in the geographical sense (except incidentally), whose inclusion in the *Bibliography* must therefore have been determined by reasons of subject matter extension. Under the headings of "Individual Motifs" and "Collective Motifs," for example, we find a large number of investigations of love, marriage, women, fathers-and-sons, children, war, professions, etc. *within* a national literature. Can the incorporation of these items in a bibliography of *comparative* literature be justified on the premise that we arc dealing here with two realms — literature and "motifs"? But motifs are part and parcel *of* literature; they are intrinsic, not extraneous. Under the headings of "*Literary Genres*" and "*Literary Currents*," we find studies on the American novel, the German Bildungsroman, the Spanish Generation of '98, etc. etc. But accounts of literary genres, movements and generations in a certain country, even if they are of a general nature, are not comparative per se. The notions of genres, movements, "schools," generations etc. are implicit in our idea of literature and literary history; they are inside, not outside of literature. We submit that, with a modicum of rationalizing, almost anything and everything in literary scholarship and criticism could lay claim to being "comparative literature" if the ultraelastic criteria of the Bibliography are accepted. Comparative literature as a quasi all-inclusive term would be close to meaningless.

Granting that there is a twilight zone where a case can be made pro and con the "comparativeness" of a given topic, we shall have to be more discriminating in the future about admitting a topic in this category to comparative literature. We must make sure that comparisons between literature and a field other than literature be accepted as "comparative literature" only if they are systematic and if a definitely separable, coherent discipline outside of literature is studied as such. We cannot classify scholarly endeavors as "comparative literature" merely because they discuss inherent aspects of life and art that must inevitably be reflected in all literature, for what else can literature be about? A paper on the historical sources of a Shakespearean drama would (unless it concentrates on another country) be "comparative literature" only if historiography and literature were the main poles of the investigation, if historical facts or accounts and their literary adaptations were systematically compared and evaluated, and conclusions arrived at which would bear on the two domains as such. A treatment of the role of money in Balzac *Père Goriot* would be comparative only if it were principally (not just incidentally) concerned with the literary osmosis of a coherent financial system or set of ideas. An inquiry into the ethical or religious ideas of Hawthorne or Melville could be considered comparative only if it dealt with an organized religious movement (e. g., Calvinism) or set of beliefs. The tracing of a character in a novel by Henry James would be within the scope of comparative literature only if it developed a methodical view of this character in the light of the psychological theories of Freud (or Adler, Jung, etc.).

(节选自：Henry H. H. Remak：*Comparative Literature*：*Its Definition and Function*. From *Comparative Literatreu*：*Method and Perspective*, Edited By Newton P. Stallknecht and Horst Frenz, Southern Illinois University Press, 1961：6-9.)

【研究范例】

中国诗与中国画（节选）

◉钱锺书

【导读】即使从世界性视野看，钱锺书的《中国诗与中国画》都可以当之无愧地称为比较文学"跨学科研究"的经典之作。这篇15000余字的论文中，钱锺书出入古今中西，广征博引，横跨文学、艺术、哲学、宗教多种学科，对诗与画的关系、对中国诗歌风格与西方诗歌风格、对中国传统诗学批评与绘画理论批评的审美理想都提出了许多精辟的见解。我们可以从三个方面来看这篇论文在比较文学"跨学科研究"中的典范式意义。

第一，诗歌与绘画的跨越性研究。钱锺书的《中国诗与中国画》要处理的是"诗"与"画"的关系问题以及"中国传统文艺批评对诗和画有不同的标准"问题，而这正是"文学"与"其他艺术"的跨界研究。从研究对象看，这完全符合比较文学美国学派关于"跨学科研究"的界定。《中国诗与中国画》通篇贯穿着"诗"与"画"这两种不同艺术门类的比较性思考。仅以"诗"与"画"的关系这个小节为例。这篇文章一开始就密集引用了大量资料，从张彦远的"诗画异名同体"，孔武仲的"无形画""有形文"等一直写到孙绍远、杨公远的"题画诗"以及吴龙翰的"诗画互足"论。紧接着，文章又引证西方美学文献，最后指出"诗和画既然同是艺术，应该有共同性；而它们并非同一门艺术，又应该各具特殊性"。

第二，文学艺术与哲学宗教的跨越性研究。"跨学科研究"不仅需要跨越文学与其他艺术的界线，还需要跨越文学与哲学、宗教、历史等人文社会科学的界线。在这方面，钱锺书的《中国诗与中国画》同样作出了表率。在讨论中国传统绘画"画分北南"命题时，钱锺书不仅分析了董其昌在《容台别集》、莫是龙在《画说》、陈继儒在《偃曝余谈》中所提出来的观点，而且还将文艺上的“南北”风格联系到学术思想上的“南北”学风进行论述。通过大量的材料，钱锺书指出，中国早在六朝时期就已经把作为地理概念的“南”和“北”当作两种思想方法或学风来进行讨论了。为了说明这个问题，钱锺书广泛地触及了中国的诗歌、画论、禅宗史和学术思想等诸学科领域的文献与资料。

第三，中西文化的跨越性研究。比较文学“跨学科研究”在跨越文学与其他知识领域进行平行比较的时候，是否需要同时跨越语言、国家与民族的界线？美国学派代表人物雷马克对此没有明确表述。从钱锺书的论文看，他很充分地体现了比较文学跨学科研究方法无限宽广的学术视野。即使在讨论中国传统文艺中“诗”“画”关系时，钱锺书也同时不忘引用西方思想资源。从古希腊诗人西摩尼得斯（Simonides of Ceos）、古罗马哲学家西塞罗（Marcus Tullius Cicero）、意达利画家达文齐（Leonardo Da Vinci，今译达·芬奇）、德国美学家莱辛（Gotthold Ephraim Lessing），到古罗马诗人霍拉斯（Quintus Horatius Flaccus，今通译贺拉斯），钱锺书以自己宽广的学术视野自觉地将文学与艺术的比较研究与中西文化的跨文明研究交错关联起来。■

二

诗和画号称姊妹艺术。有些人进一步认为它们不但是姊妹，而且是孪生姊妹。唐人只说“书画异名而同体”（张彦远《历代名画记》卷一《叙画之源流》）。自宋以后，评论家就反复强调诗和画异体而同貌。例如孔武仲《宗伯集》卷一《东坡居士画怪石赋》：“文者无形之画，画者有形之文，二者异迹而同趣”；冯应榴《苏文忠公诗合注》卷五〇《韩干马》：“少陵翰墨无形画，韩干丹青不语诗”；张舜民《画墁集》卷一《跋百之诗画》：“诗是无形画，画是有形诗”；释德洪觉范《石门文字禅》卷八：宋迪作八景绝妙，“人谓之‘无声句’。演上人戏余曰：‘道人能作有声画乎？’因为之各赋一首”；《宋诗纪事》卷五九引《全蜀艺文志》载钱鍪《次袁尚书巫山诗》：“终朝诵公有声画，却来看此无声诗。”两者只举一端，像黄庭坚《次韵子瞻、子由题憩寂图》：“李侯有句不肯吐，淡墨写作无声诗”，米友仁《自题山水》：“古人作语咏不得，我寓无声缣楮间”，周孚《题所画梅竹》：“东坡戏作有声画，叹息何人为赏音”，例子更多。舒岳祥《阆风集》卷六《和正仲送达美善归钱塘》：“好诗甚似无声画，错眼羞同没字碑”，求对仗的平仄匀称，揣“有”字为“无”字，出了毛病。“碑”照例有“字”，“没字的碑”是自身矛盾语，恰好用作比喻，去嘲笑目不识丁；“画”压根儿“无声”，说“好诗似画”，词意具足，所添“无声”两字就不免修辞学所谓“赘余的形容”（redundant epithet）了①。南宋孙绍远搜罗唐以来的题画诗，编为《声画集》；宋末名画家杨公远自编诗集《野

① 参看昆体良（Quntilian）《修辞原理》（*Instituio oratoria*）第 8 卷 6 章 40 节，《罗勃（Loeb）古典丛书》本第 3 册 324 页。

趣有声画》，诗人吴龙翰所作《序》文里说："画难画之景，以诗凑成，吟难吟之诗，以画补足。"（曹庭栋《宋百家诗存》卷一九）从那两部书名，可以推想这个概念的流行。

"无声诗"即"有形诗"和"有声画"即"无形画"的对比和西洋传统的诗、画对比，用意相类。古希腊诗人（Simonides of Ceos）早说："画为不语诗，诗是能言画。"[①]嫁名于西塞罗的一部修辞学里，论互换句法（commutatio）所举第四例就是："正如诗是说话的画，画该是静默的诗"（Item poema loquens pictura, pictura tacitum poema debet esse）。"[②]达文齐干脆说画是"嘴巴哑的诗（una poesia muta）"，而诗是"眼睛瞎的画（una pittura cieca）"[③]。莱辛在他反对"诗画一律"的名作里，引了"那个希腊伏尔太的使人眼花缭乱的对照（die blendende Antithese des griechischen Voltaire）"，也正是这句话[④]，轻轻地又把他所敌视的伏尔太带扫了一笔。"不语诗""能言画"和中国的"无声诗""有声画"是同一回事，因为"声"在这里不指音响，就像旧小说里"不则（作）声"、旧戏曲里"禁（噤）声！禁声！"的那个"声"字。古罗马诗人霍拉斯的名句："诗会像画（ut pictura poesis erit）"，经后人断章取义，理解作"诗原如画"[⑤]，仿佛苏轼《书鄢陵王主簿折枝》所谓："诗画本一律。"诗、画是孪生姊妹的说法是千余年西方文艺理论的奠基石，也就是莱辛所要扫除的绊脚石，因为由他看来，诗、画各有各的面貌衣饰，是"绝不争风吃醋的姊妹（Keine eifersuechtige Schwester）"[⑥]。

诗和画既然同是艺术，应该有共同性；而它们并非同一门艺术，又应该各具特殊性。它们的性能和领域的异同，是美学上重要理论问题[⑦]，这里不想探讨。我有兴趣的是具体的文艺鉴赏和评判。我们常听人说：中国旧诗和中国旧画有同样的风格，表现同样的艺术境界。那句话究竟是什么意思？这个意思是否能在文艺批评史里证实？

三

……

中国画史上最有代表性的、最主要的流派当然是"南宗文人画"。董其昌《容台别集》卷四有一节讲得极清楚："禅家有南北二宗，唐时始分。画之南北二宗，亦唐时分也；但其人非南北耳。北宗则李思训父子着色山水，流传而为宋之赵干、赵伯驹、伯骕以至马、夏

---

① 艾德门茨（J. M. Edmonds）《希腊抒情诗》（*Lyra Graeca*），罗勃（Loeb）《古典丛书》本第 2 册 258 页。参看哈格斯达勒姆（Jean H. Hagstrum）《姊妹艺术》10 又 58 页。

② 西塞罗（Cicero）《修辞学》（*Rhetorica ad Herennium*）第 4 卷第 28 章，罗勃本 326 页。

③ 达文齐《画论》（*Trattato della Pittura*）第 16 章，米兰奈西（G. Milanesi）编本 12 页。

④ 莱辛《拉奥孔》（*Laokoon*）《前言》（Vorrede），李拉（P. Rilla）编《全集》第 5 册 10 页。

⑤ 霍拉斯（Horace）《论诗代简》（*Ars poetica*）361 行，参看《姊妹艺术》26，37，59-61 页等。

⑥ 《拉奥孔》第 8 章，82 页。

⑦ 可参看罗西（A. Russi）《总体艺术和分门艺术》（*L'Arte e le Arti*）13-15 页；斯巴夏脱（F. E. Sparshott）《美学的结构》（*The Structure of Aesthetics*）42-57 页。

辈。南宗则王摩诘始用渲淡，一变构研之法；其传为张璪、荆、关、董、巨、郭忠恕、米家父子以至元之四大家，亦如六祖之后有马驹、云门、临济儿孙之盛，而北宗微矣。要之摩诘所谓‘云峰石迹，迥出天机，笔意纵横，参乎造化’者，东坡赞吴道子、王维画壁亦云：‘吾于维也无间然’，知言哉!”（参看同卷《文人画自王维始》一条，叙述更详）。董氏同乡书画家莫是龙《画说》一五条里有一条，字句全同；董氏同乡好友陈继儒《偃曝余谈》卷下有论旨相类的一条，坦白地把李思训、王维明白比为“禅家”北宗的神秀和南宗的惠能。南、北画风的区别，也可用陈氏推尊的话来概括，《弇州四部稿》卷一五四《艺苑卮言·附录》卷三：“吴、李以前画家，实而近俗；荆、关以后画家，雅而太虚。今雅道尚存，实德则病。”这些是明人论画的老生常谈，清人大体上相承不改，还把“南宗”的品目推广到董氏自己的书法上去：“太仆文章宗伯字，正如得髓自南宗。”（姚鼐《惜抱轩诗集》卷八《论书绝句》三）。……

把“南”“北”两个地域和两种思想方法或学风联系，早已见于六朝，唐代禅宗区别南、北恰恰符合或沿承了六朝古说①。其实《礼记·中庸》说“南方之强”省事宁人，“不报无道”，不同于“北方之强”好勇斗狠，“死而不厌”，也就是把退敛和进取分别为“南”和“北”的特征。《世说·文学》第四：“孙安国曰：‘南人学问清通简要。’褚季野曰：‘北人学问渊综广博。’支道林曰：‘自中人以还，北人看书如显处视月，南人看书如牖中窥日。’”历来引用的人没有通观上文，因而误解支道林为褒北贬南。孙、褚两人分举南、北“学问”各有特长；支表示同意，稍加补充，说各有流弊，“中人”以下追求博大，则流为浮泛，追求简约，则流为寡陋。“显处视月”是浮光掠影，不鞭辟入里，和“牖中窥日”的一孔偏面，同样不是褒词而是贬词。《隋书·儒林传》叙述经学，也说：“大抵南人约简，得其英华；北学深芜，穷其枝叶”，简直像唐后对南、北禅宗的惯评了。看来，南、北“学问”的分歧，和宋、明儒家有关“博观”与“约取”、“多闻”与“一贯”、“道问学”与“尊德性”的争论，属于同一类典型。巴斯楷尔区分两类有才智的人（deux sortes d' esprit）：一类“坚强而狭隘”，一类“广阔而软弱（l'esprit pouvant étre fort et étroit, et pouvant étre ample et faible）”②这个分歧正由于康德指出的“理性”两种倾向：一种按照万殊的原则，喜欢繁多（das Interesse der Mannigfaltigkeit, nach dem Princip der Specification），另一种按照合并的原则，喜欢一贯（das Interesse der Einheit, nach dem Princip der Aggregation）③。禅宗之有南、北，只是这个分歧的最极端、最尖锐的表现。南宗禅把“念经”“功课”全鄙弃为无聊多事，要把“学问”简至于无可再简、约至于不能更约，说什么“微妙法门，不立文字，教外别传”“经诵三千部，曹溪一句亡”“广

① 据文廷式《纯常子枝语》卷9、卷27所引道士著作，宋以后道家也分“南北宗”；区分的原则是否与此相近，没有去考究。

② 巴斯楷尔（Pascal）《思辨录》（*Pensées*）第1篇2节，季洛（V. Giraud）编本，50页。

③ 《纯理性批判》（*Kritik der reinen Vernunft*），艾尔德曼（B. Erdmann）校本，格鲁依德（W. de Gruyter）版500页，参看495页。

学知解，被知解境风之所漂溺”（《五灯会元》卷一释迦牟尼章次、卷二惠能章次、卷三怀海章次）。李昌符《赠供奉僧玄观》：“自得曹溪法，诸经更不看”；张乔《宿齐山僧舍》：“若言不得南宗要，长在禅床事更多”；都是说南宗禅不看“经”、省“事”。南宗画的理想也正是“简约”，以最省略的笔墨获取最深远的艺术效果，以减削迹象来增加意境（less is more）。和石溪齐名“二溪”的程正揆反复说明这一点；他的诗文集《青溪遗稿》冷落无闻，不妨多引一些。卷一五《山庄题画》六首之三：“铁干银钩老笔翻，力能从简意能繁；临风自许同倪瓒，人骨谁评到董源！”卷二二《题卧游图后》：“论文字者谓增一分见不如增一分识，识愈高则文愈淡。予谓画亦然。多一笔不如少一笔，意高则笔减。何也？意在笔先，不到处皆笔；繁皱浓染，刻划形似，生气漓矣。”卷二四《龚半千画册》：“画有繁减，乃论笔墨，非论境界也。北宋人千丘万壑，无一笔不减；元人枯枝瘦石，无一笔不繁。予曾有诗云”（即“铁干银钩”那一首）；《题石公画卷》：“予告石溪曰：画不难为繁，难于用减，减之力更大于繁。非以境减，减以笔；所谓‘弄一车兵器，不若寸铁杀人’者也。”卷二六《杂着》一：“画贵减不贵繁，乃论笔墨，非论境界也。宋人千丘万壑，无一笔不减，倪元镇疏林瘦石，无一笔不繁。”翁方纲《复初斋诗集》卷一二《程青溪〈江山卧游图〉》：“枯木瘦石乃繁重，千岩万壑乃轻灵”，正用程氏自己的语意；吴雯《莲洋集》卷六《题云林〈秋山图〉》：“岂但秾华谢桃李，空林黄叶亦无多”，也是赞叹倪瓒的笔墨简净。值得注意的是，程氏藉禅宗的“话头”来说明画法。“弄一车兵器，不是杀人手段，我有寸铁，便可杀人”，那是宋代禅师宗杲的名言，儒家的道学先生都欣赏它的；例如朱熹《朱子语类》卷八就引用了，卷一一五教训门徒又“因举禅语云：‘寸铁可杀人；无杀人手段，则载一车枪刀，逐件弄过，毕竟无益’。”南宗禅提倡“单刀直入”（《五灯会元》卷一一守廓章次、旻德章次）而不搬弄十八般武器，嘲笑“博览古今”的“百会”为“一尚不会”（同书卷七洛京南院和尚章次），所谓：“只要单刀直入，不要广参”（《宗镜录》卷四一）。那和“南人学问”的“清通简要”“约简得英华”，一拍即合，只是程度有深浅。同一趋向表现在形象艺术里，就是绘画的笔墨“从简”“用减”。“南宗画”的定名超出了画家的籍贯，揭出了画风的本质，难道完全“无所取义”么？

那么，能不能说南宗画的作风也就相当于最有代表性的中国旧诗的作风呢？

五

……

神韵派在旧诗传统里并未像南宗在旧画传统里那样占有统治地位。唐代司空图、宋代严羽的提倡似乎没有显著的影响，明末陆时雍评选《诗镜》的宣传，清初王士祯通过理论兼实践的鼓动，勉强造成了风气。不过，这个风气短促得可怜。不但王士祯当时已有赵执信作《谈龙录》来强烈反对，乾隆时诗人直到晚清的“同光体”作家差不多全把它看作旁门小家的诗风。这已是文学史常识。王维当然是大诗人，他的诗和他的画又具有同样风格，而且他在旧画传统里坐着第一把交椅，但是旧诗传统里排起坐位来，首席是数不着他的。

中唐以后,众望所归的最大诗人一直是杜甫。借用意大利人的说法,王维和杜甫相比,只能算"小的大诗人(un piccolo-grande poeta)"——他的并肩者韦应物可以说是"大的小诗人(un grande-piccolo poeta)"①,托名冯贽所作《云仙杂记》是部伪书,卷一捏造《文览》记仙童教杜甫在"豆垄"下掘得"一石,金字曰:'诗王本在陈芳国'",更是鬼话编出来的神话;然而作为唐宋舆论的测验,天赐"诗王"的封号和王禹偁《小畜集》卷九《日长简仲咸》:"子美集开诗世界",可以有同等价值。元稹《故工部员外郎杜君墓系铭》称杜诗"兼综古今之长",《新唐书》卷一二六《杜甫传赞》也发挥这个意思;《皇朝文鉴》卷七二孙何《文箴》说:"还雅归颂,杜统其众";晁说之《嵩山文集》卷一四《和陶引辩》:"曹、刘、鲍、谢、李、杜之诗,《五经》也,天下之大中正也;彭泽之诗,老氏也";秦观《淮海集》卷一一《韩愈论》进一步专把杜甫比于"集大成"的孔子;朱熹《朱子语类》卷一三九以李、杜诗为学诗者的"本经";吴乔《围炉诗话》卷二有"杜《六经》"的称呼;蒋士铨《忠雅堂文集》卷一《杜诗详注集成序》也说:"杜诗者,诗中之《四子书》也。"潘德舆《养一斋集》卷一八《作诗本经序》:"三代而下,诗足绍《三百篇》者,莫李、杜若也。……朱子曰:'作诗先看李杜,如士人治本经。'虽未以李、杜之诗为《经》,而已以李、杜之诗为作诗之《经》矣。窃不自量,辑李、杜诗千余篇与《三百篇》风旨无二者,题曰《作诗本经》";参照潘氏另一书《李杜诗话》卷二说杜甫"集大成"的话,此处李、杜齐称就好比儒家并提"孔、孟",一个"至圣",一个"亚圣",还是以杜甫为主的。

这样看来,中国传统文艺批评对诗和画有不同的标准;评画时赏识王世贞所谓"虚"以及相联系的风格,而评诗时却赏识"实"以及相联系的风格。因此,旧诗传统以杜甫为正宗、为代表。……

总结地说,据中国文艺批评史看来,用杜甫的诗风来作画,只能达到品位低于王维的吴道子,而用吴道子的画风来作诗,就能达到品位高于王维的杜甫。中国旧诗和旧画有标准上的分歧。这个分歧是批评史里的事实,首先需要承认,其次还等待着解释——真正的,不是装模作样的解释。

(钱锺书. 七缀集[M]. 北京:三联书店,2002:5-32.)

【延伸阅读】

1. 韦斯坦因. 文学与视觉艺术[M]//孙景尧,译. 新概念　新方法　新探索——当代西方比较文学论文选. 桂林:漓江出版社,1987.

本文主要就文学与视觉艺术进行跨学科研究,所讨论的视觉艺术主要包括绘画和

① 比尼(Walter Binni)编《对意大利古典作家历代评论提要》(*I Classici italiani nella Storia della Critica*)第2册629页。

雕塑。与钱锺书的《中国诗与中国画》不同，这篇文章以西方文学艺术史为线索进行讨论，论述材料以西方为界线，基本没有触及西方文明之外的思想资源。全文分四个部分，第二个部分中对文学与视觉艺术跨学科研究所提出的16个层面的问题值得关注。另外，韦斯坦因在文章指出跨学科研究“尚未找到恰当的方向，而且还未有固定的一套方法及完整的术语”。这个问题仍然是今天跨学科研究所需要努力完成的目标。

2. 韦斯坦因. 各种艺术的相互阐发[M]//韦斯坦因. 比较文学与文学理论. 刘象愚，译. 沈阳：辽宁人民出版社，1987.

“各种艺术的相互阐发”是韦斯坦因所著《比较文学与文学理论》一书的第七章。与《文学与视觉艺术》相比，这篇论文将跨学科研究的视野从文学与视觉艺术的关系拓展到文学与音乐、戏剧等艺术门类的关系之上。同时，文章也较详细地回顾了跨学科研究在比较文学学科发展史上的位置。其中，论文关于“跨学科研究”将在“比较文学下一个阶段占有突出位置”的预言，值得关注。

3. George Slusser and George Guffey：*Literature and Science*，见孙景尧. 比较文学经典要著研读[M]. 上海：上海文艺出版社，2006.

《文学与科学》由美国加州大学河滨分校比较文学教授乔治·斯拉塞主笔，较为详细地梳理了西方思想史上关系文学与科学关系的主要观点。论文对文学形象的科学意识、文学作品中的科学主题和科学思维对文学的影响进行了非常深入的分析，是比较文学跨学科研究中“文学与自然科学的比较”领域中的经典之作。

第四章　变异研究

比较文学的变异研究(Variation Studies)是指对文学作品在跨语际、跨文明的传播交流和相互阐发的过程中呈现出的变异现象的研究。一部文学作品在跨语际的译介和接受过程中由于接受者的文化过滤和文学误读等因素的影响,其内容、主题、形象等元素都可能会发生变异。通过考察各种文学变异现象的具体表征,探究造成这些变异的复杂背景与影响因素,进而总结文学传播与接受中产生变异的规律,对于帮助我们更好地理解不同文化的异质性,体认文化主体在异质文学的传播和接受过程中进行的选择、改造与创新,都具有十分重要的意义。变异研究的分支学科包括变异学、译介学、形象学、接受学等,研究领域则包括跨国变异研究、跨语际变异研究、跨文明变异研究、文学的他国化研究等方面。

第一节　变异学

建立比较文学变异学的理论构想由曹顺庆教授在2005年中国比较文学第八届年会暨国际学术研讨会上正式提出。同年，四川大学出版社出版的《比较文学学》将文学变异学作为独立章节，开始建构比较文学变异学的理论基础。2006年曹顺庆在《复旦学报》发表《比较文学学科中的文学变异学研究》，详尽地分析了变异学提出的理论基础、研究领域，明确了变异学的研究原则。2006年5月，由高等教育出版社发行的《比较文学教程》以影响研究、平行研究、变异研究和总体文学研究四大研究领域为主要内容，开创了比较文学学科理论教材的一个新体系。之后又有《比较文学变异学的学术背景与理论构想》等一系列论文发表，不断推进了变异学由理论建构到实践运用的发展，为比较文学学科注入了新力量。

一、比较文学变异学的理论内涵

（一）变异学的研究领域

我们可以将变异学的研究范围区分为6个层次。

第一，语言层面变异学。主要是指"文学现象穿越语言的界限，通过翻译而在目的语环境中得到接受的过程，也就是翻译学或者译介学研究。"[①]随着当代审美浪潮的袭来，翻译对传统研究模式进行了反思和质疑，极度呼唤翻译主体的能动性，推崇翻译的"创造性叛逆"，注重异质文化在翻译中出现的碰撞和交流。新时代的译介学很难在实证性的影响研究下委曲求全，此时的译介学已经超越了传统翻译、媒介学，而研究异质文化中的语言变异问题正是比较文学中变异学针对语言层面的重要课题。

第二，民族国家形象变异学。当代形象学认为，形象就其生成机制来看是创造式的，而非影响研究意义上的复制品，文本中的异国形象是作者再创造的结果。当代形象学的创新之处就在于它更多地关注了形象制作的主体——"注视者"。这样，注视

① 曹顺庆.比较文学学科中的文学变异学研究[J].复旦学报，2006(1).

者与注视对象，注视者所存在的“本土”与他者所处的“异域”构成两组二元对立的概念，在这对立统一的互动中，产生了文化过滤与文化误读的变异产物。

第三，文学文本变异研究。文学文本变异是研究文本在交往中产生的文学接受现象。不同文化下的接受者对同一文本的理解有所差异，这个差异就是接受学的研究内容。它不同于接受理论或影响研究，它将“接受者”放于主体地位。文本变异研究不仅包括因为审美趣味不同所造成的文化差异，还研究异域文学进入后是如何再创作、再发展的变异。

第四，文化变异研究。其典型理论就是文化过滤。文化过滤指的是“跨文化文学交流、对话中，由于接受主体不同的文化传统、社会历史背景、审美习惯等原因而造成接受者有意无意地对交流信息选择、变形、伪装、渗透、创新等作用，从而造成源交流信息在内容、形式发生变异。”①不同的“文化模子”催生出不同的文学观、审美观和相应的文学意义建构方式以及美学特征。“文化模子”的差异性越大，文化过滤的程度就越高。比较文学的变异研究应该重视文化过滤这一现象和作用机制，使其成为变异学的研究范围。

第五，文学的“他国化”。是指“异国文学在传播到他国后，经过文化过滤、译介、接受之后发生的一种更为深层次的变异，这种变异主要体现在传播国文学本身的文化规则和文学话语已经在根本上被他国——接受国所同化，从而成为他国文学和文化的一部分，这种现象被我们称为文学的他国化。”②文化的“他国化”道路就是对异质文化如何渗透到接受国并且产生新的话语模式的过程，为本国文化注入新活力。这就是变异学所提倡的尊重异质性，实现文化发展的多元化。

第六，跨文明研究。如今中西之间的差异大于类同，跨国研究已经不能解释文学内部的很多东西。曹顺庆在《比较文学中国学派基本理论特征及其方法论体系初探》一文中，提出“跨异质文化”的观点，认为“正在崛起的中国学派必将跨越东西方异质文化这堵巨大的墙，必将穿透这数千年文化凝成的厚厚屏障，沟通东西方文学，重构世界文学观念”。之后，为了突出不同文化圈之间文明的差异性，以及由此产生的碰撞与对话，我们把“跨文化”提升为“跨文明”。“跨文明研究”就是以异质性为出发点的对文化根性、文化过程、文化趋势的整合研究。跨文明研究以变异性为核心，研究不同文化圈之间的文化传播与变异现象，极具跨时代意义，这是中国比较研究理论创新的增长点。

---

① 曹顺庆. 比较文学学[M]. 成都：四川大学出版社，2005：273.

② 曹顺庆. 比较文学课程[M]. 北京：高等教育出版社，2006：147.

（二）变异学与影响研究

韦斯坦因在其代表作《比较文学与文学理论》中，已经有意无意地触碰到了变异问题，他指出："从原则上说，比较学者绝不应对影响中的主动（给予）和被动（接受）因素作质量上的区分，因为接受影响既不是耻辱，给予影响也没有荣耀。无论如何，在大多数情况下，影响都不是直接的借入或借出，逐字逐句模仿的例子可以说是少而又少，绝大多数影响在某种程度上都表现为创造性的转变。[①]这种"创造性的转变"，其实质就是我们说的变异。爱德华·赛义德明确指出，西方学术中的"非理性的，堕落的，幼稚的，'不正常的'"[②]的东方形象，其实大多数是一种变异了的东方，是非真实的东方，是西方话语霸权下对东方的一种歪曲。

在欧美比较文学学科理论中，比较文学的根本目的是求同，而不是求异。由于忽视异质性，法国学派与美国学派的学科理论在研究实践中都面临着无法摆脱的困境。法国学派倡导实证性的国际文学关系史的研究，但常常遇到无法实证的尴尬难题。由于历史、文化、心理等多方面因素的影响，处于传播、交流和影响中的文学必然会产生变异。比如法国学者倡导的形象学，就很难用实证性的方法来研究。法国学派在形象学研究中早就提到过文学作品中的"他国形象"问题，由于形象学涉及集体想象的因素，所以它必然会产生变异。可以说，法国的形象学研究早已突破了早期的实证性和同源性研究的范畴（详细见本教材"形象学"论述）。形象学研究对象是文学作品中的他国形象，而他国形象是一种"社会集体想象物"[③]，显然，想象只能是变异的东西。"社会集体想象物"是一种融合了主观与客观、情感与理智的对他者形象的一个生产、制作与再创造的过程，此时，客观存在的他者形象已在注视方的自我文化观念下发生了变异，而这种复杂的变异过程，是不可能用实证方法和求同的方法来完全解决的。比较文学形象学，实际上既暴露了早期法国学派实证理论的尴尬，也体现了法国学者的理论进步。形象学实际上是法国学者的自我修正。可惜的是，法国学者并没有从理论上加以进一步总结，没有提出变异学理论。

多年来，法国学派放逐文学的审美意义，注重实证，人为地缩小了比较文学研究领域，企图用一种历史的科学的实证的方法来操作饱含审美因素与心理因素的文学跨国交流现象，用尽可能多的事实的累加来证明另一事实的存在，是其遭到后人诟病最为重要的原因。如影响研究无法解释文学交流与传播过程中的接受问题，无法解释为什

---

① 韦斯坦因．比较文学与文学理论［M］．刘象愚，译．沈阳：辽宁人民出版社，1987：29．

② 爱德华·W．赛义德．东方学［M］．王宇根，译．北京：三联书店，1999：49．

③ 让-马克·莫哈．试论文学形象学的研究史及方法论［M］//孟华．比较文学形象学．北京：北京大学出版社，2001：29．

么在一种文化中处于边缘的文学作品在另一种文化中却被明显地中心化?为什么在中国文学史上不见经传的寒山诗在美国却引起广泛的接受与高度的认可?为什么日本人喜欢的不是李白、杜甫而是白居易?为什么中国的二三流作品如《好逑传》等却被歌德奉为上流作品?正如法国学者艾金伯勒质疑的,来源的研究从来就解释不了为什么一只绵羊根据不同情况被改变成一头狮子、一只老虎或一头豹,甚至一条五颜六色的岩间巨蟒。显然,实证只能证明科学事实和规律,却不能说明艺术创造与文学接受过程中出现的变异,长期以来学界对于非实证认识不足,已成立影响研究的一个先天"痼疾"。尽管后来学者都敏锐地发现了问题,却鲜有人对此开出有效的药方,比较文学变异学理论正是针对这一"痼疾"开出的良方。

(三)变异学与平行研究

同样,平行研究由于没有认识到比较文学的异质性与变异性,也面临着理论上的困惑,以美国学派所讨论的比较文学有无边界问题为例,韦勒克认为,既然比较文学是以研究文学的共同审美性和文学的共同规律为对象,那么比较文学就可以跨越语言、学科、国家、文明的边界进行比较研究。就像韦勒克自己说的:"比较文学是一种没有语言、伦理和政治界线的文学研究。"[①]他主张将全世界文学看作一个整体,并且不考虑语言上的区别,去探索文学的发生和发展,"研究各国文学及其共同倾向"[②]。很明显,韦勒克是倾向于比较文学可以跨文明的,但不同文明可以比较的前提是共通性,即人性相同。应当说,这个看法并不完全错,东海西海,心理攸同。但是,同的背后,还有差异,可惜韦勒克并没有谈到这个关键问题。而其他学者的认识与韦勒克恰恰相反,比如雷马克和韦斯坦因,他们就认为不应该扩大比较文学的学科边界,因为这样做无疑会使研究对象太过繁杂,不利于展开平行比较;韦斯坦因认为东西方没有可比性,因为东西方文学之间找不到相同性。尽管从表面上看,美国学派学者韦勒克、雷马克和韦斯坦因的主张各异,但显然他们研究的立足点都是站在"求同"的基础上的,他们都没有认识到比较文学的异质性和变异性。学者们彼此间相互对立的观点说明他们看到了比较文学学科存在的危机,即异质文明之间究竟可比与不可比的问题,但却没有解释清楚这种可比与不可比的真正深层次原因。或许因为他们处于同一西方文明圈中,没有强烈的意向来解释异质文明文学之间的可比性问题。

平行研究也存在变异,却一直未被理解和重视。通常情况下,比较文学学者认为只有影响关系研究中才存在变异,而不会想到平行研究中也存在变异。平行研究中的

---

① 韦勒克.比较文学的名称与性质[M]//干永昌,等.比较文学研究译文集.上海:上海译文出版社,1985:144.

② 韦勒克.今日之比较文学[M]//干永昌,等.比较文学研究译文集.上海:上海译文出版社,1985:165.

变异问题,是指在研究者的阐发视野中,在两个完全不同的研究对象的交汇处产生了双方的阐释变异因子。不同文明的异质性导致不同文明在交流与碰撞中必然会产生变异,而这种变异也体现在双方的阐释交汇处,这也正是平行研究的最根本之处。话语的变异是平行研究中最有代表性的变异研究。东西方文明都各自拥有一套属于自己的话语体系,有自己特有的话语规则。用西方话语来解释中国文学时,由于阐释的标准属于西方话语体系,与中国话语体系存在异质性,不仅会带给中国文学崭新的理解维度,而且西方话语本身也可能会发生变异。这一点,最明显地体现在台湾学者提出来的比较文学“阐发法”之中。这种以中释西、以西释中,或者中西双向阐发时所发生的一些误读、误解,都属于平行研究中的变异现象。例如,颜元叔用西方弗洛伊德理论来阐发李商隐的诗歌,认为李商隐诗“春蚕到死丝方尽,蜡炬成灰泪始干”中的“蜡炬”,就是男性生殖器象征,这种“创造性的阐发”引起了叶嘉莹的反驳,叶嘉莹认为颜元叔严重误读李商隐诗歌。这就是典型的阐发变异。

二、变异学的特点与可比性基础

(一)变异学的特点

影响研究求的可比性是“同源性”,即流传或渊源的同一性;平行研究求的可比性是“类同性”,即不同国家文学、文学与其他学科之间的类同性。影响研究和平行研究都认为,可比性的共同特点是求同,求不同国家中的同,在他们看来,求同才具有可比性,没有同,就没有可比性。美国学者韦斯坦因在《比较文学与文学理论》中说:“我不否认有些研究是可以的……但却对把文学现象的平行研究扩大到两个不同的文明之间仍然迟疑不决,因为在我看来,只有在一个单一的文明范围内,才能在思想、感情、想象力中发现有意识或无意识地维系传统的共同因素。……而企图在西方和中东或远东的诗歌之间发现相似的模式则较难言之成理。”①显然,西方学者大多忽略了比较中异质性与变异性的可比性问题,这是比较文学现有学科理论的一个严重不足之处。

就大的学术语境而言,解构主义和跨文明研究两大思潮都是强调差异性的,在解构主义和跨文明研究两大思潮的影响下,差异性问题已经成为当今全世界学术研究的核心问题,是全球学术界关注的焦点。而对文明差异的关注正是当下我们不得不触及的一个学术前沿问题。面对当今文化逐步趋向多元综合的发展态势,不同文明间的冲突与对话关系成为一个越来越受关注的话题。中国当下的比较文学研究应该直面异质文明间的冲突与对话问题,正是在这样的学术背景下,中国学者提出了比较文学变

---

① 韦斯坦因.比较文学与文学理论[M].刘象愚,译.沈阳:辽宁人民出版社,1987:5.

异学的理论。比较文学变异学有利于促进异质文明的相互对话，建构“和而不同”的世界，实现不同文明之间的沟通和融合。

(二)变异学的可比性基础

比较不仅仅是从“同”的角度来画出一个圈，然后在这个圈中带着镣铐跳舞。对“异”的分析和清理，其实也是一种比较。不同文明之间的异质性也具有比较的价值，也就是说异质性也具有可比性。这就是比较文学变异学的基本思路。需要明确指出的是，变异学的可比性与法美学派的同源性与类同性等可比性不是截然对立的，而是相互依赖和相互包容的。变异学并非一味强调差异，也并非主张在没有影响关系的事物之间进行一通乱比。变异学强调异质性的可比性，是有严格的限定的，这种限定是在比较文学影响研究与平行研究可比性基础之上的一次延伸与补充，即在有同源性和类同性的文学现象之间找出异质性和变异性。例如，禅宗与佛教有相当的差异，但是不管发生多少变异，它依然可以回溯到源头——印度佛教。也就是说，进行比较的两者不管表面上有多大的差异，但是有“源”与“流”的关系。在影响关系研究中，变异学追求的是同源中的变异性；如果没有“同源”，也就谈不上什么“变异”。在平行研究中，任何不同国家的文学实际上都有异质性，尤其当研究对象分属不同的文明圈时，异质性更是明显。变异学主张，在研究对象之间要首先找到类同性，然后才能进一步研究变异性，并阐释类同性背后的差异及原因。如“崇高”等西方话语与《文心雕龙》中“风骨”一词，意思虽然不完全相同①，但是它们与“风骨”并非完全没有类同性，它们还是存在某种程度上的类同关联。又如用浪漫主义来阐释李白，现实主义来概括杜甫，虽然不是绝对类同，但是李白与浪漫主义、杜甫与现实主义毕竟是有一定的类同相契之处。变异学主张在这种类同性基础之上，再进一步分析研究对象之间的异质性，阐释其中发生的变异及探索其深层文化机制。

变异学的理论核心：异质性与可比性。比较文学变异学的提出，使比较文学学科从最初求“同源性”拓展到现在求“变异性、异质性”。也就是说，比较文学变异学不仅关注同源性、类同性，更关注变异性、异质性。提出异质性是比较文学的可比性，或者说比较文学可比性的基础是异质性，这无疑是对比较文学原有学科理论的一大挑战，同时也是一大突破和转向。

异质性为何会成为比较文学可比性的基础？既然以往的比较研究都是求“同”的，现在提倡的“异”可比吗？它比较的基础何在？这是比较文学可比性原则提出的

① “风骨作为一个完整的概念，就是要求文章‘刚健既实，辉光乃新’，在思想艺术方面具有刚健，遒劲的力的表现，像鹰隼展翼疾飞那样‘骨劲而气猛’，这正是当时文艺作品普遍缺乏的。”参阅敏泽.中国文学理论批评史(上册)[M].北京：人民文学出版社，1981：3.

问题,也是比较文学变异学必须回答的问题。

弗朗索瓦·于连认为,文明的异质性,"这是一个要害问题,我们正处在一个西方概念模式标准化的时代。这使得中国人无法读懂中国文化,日本人无法读懂日本文化,因为一切都被重新结构了。中国古代思想正在逐渐变成各种西方概念,其实中国思想有它自身的逻辑。在中国古文中,引发思考的往往是词与词之间的相关性、对称性、网络性,是它们相互作用的方式。如果忽视了这些,中国思想的精华就丢掉了。"[①]所以,当下的比较文学研究就是要从中国文化自身的逻辑出发,在与西方的对话中,坚持一个自身的基本话语规范和价值立场,不能盲目用"比较"一词来否定文明之间的异质性。而于连的整个思想体系也就是围绕中国思想与西方思想的"差异性"与"无关性"来展开的,也可以说是用"差异"来进行比较的;于连在中西比较中主动求"异",通过"异"的比较来还原文明自身的原生态,让这些独立性、自主性的文明用自己的话语规则来言说,继而进行优势互补,对话融通。

【原典选读】

文学借鉴与比较文学研究

◉约瑟夫·T. 肖

【导读】约瑟夫·T. 肖的《文学借鉴与比较文学研究》收录在 1984 年出版的由北京师范大学中文系比较文学研究组编写的《比较文学资料》中,该书辑录了 34 篇文章,多是中外知名学者的代表性作品。约瑟夫·T. 肖的这篇文章一直被认为是探讨影响研究的,但观览全文,文中已透露出文学变异的成分,只是这种成分多年来没有得到相应的重视。实证性是比较文学影响研究的基本特点,但是随着比较文学学科理论的发展,尤其在 20 世纪 50 年代以来,影响研究已不再是单纯的国际间文学关系史的研究。由于接受美学的冲击,越来越多的美学因素和心理学因素加入到影响研究的具体实践当中,因此我们应该认识到比较文学影响研究所具有的双重性特点:实证性与非实证性特征。

在这篇论文里,约瑟夫·T. 肖总结了文学借鉴的 7 种术语,这其中既有影响的实证性特点又有影响的非实证特点。如在文学翻译中,肖提醒人们注意文学翻译过程中会出现的变化,认为应该将翻译作品本身看作文学作品,因为每一个译者都会使译作符合"自己时代的口味",译者选择作品进行翻译的时候有一种"选择性共鸣",这种共

---

① 秦海鹰. 关于中西诗学的对话——于连访谈录[J]. 中国比较文学,1996(2).

鸣即译者根据自己的文化传统对作品进行过滤的过程,进而在译著中体现出译者的“创造性叛逆”。译作可能偏重于一个作家的某一些作品或他创作个性的某一些方面,排斥或忽视他的另一些作品和他的创作个性的另一些方面。这种在翻译、译作中出现的变异,我们可以统称为翻译的变异。又如,在文学创作方面,约瑟夫·T.肖认为,文学的借鉴与直接的借用是文学学术研究的主要内容,并且这类研究在比较文学中具有不可替代的地位。他举例说,如果要对莎士比亚进行全面研究,就必须了解他如何借鉴薄伽丘和荷林舍德,又如何加以改造。这种在创作中出现的变异即文学文本的变异。除了以上的变异外,还有一种情况是在跨文化传播的过程中出现的语言变异,肖提醒到,“另外一种语言的辞句、隐喻、明喻、文体和语汇是不能直接借用的,必须加以变革,使之符合本民族的文学传统才行”。这就造成了跨文化传播中语言变异的必然性。

约瑟夫·T.肖又指出,“文学影响的种子必须落在休耕的土地上”,而“作家与传统必须准备接受、转化这种影响,并作出反应。各种影响的种子都可能降落,然而只有那些落在条件具备的土地上的种子才能够发芽,每一粒种子又将受到它扎根在那里的土壤和气候的影响……”因此,在影响中变异是必然的。最后,肖提出应该对作家和文学的影响加以研究,而这类研究的中心应该重在考虑哪些因素被吸收了,哪些被变革了,哪些被排斥了。这就是我们今天所说的变异研究,以往的比较文学研究过分地强调了影响研究的实证性特点,放逐了文学的审美性与文学性,事实上,影响研究还有自身的非实证性特点。■

在一些文学研究,尤其是在比较文学的研究中,文学借鉴的研究始终是一个非常重要的分支。可是,对这种研究的价值及其效果却一直存在着种种疑问,以致近来不得不对此作一番辩解了。出源考证受到反对,说是过于轻率,是为考证而考证,文学影响的研究受到多方面的攻击。有人觉得影响这个概念是“实证主义”的,据此而予以否定。决定论者也否定它:一种意见认为,有意义的是民族——社会——经济的决定作用,而不是国际的与文学的决定作用;另一种意见是纯文学的决定论,主张文学研究应该局限于技巧本身,本国文学传统中的“历史必然性”可以决定一切,包括从外国输入的影响,因此,所谓外国影响是一个毫无意义的概念。不久前,还有一种意见认为,影响只能联系作者的个性和个人心理来考虑,而他的文学创作则只能从文学传统的角度去研究,看作基本独立的东西。

然而,直接的文学关系和文学借鉴的研究却仍然是文学学术研究的主要内容,任何较新的文学研究的书目都可以表明,这类研究在比较文学中依然占有重要地位。被人认为可以取而代之的各种研究领域，无论是平行类同的研究，各种“流派”的研究，具体作品的艺术分析，或是各种主题及其在各个时代、各种文学中不同处理的研究等，都不能取消直接文学关系这一项研究存在的理由。对一位作家进行认真的研究和分析，必须考察他的作品的各个组成部分，它们的含义与相互关系，它们是怎样提供给作家的，它们对于作家和他的作品有什么意义。莎士比亚如何取材于薄伽丘和荷林舍德，又如何加以改造，即使是反对出源考证和影响研究的人，也没有一个会认为了解这一点是毫无意义的。莎士比亚、拜伦和司各特在19世纪的欧洲遐迩闻名，继而有了后来各国文学中大量作品的产生。如果没有这些英国作家的作品，或者他们没有那样闻名，那么，起码也难以想象这些国家的文学作品在形式和内容两方面会是什么样子。对于这一点，也不会有人提出疑义。《堂·吉诃德》和亨利·菲尔丁的小说之间有什么关系，仅在身世经历、社会发展、文学体裁和传统等方面去刨根问底，也是得不到恰如其分的解释的。

一些学者和批评家，包括许多研究文学借鉴的学者和批评家，觉得指出某位作家的文学借鉴似乎就会抹煞他的独创性。其实，独创性不应该仅仅理解为创新。许多伟大作家并不以承认别人对他们的影响为耻辱，许多人甚至把自己借鉴他人之处和盘托出。他们觉得所谓独创性并不仅仅包括，甚至主要并不在于内容、风格和方法上的创新，而在于创作的艺术感染力的真诚有效。没有艺术感染力的创新只有形式主义者才会感兴趣。使读者受到真切的美的感染，产生独立的艺术效果的作品，无论借鉴了什么，都具有艺术的独创性。有独创性的作家并不一定是发明家或别出心裁，而是能将借鉴别人的东西揉进新的意境，在造就完全属于他自己的艺术品的过程中获得成功的人。

一个国家的一个或几个作家被另一个国家接受，而且流行并普及开来，这就是文学之间直接的相互联系。在某一种文学或某一个时代中，外国作家被接受，成为文学鉴赏趣味直接而不可分割的一部分，就会影响到本国作家的读者群，也会影响本国作家本人的艺术和批评意识。现在已经有了研究接受和流行普及的各种复杂而依然有效的方法。报纸、刊物、日记上的评论能反映出一个作家被接受和普及的程度，文学作品中也会提及。这些在作家的作品的销量、版数和翻译情况中也能部分反映出来。

关于接受和普及，有一个方面很容易被忽略，这就是一个作家的作品在某一个国家通行的语言中的可获取程度。例如，英国文学在美国是可以接受的，反之亦然。同样，十八和十九世纪时，法国文学在俄国也可以直接接受，用其他语言写作的作家可以通过法文译本传递给对文学感兴趣的俄国人。十九世纪时，英、德、意等国文学大都是通过法文译本传到俄国上流社会的。这样，在研究接受时就必须经常考虑媒介语言的问题——什么样的作品可能被译成那种语言，在翻译过程中又会出现什么变化等。

某些作家，甚至某些文学运动，可能对社会的全部或其大部产生一种非文学或文学以外的影响。例如，伏尔泰、拜伦，或托尔斯泰的思想、行为甚至服饰，在当时或以后的各个社会中都可能有广泛的表现。这种社会行为可能有助于一个作家的社会意识的形成，而这个作家与那个外国作家的作品未必有直接的联系，但是，他却可能在文学中表现出这种社会意识。

一个作家在另一个国家被接受，会引起整个文学的相当一部分被这个国家接受。拜伦在欧洲的声誉多多少少促成了汤马斯·摩尔以及与他同时代的其他作家在欧洲的名望，在某些国家中，甚至可能间接地推动了十九世纪对莎士比亚的崇拜。屠格涅夫在西方被接受又使得托尔斯泰、陀思妥耶夫斯基以及整个俄国近代文学在西方被接受。为什么有些作家容易输出，有些却不行——为什么拜伦比他的同代人在国外的声誉更隆，这些问题倒是耐人寻味的。另一方面，一个作家或他的作品被某一作家个人或某一国文化所接受，又必须与文学影响严格加以区别，尽管这种接受确实可能推动或提供媒介物来促成文学影响的产生。一个作家可能在另一个国家相当流行，却对它的文学并不产生显著的影响。

奇怪的是，似乎还没有人把表示文学借鉴的种种术语一一对比，以便明确定义并加以区别。最需要明确定义并加以讨论的术语是翻译、模仿、仿效、借用、出源、类同和影响。

翻译（translation）是一项创造性的工作；翻译者把用另一种语言写成的、往往是不同时代的作品引进他那个时代的本国文学传统里。现代翻译家往往完全忠实于原著的形式和内容，尽力用新的语言再现原作的风貌，也许正是因为这个缘故，翻译作品没有被看作本身就是文学作品而得到足够的研究。然而，每一个翻译者多多少少都在使他的译作符合自己时代的口味，使他所翻译的过去时代的作品现代化。以往的翻译理论和实践允许对原作作一定的删节、增补和释义，形式可以改动，文体也往往可以变化。波齐奥里教授认为译者对原作有一种“选择性共鸣”（elective affinity），即使他的译文不能尽原文之妙，他选择哪一部作品进行翻译，至少可以反映出他对这部作品的共鸣。因此，翻译不仅属于某一外国作家在某种文学中被接受情形的研究范畴，而且也属于文学本身的研究范畴。它们提供了外国作品与本国作品之间最好的媒介，外国作品的形式和内容往往要经过更改和翻译，对本国文学才能发挥最大的影响，因为只有这种形式才能被文学传统直接吸收，其实，它本身就已经成了这个文学传统的一部分。

所谓模仿（imitation），就是说，作家尽可能地将自己的创造个性服从于另一个作家，一般是服从于某一部作品，但又不像翻译那样在细节上处处忠实于原作。模仿往往是艺术家发展过程中的一种学习手段。学者和批评家们往往对此嗤之以鼻，然而，它却有其独立的美学价值。普希金曾指出，模仿并不一定是“思想贫乏”的表现，它可能标志着一种“对自己的力量的崇高的信念，希望能沿着一位天才的足迹去发现新的世界，或者是一种在谦恭中反而更加高昂的情绪，希望能掌握自己所尊崇的范本，并赋予它新的生命。”仿作可能是整部的作品，也可能是局部；偶尔也可能是对一个作家总的风格的模仿，而不限于具体的细节。

与模仿有关却又最好加以区分的是仿效（stylization）。出于某种艺术目的，作家的风格和内容表现出别的作家、别的作品，甚或某一时期的风格特征。例如，普希金常常用仿效的手法传达某种气氛或背景。他在《波尔塔瓦》中表现彼得大帝时就稍稍仿效了十八世纪的英雄诗体。普希金的《致大海》是他为悼念拜伦而作的唯一的悼亡诗。其中一段使人联想起拜伦，流露出他对拜伦的几分赞颂；当然，全诗与拜伦的风格相去甚远，此时的普希金也已经改变了他早年对这位同时代的英国诗人的赞赏态度。

借用（borrowing）是作家取用现成的素材或方法，特别是格言、意象、比喻、主题、情节成分等。借用的来源可以是作品，也可以是报纸、谈话报道或评论。借用可以是一种暗指，隐隐约约表明其文学上的出处；也间或有某种仿效的成分。古代和现代的许多老练的作家都认为他们的读者能够从字里行间辨别它们，批评家和学者的任务则是指出新作中借用的素材与老作品有什么关系——借用的巧妙之处。

出源（source）这个词经常用来表示借用的出处。在文学研究中，“出源”的这一用法似乎应该与为某作品提供素材或基本素材——尤其是情节这一意义上的“出源”明确区分开来。这里所谓的出源不一定为一部作品提供，甚或启发作品的形式，一般说来，出处提供的素材与作品的形式是两码事。普希金的《鲍里斯·戈都诺夫》的出源是卡拉姆辛的《编年史》，莎士比亚的出源是荷林舍德和薄伽丘，而他们的艺术手法都来自别处。

以上种种术语都表示文学作品中的一种直接联系。平行类同（parallels）是另一个有研究价值又很有意思的题目。有时，一部作品同时与几部作品在素材上类似，借用的直接出源发生疑问，这时，只有足够的排斥其他可能性的类同之处才能决定其确凿的出源，就像日尔蒙斯基教授论证普希金所运用的拜伦式浪漫诗体小说是直接来自拜伦那样。除了这一类平行类同之外，还有不同作家、不同文学，或者不同时代之间在形式和内容方面的相似现象，它们之间并没有明显的直接联系。比较类似作品对于其中每一部作品的评论来说是非常有趣又非常有价值的。这些平行类同的作品可能有共同的出源，也可能没有。它们经常包含在文学运动中，显然由不同的文学产生，一般说来，主要是各自的文学传统作用的结果，例如狄更斯和果戈理的情形就是这样。平行类同的研究，如同其他文学现象的研究一样，其价值在于帮助我们更好地理解具体作品的质量和优劣，也有助于揭示各民族文学传统之间的异同。研究平行类同的作品时，直接影响的可能性当然应该加以考虑。最近，一位对莱蒙托夫的《恶魔》与维尼的《埃罗阿》作比较研究的作者，竟然连莱蒙托夫是否读过维尼的作品都未加以考虑，更不必说那些异同点是否是有意识的反应了。

一位作家和他的艺术作品，如果显示出某种外来的效果，而这种效果又是他的本国文学传统和他本人的发展无法解释的，那么，我们可以说这位作家受到了外国作家的影响（influence）。影响与模仿不同，被影响的作家的作品基本上是他本人的。影响并不局限于具体的细节、意象、借用，甚或出源——当然，这些都包括在内——而是一种渗透在艺术作品之中，成为艺术作品有机的组成部分，并通过艺术作品再现出来的东西。仍然以普希金的《鲍里斯·戈都诺夫》为例，主要的影响并不是出源——卡拉姆辛的《编年史》，而是莎士比亚的人物塑造，情节安排和戏剧形式。一个作家所受的文学影响，最终将渗透到他的文学作品之中，成为作品的有机部分，从而决定他们的作品的基本灵感和艺术表现，如果没有这种影响，这种灵感和艺术表现就不会以这样的形式出现，或者不会在作家的这个发展阶段上出现。文学影响的种子必须落在休耕的土地上。作家与传统必须准备接受、转化这种影响，并作出反应。各种影响的种子都可能降落，然而只有那些落在条件具备的土地上的种子才能够发芽，每一粒种子又将受到它扎根在那里的土壤和气候的影响，或者，换一个比方，嫁接的嫩枝要受到砧木的影响。

当民族文学刚刚诞生，或当某一文学的传统发生方向上的突变时，文学影响显得最为频繁，成效也最为显著。它还可能伴随着社会政治运动，尤其是动乱发生。如同一切文学现象那样，它不仅具有文学的背景，而且具有社会的，甚至常常是政治的背景。文学形式与美学情趣一旦落伍过时，作家们就可能从本国文学过去的表现形式中去寻求适应眼前需要的答案；他们也可能向国外探索，去发现能表现和满足他们的文学意愿的东西。民族文学刚刚诞生时，作家们会去寻求那些略加改变即能适应他们的觉悟、时代和民族意识的内容和表现形式。一般说来，国内外相互对立的文学运动和代表人物这时会同时出现，各种不同的、可能被吸收的国外影响会纷至沓来。例如，在十八、十九世纪，法国、德国和英国的作家和文学就相继或同时影响过俄国的作家和文学传统。

有意义的影响必须以内在的形式在文学作品中表现出来，它可以表现在文体、意象、人物形象、主题或独特的手法风格上，它也可以表现在具体作品所反映出的内容、思想、意念或总的世界观上。当然，列出令人信服的作品之外的证据来说明被影响的作家可能受产生影响作家的影响，是完全必要的。为此，各种文献记载、引语、日记、同代人的见证和作者的阅读书目等都必须加以运用。可是，最基本的证明又必须在作品的本身。具体的借用是否表现为影响，取决于它们在新作中的作用和重要程度；而影响并不一定包括具体的借用。考察一位作家的发展过程时，影响研究显得格外有趣。例如，普希金在自己的文学生涯的每个阶段中，就吸收发展了拜伦的浪漫诗体小说、莎士比亚的历史悲剧和司各特的历史小说。影响可能局限在某种体裁之内，也可能超出它的范围之外。在一部作品中可能同时存在一系列的影响，例如在《卡拉玛佐夫兄弟》中，陀斯妥耶夫斯基在塑造梯米特里、伊凡和佐西玛神父的形象时就分别受席勒、歌德和《帕芬尼修道士的游历》的影响，但整个作品又完全是他本人的，他所运用的这些影响只是大大丰富了这部作品。

文学作品对文学作品的影响，论证起来也许最能令人信服，在美学研究上也最有兴味。此外，还有一种对作家个人的影响。这种影响可能来自一位文学家，也可能来自非文学家；它往往表现在内容方面，而不在体裁和风格方面。正如特鲁门·卡波特最近对一批俄国作家所指出的，非文学家弗洛伊德就是对西方文学产生了最大影响的人物之一。从柏拉图和亚里士多德到托玛斯·阿奎那、黑格尔、阿尔弗莱德·诺斯·怀特海德和卡尔·马克思，哲学家和思想家们对作家都往往发生影响。个人影响与文学影响有时会重合一致，例如马拉美和瓦勒里的情况就是这样。作家的国际声誉和影响在很大程度上取决于他们对世界观、对一个国家和一个时期的文学传统所提供的或被认为提供了的答案。

文学影响的研究中，最复杂的问题之一是所谓直接影响和间接影响的问题。一个作家将一个外国作家的影响引入文学传统，然后，如同俄国的拜伦式传统那样，它就会随着本国作家的影响而向前发展。随着这种传统的继续，另一个本国作家又会去向这个外国作家索求第一个作家没有采用的素材、色调、意象或效果，于是，这种影响又被进一步丰富了。例如，莱蒙托夫受到普希金和其他俄国作家的拜伦式诗体小说的影响，可是，他又回到拜伦那里，直接寻求那些被普希金忽略或更改过的特点。

在比较文学中，文学影响有一些特别的方面，其中之一与翻译有关，我们已经讨论过翻译问题，然而仍有必要再看一看。即使有了一个能够阅读外国作品原著的读者群，或者一个通过媒介语言能够阅读原著的读者群，一部作品在被翻译之前，在本国传统中为它找到适当的文体、形式和语汇之前，仍不真正属于这个民族的传统。作品经过了翻译，经常会有一些人为的更动，也会有一些释义，然而，在吸收和传递文学影响方面，译作却有着特殊的作用。直接影响往往产生于译作而不是原作。译作可能偏重于一个作家的某一些作品和他的创作个性的某一些方面，排斥或忽视他的另一些作品和他的创作个性的另一些方面。例如，拜伦作品最早的诗体翻译是茹柯夫斯基的《希隆的囚徒》和科兹洛夫的《阿比多斯的新嫁娘》，这一点对于拜伦传统在俄国的进一步发展有着非常重要的意义。

不同语言之间的文学语汇和文体的影响问题，大概迄今为止还没有得到足够的研究。每一个时代都会产生自己的文学语言，它既有继承本民族文学传统的成分，也有与传统相对立的成分。在模仿和翻译外国作家时，作家的任务是将原作的文体和语言加以变革，以适应他自己的时代、语言和文学传统的需要。模仿者和翻译家在这种变革过程中往往为他的文学传统带进一些新东西，不但在体裁和内容方面，也在文体和语汇方面。另外一种语言的辞句、隐喻、明喻、文体和语汇是不能直接借用的，必须加以变革，使之符合本民族的文学传统才行。

在比较文学中，一个特殊的影响问题是关于接受与影响的时间问题。十九世纪时，莎士比亚影响了英国文学，也影响了许多外国文学，在这些影响中，对莎士比亚的鉴赏和重新解释可能有不少共同点。然而，莎士比亚在十九世纪的法国或俄国的影响与在英国的影响却大不相同，因为莎士比亚在本国始终闻名，并具有一定的影响。重新评价并不等于新发现。莎士比亚在十九世纪英国文学传统中的位置与他在其他国家文学传统中的地位是迥然有别的。产生影响的作家必须与他从事写作、发生影响的文学传统联系起来加以研究。每个时代和国家的文学背景不同，一个作家或一种文学产生的影响也将随着不同的时代要求而变化。文学中的新成分与那些始终存在并为人熟知的成分有质的不同，后者只是相对的不活跃而已。

我相信，这一番对文学关系的浏览表明，对接受和普及的研究，对各种直接的文学借鉴包括文学影响在内的研究，仍然是大有必要的。只要严谨、慎重，这种研究对于了解作家、作品和文学运动都有帮助。最容易收到成效的有待于进一步研究的领域也许是那些新近崭露头角的民族文学。最近，越来越多的材料已将这些研究不断推向过去；有人已经提出了这样的疑问，为什么这种研究通常总是只从文艺复兴或文艺复兴之后才开始。

我认为，甚至是最好的文学借鉴的研究对具体作品之间内在关系仍旧钻研得不够深入细致。例如，埃斯代夫关于拜伦在法国的极为重要的研究，无疑是接受和普及的最好的比较研究之一，它出色地阐述了拜伦在法国被接受的过程，讨论了拜伦的哪些方面对哪些法国作家产生了影响，可是，一旦人们想了解具体作品之间的关系，想评价和分析接受了拜伦影响的作品时，就会觉得它非常令人失望。在研究得最多的文学接触中，一般的结论都是非常正确的，然而，许多有价值的独到见解仍然有待于发掘。

对作家和文学的影响应该研究，这是理解二者的需要。这种研究应该考虑哪些因素被吸收了，哪些被变革了，哪些被排斥了。注意力的重心应该放在借用或受影响的作家所吸收的东西干了些什么，对完成的文学作品又产生了什么效果。在理解和评价一部作品时，不但要将它置于文学传统之中，而且要给它下一个确切的定义，说明它所要达到的目的，以及它的成功之处在哪里。要做到这些，直接的文学关系和文学借鉴的研究是必不可少的。

（北京师范大学中文系比较文学研究组. 比较文学资料[M]. 盛宁，译. 1984.）

比较文学学科中的文学变异学研究（节选）

◉曹顺庆　李卫涛

（一）

将“文学变异学”作为比较文学的一个研究领域，是一个新的提法。这个研究领域的确立，是从比较文学学科领域的现状、文学发展的历史实践以及比较文学学科理论的拓展几个方面来综合考虑的。

首先，所谓当下比较文学学科研究领域的失范是指比较文学自身的研究领域没有一个明确的研究对象和研究范围，而且有些理论阐述还存在很多纷乱之处。其中存在于影响研究中的实证性与审美性的纷争中就突出地表现了这种比较文学学科领域的失范现象。

影响研究的法国学派最初之所以提出国际文学关系史理论，一方面回应了当时克罗齐等人对比较文学的非难，另一方面也考虑到作为一个学科必须有一个科学性基础，所以他们提出比较文学不是文学的比较，而是一种实证性的国际间文学关系史的研究。但是，后来美国学者却质疑了法国学派的影响研究单纯强调科学实证而放逐审美价值的学科定位，认为他们的影响研究是僵硬的外部研究和文学史研究，提出要“正视‘文学性’这个问题”①，因为“文学性”是美学的中心问题，是文学艺术作品得以存在的内在规定性。也就是说，比较文学应该把美学价值批评重新引进比较文学学科领域之中。

但是，一旦文学性介入比较文学的影响研究实践之中，就使得我们面前的比较文学研究出现了新的困扰。这主要是因为传统的影响研究以实证性探寻为研究定位，当然如果仅仅对于“国际文学关系史”②的研究来说，这种实证性的影响研究本来也无可厚非，但是对于一种文学的比较研究来说，它却存在着一定的缺陷。这主要是因为，实证性的影响研究想要求证的是人类的美学艺术创作过程中存在的接受和借鉴规律，“实证能证明科学事实和科学规律，但不能证明艺术创造与接受上的审美意义”③。也就是说，要从文学艺术的外部研究来揭示其文学内部的规律性，这当然是非常困难的。所以，影响又被称为是“像难以捉摸而又神秘的机理一样的东西，通过这种机理，一部作品对产生出另一部作品而作

---

① 韦勒克. 比较文学的危机[C]//干永昌，等. 比较文学研究译文集. 上海：上海译文出版社，1985：30.

② 马·法·基亚. 比较文学[M]. 颜保，译. 北京：北京大学出版社，1983：1.

③ 陈思和. 20世纪中外文学关系研究中的“世界性因素”的几点思考[J]. 中国比较文学，2001(1)：18.

出贡献”①。就连强调实证影响研究的伽列(Carte 又译卡雷)都认为影响研究“做起来是十分困难的,而且经常是靠不住的。在这种研究中,人们往往试图将一些不可称量的因素加以称量”②。

所以说,文学审美性介入比较文学研究之后,影响研究就不应该还是一种单纯的文学关系史研究了。然而,当下我们的许多比较文学教材在处理影响研究的时候还没有很好地解决文学史研究和文学性研究的关系问题,还是将二者纠结在一起。比如在阐释媒介学的时候,还是把实证性的文学媒介考证与译介学混杂在一起,这样造成的后果就是没有办法真正把译介学出现的非实证性“创造性叛逆”说清楚。可以说,当下的译介学已经不是简单的语词翻译了,它更关注于文学性因素在不同语言体系中出现的变异现象。但是由于以前的影响研究特征过于模糊,所以就造成了译介学无法获得恰当的研究定位。实际上,比较文学中的实证性研究和审美性研究并不是不可两全的,我们没有必要将二者在影响研究中纠缠不清,完全可以将二者分为两个不同的研究领域。一个是实证性的文学关系史研究领域;另一个则不再只注意文学现象之间的外部影响研究,而是将文学的审美价值引入比较研究,从非实证性的角度来进一步探讨文学现象之间的艺术和美学价值上新的变异所在,是属于文学变异学研究领域。

其次,提出文学变异学的研究领域,是有充分的文学历史发展实践的支持的。这是因为,从人类文学的历史发展形态上看,文学形式和内容最具有创造力和活力的时代,往往是不同国家民族文学,乃至不同文化/文明之间碰撞、互相激荡的时代。这些时期的社会文化和文学不会保持静态,它往往表现为不同体系的文化和文学之间碰撞激荡、交流汇聚、相互融合的状态,它是各种文学基因发生“变异”并形成新质的最佳时期。所以,这些时期会在文学上呈现出生机勃勃、丰富多彩、新异多变的创造性面貌。比如中国魏晋南北朝时段的文学局面就是一个典型的例证。虽然此一时期社会动荡不安,甚至战乱频仍,但是正是由于印度佛教文化/文学因素大量被引入中土,刺激了中国本土的文学创造力,当然还有中国南北朝文学的彼此交流和融合,所以在文学和文学理论方面都留下了许多不朽的篇章。探究这种文学横向发展现象的内在实质,就是不同文化/文学体系之间的冲突和交流,“能够激活冲突双方文化的内在的因子,使之在一定的条件中进入亢奋状态。无论是欲求扩展自身的文化,还是希冀保守自身的文化,文化机制内部都会发生一系列的‘变异’”③。本土文化/文学体系自身出现的变异因素往往就是文化与文学新质的萌芽,而这种具有创造力的新因素最终推动了文学的发展。

---

① 布吕奈尔,等.什么是比较文学[M].葛雷,等,译.北京:北京大学出版社,1989:74.

② J-M.伽列.比较文学初版序言[M]//北京师范大学中文系比较文学研究组.比较文学研究资料.北京:北京师范大学出版社,1986.43.

③ 严绍璗.论“文化语境”与“变异体”以及文学的发生学[J].中国比较文学,2000(3):10.

而且,这种外来的异质性文学因素所引起的文学变异现象甚至使得本土固有的传统得以变迁,这样的文学变异就成为一个复杂的动态过程。变异的文学现象促进了本土文学的发展,并逐渐融入本土文学的传统中,形成后世文学的典范。比如闻一多在论及中国古代文学史的时候,肯定了佛教文学对中国文学产生的重大推动作用,认为如果没有外来的文学因素的介入,中国本土文学就不会有那么多变异性的发展,北宋以后的“中国文学史可能不必再写”①。确实,魏晋以降的佛教文学流传进入中土,中国古代文学在这种横向的冲击下,吸收和借鉴,产生了新的文学变异因素,我们今天所说的深受外来文学因素影响的中国禅宗以及变文、小说、戏剧早已成为中国文学自身的固有传统。而且,每个国别文学体系中出现的文学变异现象都是丰富而复杂的,因此对文学变异现象的研究理应成为比较文学研究的主要视角之一。

最后,提出文学变异学领域的原因还是因为我们当下的比较文学学科拓展已经改变了最初的求同思维,而走入求异思维的阶段。比较文学的法、美学派理论都是在单一的文明体系内部进行的,他们都是从求同思维来展开比较文学的研究。尤其对于没有实际关联的不同文明体系的文学现象之间的比较,美国学派的平行研究更是从一个共通的“文学性”层面出发,来研究它们之间的共同点的。它注重强调没有实际影响关系的文学现象之间的“某种关联性”②,这种所谓的关联性也就是韦斯坦因(Ulrich Weisstein)所谓的类同或者平行研究中存在的“亲和性”③。无论是“关联性”或是“亲和性”,都是一种以求同思维为中心的比较文学研究模式,这在单一的西方文学/文明体系中是很实际的一种研究范式。然而,当我们将比较文学的研究视野投向不同的文明体系中的文学比较的时候,就会发现除了一些基本的文学原则大致相同外,更多的是异质性的文学表现,更多的是面对同一个文学对象而形成的不同的文学表达形式或观念的变异。对不同文明体系的文学变异现象的研究曾被韦斯坦因等西方学者的求同思维所怀疑,这种“迟疑不决”④的心态正是比较文学求同思维的具体写照。那么,我们现在要做的就是要走出比较文学的求同,而要从异质性与变异性入手来重新考察和界定比较文学的文学变异学领域。而文学变异学的提出正是这种思维拓展的最好体现。

从上面三个方面来说,我们提出比较文学的变异学研究领域是对颇受争议的影响研究的研究对象和范围的重新规范,并且变异学还有古今中外的文学横向交流所带来的文

---

① 闻一多.文学发展中的予和受[M]//约翰·迪尼,刘介民.现代中国比较文学研究(第一册).成都:四川人民出版社,1988:214.

② 亨利·雷马克.比较文学的法国学派和美国学派[M]//北京师范大学中文系比较文学研究组.比较文学研究资料.北京:北京师范大学出版社,1986:71.

③ 乌尔利希·韦斯坦因.比较文学与文学理论[M].刘象愚,译.沈阳:辽宁人民出版社,1987:5.

④ 乌尔利希·韦斯坦因.比较文学与文学理论[M].刘象愚,译.沈阳:辽宁人民出版社,1987:36,5.

学变异实践作为支持，它更和当下比较文学跨文明研究中所强调的异质性的研究思维紧密结合。所以，比较文学的文学变异学的研究领域有着坚实的理论和实践基础。

（二）

如果将文学变异学作为比较文学的研究领域之一，那么，它在比较文学整个学科建构中的地位是怎样的呢？它和比较文学学科其他研究领域的彼此关系是如何的呢？这些都是我们需要给以明确界定的。

由此可见，跨越性和文学性作为比较文学的两个不可或缺的学科特质，也同样规定着比较文学学科研究领域的划分。如果说，法国学派的文学关系史的研究和美国学派的跨学科研究等都强调了对文学现象的跨越性研究，而成为比较文学的学科领域；那么，比较文学变异学研究领域刚好就是从跨越性和文学性这两点上面生发出去的，它是文学跨越研究和文学审美性研究的结合之处。因为最为切近比较文学的这两个学科特质，所以成为一个更为稳固的学科研究领域。和文学关系史研究相比较，它更为突出文学比较的审美变异因素，不但注重对有事实影响关系的文学变异现象的比较研究，而且也研究那些没有事实关系的，以及以前在平行研究中人们对同一个主题范畴表达上面出现的文学或者审美异质性因素，所以说，文学变异学研究领域是更为开阔的。

那么，从上文的这些论证中，我们就可以得出比较文学变异学的定义：比较文学变异学将比较文学的跨越性和文学性作为自己的研究支点，它通过研究不同国家之间的文学现象交流的变异状态，以及研究没有事实关系的文学现象之间在同一个范畴上存在的文学表达上的异质性和变异性，从而探究文学现象差异与变异的内在规律性所在。

（三）

分析了比较文学变异学提出的原因，以及真正的含义之后，那么作为一个比较文学学科的固定的研究领域，文学变异学也应该有自身明确的研究对象和研究范围。我们将从四个方面来辨析文学变异学可能的研究范围。

第一是语言层面变异学。它主要是指文学现象穿越语言的界限，通过翻译而在目的语环境中得到接受的过程，也就是翻译学或者译介学研究。国内一般的比较文学教材都沿用法国学派的观点，将译介学放入媒介学的研究范畴之中，但是由于媒介学属于传统实证的影响关系研究，而译介学却涉及了很多跨越不同语言与文化层面的变异因素在里面，所以我们很难将译介学归入此类。也就是说，“译介学最初是从比较文学中媒介学的角度出发、目前则越来越多是从比较文化的角度出发对翻译（尤其是文学翻译）和翻译文学进行的研究。”①由于当下视野中的译介学研究已经超越了传统的语词翻译研究的范畴，所强

① 谢天振. 译介学[M]. 上海：上海外语教育出版社，1999：1

调的已不是传统的“信、达、雅”，而是“创造性叛逆”。已经从传统的实证性研究，走向了一种比较文学视野下的文化与文学研究，那么译介学就不能用简单的实证影响关系来作为研究范式了，它已经超出了媒介学研究的范畴。而在这其中，我们要把研究的注意力从语词翻译研究转向那些语词的变异本身，也就是将文学的变异现象作为首要的研究对象。

第二是民族国家形象变异学研究，又称为形象学。形象学产生在20世纪的中叶，基亚（Guyard M. F.）在其《比较文学》一书中就专列一章“人们看到的外国”来论述形象学，并称之为比较文学研究“打开了一个新的研究方向”①。虽然后来韦勒克（Rene Wellek）以形象学是一种“社会心理学和文化史研究”来否定伽列和基亚的尝试②，但随着社会科学新理论的出现，形象学逐渐成为比较文学研究的分支之一。当然，形象学也从最早的实证性关系研究，而走入对一种文学和文化研究的范畴里面。形象学主要研究目的就是要研究在一国文学作品中表现出来的他国形象。在这里，他国形象只是主体国家文学的一种“社会集体想象物”③，正因为它是一种想象，所以使得变异成为必然。比较文学对于这个领域的研究显然是要注意这个形象产生变异的过程，并从文化/文学的深层次模式入手，来分析其规律性所在。

第三是文学文本变异学研究。比较文学研究的基点是文学性和文本本身，所以文学文本之间产生的可能的变异也将必然成为比较文学研究的范畴。首先它包括有实际交往的文学文本之间产生的文学接受的研究领域。文学接受是一个很热门的研究领域，正如谢夫莱尔（Yves Chevrel）所说，“‘接受’一词成为近15年来文学研究的主要术语之一”④。国内的多本比较文学概论也列出了专章来处理接受研究的问题，但问题是，接受研究目前还没确定一个明确的研究定位。它是影响的一种变体呢，还是不同于影响研究的新研究范式，它和影响研究的异同又在哪里呢？实际上，从变异学和文学关系学的角度来看文学接受学，问题就非常清楚了。它不同于文学关系研究，主要是因为后者是实证性的，而文学接受的过程却是有美学和心理学因素渗入，而最终无法证实的，是属于文学变异的范畴。其次，文学文本变异学研究还包括那些以前平行研究范畴内的主题学和文类学的研究。主题学和文类学虽然研究范围不同，但它们有一个共同点，就是二者都有法、美学派追求“类同”或者“亲和性”研究的影子。而实际上传统的主题学、文类学研究中，已经不可避免地涉及主题变异和文类变异问题，尤其在不同文明体系中，文本之间的主题和文类

① 马·法·基亚．比较文学［M］．颜保，译．北京：北京大学出版社，1983：1，170

② 韦勒克．比较文学的危机［M］//干永昌，等．比较文学研究译文集．上海：上海译文出版社，1985：125.

③ 让-马克·莫哈．试论文学形象学的研究史及方法论［M］//孟华．比较文学形象学．北京：北京大学出版社，2001：29.

④ 伊夫·谢夫莱尔．从影响到接受批评［M］//金丝燕，摘译．转引自乐黛云．比较文学原理．长沙：湖南文艺出版社，1988：245.

在类同之外，更多的却是不同之处，那么我们的比较文学研究的任务就是“不仅在求同，也在存其异”①。而且通过不同的文学主题和文类变异现象的研究，我们可以更为有效地展开不同文明体系间的文学对话，从而更为有效地总结人类的文学规律。

第四是文化变异学研究。文学在不同文化体系中穿越，必然要面对不同文化模式的问题。也就是说，“文化模子的歧异以及由此而起的文学的模子的歧异”②是比较文学研究者必然要面对的事情，文学因文化模子的不同而产生的变异是不可避免的事情。这其中，以文化过滤现象最为突出。文化过滤是指文学交流和对话过程中，接受者一方因为自己本身文化背景和传统而有意无意地对传播方文学信息进行选择、改造、删改和过滤的现象。文化过滤研究和文学接受研究很容易混淆，但是最为关键的，就是文化过滤主要是指由于文化“模子”的不同而产生的文学变异现象，而不是简单的文学主体的接受。同时，文化过滤带来一个更为明显的文学变异现象就是文学的误读，由于文化模式的不同造成文学现象在跨越文化圈时候造成一种独特的文化过滤背景下的文学误读现象。那么文化过滤和文学误读是怎么样的关联，它们彼此之间关系如何，它们是如何成对发生的，它们所造成的文学变异现象内在的规律性是什么，这都将是文化过滤和文学误读所主要探讨的问题。

这四个层面的变异研究共同构成了比较文学的文学变异学的研究领域。当然，作为一个全新的学科视角，变异学研究中还存在很多问题等待梳理，但可以肯定地说，文学变异学的研究范畴的提出，对于比较文学学科领域的明确，以及对于比较文学学科危机的解决无疑是一种有益的尝试。

（原载《复旦学报》2006 年 1 期）

【延伸阅读】

1. 曹顺庆. 南橘北枳：曹顺庆教授讲比较文学变异学[M]. 北京：中央编译出版社，2014.

《南橘北枳》是“比较文学与世界文学名家讲堂”20 卷丛书之一。本书是曹顺庆教授关于比较文学变异学的演讲稿与论文选集，是作者关于比较文学变异学学科理论在国内的第一次集中展现。《南橘北枳》全面集中地介绍了作者所提出的比较文学变异学的基本理论、意义与价值、研究领域及方法等。

---

① 张隆溪. 钱锺书谈比较文学与“文学比较”[M]//北京师范大学中文系比较文学研究组. 比较文学研究资料. 北京：北京师范大学出版社，1986：94.

② 叶维廉. 东西方文学中“模子的应用”[M]//温儒敏，李细尧. 寻求跨中西文化的共同文学规律——叶维廉比较文学论文选. 北京：北京大学出版社，1987：3.

2. Shunqing Cao, *The Variation Theory of Comparative Literature*, Berlin & Heidelberg: Springer, 2014.

曹顺庆教授英文专著《比较文学变异学》于2014年3月由世界知名出版机构Springer在德国海德堡、英国伦敦、美国纽约同时出版，受到世界学界的关注。此著作是比较文学中国学派的代表之作，世界比较文学学会前会长、荷兰乌特勒支大学教授佛克玛为此书作序，提出"比较文学变异学是对已有研究范式——'影响研究'和'平行研究'不足的回应"。

第二节 形象学

作为比文学变异学的一个研究领域，形象学（Imagologie）研究的是文学作品中以他者面目出现的民族国家形象，如"晚清文学中的西方人形象"或"战后日本文学中的美国形象"。作家在作品中展示的异国异族形象凝聚了作家个人的复杂情感，体现出的是不同国家、不同民族的巨大文化差异，这样的异国异族形象是作家对他者曲解、夸张与想象的产物。形象学不索隐求证这些形象的假与真，探究的是异国异族形象的创造过程和规律，分析其中包蕴的民族心理以及深层文化意蕴。

一、形象学的产生

"形象（Image）"及相关话题已经遍布世界的每一个角落，影响着我们的生活。所以，后现代理论家詹姆逊（Fredric Jameson）说："后现代主义文化也被称为形象文化。"[①]学术界针对现实生活中发达的形象文化，目前正逐步形成以形象设计及应用为宗旨的普通（一般）形象学。与文学相关的形象学应属于特殊形象学，它可以从普通形象学的学科理论和研究方法中获取本体论意义上的支持。

形象学随着比较文学学科的发展逐渐走向成熟。它萌芽于法国学派的影响研究，被法国学者划入"国际文学关系研究"范畴，是深受法国学派垂青的研究领域，也是受

① 许钧，等. 文学翻译的理论与实践——翻译对话录[M]. 北京：译林出版社，2001：257.

到美国学派韦勒克严厉批判的一个领域。法国比较文学学者让-玛丽·卡雷(Jean-Marie Carré)是把形象研究单独提出来的第一人。他为形象研究划定了研究区域,倡导在研究国际文学关系时,不拘泥于考证,而是注重探讨作家间的互相理解,大众间的相互看法、游记、幻象等,认为形象研究是要揭示"各民族间的、各种游记、想象间的互相诠释"①。对于比较文学学科而言,卡雷的主要功绩在于,他通过形象研究为以往难以把握的影响研究赋予了直观性和实践上的可操作性,揭示了形象研究的跨学科特征。到了20世纪50年代,法国学派的基亚(Marius-François Guyard)在其著作中设专章探讨了形象研究,进一步阐发卡雷的形象研究理论,提出不要再去追寻一些让人产生错觉的总体影响,而是努力更好地揭示出在个人和集体意识中,具有很大影响力的民族神话是如何被制作出来,又是如何流传下来的。这些理论阐发为比较文学研究拓展出一个新的研究方向。

在20世纪50—60年代的比较文学学科危机中,韦勒克等学者对形象学提出了严厉批评,认为考据的,甚至是后实证主义的研究类型"代表了比较文学中臭名昭著的'法国学派'"②。形象研究的支持者在坚持其研究方向,同时反思研究路径存在过分使用历史和文化分析来研究文学文本,把文学文本简化为外国形象的清单等问题,从而使危机转变为促进形象学研究发展的契机。20世纪下半叶,研究者们大胆从接受美学、符号学以及当代心理学和哲学中广泛吸收最新研究成果,借鉴当时蓬勃兴起的人文及社会科学中的研究新思路、新方法,夯实了形象研究的理论基础。经过巴柔、莫哈、基亚、卡多、德特利、迪赛林克和布吕奈特等名家的努力,形象研究的相关论断日渐合理,形象研究被定义为以文学作品为主要研究资料,挖掘文学作品中展示的异国形象,这些形象是"在文学化,同时也是社会化的过程中所得到对异国看法的总和"③。所以,应把异国形象作为一个广泛而复杂的总体想象的一部分来研究。更确切地说:"所有的形象都源自一种自我意识(不管这种意识是多么微不足道),它是对一个与他者相比的我,一个与彼此相比的此在的意识。形象因而是一种文学的或非文字的表述,它表达了存在于两种不同的文化现实间的、能够说明符指关系的差距。"④因此,可以说,"比较文学形象学并不完全等同于一般意义上的形象研究,它是对一部作品、一

---

① 卡雷.《比较文学》前言[M]//孟华.形象学.陈惇,等.比较文学.北京:高等教育出版社,2004:165.

② 达尼埃尔-亨利·巴柔.从文化形象到集体想象物[M]//孟华.比较文学形象学.北京:北京大学出版社,2001:118.

③ 达尼埃尔-亨利·巴柔.从文化形象到集体想象物[M]//孟华.比较文学形象学.北京:北京大学出版社,2001:120.

④ 达尼埃尔-亨利·巴柔.从文化形象到集体想象物[M]//孟华.比较文学形象学.北京:北京大学出版社,2001:121.

种文学中异国形象的研究”[①]。

形象学最终被定义是对文学作品中他者形象的研究，所谓的他者并非客观存在的他者，他者的塑造源于一种自我意识，他者的主观虚构成分较为明显。他者形象的生成过程实际上是通过相应的心理机制完成的、对异域历史文化现实的变异过程。因此，把形象学纳入比较文学变异学的理论框架之中最合理不过。中国比较文学学会第六届年会把“文学中的异国形象”作为年会专题之一，第七届年会也设置了分议题“形象学专题”，学会对形象学的极度关注从侧面反映出形象学在比较文学学科中所占的重要地位。目前的形象学研究的重点和方法论都得以全面更新，形象学研究获得前所未有的进展，已成为比较文学变异学视野观照下的一个极具研究前景的跨学科、多元化的研究领域。

二、形象学的理论内涵

所有形象都是个人或者集体通过言说、书写而创造出来的，是情感与思想的混合物，并不遵循真实原则，不忠实展示现实存在的那个“他者”。他者形象的建构过程是注视者借助他者发现自我和认识自我的过程，注视者对他者的情感态度是狂热、憎恶或者亲善也由此体现。因为形象是注视者一方展示的，所以具有很强的主观性。“比较文学意义上的形象，并非现实的复制品（或相似物），它是按照注视者文化中的模式、程序而重组、重写的，这些模式或程序均先存于形象”，[②]其实，他者形象是一种文化以自我为中心塑造出来的。如此呈现的形象初期是扁形的、一维的，随着时间的推移，立体的、多维的形象可能会出现。而且，在特定时期内，在某一特定文化中，大众对“他者”不能任意说、任意写。

法国学者莫哈在《试论文学形象学的研究史和方法论》一文中指出：“文学形象学研究的一切形象，都是三重意义上的某个形象：它是异国的形象，是出自一个民族（社会、文化）的形象，最后是由一个作家特殊感受创作出的形象。”[③]这句话包含三层语义：第一层语义强调的是形象的现实性，关注的是形象中稳定和忠实的成分。第二层语义也是形象学研究重视的，“出自一个民族（社会、文化）的形象”，关注创造了他者形象的文化。于是，他者形象被纳入了想象的传统之中。第三层语义，我们关注创造形象的作家的特殊感受，即创作过程中作家的主体性在其塑造的形象上的反映。由形

① 曹顺庆.比较文学教程[M].北京:高等教育出版社,2006:122.

② 达尼埃尔-亨利·巴柔.形象[M]//孟华.比较文学形象学.北京:北京大学出版社,2001:156-157.

③ 让·马克·莫哈.试论文学形象学的研究史及方法论[M]//孟华.比较文学形象学.北京:北京大学出版社,2001:25.

象的概念内涵可以看出，第二、三层面的形象研究远比第一层面值得重视，因为这两个层面把异国的文学描写视作一种创造和再创造，与引发出形象制作过程的原始认知相去甚远。换句话说，一个作家在创造异国的时候，并非直接去感知异国，而是依据自己的体悟来创造它。①由此我们说，形象学研究关注和强调的重点是其创造和再创造过程中形象自身的变异性，也就是与原始形象认知的差距。在形象创造过程中，由于对异国形象的主观想象引发了形象变异，这种变异才是形象学研究关注的焦点，通过考察这样的经由创造和再创造变异的“异国”，我们才能看出一个社会更深层次的界限和真实状况：他将什么拒之门外，从而也就说明了它本质上是什么。

1. **套话**

套话(Stéréotype)大量存在，它是形象的一种特殊存在形式。Stéréotype 原指印刷业中的铅板，后来引申出“陈词滥调”“老套”等义，此处转义为套话，是指一个民族在长时间内反复使用、用来描写异国或异国人的约定俗成的词组，用法国符号学家吕特阿莫希的话说，套话就是人们“现成的套装”，也即人们对各类人物的先入之见。比如欧洲人常用来指称犹太人的“鹰钩鼻”，中国人用来指称西方人的“老毛子”“大鼻子”等。

套话的产生有混淆表语与主要部分、混淆自然属性与文化特征等多种方式。套话一旦建立，事实上就把世界与一切文化分了等级。套话暗含的是一种对立，是对他者的一种固化的看法，拒绝、排斥一切可能的批评。②从“老毛子”等例证可以看出，套话会把总体的、抽象的、模糊的形象化为一个个语义相对简单的词汇，是“单一形态和单一语义的具象”。更进一步说，“套话是对一种文化的概括，它是这种文化标志的缩影”“作为他者定义的载体，套话是陈述集体知识的一个最小单位，它希望在任何历史时刻都有效。套话不是多义的，相反，它却具有高度的多语境性，任何时刻都可使用”，如法国人喝葡萄酒，德国人喝啤酒，英国人喝茶等。③在一定历史时段内，套话具有较高的稳定性，表现的是注视者群体对他者的一个相对固定的思维模式。通过套话研究可以考察一定时期内的民族心态史，使形象学研究和更为广泛的社会科学研究结合起来。

2. **社会集体想象物**

作家(读者)对异国现状的感知与其隶属的群体或社会的想象联系密切，关注群

---

① 让·马克·莫哈. 试论文学形象学的研究史及方法论. 孟华，译. 中国比较文学，1995(2)：144-158.

② 达尼埃尔-亨利·巴柔. 形象[M]//孟华. 比较文学形象学. 北京：北京大学出版社，2001：159-162.

③ 达尼埃尔-亨利·巴柔. 形象[M]//孟华. 比较文学形象学. 北京：北京大学出版社，2001：160.

体或社会的想象就很有必要。社会集体想象物(imaginaire social)是指一个社会对另一个集体、社会文化整体的阐释与想象,也即是一种变异了的形象。对社会集体想象物的研究主要在文学文本之外展开,是对文学形象做一种扩展了的社会文化语境研究。作家与社会集体想象物之间具有引导、复制、批判三种关系形态,借用利科《从文本到行动》中的理论来讲,多样的社会集体想象物处在意识形态与乌托邦构成的区间范围之内。

在形象学研究领域中,意识形态是与"任何自塑自我形象、进行戏剧意义上的'自我表演'、主动参与游戏和表演的社会群体的需求"相连。它"被当作集体记忆联接站,以便使开创性事件的创始价值成为整个群体的信仰物",具有整合功能。意识形态是在肯定群体自身历史、特性及在文明发展中所占地位的主导型阐释。简言之,是从自我肯定的角度塑造异国,群体借此再现了自我存在并以此强化自我的身份。[①]如J. 布鲁斯、热拉尔·德·维利叶等在1945年以后写的法国间谍小说,把第三世界塑造为混乱、暴力、共产主义阴谋充斥的土地。

处于利科提到的另一极的乌托邦也是一种变异了的形象。与意识形态的整合功能相反,在"乌托邦本质上是质疑现实的",带有乌托邦色彩的异国形象描写常常具有颠覆群体价值观的功能。赫尔曼·黑塞在作品《东方之旅》《希德哈达》中再现的亚洲,17世纪欧洲的"中国热"风潮中虚构的中国"理想国"形象,都是乌托邦幻象的样本。

需要说明的是,虽然乌托邦起到的是离心作用,而意识形态起到的是凝聚人心的作用,但意识形态与乌托邦二者之间并非总是泾渭分明。比如,基歇尔的《中国图说》的中国形象尽管有乌托邦的因素,但描述的基本框架仍是意识形态的。[②]

三、形象学研究内容及研究方法

比较文学形象学研究是在变异学的理论框架之内进行的。因为他者形象是经过文化过滤的形象,是他者缺席状态下虚构的形象,是注视者文化的投射物,变异现象伴随着他者形象塑造与接受的整个流程。其中,文化过滤对他者形象的改变起着重要作用,研究中要充分关注。而文化过滤本身就是变异学研究的一个方面,因此,只有充分运用好变异学的相关理论才能做好相关研究工作。

没有注视者,他者形象则无法建构;没有作为他者存在的异国,他者形象更无从谈

---

① 让·马克·莫哈.试论文学形象学的研究史及方法论[M]//孟华.比较文学形象学.北京:北京大学出版社,2001:32.

② 汪介之,唐建清.跨文化语境中的比较文学[M].北京:译林出版社,2004:548-549.

起。形象学研究紧紧围绕注视者与他者这两个方面展开，既对二者分别进行研究，也关注二者之间的关系。注视者是当代形象学研究的重心。既然他者形象是注视者假借他者发现自我和认识自我的过程，注视者在建构他者形象时就毫无例外地受到注视者与他者相遇时的先见、身份、时间等因素的影响。生活在一定文化传统中的注视者，先于注视者存在的历史与传统构成了注视者的先见。注视者的身份既包含血缘、种族、性别等天赋成分，也有职业、社团成员等后天成分；不同身份必然构建出不同的他者形象。时间是一个开放系统，他者形象的历史感是浸润在时间中的东西，身处不断变化的历史语境中的注视者注视他者愈久，注视者体现出的个体反思精神愈加强劲，立体的、多维的他者形象也会日益凸显，老舍写于不同时期的《二马》与《英国人》中塑造的不同的英国人形象就说明了这一点。

比较文学形象学中所指他者形象不仅指涉人物形象，文学作品及相关游记、回忆录等各种文字材料中的异国肖像、异国地理环境、异国人等，都属于比较文学形象学的研究范围。比如国际交流中常见的异国绘画、瓷器、挂毯甚至园林等，其中都对异国形象的感知与塑造起着重要影响；人种（黄种人、黑种人、白种人）因素也会也是异国形象研究需要关注的一个方面。

概括地讲，比较文学形象学的研究方法可分为文本外部研究与文本内部研究两种。文本外部研究具有跨学科性质，属于文学社会学研究。因吸纳了年鉴派重视互文性、人类学重视遗传—生理作用、接受美学重视接受主体的作用等理论精华，拓宽了比较文学形象学的学术视野，文本外部研究从中获益甚多。文本外部研究又分为社会集体想象物、作家、作家想象的异国形象与真实的异国关系三个层面。比较文学形象学研究不局限于文学，关注文学形象产生、传播的文化语境，但并未放弃文本内部研究。对文学文本的研究从套话、文本中注视者与他者的等级关系、模式化的故事情节三个层面展开。随着形象学研究的日趋深入，形象学研究日益呈现出广阔的发展前景。因其跨学科的特性，与历史学、文化地理学、民族学、人类学等有着难以割裂的亲缘关系，恰当地把这些学科的相关理论运用到形象学的研究之中，必然会拓展形象学的研究方法，完善形象学的理论框架，推动形象学研究向纵深发展。

【原典选读】

试论文学形象学的研究史及方法论（节选）

◉让·马克·莫哈

【导读】《论文学形象学的研究史和方法论》是法国比较文学家让·马克·莫哈（Jean-

Marc Moura)的一篇重要论文,原载1992年第3期的法国《比较文学杂志》,孟华将之翻译为中文并编入其主编的文集《比较文学形象学》。本篇论文分为两大部分。第一部分总结了比较文学形象学学科的发生、发展史,认为形象学具有跨学科性,在研究实践中要动用符号学、接受美学等多种理论;从形象本身、形象与社会集体想象物的关系、在具体文本中分析形象的适当方法三个方面对他者形象进行定义。第二部分界定了形象、社会集体想象物、意识形态和乌托邦四个概念,以此完成了对形象学理论特质的阐发。■

大家知道,文学形象学的定义是研究文学作品中所表现的异国。它有两个主要的研究方向:一是研究"游记这些原始材料";但主要还是研究"文学作品,这些作品或直接描绘异国,或涉及或多或少模式化了的对一个异国的总体认识"。(p. 17)

1/形象被理解为"在文学化但同时也是社会化的过程中得到的对异国的总体认识",最典型的例子是有关异国的固定模式,它是"一种文化的象征性表现",即使是在文学文本中,这种固定模式也与大量的意识形态问题相联。(p. 23)

2/这一形象"源自一个宽泛且复杂的总体:整体想象物。更确切地说,是社会整体想象物"。而社会整体想象物是"全社会对一个集体、一个社会文化整体所作的阐释,是双级性(同一性/相异性)的阐释"。它显然部分地"与事件、政治、社会意义上的历史"相联。形象学研究的主要困难在于找到"想象他者"时所特有的规律、原则和惯例。就像人们所说的,这种想象在一定程度上是与历史铰接在一起的,但它并非历史的"代用品",更非历史的影像。(p. 24)

3/分析形象采用的方法依托于形象与社会整体想象物的关系。由于每一具体问题与历史语境铰接的方式不同,因而就不可能硬性规约使用的方法。(p. 24)

文学形象学所研究的一切形象,都是三重意义上的某个形象:它是异国的形象,是出自一个民族(社会、文化)的形象,最后,是由一个作家特殊感受所创作出的形象。……事实上,所有具学术价值的形象学研究一般都注重第二点,即注重研究创造出了形象的文化。(pp. 25-26)

对社会集体想象物的研究代表了形象学的历史层面。与其他描述相比,这种研究并不注重文学描述。……然而,文学史家仍可将社会集体想象物等同于文化生活范畴,并把它定义为"是对一个社会(人种、教派、民族、行会、学派……)集体描述的总和,既是构成,亦是创造了这些描述的总和"。(pp. 29-30)

因此,意识形态较少由内容来定义,而主要由它对一个特定群体所起的整合功能来定义。我们看到什么样的异国描写就可被称为意识形态的。这是对相异性进行“整合”后的形象,它使人们从该群体关于自身起源、身份,并使其确信自我在世界史中地位的观念出发去读解异国。其目的是使想象出的本群体的身份支配被描写的相异性(冒着使用异国情调套话的危险)。(pp. 32-33)

我们最感兴趣的是其中最基本的一个层面:乌托邦本质上是质疑现实的,而意识形态恰要维护和保存现实。乌托邦具有“社会颠覆的功能”。卡尔·曼海姆对此曾有过精辟的论述,他将乌托邦定义为“在想象和现实之间的一道壕沟,它对这个现实的稳定性和持久性构成了一种威胁”。(pp. 33-34)

凡按本社会模式、完全使用本社会话语重塑出的异国形象就是意识形态的;而用离心的、符合一个作者(或一个群体)对相异性独特看法的话语塑造出的异国形象则是乌托邦的。(p. 35)

形象学自视为国际关系史和文学史,它研究文化和文学领域内相同性/相异性的辩证关系,简言之,形象学研究要靠总体文学和比较文学在原理的普遍性和博学的专门化之间的持久来支持。因此,我们有充足的理由将形象学视为关于异国的幻象史。只要观察一下这些幻象都是自我幻象的反面,我们即可懂得在这里形象学甚至触及了整个文学的核心问题。(p. 40)

(孟华. 比较文学形象学[M]. 北京:北京大学出版社,2001.)

从文化形象到集体想象物(节选)

◉达尼埃尔-亨利·巴柔

【导读】《从文化形象到集体想象物》是法国比较文学家达尼埃尔-亨利·巴柔所著,原载布吕奈尔、谢夫莱尔主编的《比较文学概论》(*Précis de literature comparée*),孟华将之翻译为中文并编入《比较文学形象学》。本文总结了形象学早期研究把文学文本转化为外国形象的清单等弊端;重点论述了文学形象的概念内涵,认为形象皆来自自我意识,是情感与思想的混合物,研究形象就要研究注视者的文化构成、运行机制等内容;同时,文章也阐发了文学形象与集体想象物之间的关系。■

当这种跨学科性尚未正式确立时,形象学研究,特别是在法国,曾受到了来自两种极端行为的损害:一方面,是过分使用历史和文化分析来研究的文学文本;与此相反,另一种

是过于简化了文学文本的阅读，将之转化为外国形象的清单。（p. 119）

这并不是为了忘记文学研究，把自己的领域无限扩大；而是为了将自己的方法与其他方法相对照，特别是将“文学”形象与其他平行的、同时代的证据（报刊、副文学、图片、电影、漫画等）进行比较。这里涉及的显然是将文学思考重新置放于对一个或多个社会的文化进行的总体分析中。

……如此设计出的“文学”形象被视为在文学化，同时也是社会化的过程中所得到的关于异国看法的总和。这一新的视域要求研究者不仅考虑到文学文本，其生产及传播的条件，且要考虑到人们写作、思想、生活所使用的一切文化材料。此类工作将研究者导向了一个或然问题的十字路口，而形象在这里就像一个启示者，它把意识形态（如种族主义、异国情调等；这里仅举此两例，以使所讨论的问题紧扣住“人们看到的异国”）的运作机制特别清晰地揭示了出来。（p. 120）

所有的形象都源自一种自我意识（不管这种意识是多么微不足道），它是对一个与他者相比的我，一个与彼处相比的此在的意识。（p. 121）

形象是描述，它是感情和思想的混合物，必须抓住其情感和意识形态的反响。以上这些建议的直接后果是取消了一个伪问题，形象研究经常陷入其中：讨论一个形象与“被注视”国相比是否“错误”或其“忠实程度”的问题，就好像形象是现实的一个“相似物”一样（由此而来的是“感觉”的诸种错误）。这就跌入了参考系错觉的陷阱之中，而此类幻觉是经常被揭露的。我们以何客观条件为准来判断形象是否忠实于人们称为现实的东西呢？事实上，对形象的研究应该较为注重探讨形象在多大程度上符合在注视者文化，而非被注视者文化中先存的模式、文化图解，而非一味探究形象的“真实”程度及其与现实的关系。因此，我们就必须了解注视者文化的基础、组成成分、运作机制和社会功能。（pp. 122-123）

我“看”他者；但他者的形象也传递了我自己的某个形象。在个人（一个作家）、集体（一个社会、一个国家、一个民族）或半集体（一种思想流派、一种“舆论”）的层面上，他者形象不可避免地同样要表现出对他者的否定，对我自身、对我自己所处空间的补充和外延。我想言说他者（最常见的是由于专断和复杂的原因），但在言说他者时，我却否认了他，而言说了自我。我也以某种方式同时说出了围绕着我的世界，我说出了“目光”来自何处及对他者的判断：他者形象揭示出了我在世界（本土和异国的空间）和我之间建立起的各种关系。……这些关系主要不是言说者（注视者）社会与被注视者社会间实际存在的，而是经过重新思索、被想象出来的关系。（pp. 123-124）

套话被视作形象的一种基本形态，甚至是漫画了的形态。（p. 125）

但他者不仅仅“被注视”，而且必须缄口不语。（p. 141）

一切文化都是在与其他文化相对立、相比较中而确定的。如果人们同意此说，那么对他者的（文学的或非文学的）描述就会变得与一切文化都不可分，同时又会成为下述现象的基本形式：无法抵御的社会在场及社会的整个倾向——对他者的梦想。异国形象这些特殊的凝结物构成了社会集体想象物，而形象学研究从一开始就将此确定为自身的研究前景。（p. 144）

（孟华. 比较文学形象学［M］. 北京：北京大学出版社，2001.）

【研究范例】

19 世纪西方文学中的中国形象（节选）

◉米丽耶·德特利

【导读】《19 世纪西方文学中的中国形象》是法国比较文学家米丽耶·德特利完成的一篇论文，文章言明本文所谓的“19 世纪西方文学中的中国形象”主要指的是从 1840 年到 20 世纪前十年西方文学中的中国形象，因为从 18 世纪末期中国闭关锁国到第一次鸦片战争这段时期史料不够丰富，而鸦片战争为起点的第二阶段则“相关的史料极为丰富，其中的统一性也是第一阶段所不具备的”。作者简单回顾了欧洲人通过亚洲游记等材料获取的早期亚洲人的形象的变迁史。纵观全文，西方文学中的中国形象时好时坏，但无论好与坏，形象背后总是可见出西方文明以及西方人的影子：或通过塑造坏的中国形象来抬高自己，实现自我的精神胜利；或者塑造好的中国形象，透露出对西方人自身文明的失望，表达想要走近中华文明的愿望，等等。言说他者时带出的情感因时因人会有所变化。■

欧洲人最早读到的亚洲游记是圣方济各会修士让-杜·布朗·卡尔班和纪尧姆·德·卢布鲁克撰写的。两位修士曾于 13 世纪上半叶深入喀拉昆仑山，进入蒙古可汗的宫廷。他们的游记在时人的思想中留下深刻的烙印，使人认为远东各民族生性凶残，在各方面都与欧洲人迥异，因之成其心患。……马可·波罗曾在蒙古统治下的中国长期居住，他的游记反而传述了一个极度文明、和平而繁荣的民族，“尽管他们不知道上帝，却在许多方面值得尊敬”。许多世纪以来，欧洲人对黄色人种（中国人、蒙古人和满族人甚至日本人都混为一谈）的态度是游移不定的，有时一种态度占上风，有时又是另一种。（p. 241）

总的来说,19 世纪初期欧洲文学中的中国人形象多是表面化、漫画式的;它退化到一些衣着饰品的细节描写(男人穿着妇女们才穿的彩色长袍,带着阳伞、扇子),以及一些外形特征(女人的小脚、男人的辫子、黄皮肤、长指甲、吊眼睛——此时尚未用"有蒙古褶的眼睛"一词)和一些琐碎小事(爱情、诗歌、漫步、梦幻)。其中对中国人精神状态的勾画往往自相矛盾(对旧事和诗歌的趣味、对外表的关心、无所事事、懒散、专制、文雅、感情细腻、无动于衷、怯懦等等)。(p. 248)

1840 年以来描写中国的文学大量涌现(随着中国国门被迫打开,涌现了大量游记以及从游记中汲取灵感的虚构作品),这些作品给人的印象是无休止地和过去的文学作品进行清算:因为它们不断地有意无意地对照耶稣会士和启蒙哲学家塑造的理想的中国人形象,建立一个完全相反的新形象。对中国事物的态度由喜好到厌恶,由崇敬到诋毁,由好奇到蔑视。(p. 248)

19 世纪,无论是"善良的野蛮人"还是"高尚的中国人"的神话都不再时兴了。在欧洲人看来,中国人都是些恶人:他们极不诚实,礼貌只是出于虚伪,微笑都是鬼脸怪相。如此普遍的弑婴和乞讨行为都证明了他们是些麻木、冷漠、自私并且毫无慈悲之心的人。(p. 250)

"野蛮""非人道""兽性",这些形容词通常被 19 世纪的人们用来总结对中国人的看法。同样,他们在提到中国人时也很少把他作为可与之建立人与人关系的个体(缺少个性也被看作中国人的另一性格特征):通常人们说起"中国人"时,把他当作一个密集的、不可数的、模糊的整体,或是"中国人群"。人们通常用动物和他们作类比:"蚂蚁"是最常见的比喻。(p. 251)

因此中国人形象映射出了世纪末欧洲人的发展方向。由于它对欧洲人所具有的劝诫作用,中国人形象就更镀上了一层晦暗而令人生厌的色彩。这其实就是这些世纪末法国小说的真正功能,它们争相挥舞着这样一个丑恶吓人的中国人形象:退化、险恶、麻木、对自己的卑下一无所知。(p. 261)

为了捍卫自己的身份,欧洲人于是一刻不停地贬低、摧毁中国人,针对的不仅仅是中国的文明,甚至是中国的人。这种有条不紊地对他者进行诋毁和否定的行动并非毫无恶意,但白人教化行动的神话却对此保持沉默。然而,人们无法阻止一种情绪渗入良知之中:表面上似乎是担心有仇必报的复仇的中国人要求算账,实际上是对自己产生了忧虑和怀疑。因此,就在人们能够确信他者已被消灭的时候,他者却如同一阵强烈的悔恨,突然

又冒了出来,欧洲人惊恐地发现他很像自己。(p.262)

(孟华.比较文学形象学[M].北京:北京大学出版社,2001.)

文化对话与世界文学中的中国形象(节选)

◉乐黛云

【导读】《文化对话与世界文学中的中国形象》(*Cultural Dialogue and the Image of China in World Literature*)是乐黛云在中国召开的哈佛—燕京学社学者第一次研讨会上所作的报告,后被收入刘海平主编的《中美文化的互动与关联》论文集。文中的"世界"主要是指西方,作者从西方学术著作与西方文学作品两方面入手,初步勾勒出中国形象的发展史,展示了中国形象的复杂性。同时,作者提及西方人在不同时段塑造的不同中国形象的背后所隐藏的欧洲社会现实,印证了形象学所谓的言说他者与展示自我同步这一理论。■

西方关于中国形象的第一本著作可以说是西班牙人门多萨(Mendoza)1585年应罗马教皇的要求撰写的《大中华帝国史》。这部上溯到唐尧时代,把中国描写为极其强大、发达一体化大帝国的编年史,七年中竟以七种欧洲主要语言,出版了四十六版,可见欧洲当时对中国信息极感兴趣之一斑。(p.44)

如果说学术著作由于中国的遥远和复杂难懂不能不掺进大量作者主观推理和想象,那么,在虚构文学中,这种情况就更其严重了。在这里,我们更可以清楚地看到遥远的异国他乡是如何作为一种与自我相对立的他者而存在,凡自我所渴求的、所构想的,以及在现实中无法满足的都会幻化而投射于对方。16世纪以来,英国作家克里斯多夫·马罗(Christopher Marlowe)的名作《帖木儿》、意大利作家阿利瓦本尼(Arivabene)的戏剧《伟大的尧》、英国浪漫主义诗人柯勒律治(Samuel Coleridge)的《忽必烈》都曾夸张地描写了中国的强大、奢侈、专制和智慧,虽然他们不免把中东、蒙古、中国混为一谈。(p.44)

在歌德之后,以中国为题材的20世纪作品有了完全不同的面貌。庞德(Ezra Pound)在他的《诗篇》中把中国和西方联结在一起,致力于把中国纳入他的诗体形式的人类文明的历史图景。一批描写中国现实生活的作品产生了:谢阁兰(Victor Segalen)的《雷内·雷》(1913)通过一位在清朝皇室担任教师,同时为多方面充当密探的年轻法国人的经历,描写了当时的宫廷生活和辛亥革命的山雨欲来。……无论是写中国现实,或是写一种中国精神,以上这些作品都把中国作为世界的一部分,或揭示人类共同面临的官僚体制,革命、战争等严重问题;或探索善恶、意义、过去和未来等全人类都正在苦苦思索的问题,这与十七八世纪的作品,单纯把中国作为一个与“我”相对的“他”来理解有了很大的区别。(pp. 49-50)

从以上这样一个非常简略的历史追溯,可以清楚地看到有中国形象的描写,从最富于意识形态意味的“求同”到最富于乌托邦意味的理想的寄托;从最遥远的完全相异,到对人类共同困惑的求索,排成了非常丰富复杂的光谱,而这光谱的貌似无常的变幻又时隐时现地与社会的变化相关。例如,17 世纪最初 20 年出现了赞扬中国的第一个高潮,当时欧洲正处于 30 年战争前夜,那是暴虐横行,人们对现实极为不满的年代。西方对中国极感兴趣的另一个高潮则是以第一次世界大战后西方普遍感到的沮丧和绝望为背景。这种时刻,人们最需要通过“他者”,创造一个“非我”来发泄不满和寄托希望。中国正是作为这样一个极富魅力的“异域”面被探索的。目前,世界正处于一个极富挑战意义的,正待开垦的领域,事实上,一个研究中国的新的高潮正在掀起。我们应积极参与这一已经进行了四百余年的文化对话,以一种“互为主观”的方法重新认识别人,也重新认识自己,这不仅对中国文化的重构,而且对世界文化的发展都具有十分重要的意义。(p. 50)

(刘海平. 中美文化的互动与关联[M]. 上海:上海外语教育出版社,2003.)

【延伸阅读】

1. 孟华. 比较文学形象学[M]. 北京:北京大学出版社,2001.

本书共收入了欧洲大陆比较文学学者 13 篇论述形象学或进行形象学研究的论文,既有理论和方法的探讨与阐发,也有具体的研究实例。阅读本书可使读者清楚地把握形象学发展的脉络及其理论来源,了解当代形象学的基本理论和研究方法。

2. 周宁. 跨文化形象学[M]. 上海:复旦大学出版社,2014.

跨文化形象学起于当下中国文化自觉的问题,作者从解构西方的中国形象入手,揭示其中知识与权力的关系,进而提出“三组课题”。按三组课题清理跨文化形象学的基本研究思路与体系,可发现其理论困境:面对西方现代性,中国现代性自我想象的困境不仅在知识与观念上,还在价值与权力上;真正需要解构的,不是西方现代性及其构建的中国形象的知识—权力网络,而是中西方二元对立的现代性思维模式。在这一思维模式中,我们不可能摆脱西方这一巨大的他者进行现代性自我确认,即使是用后现代的话语理论解构西方现代性,质疑西方的中国形象构成中国现代性自我想象的他者,也最终会落入后现代的话语理论的陷阱,因为没有他者便没有自我。三组课题出现的理论困境,将直接质疑跨文化形象学的前提与意义。

第三节　接受学

比较文学接受学，又称接受研究，它是在西方解释学文论和接受美学影响下建立的一种比较文学变异研究模式，主要研究他国读者、社会对一个国家的作家作品接受过程中出现的变异。1979 年 8 月，在奥地利因斯布鲁克召开了国际比较文学第九届大会，会上以"文学的传播与接受"为题展开讨论，接受研究作为比较文学研究的一个新范式被世界比较文学界所承认。接受研究不是孤立地看待作品本文，而是把它作为人与人之间的交流活动，这样，作品不是一个永远不变的客观存在，而是在读者参与创作的基础上呈现出意义。

一、接受研究的产生与理论内涵

比较文学接受学是在接受理论之后出现的。接受理论于 20 世纪 60 年代中期产生，以德国康斯坦茨大学的姚斯、伊瑟尔、福尔曼等学者为代表，由于他们重视研究读者对作品接受的反应、规律及对文本意义生成的重要作用，因而被称为"接受理论"。吸收了接受理论成果的接受研究扩大了文学研究的范围，如果说影响研究主要着眼于已经完成的文学作品之间的关系，而接受研究"则可以指明更广大的研究范围，也就是说，它可以指明这些作品和它们的环境、氛围、读者、评论者、出版商及周围情况的种种关系。因此，文学'接受'的研究指向了文学的社会学和文学的心理范畴"①。处于不同文明、文化系统中的读者，具有不同的文化形态和心理结构，被接受对象在接受者那里必然会有所选择、过滤、修正。因此，文本尽管还是那个文本，但经过不同时代、不同民族的读者的阐释，已形成不同的作品。这样，接受理论与比较文学在这个基点上契合了。

比较文学接受学是建立在接受理论之上的研究范式，接受学从接受理论那里吸收了不少理论养分。接受理论又叫接受美学，它把读者研究置于非常重要的地位，与文

① 韦斯坦因.比较文学与文学理论[M].刘象愚，译.沈阳：辽宁人民出版社，1987：47.

本中心论相对，提出读者中心论。接受理论认为，文学作品不是以同样的面貌呈现在所有时代、所有读者面前的，相反，作品意象与表现形式有赖于读者完成。可见，接受理论研究的读者，不是一般意义上的观众或作品的阅读者，而是文学的一个组成部分，是艺术思维的又一个环节。比如，文学史在西方一直局限在作品与作者的范围研究，而很少从读者角度研究，姚斯提出，要重写文学史，文学史研究必须寻找当年读者对文学作品的反应，不同时代的读者对同一部作品产生不同意见的原因，不同时代不同背景下的读者们对作品的期待心理、审美情趣、阅读习惯及由此造成的对创作的影响，这样，形成作者、作品、读者"三位一体"的研究文学史的全方位结构。

当接受理论从文本中心转到读者中心后，就取得了与传统文学观念截然不同的理论建树。接受理论认为，读者不是被动的接受者，而是能动的因素，读者的阅读是创造性的阅读，是文学作品能否流传的决定性力量。由于读者参与作品价值的建构，文本在不同的时空中不断演化，也就没有所谓独立、绝对的文本。文本只有经过读者阅读才成为作品，并决定其价值。读者对作品文本的接受是一种阐释活动，在作品文本里，有许多"意义空白"，即没有交代清楚的地方，这就需要读者凭自己的生活经验、知识与想象力，进行创造性的填补，使之具体化。从作家的角度看，作家在创作时文学接受已经对其产生影响，因为作家必须考虑读者的"期待视野"，即作家要关注自己正在创作的作品能否被读者理解和接受。"期待视野"是读者在阅读之前对作品显现方式的定向性期待，期待视野有两大形态，其一是既往的审美经验，其二是既往的生活经验。因此，一部文学作品，以唤醒读者以往的阅读记忆而使这类文本的流派和风格被完整地保持，或被改变、重新定向，或讽刺性地获得实现。比如，塞万提斯的《堂吉诃德》模仿骑士传奇，就是为了唤起读者对骑士传奇的期待视野，但又以主人公荒诞不经的经历讽刺了骑士传奇，从而改变了当时读者对这一文学类别的印象。同时，随着时间的推移，"作品的接受经验会被历代读者加深、发展、修正甚至推翻"①。

接受理论认为，文学的接受包含垂直接受和水平接受，垂直接受是从历史的纵向考察读者接受作品的情况；水平接受是考察同一时代的不同读者对作品的接受情况。不同时代的读者由于"期待视野"的变化，并不断发现作品潜在的含义，因此出现不同的接受情况。同一时代的读者因其身份、文化等的差异，对同一作品的接受也会有所不同。读者的这种能动性，也会影响作家的创作。同样，文学效果不仅仅取决于作品本身的内涵，更取决于读者参与文学作品的创造。读者的能动创造作为潜在的力量，改变了传统的观念，改造了社会，影响了历史。

---

① 陈惇，孙景尧，谢天振. 比较文学[M]. 北京：高等教育出版社，1997：475.

当接受理论被运用于比较文学领域时,即“以比较文学的目光审视接受理论视域中的文学活动,不难发现它并非是一种指向作为客体的、物的对象性活动,而是将它处理成一种作为整体的人与人之间关系的沟通活动,是联接人与人之间的思想、情感和认识的一种‘人际交流活动’。接受理论中的文学的这种人际交流的性质,决定了文学难以摆脱其观察者而独立存在。因为读者是参与创作的力量,作品的意义要通过读者的接受才能显现出来。这种研究趋势进入比较文学研究领域时,一种新的比较文学研究类型——接受研究就出现了”①。比较文学接受学将读者对作品的阅读与接受置于重要的研究位置,强调读者对作品意义的建构作用。但接受学与接受理论又存在区别,“接受理论极为重视读者在文学中的地位和作用,强调读者在文学活动中的中心意识;而接受学更注重读者对文本的理解和阐释本身”②。同时,接受学强调读者对跨文明、跨文化的文学接受研究,即读者对异域(国)、异质文化的作家作品的接受和反应。比如,中国读者对法国作家司汤达的《红与黑》的接受就属于接受学研究的范围,但法国读者对《红与黑》的接受就不属于此列,而接受理论则没有异域接受的限制。正因为如此,比较文学接受学更多的是求异,而不是求同。

二、比较文学接受学与影响研究

人类文化的传承与发展,使得一个作家、一部作品必然接受了他人的影响并存在影响他人的因素。接受和影响是一个问题的两面。“播送者对接受者来说是‘影响’,接受者对播送者来说是‘接受’。过去的影响研究只研究 A 如何影响 B,很少研究 B 对于 A 如何接受。”③意大利学者弗朗科·梅雷加利也论及接受学与影响研究的区别:“‘接受’这个术语跟信息与接受者之间的关系紧密相连。但是必须注意到,这种关系可以用两种不同的方式、两种不同的矢量前景去考察:可以把交流作为信息对接受者的影响加以研究,也可以把它作为接受者对信息的影响加以研究;也就是说,存在着两种方向,一种是‘信息→接受者’,另一种是‘接受者→信息’。接受美学的代表理论家在论及接受时主张第二种方向,第一种方向可以称为‘影响’。”④除此以外,接受学还扩大了研究的范围,它关注接受的历史、现实背景和文化状况,从而使文学研究与社会学、心理学、民族审美特点联系起来了。正如韦斯坦因所说:“影响,应该用来指已经

① 陈惇,孙景尧,谢天振.比较文学[M].北京:高等教育出版社,1997:479.

② 曹顺庆.比较文学教程[M].北京:高等教育出版社,2006:139.

③ 乐黛云.中西比较文学教程[M].北京:高等教育出版社,1988:111.

④ 弗朗科·梅雷加利.论文学接受[M]//干永昌,等.比较文学研究译文集.上海:上海译文出版社,1985:406.

完成的文学作品之间的关系，而‘接受’则可以指明更广大的研究范围，也就是说，它可以指明这些作品和它们的环境、氛围、读者、评论者、出版商及周围情况的种种关系。因此，文学‘接受’的研究指向了文学的社会学和文学的心理范畴。”①接受学肯定了接受者的主体地位，关注接受者对被接受对象如何选择、调适，以及经过文化过滤后产生的变异。

从某种意义上讲，比较文学接受学是对影响研究的纠正和超越。影响研究虽然是比较文学最早的研究方法之一，但长期以来遭到学者们的非难。影响研究通过实证来证明某个作家与他国作家、思想家之间的关联，被认为只属于外缘研究，而不是关注文学本体及其美学价值，它以文学受到的外部影响取代了文学本体的内部发展规律，让人难以信服。接受研究不是孤立地研究作品文本，而是将作品、社会、作家、读者联系起来，将文学作品放在纵向“垂直接受”与横向“水平接受”的坐标上，立足于文学性进行研究，为比较文学开辟了一片新天地。具体而言，接受学与影响研究有以下区别：

首先，接受学关注的是文学在域外的变异，影响研究关注的是事实联系。接受学在现代阐释学和接受理论的影响下，主要研究域外读者对文本的接受和阐释，特别是因文化的差异产生的变异。影响研究立足于实证主义，以具体的文献资料证明异域作家、作品之间存在的事实上的联系，更多的属于外部研究的范围，而不是对文学内在审美性的研究。

其次，接受学研究的重心是读者，影响研究的重心是文本。当接受学以读者作为切入点时，发现每个读者在一个纵的文化历史发展与横的文化接触面构成的坐标之中构成其独特的，包含文化修养、知识水平、欣赏趣味以及个人经历等因素的“接受屏幕”。这个“接受屏幕”决定了读者如何去阐释和理解某个文本。处于不同文化系统的读者具有不同的文化形态和心理结构，其“接受屏幕”自然也就不同，接受学则研究域外读者对同一文本的不同阐释及原因，探讨其规律，所以，读者是接受学研究的核心。影响研究则以文本为研究的核心，“侧重对域外文学的借鉴、模仿，以及素材源泉等事实联系的梳理，研究视点主要集中在作品上”②。影响研究研究作家作品之间存在的事实联系，关注文本中具有的外来因素。

第三，接受学是影响研究的延伸。影响研究关注文学传承中的机械的因果关系，脱离了文学本体，颠倒了主体、客体的位置，越来越走向僵化，接受学调整了主客体的

---

① 韦斯坦因．比较文学与文学理论［M］．刘象愚，译．沈阳：辽宁人民出版社，1987：47.

② 陈惇，孙景尧，谢天振．比较文学［M］．北京：高等教育出版社，1997：479.

位置，是对影响研究的延伸。它强调不同文化传统的读者对异域作家、文本的创造性接受与阐释，研究某国文学在接受异域文学之后产生的种种变体，以及考察接受方的种种文化的、心理的、艺术气质的等方面的情况，是对影响研究在理论上的推进和实践上的拓展。

三、比较文学接受学的特点和研究方法

比较文学接受学在吸收、融合了接受理论后，形成了新的比较文学变异学研究范式，它与影响研究、平行研究具有明显的差异，使比较文学扩大了自己的研究领域和关注的对象，为比较文学注入了新的活力。

比较文学接受学与接受理论都将读者置于研究的重心，但接受理论没有对读者作限定，而接受学强调读者的跨文明/文化、跨民族、跨语言的要求，即读者对域外作家、作品接受时的反应。由于异域读者心中的接受屏幕不同，其对某部作品的接受与本土读者会有所差异，比如列夫·托尔斯泰的小说《安娜·卡列尼娜》，在中国 20 世纪 40—80 年代的读者一般把安娜看作反抗封建包办婚姻，追求自由爱情的伟大女性，而对小说中表现的宗教思想、宗教情感基本上不涉及，这是中国读者普遍宗教观念淡漠所致，说明读者与作者之间存在某种文化传统的断裂层。随着 90 年代以来，中西方文化交流频繁，西方 20 世纪各种文论进入中国，中国读者对安娜的解读呈现多元化和纵深化趋势，如从宗教、心理批评、女性主义等不同角度进行分析，说明读者的接受有历时性的变化。正如法国比较文学学者谢弗莱尔所说："关键是要从诸如'期待视野''美学法则'及'视野转换'等概念中得出结论并进一步将研究的重点放在接受者上，应该把共时性研究与大量的历时性研究结合起来。"①建立在不同文化传统的审美原则和时代特点，潜移默化在读者的内心，对其接受活动发生影响。

接受学还要考查异域文学进入本土后被翻版、改写、再创造的过程，并终至发生变异。运用接受学的研究方法，可以了解哪些成分被读者接受，哪些内容被读者忽略，哪些因素经读者过滤后改写，了解读者对域外作家作品、文学现象的印象、态度、感受等。五四时期，中国作家不同程度地受到外国作家作品的影响，并在创作上显现出自身的特点，如冰心接受了泰戈尔的泛爱思想，文章显得平和恬淡，充满爱心和童心；鲁迅接受了 19 世纪俄国文学的一些因素，形成其小说为人生、关注"小人物"等特点。对异域文学的接受反过来使读者对本土文学产生新的理解和感受，如郭沫若虽然从小熟读

① 乐黛云. 比较文学原理：附录二[M]. 长沙：湖南文艺出版社，1988：256.

中国诗歌，但他走上诗人道路的却是受到外国诗歌的影响，他读了美国诗人郎费罗的《箭与歌》，“感觉着异常的清新”“就好像第一次才和‘诗’见了面”。正是受到这首诗的感悟，在“那读的烂熟，但丝毫也没感觉着它的美感的一部《诗经》中，尤其《国风》中，才感受到了同样的清新，同样的美妙”①。这说明，读者的接受是接受主体积极参与的过程，而不是被动受其影响。再如 20 世纪西方意象派诗人对中国古典诗歌的接受，亦是主动的借鉴，“意象派诗人之所以迷恋于中国古典诗，并非纯为猎奇，或给自己的诗添些异国味，他们觉得中国古典诗歌与意象派的主张颇为吻合，可以引这个有几千年历史的文明来为自己的主张作后盾”②。正因为如此，中国古典诗歌在他们那里发生了变异，从而使熟知古典诗词的中国读者也感到新奇。

因此，比较文学接受学以研究异域文学在他国的变异为重心，深化了比较文学研究，并与影响研究区分开来，将比较文学接受学纳入文学变异学范畴，丰富了比较文学学科理论的建设。关注文学之同中之异，文学相互影响之下的变化、改造，更能发现各种文学的民族特性，更接近文学的本质。“在多元文化共存的时代，注重变异研究的比较文学接受学必将对异质文化之间的平等互识、互证、互补产生积极作用。”③

从比较文学的研究方法看，“可以采用实证的方法，也可以采用审美的方法，只不过它常常是以审美方法为主，以实证方法为辅。比较文学接受学的研究也可以是历史的方法、哲学的方法，还可以运用文学社会学、文学心理学的方法等，也可以多种方法综合运用”。④如韦建国、户思杜的《西方读者视角中的贾平凹》，主要运用了审美的方法，阐述西方读者对贾平凹作品的分析、评价。赵毅衡的《意象派与中国古典诗歌》则既有审美的方法，也有实证的方法，并对意象派对中国古典诗歌的接受、误读、改写进行了细读式研究。伍晓明的《中国文学中的现代思潮概观》，则综合运用了社会学、历史学的方法，阐述了中国新文学接受西方现代文艺思潮的历史条件，探讨了中国新文学作家群体对西方浪漫主义的不同接受等。可见，较之传统影响研究主要以实证为主，接受学的研究方法更加多样，真正达到了理论上的刷新与实践上的拓展。

---

① 郭沫若. 沫若文集·第 11 卷[M]. 北京：人民文学出版社，1969：138-139.

② 赵毅衡. 意象派与中国古典诗歌[J]. 外国文学研究，1979(4)：4.

③ 曹顺庆. 比较文学教程[M]. 北京：高等教育出版社，2006：146.

④ 曹顺庆. 比较文学教程[M]. 北京：高等教育出版社，2006：144.

【原典选读】

走向接受美学（节选）

◉姚斯

【导读】《走向接受美学》是接受美学的创始人、德国著名学者汉斯·罗伯特·姚斯的经典著作，阐述了接受美学的基本理论和基本方法。

全书包括五章的内容，第一章“文学史作为向文学理论的挑战”，被看作接受美学的纲领性文献。姚斯在批判以杰文纳斯为代表的目的论历史观和以冯·兰克为代表的历史循环论的基础上，认为文学史应是文学作品的接受史，力图从读者或消费者的角度建立一种新的文学史观念。第二章“艺术史与实用主义历史”则探讨艺术史与一般历史的区别。认为文学史是与不同时代读者的接受史融合在一起的，而一般历史只是文献的汇编。第三章“类型理论与中世纪文学”，姚斯以接受美学的观念研究了中世纪文学，以此建立区别于传统文学理论和结构主义的类型理论，即历史系统学。第四章“歌德的《浮士德》与瓦莱里的《浮士德》：论问题与回答的解释学”是在接受美学理论指导下进行的个案分析。第五章“阅读视野嬗变中的诗歌文本：以波德莱尔的诗“烦厌（Ⅱ）为例”以具体实例建构接受美学的文学解释学理论。

总的来看，姚斯的《走向接受美学》反对以“新批评”、结构主义为代表的当代西方文学批评中的文本中心论，试图建立以读者为中心的文学研究新范式。姚斯认为，文学史不是作家生平加作品的资料汇编，也不是相对主义的循环或者精神史，而是文学作品的消费史，即消费主体的历史。读者阅读作品时，必然与以前的作品进行对比，从而对现时的接受进行调节。作品因读者的接受理解而存在，文学史就是文学接受史，甚至任何文学研究本质上就是文学史研究。姚斯还提出“期待视野”这个文学史理论中的重要概念。“‘期待视野’是阅读一部作品时读者的文学阅读经验构成的思维定向或先在结构。”①期待视野是读者在阅读理解之前对作品显现方式的定向性期待，读者以往的审美经验和生活经验相互交融形成具体的阅读期待。对作品的理解就是期待视野对象化的过程，一部作品可能与读者的期待视野一致，也可能不一致，因此，文学作品的接受史表现为读者期待视野的构成、作用及变化史。■

艺术作品的历史本质不仅在于它再现或表现的功能，而且在于它的影响之中。领悟

① H. R. 姚斯，等. 接受美学与接受理论：译者前言[M]. 周宁，金元浦，译. 沈阳：辽宁人民出版社，1987：6.

到这一点，对建立一种新的文学史基础有两点作用。一方面，假如作品生命的产生“不是来自于作品自身的存在，而是来自于作品与人类之间的相互作用”，这种不断的理解和对过去的能动的再生产就不能被局限于单个作品。相反，现在必须把作品与作品的关系放进作品和人的相互作用之中，把作品自身中含有的历史连续性放在生产与接受的相互关系中来看。换言之，只有当作品的连续性不仅通过生产主体，而且通过消费主体，即通过作者与读者之间的相互作用来调节时，文学艺术才能获得具有过程性特征的历史。另一方面，假如“人类现实不仅是新事物的产生，而且也是一种对于过去（批判的、辩证的）再生产”，只有将其独立出来，我们才能观察到艺术在这一不间断的总体化的过程中的功能。因为艺术形式的特殊成就不再被定义为模仿，相反被辩证地视为一种能够形成和改变感觉的媒介，艺术过程中首先发生的是“感觉的形成”。（p. 19）

即使对于判断一部新作品的批评家来说，那些根据对先前著作的肯定或否定的标准来设计自己作品的作者，以及按其传统将作品归类并历史地予以解释的文学史家，在他们对文学的反映关系变成再生产之前，也都是最早的读者。在这个作者、作品和大众的三角形之中，大众并不是被动的部分，并不仅仅作为一种反应，相反，它自身就是历史的一个能动的构成。一部文学作品的历史生命如果没有接受者的积极参与是不可思议的。因为只有通过读者的传递过程，作品才进入一种连续性变化的经验视野。在阅读过程中，永远不停地发生着从简单接受到批评性的理解，从被动接受到主动接受，从认识的审美标准到超越以往的新的生产的转换。文学的历史性及其传达特点预先假定了一种对话并随之假定在作品、读者和新作品间的过程性联系，以便从信息与接受者、疑问与回答、问题与解决之间的相互关系出发设想新的作品。如果理解文学作品的历史连续性时像文学史的连贯性一样找到一种新的解决方法，那么过去在这个封闭的生产和再现的圆圈中运动的文学研究的方法论就必须向接受美学和影响美学开放。（p. 24）

文学与读者的关系有美学的，也有历史的内涵。美学蕴涵存在于这一事实之中：一部作品被读者首次接受，包括同已经阅读过的作品进行比较，比较中就包含着对作品审美价值的一种检验。其中明显的历史蕴涵是：第一个读者的理解将在一代又一代的接受之链上被充实和丰富，一部作品的历史意义就是在这过程中得以确定，它的审美价值也是在这过程中得以证实。在这一接受的历史过程中，对过去作品的再欣赏是同过去艺术与现在艺术之间、传统评价与当前的文学尝试之间进行着的不间断的调节同时发生的。文学史家无法回避接受的历史过程，除非他对指导他理解与判断的前提条件不闻不问。（pp. 24-25）

论题 1. 文学史的更新要求建立一种接受和影响美学，摒弃历史客观主义的偏见和传统的生产美学与再现美学的基础。文学的历史性并不在于一种事后建立的“文学事实”的

编组,而在于读者对文学作品的先在经验。(p.26)

论题2.从类型的先在理解,从已经熟识作品的形式与主题,从诗歌语言和实践语言的对立中产生了期待系统。如果在对象化的期待系统中描述一部作品的接受和影响的话,那么,在每一部作品出现的历史瞬间,读者文学经验的分析就避免了心理学的可怕陷阱。(p.28)

一部文学作品,即便它以崭新面目出现,也不可能在信息真空中以绝对新的姿态展示自身。但它却可以通过预告、公开的或隐蔽的信号、熟悉的特点或隐蔽的暗示,预先为读者提示一种特殊的接受。它唤醒以往阅读的记忆,将读者带入一种特定的情感态度中,随之开始唤起“中间与终结”的期待,于是这种期待便在阅读过程中根据这类本文的流派和风格的特殊规则被完整地保持下去,或被改变、重新定向,或讽刺性地获得实现。(p.29)

论题3.按照这样一种方法重新结构——一部作品的期待视野允许人们根据它对于一个预先假定的读者发生影响的种类和等级来决定它的艺术特性。假如人们把既定期待视野与新作品出现之间的不一致描绘成审美距离,那么新作品的接受就可以通过对熟悉经验的否定或通过把新经验提高到意识层次,造成“视野的变化”,然后,这种审美距离又可以根据读者反应与批评家的判断(自发的成功、拒绝或振动,零散的赞同,逐渐的或滞后的理解)历时性地对象化。(p.31)

论题4.面对过去人们对一部作品的创造和接受,期待视野的重构使得人们从另一方面提出问题以求本文给出回答,从而去发现当代读者是如何看待和理解这一作品的。这一途径校正了最难以认识的古典主义标准及现代化的艺术理解,避免诉诸于普遍的“时代精神”的循环。它揭示了一部作品以前理解和目前理解的诠释的差异性,建立起调节二者地位的接受史意识,并因之回归于柏拉图式的语言学形而上学的教条。这一明显的自我确证要求:在文学本文中,文学永远是表现,而被一次性决定的客观意义对于阐释者在任何时代都是可以马上接受的。(pp.35-36)

论题5.接受的审美理论不仅让人们构想一部文学作品在其历史的理解中呈现出来的意义和形式,而且要求人们将个别作品置于所在的“文学系列”中从文学经验的语境上去认识历史地位和意义。从作品接受史到文学事件史,在这一步中后者表现为一个过程,在此过程中作者只是被动地接受。易言之,后继作品能够解决前一作品遗留下来的形式的和道德的问题,并且再提出新问题。(p.40)

把“文学演变”建立在接受美学上,不仅重建了文学史家失去的作为立足点的历史发展方向,而且还拓展了文学经验的时间深度,使人们能够认识到一部文学作品的现实意义

与实质意义之间的可变的距离。这就意味着，一部作品的艺术特点在其初次显现的视野中不可能被立即感知到。（p. 43）

论题6. 语言学区分历时性分析与共时性分析两种方法论上的相关方法，其成就在于打破了单一的历时性角度——以前人们唯一使用过的——在文学中具有相同意义。我们一旦考虑到审美态度的变化，新作品的理解与旧作品的意义之间的功能联系便与接受史的角度相抵触。我们还可以利用文学发展中一个共时性的横切面，同等安排同时代作品的异质多重性，反对等级结构，从而发现文学的历史时刻中的主要关系系统。从这里出发，一种新文学史的缩写原则得以发展。假如进一步将这一横断面的以前和以后都作这样的历时性安排，那么文学结构的演变在其开创新纪元的瞬刻，便被历史地结合起来了。（pp. 44-45）

论题7. 只有当文学生产不仅仅在其系统的继承中得到共时性和历时性的表现，而且也在其自身与“一般历史”的独特关系中被视为“类别史”时，文学史的任务方可完成。这一关系并未结束这样的事实：在所有时代的文学中均能发现的一种典型的、理想化的、讽刺的或者乌托邦式的社会生活幻想。这种文学的社会功能，只有在读者进入他的生活实践的期待视野，形成他对世界的理解，并因之也对其社会行为有所影响，从中获得文学体验的时候，才真正有可能实现自身。（pp. 48-49）

一种理论打算摧毁物质主义的传统思想，并代之以历史的功能思想，那就必然会招致责难，人们将会反对它在文学艺术范围内的片面性。放弃这一语言学方法的潜在的柏拉图主义，摒除虚幻的艺术作品的永恒本质以及观察者永恒的立足点，并开始把艺术史当作一个生产和接受的双向过程，其中，生产和接受并不是具有同等的功能，而是以问题与回答的对话的结构来调节过去与现在，不管谁这样做，都会冒着失去特殊的艺术体验的危险，而这种特殊的艺术体验显然处于历史性的对立面。艺术史编撰工作遵循着开放性结构和作品的不完全的感觉性阐释的原则，统一于对生产的理解和批评的再阐释过程。这一文学史学首先关系到艺术的知识功能和解放功能。所以，从狭义上看，新史学并不一定要忽视艺术的社会特点和审美特点——文学的批评、交流和社会影响功能，还有下述成就：文学艺术能使饱经苦难的人们经验到狂喜、愉快、游戏的冲动。这些冲动能使他脱离其历史存在和社会环境。（pp. 93-94）

文学解释学已不再对发现本文中暗藏的唯一的真理——阐释本文感兴趣了。巴尔特把文学解释学当作“反神秘的密码”，绝非随意之言。“多元本文”的理论主张“互文性”，即无限的、随意的意义可能性的产生和随意的阐释。文学解释学与之针锋相对，提出这样一个前提，文学作品意义的具体化是一个历史进程，它遵循着沉淀在审美原则的形成与变化中的特定“逻辑”。文学解释学进而又假定,在阐释视野的变化中,人们可以清清楚楚地区分开随意的阐释和规范构成性的阐释。支持这一假设的基本理论只能存在于本文的审美特性中:如同一个有序原则,阐释依靠它存在,而阐释的具体化的意义也改进、完善了这一原则。(p.185)

(H. R. 姚斯,R. C. 霍拉勃. 接受美学与接受理论[M]. 周宁,金元浦,译. 沈阳:辽宁人民出版社,1987.)

接受理论(节选)

◉霍拉勃

【导读】《接受理论》是美国学者罗伯特·C. 霍拉勃对接受美学的研究著作,研究了接受美学的产生条件、基本理论、发展过程、自身价值及发生的影响,是对接受美学的整体面貌较全面的把握。

《接受理论》也包括五章的内容,它首先阐述了接受理论作为一种新的批评范式的基本情况,接着介绍了接受理论受到的影响及先驱人物,如俄国形式主义、布拉格结构主义、文学社会学以及罗曼·茵格尔顿及汉斯-乔治·伽达默尔的理论。该书对接受理论的代表人物主要选择了姚斯和伊瑟尔进行介绍,并对接受理论与一般交流理论的关系,接受理论中马克思主义接受理论与经验主义接受理论作了分析和阐述。最后,作者对接受理论存在的问题及面临的挑战表达了自己的看法。■

汉斯·罗伯特·姚斯在1969年的一篇题为《文学学范式的改变》的论文中,勾画出文学方法的历史,从而预示了当代文学研究中一场“革命”的开始已近在咫尺。姚斯从托马斯·S. 库恩的著作中借用了“范式”和“科学革命”的理论,揭示出文学研究有着与自然科学相似的发展过程。他论证道,文学研究并不是一个事实与证据日积月累的过程,也不是亟待接近对文学本质的认识或正确地理解个体文学作品的过程。反之,文学研究的发展特点恰恰在于质的飞跃、间断的和分离的创造。一种曾经指导过文学研究的范式,一旦不再能够满足研究作品的需要,就要被废弃,被一种新的范式,一种更适应于文学研究的、独立于旧范式的新范式取而代之,直到这种新范式又无法实现其对旧作品作出新解释的功能为止。(pp.275-276)

文学研究的新途径的出现,尤其是具有范式地位的新途径的出现,不可避免地导致一系列为它追根溯源的研究,从而使其独创性黯然失色。在某种意义上我们可以说:理论创造了自己的先驱。这一格言对接受理论同样适用。的确如此,在接受理论崭露头角的那几年,有些研究就力图证实它对前代思想的依附。一般说来,先驱并不难找。亚里士多德的《诗学》将净化归结为审美经验的核心范畴,这可被看作观众反应在其中起到重要作用的理论的最早例证。事实上,整个修辞学传统及其与诗学理论的关系,都把着眼点放在口头或书面交流对听众或读者的影响上,这同样可被视为先驱。在德国理论传统中,莱辛对亚里士多德诗学范畴的注释也许是理论转移的最著名的例证。在其理论中,戏剧对观众个人的影响受到实质性的重视。广言之,从 1750 年鲍姆嘉通的论著《美学》始,美学作为哲学研究的一个分支,直到康德的《判断力批判》,整个 18 世纪的美学传统都建立在艺术品是什么、做什么的思想上。……

在此基础上,我们须注意到具有先导性质的五种影响:俄国形式主义、布拉格结构主义、罗曼·茵格尔顿的现象学、汉斯-乔治·加达默(Hans-Georg Gadamer)的解释学,还有"文学社会学"。它们之所以被选中,是因为一则它们对理论的发展具有显著的影响,在接受理论主要理论家的脚注和理论来源中就足以获得证明;二则,如上所述,它们都重新着眼于本文—读者的关系,从而有助于解决文学研究中的危机。在大部分情况下,所谓的康斯坦茨学派的理论家多受其直接影响。(pp. 289-291)

姚斯试图克服马克思主义的二难境界,从读者或消费者的观点来看文学。60 年代末、70 年代初,姚斯把他的理论称为"接受美学"(Rezeptions ästhetik),主张艺术作品的历史本质,绝不能被单纯的艺术品生产的考察和作品描述所抹杀。相反,我们应把文学看成生产和接受的辩证过程。"只有当作品的延续不再从生产主体思考,而从消费主体方面思考,即从作者与公众相联系的方面思考时,才能写出一部文学和艺术的历史。"姚斯把文学置于较大的事件过程中,以迎合马克思的历史思考;把观察主体置于其研究的核心,以保持形式主义所取得的成就。历史和美学就这样被联系起来:

"美学意义蕴含于这一事实中,读者首次接受一部文学作品,必然包含着与他以前所读作品相对比而进行的审美价值检验。其中明显的历史意义是,第一位读者的理解,将在代代相传的接受链上保存、丰富,一部作品的历史意义就这样得以确定,其审美价值也得以证明。"

因此,注意的转移还孕育着一种新型的文学史。姚斯展示的是一种在过去与现在之间具有有意识的调节作用的历史编纂工作。它并不简单地接受既定的传统,研究文学接受史的人,必须以作品如何影响当时的条件和事件,又如何被它们所影响作为指针,不断地重新思考作品。(pp. 239-240)

70 年代中期以来,接受理论中经验主义的研究盛行一时,这是接受理论遇到更大危机的征兆。奠基于自然科学的经验方法之上的经验主义研究,在解释学与现象学的出发点上就退却了。它们认为自己只是为更加面面俱到的文学范型提供资料与数据结果。但不管怎么说,他们绝没有在康斯坦茨学派的伦理上推进半步,尽管在过去几年中,站在理论前线的非经验主义的最知名的理论家也同样无所建树。斯梯尔和伊瑟尔的最后一部力作分别发表于1975年和1976年。虽然姚斯的《审美经验》的修订版最近在德国出版,但其中并没有任何重大的理论突破。

……

然而,我们也可以认为,新理论发生饥荒,是由各种不同的困境造成的,接受理论的基本假设,一经逻辑的延伸,困境便接踵而至。接受理论无疑在引导文学研究的途径上具有巨大的冲击力,左右了文学研究的方法。但接受理论探索的这条道路并没有像我们原先想象的那样开阔和具有多产性。常常令人百步九折,盘旋迂回,或者步入死胡同。而接受理论一旦面临着结构主义、后结构主义以及法国和美国的“先锋派”等各种不同的理论时,这一点便更加昭然若揭了。(pp. 436-437)

(H. R. 姚斯,R. C. 霍拉勃. 接受美学与接受理论[M]. 周宁,金元浦,译. 沈阳:辽宁人民出版社,1987.)

【研究范例】

意象派与中国古典诗歌

◉赵毅衡

意象派,是本世纪初由一些英美青年诗人组成的诗派,1910—1920年活动于伦敦。意象派历史不长,创作成果不大,却造成巨大的影响,尤其在美国,这影响至今没有消失。因此,意象派被称为“美国文学史上开拓出最大前景的文学运动”①,很多文学史著作把它作为英美现代诗歌的发轫。

意象主义,是这批青年诗人对后期浪漫主义(即所谓维多利亚诗风)统治英美诗坛感到不满,在多种国外影响之下开创出来的新诗路。他们反对诗歌中含混的抒情、陈腐的说教、抽象的感慨,强调诗人应当使用鲜明的意象——描写感觉上具体的对象——来表现诗意。

当然,诗歌一向都是使用意象的,但往往在一段具体描写之后就要引出抽象的、“提高一层次”的发挥。而意象派强调把诗人的感触和情绪全部隐藏到具体的意象背后。意象派把注意力集中在事物引起的感觉上,而不去探求事物之间的本质联系,也不去阐发这联系的社会意义。但是,在诗歌艺术技巧上,意象派作了十分有意义的开拓工作。意象派

① Howard Munford Jones《Guide to American Literature and Its Background Since 1890》(Harvard University Press, Cambridge 1959 二版)p140.

所探索的，实际上是形象思维在诗歌创作中的某些具体规律。因此，它是值得我们重视的一个诗派。

东方诗歌（中国古典诗歌、日本古典诗歌）对意象派起了很大影响。日本文学界对意象主义及其日本渊源作了很多研究工作，而对意象派所受的中国诗歌影响我们至今没有加以研究。实际上，意象派受中国古典诗歌之惠远比受之于日本诗者更为重要。

开风气之先的是意象派前期主将埃兹拉·庞德①。1915 年他的《汉诗译卷》（*Cathay*）问世，这本仅有十五首李白和王维短诗译文的小册子，被认为是庞德对英语诗歌“最持久的贡献”②，是“英语诗歌经典作品”③，其中《河商之妻》（即李白《长干行》）、《南方人在北国》（即李白《古风第八》）等篇章脍炙人口，经常作为庞德本人的创作名篇而选入现代诗歌选本，美国现代文学史上也常要论及，从而使庞德从 T. S. 爱略特手中得到“为当代发明了中国诗的人”的美名。一个国家的现代文学受一本翻译如此大的影响，这在世界范围内是很少见的事。

这本译诗触发起英美诗坛翻译、学习中国古典诗歌历久不衰的热潮。意象派后期挂帅人物、美国女诗人爱米·洛威尔邀人合译了中国古典诗歌一百五十首，于 1920 年出版《松花笺》（*Fir-Flower Tablets*），爱米·洛威尔直到临死还在计划继续译中国诗。在庞德译诗出版后的五年之内出现的中国古典诗歌英译本至少不下十种。文学史家惊叹，这些年月，中国诗简直“淹没了英美诗坛”④。

意象派诗人之所以迷恋中国古典诗歌，并非纯为猎奇，或给自己的诗添些异国味，他们觉得中国古典诗歌与意象派的主张颇为吻合，可以引这个有几千年历史的文明来为自己的主张作后盾。庞德说：“正是因为有些中国诗人，满足于把事物表现出来，而不加说教或评论，所以人们不辞繁难加以迻译。”⑤所以，意象派之与中国古典诗歌结合，是有一定姻缘的。“按中国风格写诗，是被当时追求美的直觉所引导的自由诗运动命中注定要探索的方向”。⑥而著名汉诗翻译家卫律（Avthur Waley）在 1918 年出版的《中国诗 170 首》甚至被

---

① 埃兹拉·庞德（Ezra Pound），美国现代重要诗人。此人“第二次世界大战”时期投靠墨索里尼，战后被美军逮捕，以叛国罪受审。但他是现代诗歌一些重要运动的发起者，在美国诗坛的影响近年来越来越大。对他的诗歌创作和理论，有必要作认真研究。

② 《Literary History of the United States》by Robert E. spillev Willar Thorp 等.（Mac Millan & Co. 1974，四版）p. 1338.

③ Kenneth Rexroth《100 chinese poews》附文献书目注释。

④ 《Digest of World Literature》卷四，Poetry of Ezra Pound.

⑤ Ezra Pound《Chinese Poetry》，转引自 Wai-Lim Yip《China Poetry—Major Modes and Genres》（University of Califonia Press，1977）p. 29.

⑥ Hugh Kenner《The Pound Era》（Faber & Faber，London，1972）p. 196.

文学史家认为是“至今尚有生命力的唯一意象派诗歌”①。

意象派从中国古典诗歌学到的技巧可以归结为以下三点：

一、“全意象”

庞德对汉语文字学的无知引出非常有趣的结果。当时庞德对汉字可以说目不识丁，他是根据一个研究日本文学的“专家”费诺罗萨死后留下的对汉诗逐字注释的笔记进行翻译的。据费诺罗萨的观点，中国诗中的方块字仍是象形字，每个字本身就是由意象组成的，因此中国作家在纸上写的是组合的图画。例如太阳在萌发的树木之下——春；太阳在纠结的树枝后升起——东。这样中国诗就彻底地浸泡在意象里，无处不意象了。于是庞德找到了扫荡浪漫主义诗歌抽象说理抒情的有力武器，②而为意象主义最早的理论家赫尔姆的想入非非的主张“每个词应有意象粘在上面，而不是一块平平的筹码”③找到了有力根据。1920 年庞德发表《论中国书面文字》(*Essay on Chinese Written Characters*)一文，详细阐明了他的看法，引起学界哗然。

但是庞德不顾汉学家的批评，坚持他的看法。虽然比他早几个世纪培根和莱布尼茨就对中国字大感兴趣，但庞德搞出了对中国字魔力的崇拜。他的长诗《诗章》中经常夹有汉字，好像方块字有神秘的象征意义。

但他更经常做的是从方块字的组成中找意象。《论语》的“学而时习之，不亦乐乎”，被他反用入诗句：

> 学习，而时间白色的翅膀飞走了，
> 这不是让人高兴的事。
>
> 《诗章》第七十五章

这个“白色的翅膀”是他从習字中化出来的。

甚至在翻译中庞德也这样搞。1954 年他出版《孔子颂诗集》，即《诗经》译文。《大雅·崧高》首句：“崧高维嶽”被他译成：

> 高高地，盖满松林的山峰，充满回音……

“崧”字中，被他抓出了“松树”与“山”，而“嶽”中被他挖出了“言”。这句诗挺美的，只是作为翻译未免太过。幸好，庞德翻译著名的《汉诗译卷》时，还未能自己辨认汉字，只

---

① 《The Concise Encyclopedia of Modern World Li terature》1963，p. 458.

② 《Guide to American Literature from Emily Dickenson to the Present Day》by James T. Callow, Robert J. Reilly, 1973.

③ 见 Hulme 笔记，转引自《Imagism and the Imagists》by, Glenn Hughes(Bowes & Bowes, London, 1960) p. 20.

是根据别人的注释翻译,所以没有过分失真。

庞德虽然把中国古典诗歌"意象主义"的原因搞错了,但他的错误是个幸运的错误,他的直觉是正确的,他敏感地觉察到中国诗是意象派应该学习的范例。不少中国古诗,尤其是唐诗,的确是浸泡在意象之中。我随便举一些选本必录的名诗为例:刘长卿《送灵彻》,韦承庆《南行别第》,韦应物《滁州西涧》,张继《枫桥夜泊》,杜牧《山行》、《寄扬州韩绰判官》,温庭筠《咸阳值雨》等,这些诗都可入意象派诗集。我们可以发现唐诗中的"意象诗"大多是绝句,律诗起承转合结构分明,往往必须从具体意象"拔高",而绝句比较自由,可以只在意象上展开。宋之后,以理入诗,"意象诗"就少了。同样情况也在词中出现:小令比长调多"意象诗"。

庞德的错误之所以是"幸运"的,其第二个原因是,从汉语文字学称为"会意字"的那一部分字的象形构成中,的确能够发掘出新鲜而生动的意象。让我们看意象派诗人弗莱契描写黄昏的诗句:

现在,最低的松枝

已横画在太阳的园面上。

《兰色交响乐》第五章

显然,他是从"莫"(暮)字中得到启发。类似的例子使评家说他写此诗时"处在中国诗决定性的影响之下"①。

二、"脱节"

1913 年意象派诗人弗林特在《诗歌》杂志上发表文章,提出著名的意象派三原则,要求"绝对不用无益于表现的词"。这条过分严酷的原则,意象派诗人自己也无法贯彻初衷,所以后来再不见提起。但是汉语古典诗歌,由于其特别严谨的格律要求以及古汉语特殊的句法形态,往往略去了大部分联结词、系词以及各种句法标记,几乎只剩下光裸裸的表现具体事物的词。这样,中国古典诗歌就取得了使用英语的意象派无法达到的意象密度。

这种情况,使意象派诗人十分兴奋。但接着就出现了如何把中国诗的这种特殊品质引入到英语中来的问题。庞德这样翻译李白的诗《古风第六》中"惊沙乱海日"一句:

惊奇。沙漠的混乱。大海的太阳。②

开创了"脱节"翻译法的先例。

---

① 见 Hulme 笔记,转引自《Imagism and the Imagists》by, Glenn Hughes(Bowes & Bowes, London,1960)p. 137.

② 原文:Surprised. Desert turmoil. Sea sun.

对于这个问题，加利福尼亚大学中国文学与比较文学副教授、华裔学者叶维廉最近作了仔细的研究。他举出杜审言的两句诗为例：

云霞出海曙，梅柳渡江春。

他觉得可以译成：

云和雾在黎明时走向大海，
梅和柳在春天越过了大江。①

但不如译成：

云和雾
向大海；
黎明。

梅和柳
渡过江；
春。

为什么？因为“缺失的环节一补足，诗就散文化了。”②的确，翻译时，加上原诗隐去的环节，就是解释词之间的关系，而解释是意象派诗人最深恶痛绝的事。赫尔姆说：“解释，拉丁文 explane，就是把事物摊成平面，”③因此不足取。

但问题是，中国古典诗歌是不是真正“脱节”的？大部分古典汉诗的诗句，词之间的句法关系虽然没有写出，却是明摆着的，古典汉诗的特殊句法规定不必在字面上表达这些联系，但翻译时只有补起来才是忠实于原文。例如“惊沙乱海日”一句，就连鼓吹“脱节”译法的叶维廉自己的译本中也译作：

惊起的沙迷乱了“瀚海”上的太阳……④

但是他却认为柳宗元的《江雪》应译成：

---

① 据《唐诗选》（余冠英等注，人民文学 1978 年版）. 杜审言此二句诗应解为：“破晓时云气被朝阳照耀好像与旭日一起从海中升出；到江南见梅柳开花抽芽，似乎大自然一过长江就换上春装。”

② Ezra Pound《Chinese Poetry》，转引自 Wai-Lim Yip《China Poetry—Major Modes and Genres》（University of Califonia Press，1977）p. 9.

③ Halme《Further Speculation》（Lincoln Neb. 1955）.

④ 英文：Startliug sand confounds the sun above the “Vast sea”.

孤独的船。竹笠。一个老人，
钓着鱼:冰冻的河。雪。

这是不足为法的。“脱节”法只有在个别情况下是我们欣赏诗歌时的惯例，也是翻译中应使用的办法:第一种如“枯藤老树昏鸦，小桥流水人家”，这些诗句本来就是由孤立的意象并列而成的;第二类如“人闲桂花落，夜静春山空”“星垂平野阔，月涌大江流”，这些诗句一句之中压入了两个基本上各自独立的意象，他们之间有点关系，但不必要去点明，我们欣赏诗歌时，能自动把两个意象联系起来，却不一定需要弄清二者究竟是什么句法关系;第三类如上文谈到的杜审言的诗句“云霞出海曙，梅柳渡江春”隐去的环节很玄妙，不是加几个词能解决的，这就强迫我们使用“脱节”译法。我们可以猜想，庞德当初写出“惊奇。沙漠的混乱……”这妙句，是因为他在费诺罗萨笔记上只看到每个字的解释，在“海”字上碰到难关而无法串解全句，这才想出的绝招。

同样的“脱节句”也出现在李白古风第十四首(庞德改题为《边卒怨》)的译文之中。“荒城空大漠”一句被译成:

荒凉的城堡，天空，广袤的沙漠。

这可能是原文“空”字过于难解而逼出来的翻译法。不管庞德的动机是什么，这样解除了句法环节只剩下名词的诗句，对于句法标记十分明确的印欧语系各语言，的确是叫人瞠目结舌的新东西。

庞德马上觉悟到他“以李白为师”学到了一种十分奇妙的诗歌技巧，他把这方法用到创作中去:

雨;空旷的河，一个旅人。
……
秋月;山临湖而起。

《诗章》第四十九

但在英语中，这样只剩下孤立名词的诗句，终嫌不自然。因此，中国古典诗歌的“脱节”法在意象派诗人手里朝另一个方向发展:保留一些句法关系标记，但在诗行写法上把它打散。庞德的名诗《地铁站台》当初在《诗歌》杂志上刊登时是这样写的:

人群中　出现的　那些脸庞:
潮湿黝黑　树枝上的　花瓣。

评者认为这是明显地想追求方块字意象脱节的效果。[①]另一种是拆成短行的办法，这在意象派诗人中十分盛行。而威·卡·威廉斯这首诗把每行压到只剩一个词(而且大部分是单音节词)，似乎走极端，但实际上是实践了庞德的想法。

《槐花盛开》

就在
那些
翠绿

坚硬
古老
明亮

折断的
树枝
中间

白色
芳香的
五月

回来吧。

而庞德这首诗采用梯形写法：

忘川的形象，
　　　　　　　　布满微光的
田野，
　　　　　金色的
　　灰悬崖，
　　　　　下面

① Ezra Pound《Chinese Poetry》，转引自 Wai-Lim Yip《China Poetry—Major Modes and Genres》(University of Califonia Press，1977) p. 20.

是海

硬过花岗岩……

《大战燃眉·阿克塔孔》

在美国,“梯形诗”不是“马雅柯夫斯基体”,是威·卡·威廉斯首先在较长的诗中稳定地采用这种写法,或许应该称“威廉斯体”。

间隔、短行、梯形三种写法,同样是追求使意象“脱节”孤立起来的“聚光灯”效果,加强每个意象的刺激性,同时使人感到意象之间的空间距离。这样,虽然句法联系标记保留了,但读者被引导去体会意象之间比句法关系更深一层的联系。

三、“意象迭加”

然而,意象派师法中国古典诗歌还学到更多的法宝。

1911 年某一天,庞德在巴黎协和广场走出地铁,突然在人群中看到一张张美丽的面容,他怦然有所动。想了一天,晚上觉得灵感来了,但脑中出现的不是文词,而是斑驳的色点形象。他为此写了三十行诗,不能尽如人意;六个月后,改成十五行,仍不能满意;一年之后,他把《地铁站上》这首诗写成目前的形式:只有两行。

人群中出现的这些脸庞:

潮湿黝黑树枝上的花瓣。

这首极短的诗,是意象派最负盛名的诗作,“暗示了现代城市生活那种易逝感,那种非人格化。”①从诗的意象本身看不出这种“暗示”,这些丰富的联想大部分产生自这首诗奇特的形式。

有人认为这首诗是学的日本俳句②,这只是从表面上看问题,实际上这种技巧是从中国诗学来的。早在得到费诺罗萨的笔记之前,庞德就对中国诗如痴如醉,那时他从翟理斯的《中国文学史》③中直译的诗歌译文中找材料进行改译。让我们将他改译的一首诗逐字反译成现代汉语:

丝绸的窸窣已不复闻,

尘土在宫院里飘荡,

---

① Hugh Kenner《The Pound Era》(Faber & Faber, London, 1972) p. 79.

② Earl Miner《The Japanese Tradition in British and American Literature》(Princeton University Press, Naw Jersey, 1958) p. 117.

③ Herbert A. Giles《A History of Chinese Literature》,此书与法国 Judith Gautier 所作《Le Livre de Jade》同为意象派学习中国古典诗歌的教科书。

听不到脚步声，而树叶
卷成堆，静止不动，
她，我心中的欢乐，长眠在下面：

一张潮湿的树叶粘在门槛上。

这最后一句显然是个隐喻，但采用了奇特的形式：它舍去了喻体与喻本之间任何系词，它以一个具体的意象比另一个具体的意象，但两个意象之间相比的地方很微妙，需要读者在想象中作一次跳跃。庞德称他在中国诗里发现的这种技巧为“意象迭加”（Supes-posifion），《地铁站上》就是袭用这种技巧的，因此有的文学史家称这首诗是应用中国技巧的代表作品。①

庞德认为这种迭加，才是“意象主义真谛”②——“意象表现瞬间之中产生的智力和情绪上的复合体。”作为意象的定义，庞德的说法是错误的：意象不一定要有比喻关系，很多意象是直接描写事物的所谓“描述性意象”，更不能说只有这种形式特别的隐喻才是真正的意象。

但是，这种意象迭加手法，的确有奇妙的效果：它使一个很容易在我们眼前一滑而过的比喻，顿时变得十分醒目，迫使读者在一个联想的跳跃后深思其中隐含的意味。

让我们看庞德那首译诗的原文：据传为汉武帝刘彻所作的《落叶哀蝉曲》③

罗袂兮无声，玉墀兮尘生。虚房冷而寂寞，落叶依于重扃。望彼美之女兮安得，感余心之专宁。

这里，“落叶依于重扃”嵌在诗当中，乍一看似乎是实写景，并不是隐喻。但这可能正是我们对我国古典诗歌中一些意象技巧的敏感性反不如意象派诗人的地方，意象派诗人在选取最富于诗意的意象上，的确独具慧眼。

“迭加”在中国古典诗歌中，并不是罕见的例子。很多诗句中的“迭加”，不需要意象派诗人用冒号、破折号、分行、空格等办法来提醒注意，我们也认得出。下面是随手采集的一些

---

① 《Digest of World Literature》卷四，Poetry of Ezra Pound.

② 1913年意象派诗人弗林特在《诗歌》杂志上发表文章，形式上是与一个意象派诗人（即庞德的化身）的对话，文中提出了著名的意象主义三原则。但之后被访者又提到一个“意象主义真谛”，问者求一解释，而对方故作神秘默而不答。直到1915年庞德已脱离意象派后，才在一篇回顾性的文章中解释了这种“复合体”概念。

③ 此诗据说是汉武帝思怀李夫人所作，见于前秦方士王嘉所撰《拾遗记》，该书语多荒诞，这首诗恐怕为后人依托。但近人也有认为并非伪作的。

例子。[因为只录下个别诗句,上下文意义不分明,我在迭加部分(喻体)下画一条线。]
有正常次序的:

照影溪梅,怅绝代佳人独立。

辛弃疾《满江红·题冷泉亭》

有倒过来的:

雨中黄叶树,灯下白头人。

司空曙《喜外弟卢纶见宿》

落叶他乡树,寒灯独夜人。

马戴《灞上秋居》

也有与喻本挤入一句之中的:

自把玉钗敲砌竹,
清歌一曲月如霜。

高适《听张立本女吟》

这种手法,一经庞德倡用,其他意象派诗人也竞相采用。我们可以举奥尔丁顿的诗为例:

《R.V 和另一个人》
你是敏感的陌生人
在一个阴霾的城里,
人们瞪眼瞧你,恨你——

暗褐色小巷里的番红花。

爱米·洛威尔下面二首诗把喻体放在前面:

《日记》
狂风摇撼的树丛里,颠荡着银色的灯笼,
老人回想起
他年轻时的爱情。

《比例》
天空中有月亮,有星星;

我的花园中有黄色的蛾
围着白色的杜鹃花扑腾。

赫尔姆曾要求:“两个视觉意象形成我们可以称之为视觉和弦的东西,联合起来提示一个与二者都不同的意象。”“视觉和弦”这个名称倒也生动。意象派诗人在中国古典诗歌中找到了把一个寻常比喻变成含不尽意于言外的“视觉和弦”的技巧,并给予更醒目、更生动,也更富于诗意的形式。

总的来说:中国古典诗歌给意象派带来的影响是健康的、有益的。除了上面说的三点具体处理意象的技巧外,我们还应当指出下列两个问题:

1912 年费诺罗萨的寡妻在《诗歌》杂志上读到庞德的意象主义诗作,觉得写出这种风格的诗的人,是完成其丈夫遗业的合适的人选,因此,她把 150 本笔记本交到了庞德手中,庞德这才开始翻译中国诗。

我们不能说意象派是从中国古典诗歌发源的,只能说中国诗丰富了意象派诗人的技巧,加强了他们的信念。

意象派在英美兴起时,正是欧洲大陆上后期象征主义向达达主义和超现实主义过渡而执欧洲诗坛牛耳的时期,意象派诗人不可避免要以法国象征主义为师,但意象派的诗歌与象征主义很不相同:意象派诗歌大都色彩比较明朗、清晰、诗情藏而不露却并不难懂,很少如象征主义诗歌那样的晦涩,那样充满过于费人猜想的象征。这显然与中国古典诗歌意象的轻捷明快有关。“中国诗歌的自由诗译文是对后期象征主义趋势的矫正剂。”①

意象派诗人不仅热衷于翻译、改作、模仿中国诗,不仅向中国诗学技巧,进而在选材上、意境上向中国古典诗歌学习。爱米·洛威尔甚至写了一组著名的诗,《汉风集》(*Chinoi series*)。我们试举一首为例:

《飘雪》
雪在我耳边低语。
我的木屐,
在我身后留下印痕。
谁也不打这路上来,
追寻我的脚迹。
当寺钟重新敲响,
就会盖没,就会消失。

① Hugh Kenner《The Pound Era》(Faber & Faber, London, 1972) p. 196.

虽然木屐是日本货，这首诗仍有点李清照的情调。的确意象派诗人学中国诗，企图超出形似而追求神似的努力，似乎没有白费。

同时意象派学中国诗并非一味效颦。中国古典诗歌几乎全部意象是从大自然景色中选取的，这是几千年农业社会经济生活的反映。作为现代诗人，就不能讳言城市生活。我们在意象派诗人的作品中看到不少将城市意象与大自然意象糅合入诗的好例。庞德的《地铁站上》效果奇妙原因之一就是将一个大自然意象贴合在一个城市意象上，充分利用了情调上的对比。弗莱契《幅射》中的某些章节也是二种意象糅合比较成功的例子。此外，意象派诗歌全部是自由诗，却比英语格律诗更好地表现了格律严谨的中国古典诗歌的风貌，这也是意象派的一个成功的探索，开了汉诗翻译一派的先河。

意象派诗作之短小凝练也与东方诗歌有关。固然，意象派的原则——以情绪串接意象——使他们的诗能展开的长度和深度都很有限，难以对生活中的重大课题作深入探讨，但就某些题材来说，抒情诗的短小又何尝不是优点？《地铁站上》定稿那两行不比初稿的三十行更令人激赏？

固然古希腊有二三行的短诗，但在罗马人手里短诗就成了写讽刺诗的专用形式。英国首先学拉丁诗的本·江生和海利克等人更把短诗搞成俏皮的警句诗。浪漫主义诗人雨果等开始写严肃题材的短诗，但短诗之盛行，是在东方诗歌影响下形成的。十九世纪法国人对俳句之醉心，有如文艺复兴时代英国人对十四行诗的热狂。而俳句促进了法国现代诗歌走向凝练的趋势。① 固然，很早就有人提出所有真正的诗必须是短诗，但那是针对密尔顿的《失乐园》或华滋华斯的《序曲》那样太冗长的诗而言的。② 大量抒情诗短到只有二至五行，这是东方诗歌形式的影响所致。

意象派诗人向东方诗学习，首先从日本诗开始，这有历史原因。十九世纪上半期（约1800—1870）法国文艺界盛行中国热，而下半期（约1865—1895）盛行日本热。意象派受到法国诗歌影响，首先搬过来的自然是日本热。

但意象派主要迷恋于日本诗形式的精巧简练，无韵的日本诗又似乎可为他们的自由诗主张张目。自从庞德倡学中国诗后，意象派发现中国诗内容和技巧都更丰富，因此出现了一个矛盾的情况：爱米·洛威尔把自己的一本诗集取名为《飘浮世界的图景》，名字套自日本传统版画名称“浮世绘”，弗莱契的诗集干脆名之为《日本版画》，但评者认为其中的诗“与其说是像日本诗，不如说像中国诗。”③

---

① Earl Miner《The Japanese Tradition in British and American Literature》(Princeton University Press, Naw Jersey, 1958) p. 129 引 Schwatz 语.

② 参见 T. S. Eliot《Poetry and Prose》一文，又见《Guide to American Literature from Emily Dickenson to the Present Day》by James T. Callow, Robert J. Reilly, 1973, p. 76.

③ 见 Hulme 笔记，转引自《Imagism and the Imagists》by, Glenn Hughes(Bowes & Bowes, London, 1960) p. 137.

意象派学日本诗是承法国余风，而学中国诗基本上是独辟蹊径，他们在这里得到更大的收获。意象派是如此深地打上中国印记，以致有的文学史干脆名之以“意象主义这个中国龙”，来与“象征主义这条法国蛇”并称，①作为现代美国诗歌国外影响的两个主要来源。

说清这个问题，倒不是与日本人争强赌胜，而是还历史本来面目。我们民族文化对世界的影响，这个荣誉，不便拱手让人。

而意象派学中国诗的经验，对我们今天研究我国古典诗歌是很好的借镜。我们的新诗向古典诗歌学习至今难说已有很大成效。有的人刻意模仿，却把古典汉语也搬了进来，弄得半文不白；有的诗作意象陈旧，像仿古的园林，放不进现代建筑。意象派当然也有学得很肤浅的作品，但他们深入解剖中国古典诗歌的“意象元件”，在创作中发展中国诗的技巧；他们能用自由诗形式表现中国古诗意趣；他们把中国诗式的大自然意象与现代城市风光糅合——这些，都应当对我们有所启发。

（载《外国文学研究》1979 年第四期）

【延伸阅读】

1. 金丝燕. 文学接受与文化过滤——中国对法国象征主义诗歌的接受[M]. 北京：中国人民大学出版社，1994.

金丝燕的《文学接受与文化过滤——中国对法国象征主义诗歌的接受》一书共七章，是 20 世纪 90 年代国内最丰富最全面的法国象征主义研究成果，介绍了法国文学批评和文学史关于象征主义的研究成果，并描述了法国象征主义诗歌在中国的接受、中国新诗评论的期待视野、中国象征派诗歌的音乐性。

2. 汪介之. 文学接受与当代解读：20 世纪中国文学语境中的俄罗斯文学[M]. 北京：北京师范大学出版社，2010.

中国文学界和广大读者所面对的俄罗斯文学，其本身是一种丰富多样、异彩纷呈的客观存在，又是一个处于不断发展变化中的实体，而中国文学对它的接纳，则显示出作为接受主体（接受者民族）进行选择的目光，并且在总体上呈现出随着历史的变迁而转换的阶段性特征。本书包括 20 世纪中国文学对俄罗斯文学的接受，重新审视 20 世纪俄罗斯文学的中国视角，当代中国语境中的俄罗斯文学研究，中国文学视野中的俄罗斯经典作家作品解读和俄罗斯文学的文化阐释等五部分内容。

---

① 《From Whitman to Sandburg in American Poetry》by Bruce Weirick.（New York 1934）p. 145.

第四节　译介学

翻译作为文化传播的工具，不但承载着种种变异现象的发生，而且其本身就是变异发生的机制。基于此，我们给“译介学”下的定义是：“译介学是比较文学变异学中研究语言层面变异的学科，它关注的是跨语际翻译(Interlingual Translation)过程中发生的种种语言变异现象，并探讨产生这些变异的社会、历史以及文化根源。”

一、译介学的发展历史

20世纪前期，“译介学”在传统的比较文学学科理论里划分在“媒介学”的研究范围内。如梵·第根在1931年出版的《比较文学论》一书中，把“译本和翻译者”放在第七章“媒介”中加以讨论。[①]1934年，日本学者野上丰一郎在《比较文学论要》中把翻译作为媒介学研究的主要问题来进行论述。[②]

受国外学者的影响，在中国比较文学刚刚兴起的20世纪80年代，学界也在媒介学的范畴内讨论翻译问题。如卢康华、孙景尧的《比较文学导论》[③]，乐黛云主编的《中西比较文学教程》[④]，陈惇、刘象愚的《比较文学概论》[⑤]等比较文学教材都把译介学视为媒介学下面的一个支系。也正是在此时，“译介学”这个名称正式出现。不过其更多的是强调文学传播和交流过程中的实证关系。

20世纪70年代以来，西欧学界兴起了以后结构主义、解构主义为核心理论的“翻译研究(Translation Studies)”，这对于传统的翻译研究形成了突破，也直接促成了译介学的独立。这一新兴的翻译研究不再将“原文”及其作者作为出发点和判断标准，也不再将“译文”是否对“原文”进行了准确翻译作为主要关切点；而是转向以译者和译

① 梵·第根．比较文学论[M]．戴望舒，译．台北：台湾商务印书馆，1995：163.

② 野上丰一郎．比较文学论要[M]//刘介民．比较文学译文选．长沙：湖南人民出版社，1984：84.

③ 卢康华，孙景尧．比较文学导论[M]．哈尔滨：黑龙江人民出版社，1984.

④ 乐黛云．中西比较文学教程[M]．北京：高等教育出版社，1988.

⑤ 陈惇，刘象愚．比较文学概论[M]．北京：北京师范大学出版社，1988.

文为中心，将“翻译”这一媒介从“原文”对其的羁绊中解放出来，视为独立的主体，讨论翻译的行为、译本的效果是在何种社会文化机制下得以运作的。

20世纪90年代，“翻译研究”介绍到中国以后，引起了中国比较文学学者的重视。这个时期出版的比较文学理论和教材都把译介学从媒介学的框架里划分出来单独介绍。如1997年陈惇、孙景尧、谢天振主编的《比较文学》，就用专章讨论了译介学。①1999年谢天振出版了我国第一部系统论述译介学学科历史和理论的专著《译介学》，借用翻译研究的视角，对译介学进行了重新阐释。他认为：“译介学最初是从比较文学中媒介学的角度出发、目前则越来越多是从比较文化的角度出发对翻译（尤其是文学翻译）和翻译文学进行的研究。严格而言，译介学的研究不是一种语言研究，而是一种文学研究或者文化研究，它关心的不是语言层面上出发语与目的语之间如何转换的问题，它关心的是原文在这种外语和本族语转换过程中信息的失落、变形、增添、扩伸等问题，它关心的是翻译（主要是文学翻译）作为人类一种跨文化交流的实践活动所具有的独特价值和意义。”②这一定义标志着中国比较文学学界对译介学的研究从实证性的事实关系研究转向了文化研究。

进入21世纪，随着中国比较文学学科理论的发展，中国学者从变异学的角度对译介学进行了丰富和深化。曹顺庆主编的《比较文学教程》指出，在比较文学的学科发展历史上，法国学派的影响研究注重“求同”；而在当代全球化交流加深的背景下，文化在传播过程中的嬗变成了常态，因此，比较文学应当勇于研究各种“变异”的现象。③为此，我们将译介学纳入变异研究的范畴。

二、译介学的理论内涵

研究译介学变异性的理论前提，来自20世纪后半期欧洲的几位后结构主义和解构主义的文学理论家。首先是语言学家雅各布森对翻译地位的提升。他从语言学的层面区分了三种翻译类型：语言内翻译、跨语际翻译和符号间翻译。他把跨语际翻译视为翻译自身，把语言内翻译和符号间翻译分别称为“重新措辞”和“变形”。④这就肯定了翻译必然带来语言变异的性质。接着，本雅明、罗兰·巴特从不同的角度质疑了原文的合法性，提升了译文的地位。本雅明指出，翻译是在语言之间进行的，而人类的

---

① 陈惇，孙景尧，谢天振．比较文学[M]．北京：高等教育出版社，1997．

② 谢天振．译介学[M]．上海：上海外语教育出版社，1999：1．

③ 曹顺庆．比较文学教程[M]．北京：高等教育出版社，2006：97．

④ Roman Jacobson, "On Linguistic Aspects of Translation", in Reuben A. Brower (ed.), *On Translation*. Cambridge, MA: Harvard University Press, 1959: 232-39.

语言作为一种表达模式，相互之间就具有亲缘性。不过，这种亲缘性并非是要追求译作对原作的本质性的相似，“而是在一切形式中追求翻译的自我”。具体地说，“译者的工作是在译作的语言里创作出原作的回声，为此，译者必找到作用于这种语言的意图效果，即意向性”。也就是说，翻译是在忠实原文意义的基础上进行的自由创作。[①]在此，本雅明毫不讳言提出“翻译”的自由度的问题，从而肯定了翻译不是复制，而是一种创造。罗兰·巴特的解构主义诗学贡献了“作者已死”的理论，消解了作者对文本的绝对统治权，从而也就把文本的意义从探寻作者的意图之下解放出来，肯定阅读者和阐释者的对文本意义的重构。这对翻译研究的启示是，翻译不再是原作的附庸，而是原作意义的重新创造。进一步地，雅克·德里达深入到原文的结构中去阐述，认为原文本身就存在着翻译的要求，否则其自身是匮乏的。因此不是原文衍生了翻译，而是原文的意义结构中本来就包含了翻译。[②]这个观点更彻底地把译作提升到和原作同等重要的地位上。

在这些理论前提下，译介学不再以字面意思的“对”与“错”来研究翻译，而是从文化语境的角度来考察翻译中的变异问题。

在翻译文本研究的层面上，译介学以“翻译的叛逆性”代替了传统对“误译”的判断。所谓“翻译的叛逆性”，即承认翻译不可避免地总是一种“叛逆”原文的行为。在英文中，翻译的单词是 translation，叛逆是 treason，两个单词读音接近，因此正可以作为“翻译是叛逆”的比喻。而这种叛逆的原因，来自于深层的文化、政治因素的影响和个体的语言创造，故称为“创造性叛逆（creative treason）”。

关于创造性叛逆，法国文学社会学家罗贝尔·埃斯卡皮（Robert Escarpit）指出：“说翻译是叛逆，那是因为它把作品置于一个完全没有预料到的参照体系（指语言）里；说翻译是创造性的，那是因为它赋予作品一个崭新的面貌，使之能与更广泛的读者进行一次崭新的文学交流，还因为它不仅延长了作品的生命，而且赋予它第二次生命。”[③]谢天振认为，创造性叛逆可从媒介者、接受者和接受环境的创造性叛逆三个方面加以分析。[④]他认为，“……创造性叛逆已经超出了单纯的文学接受的范畴，它反映的是文学翻译中的不同文化的交流和碰撞，不同文化的误解与误

① Walter Benjamin. “The Task of the Translator”, Lawrence Venuti. *The Translation Studies Reader*. London and New York: Routledge, 2000.

② 德里达.巴别塔[M]//郭军，曹雷雨.论瓦尔特·本雅明：现代性、寓言和语言的种子.长春：吉林人民出版社，2003.

③ 埃斯卡皮.文学社会学[M].王美华，王沛，译.合肥：安徽文艺出版社，1987：137-138.

④ 谢天振.译介学[M].上海：上海外语教育出版社，1999：144-173.

释"。[①]这说明,创造性叛逆是翻译中客观存在的,也是不可避免的问题,体现了跨文化交流中的规律。

例如,清末民初时林纾对西洋小说的翻译,曾在翻译史上受到极大诟病。他本人不懂任何一门欧洲语言,却一边听助手口译,一边笔译了大量的欧洲小说。在翻译的过程中,他常常不尊重作者原意,而经常对原作进行删节、改写、增补和改译。因此,他的翻译小说一度遭受很多人的批评,认为不值得阅读。但在译介学的重新审视下,林纾的翻译恰恰构成了非常有趣的现象。林译小说体现了中国在首次引进西方小说时,译者面临着中国特殊的社会语境,不得不作出的文本改变。如删除西方小说中基督教色彩浓郁的词汇,"漏译"某些琐碎的情节,都是为了照顾中国读者的阅读习惯,使之不因不理解、不耐烦异国文化和枝蔓的情节而将有价值的小说弃之不理。又如林纾常常把翻译视为自己著述,情不自禁地在译文中夹入自己对社会时势的看法。这说明他是借翻译来传达对社会的批判和进行民智的开启。联系到当时的严复、梁启超等从事的翻译也有类似的现象,可知,这是一代学人有意选择的翻译策略。因此,这种变异现象意味深长地体现了当时中国知识界的知识生产机制和翻译者的主体选择。

在翻译文学史的层面上,译介学的研究提高了翻译文学的地位,将其视为他国文学的一部分。

从20世纪前半期开始,就有中国学者尝试研究中国的翻译文学。1938年,阿英写作了《翻译史话》,虽是未完稿,但体现了中国学者对翻译活动的探索。1960年,北京大学西语系法文专业57级编写了《中国翻译文学简史》,梳理了自汉朝以来的中国文学翻译史,包括佛经翻译和当代的外国文学翻译。1989年中国第一部研究中国现代翻译史的著作《中国翻译文学史稿》出版,本书回顾了晚清以来中国对外国文学的翻译状况,总结了不同时期的文化机构、文学社团和主要翻译家对翻译文学采取的主张和策略,肯定了"翻译文学在我国近代、现代和当代文学史上都占有重要的地位,并且对我国新文学的发展起了重要作用"[②]。

20世纪最后10年以来,翻译文学研究领域既出现了更全面的历史研究成果,也涌现了分国别总结的著作。前者如谢天振、查明建主编的《中国现代翻译文学史(1898—1940)》[③],孟昭毅、李载道主编的《中国翻译文学史》[④];后者如孙致礼的

① 谢天振.译介学[M].上海:上海外语教育出版社,1999:141.

② 陈玉刚.中国翻译文学史稿[M].北京:中国对外翻译出版公司,1989:11.

③ 谢天振,查明建.中国现代翻译文学史(1898—1940)[M].上海:上海外语教育出版社,2004.

④ 孟昭毅,李载道.中国翻译文学史[M].北京:北京大学出版社,2005.

《1949—1966：我国英美文学翻译概论》[①]，卫茂平的《德语文学汉译史考辨》[②]，孟昭毅的《俄苏文学及翻译研究》[③]，韩一宇的《清末民初汉译法国文学研究（1897—1916）》[④]，等等。

除了对翻译文本和翻译文学史的研究，近年来，翻译研究在后殖民主义理论的带动下也产生了理论性的突破。在后殖民语境中，翻译先是被视为语言殖民的工具，体现了殖民帝国和被殖民地权力不对等的关系。随着后殖民地国家理论家的参与，译者和被译语国家的文化被凸显出来，翻译被视为一种解殖化的途径。如巴西的翻译理论家以坎泼斯（Haroldo de Campos）提出“翻译创造（transcreation）”的思想，即翻译是从原文向译语国家文化输血，使译语文化获得健康。因此他提倡翻译时要保持本国的语言和文化特色。又如意大利裔美国翻译理论家韦努蒂（Lawrence Venuti）指出，翻译最重要的作用是对文化身份的塑造。它所塑造出的异国他乡的形象，反映的是本土的政治和文化价值；同时，翻译“也建构了一个本土立场，这是一个可资理解的位置，同时也是一种意识形态的立场”[⑤]。这两位理论家都提出自己本国的语言文化面对英语的强势地位时应采取的策略，是重视本土立场，巧妙地通过翻译来达到解殖化的目的。

在美国的华裔学者也试图从后殖民翻译理论的角度来重新解读中国对西方的翻译。如刘禾在《语际书写》和《跨语际实践》中，通过研究中西文化交往历史上的不同个案，研究翻译所引发的中国思想史的嬗变。例如，她考察了晚清对“国民性（national character 或 national characteristic）”话语的翻译，看到这个词汇携带着以欧洲中心为视角来区分种族差异的含义来到中国，在中国学者的翻译和使用之下，成为了中国人批判中国“国民性”的一个真理性概念，从而改变了中国人自我认知的方式。[⑥]从而，刘禾认为，“翻译已不是一种中性的、远离政治及意识形态斗争和利益冲突的行为。相反，它成了这类冲突的场所，在这里被译语言不得不与译体语言面对面遭逢，为它们之间不可简约之差别决一雌雄，这里有对权威的引用和对权威的挑战，对暧昧性的消解或对暧昧的创造，直到新词或新意义在译体语言中出现”[⑦]。因此，翻译不是对外国语言的再现，而是在新的文化机制和地域环境中进行了新的

① 孙致礼. 1949—1966：我国英美文学翻译概论[M]. 北京：译林出版社，1996.

② 卫茂平. 德语文学汉译史考辩[M]. 上海：上海外语教育出版社，2004.

③ 孟昭毅. 俄苏文学及翻译研究[M]. 北京：中国社会科学出版社，2011.

④ 韩一宇. 清末民初汉译法国文学研究(1897—1916)[M]. 北京：中国社会科学出版社，2008.

⑤ 劳伦斯·韦努蒂. 翻译与文化身份的塑造[M]//徐宝强，原伟. 语言与翻译的政治. 北京：中央编译出版社，2001：358-360.

⑥ 刘禾. 语际书写[M]. 北京：三联书店，1999：65-104.

⑦ 刘禾. 语际书写[M]. 北京：三联书店，1999：36.

语言创造。从这个角度来重新考察中国思想的变迁，不但可以看到中国进入世界性的思想文化场域的轨迹，还可以看到西方帝国主义话语是如何经由翻译来配置其意识形态。

译介学的变异性研究作为比较文学的新兴研究领域，为中国比较文学研究注入了新的活力。在当代多元文化交流的语境中，译介的实践活动将会更深入地改变文化交流的面貌，而更多更新的问题也会随之提出和等待解答。

【原典选读】

翻译的政治（节选）

◉斯皮瓦克

【导读】印度裔的美国学者盖亚特里·查克拉沃蒂·斯皮瓦克（Gayatri Chakravorty Spivak）是蜚声国际的文学理论家，在后殖民主义理论、马克思主义理论、女性主义理论等研究领域颇有建树。这些理论资源也贯穿于她的翻译实践和翻译研究中，受到国际学界的重视。

斯皮瓦克关于翻译的表述和研究主要集中在以下篇目中：德里达《论文字学》的"译者前言"，以及《翻译的政治》《作为文化的翻译》《被问及翻译：游移》《后殖民理性批评》。其中，《翻译的政治》（*The Politics of Translation*）是体现她主要翻译思想的代表作。

《翻译的政治》收录于1993年出版的《教学机器内外》一书。这篇文章把"翻译"置于女性主义、解构主义的视角内进行考察，颠覆了传统的翻译理论，首次对翻译中权力问题进行了全面的探讨。西方传统翻译理论认为，翻译通过对原文的逻辑的把握，能够用另一种语言传达出原文的意义。但斯皮瓦克站在解构主义的立场，提出语言具有"三重结构"：逻辑、修辞和静默。而语言的修辞性特点应高于逻辑性的特点。因此，文本的意义就不总是清晰的、有逻辑性的，而是受到修辞干扰的。而意义受到修辞干扰的文本，就被解除了意义的疆界，呈现出在差异中散播的特性。由此，翻译不但不能限定文本的意义，相反，翻译可以接近修辞的延散。译者的任务，也就是促进文本意义散佚的发生。

斯皮瓦克进一步指出，在促进意义散播的过程中，由于受到历史框架、知识—权力机制的影响，翻译成为了压迫"他者/她者"的暴力工具。例如，第三世界的妇女文本被翻译成英文时，第一世界的女性往往把自身的历史和话语模式置于第三世界的女性文本上，这就取消了原文特有的修辞意义和性别差异，使第三世界的女性文本在第一世界的女性面前失去了"她性"，是一种"新殖民主义的构建"。

为了保证第三世界文本的独立性，斯皮瓦克提出"作为阅读的翻译"的概念。她把翻译视为最亲密的阅读行为，即关注语言修辞性的阅读行为。在这种阅读中，译者克制自我，服帖于文本，与文本之间产生爱的交流，让"他者/她者"完全以本来的面目出现，而非以译者的形象出现，从而实现对他者/她者的尊重。

讨论了狭义的"翻译"之后，斯皮瓦克还探讨了广义的"翻译"含义。在她看来，阅读也是翻译。当然，这里的"阅读"是广义的阅读概念，包括对各种形式的文本的阅读。她建议第三世界的女性在阅读第一世界的白人的理论时，不是采取服帖于文本的方式，而是对文本保持距离，站在第三世界的立场上进行独立思考。

斯皮瓦克的"翻译的政治"的观点，不仅充实了后殖民主义理论，而且提供了重审翻译理论的新视角。她的翻译研究为第三世界文本进入强势的英语世界提供了理论依据和实践方向，对于中国的汉语文学传播现实，也有着重要的参考意义。■

How does the translator attend to the specificity of the language she translates? There is a way in which the rhetorical nature of every language disrupts its logical systematicity. If we emphasize the logical at the expense of these rhetorical interferences, we remain safe. "Safety" *is* the appropriate term here, because we are talking of risks, of violence to the translating medium.

I felt that I was taking those risks when I recently translated some late eighteenth-century Bengali poetry. I quote a bit from my "Translator's Preface":

> I must overcome what I was taught in school: the highest mark for the most accurate collection of synonyms, strung together in the most proximate syntax. I must resist both the solemnity of chaste Victorian poetic prose and the forced simplicity of "plain English", that have imposed themselves as the norm... Translation is the most intimate act of reading. I surrender to the text when I translate. These songs, sung day after day in family chorus before clear memory began, have a peculiar intimacy for me. Reading and surrendering take on new meanings in such a case. The translator earns permission to transgress from the trace of the other—before memory—in the closest places of the self. ①

Language is not everything. It is only a vital clue to where the self loses its boundaries. The ways in which rhetoric or figuration disrupt logic themselves point at the possibility of random contingency, beside language, around language. Such a *diss*emination cannot be under our control. Yet in translation, where meaning hops into the spacy emptiness between two named historical languages, we get perilously close to it. By juggling the disruptive rhetoricity that

---

① Forthcoming from Seagull Press, Calcutta.

breaks the surface in not necessarily connected ways, we feel the selvedges of the language-textile give way, fray into *frayages* or facilitations. ① Although every act of reading or communication is a bit of this risky fraying which scrambles together somehow, our stake in agency keeps the fraying down to a minimum except in the communication and reading of and in love. (What is the place of "love" in the ethical?) The task of the translator is to facilitate this love between the original and its shadow, a love that permits fraying, holds the agency of the translator and the demands of her imagined or actual audience at bay. The politics of translation from a non-European woman's text too often suppresses this possibility because the translator cannot engage with, or cares insufficiently for, the rhetoricity of the original.

The simple possibility that something might not be meaningful is contained by the rhetorical system as the always possible menace of a space outside language. This is most eerily staged (and challenged) in the effort to communicate with other possible intelligent beings in space. (Absolute alterity or otherness is thus differed-deferred into an other self who resembles us, however minimally, and with whom we can communicate.) But a more homely staging of it occurs across two earthly languages. The experience of contained alterity in an unknown language spoken in a different cultural milieu is uncanny.

Let us now think that, in that other language, rhetoric may be disrupting logic in the matter of the production of an agent, and indicating the founding violence of the silence at work within rhetoric. Logic allows us to jump from word to word by means of clearly indicated connections. Rhetoric must work in the silence between and around words in order to see what works and how much. The jagged relationship between rhetoric and logic, condition and effect of knowing, is a relationship by which a world is made for the agent, so that the agent can act in an ethical way, a political way, a day-to-day way; so that the agent can be alive, in a human way, in the world. Unless one can at least construct a model of this for the other language, there is no real translation.

Unfortunately it is only too easy to produce translations if this task is completely ignored. I myself see no choice between the quick and easy and slapdash way, and translating well and with difficulty. There is no reason why a responsible translation should take more time in the doing. The translator's preparation might take more time, and her love for the text might be a matter of a reading skill that takes patience. But the sheer material production of the text need not be slow.

Without a sense of the rhetoricity of language, a species of neo-colonialist construction of the non-western scene is afoot. No argument for convenience can be persuasive here. That is always the argument, it seems. This is where I travel from Michèle Barrett's enabling notion of the question of language in poststructuralism. Post-structuralism has shown some of us a staging of the agent within a three-tiered notion of language (as rhetoric, logic, silence). We must attempt to

---

① "Facilitation" is the English translation of the Freudian term *Bahnung* (pathing) which is translated *frayage* in French. The dictionary meaning is: Term used by Freud at a time when he was putting forward a neurological model of the functioning of the psychical apparatus (1895): the excitation, in passing from one neurone to another, runs into a certain resistance; where its passage result in a permanent reduction in this resistance, there is said to be facilitation; excitation will opt for a facilitated pathway in preference to one where no facilitation has occurred (J. B. Pontalis, *The language of Psychoanalysis*[London: Hogarth Press, 1973], p. 157).

enter or direct that staging, as one directs a play, as an actor interprets a script. That takes a different kind of effort from taking translation to be a matter of synonym, syntax and local colour.

To be only critical, to defer action until the production of the utopian translator, is impractical. Yet, when I hear Derrida, quite justifiably, point out the difficulties between French and English, even when he agrees to speak in English—"I must speak in a language that is not my own because that will be more just"—I want to claim the right to the same dignified complaint for a woman's text in Arabic or Vietnamese. ①

It is more just to give access to the largest number of feminists. Therefore these texts must be made to speak English. It is more just to speak the language of the majority when through hospitality a large number of feminists give the foreign feminists the right to speak, in English. In the case of the Third World foreigner, is the law of the majority that of decorum, the equitable law of democracy, or the "law" of the strongest? We might focus on this confusion. There is nothing necessarily meretricious about the western feminist gaze. (The "naturalizing" of Jacques Lacan's sketching out of the psychic structure of the gaze in terms of group political behaviour has always seemed to me a bit shaky.) On the other hand, there is nothing essentially noble about the law of the majority either. It is merely the easiest way of being "democratic" with minorities. In the act of wholesale translation into English there can be a betrayal of the democratic ideal into the law of the strongest. This happens when all the literature of the Third World gets translated into a sort of with-it translatese, so that the literature by a woman in Palestine begins to resemble, in the feel of its prose, something by a man in Taiwan. The rhetoricity of Chinese and Arabic! The cultural politics of high-growth, capitalist Asia-Pacific, and devastated West Asia! Gender difference inscribed and inscribing in these differences!

For the student, this tedious translatese cannot compete with the spectacular stylistic experiments of a Monique Witting or an Alice Walker.

Let us consider an example where attending to the author's stylistic experiments can produce a different text. Mahasweta Devi's "Stanadāyini" is available in two versions. ② Devi has expressed approval for the attention to her signature style in the version entitled "Breast-giver". The alternative translation gives the title as "The Wet-nurse", and thus neutralizes the author's irony in constructing an uncanny word; enough like "wet-nurse" to make that sense, and enough unlike to shock. It is as if the translator should decide to translate Dylan Thomas's famous title and opening line as "Do not go gently into that good night". The theme of treating the breast as organ of labour-power-as-commodity and the breast as metonymie part-object standing in for other-as-object—the way in which the story plays with Marx and Freud on the occasion of the woman's body—is lost even before you enter the story. In the text Mahasweta uses proverbs that are startling even in the Bengali. The translator of "The Wet-nurse" leaves them out. She decides not to try to translate these hard bits of earthy wisdom, contrasting with class-specific access to modernity, also represented in the story. In fact, if the two translations are read side by side, the loss of the rhetorical silences of the original can be felt from one to the

---

① Jacques Derrida, "The Force of Law," p. 923.

② "The Wet-Nurse," in Kali for Women, eds.

other.

First, then, the translator must surrender to the text. She must solicit the text to show the limits of its language, because that rhetorical aspect will point at the silence of the absolute fraying of language that the text wards off, in its special manner. Some think this is just an ethereal way of talking about literature or philosophy. But no amount of tough talk can get around the fact that translation is the most intimate act of reading. Unless the translator has earned the right to become the intimate reader, she cannot surrender to the text, cannot respond to the special call of the text.

The presupposition that women have a natural or narrative-historical solidarity, that there is something in a woman or an undifferentiated women's story that speaks to another woman without benefit of language-learning, might stand against the translator's task of surrender. Paradoxically, it is not possible for us as ethical agents to imagine otherness or alterity maximally. We have to turn the other into something like the self in order to be ethical. To surrender in translation is more erotic than ethical. ① In that situation the good-willing attitude "she is just like me" is not very helpful. In so far as Michèle Barrett is not like Gayatri Spivak, their friendship is more effective as a translation. In order to earn that right of friendship or surrender of identity, of knowing that the rhetoric of the text indicates the limits of language for you as long as you are with the text, you have to be in a different relationship with the language, not even only with the specific text.

My initial point was that the task of the translator is to surrender herself to the linguistic rhetoricity of the original text. Although this point has larger political implications, we can say that the not unimportant minimal consequence of ignoring this task is the loss of "the literarity and textuality and sensuality of the writing" (Michèle's words). I have worked my way to a second point, that the translator must be able to discriminate on the terrain of the original. Let us dwell on it a bit longer.

I choose Devi because she is unlike her scene. I have heard an English Shakespearean suggest that every bit of Shakespeare criticism coming from the subcontinent was by that virtue resistant. By such a judgement, we are also denied the right to be critical. It was of course had to have put the place under subjugation, to have tried to make the place over with calculated restrictions. But that does not mean that everything that is coming out of that place after a negotiated independence nearly fifty years ago is necessarily right. The old anthropological supposition (and that is bad anthropology) that every person from a culture is nothing but a whole example of that culture is acted out in my colleague's suggestion. I remain interested in writers who are against the current, against the mainstream. I remain convinced that the interesting literary text might be precisely the text where you do not learn what the majority view of majority cultural representation of self-representation of a nation state might be. The translator has to make herself, in the case of Third World women writing, almost better equipped than the translator who is dealing with the western European languages, because of the fact that there is so much of the old colonial attitude, slightly displaced, at work in the translation racket. Post-structuralism *can* radicalize the field of preparation so that simply boning up on the language is not enough; there is also that special relationship to the staging of language as the production of agency that one must attend to. But the agenda of poststructuralism is mostly elsewhere, and the resistance to theory among metropolitan feminists would lead us into yet another narrative.

The understanding of the task of the translator and the practice of the craft are related but different. Let me summarize how I work. At first, I translate at speed. If I stop to think about what is happening to the English, if I assume an audience, if I take the intending subject as more than a springboard, I cannot jump in, I cannot surrender. My relationship with Devi is easygoing. I am able to say to her: I surrender to you in your writing, not you as intending subject. There, in friendship, is another kind of surrender. Surrendering to the text in this way means, most of the time, being literal. When I have produced a version this way, I revise. I revise not in terms of a possible audience, but by the protocols of the thing in front of me, in a sort of English. And I keep hoping that the student in the classroom will not be able to think that the text is just a purveyor of social realism if it is translated with an eye toward the dynamic staging of language mimed in the revision by the rules of the in-between discourse produced by a literalist surrender.

Vain hope, perhaps, for the accountability is different. When I translated Jacques Derrida's *De la grammatologie*, I was reviewed in a major journal for the first and last time. In the case of my translations of Devi, I have almost no fear of being accurately judged by my readership here. It makes the task more dangerous and more risky. And that for me is the real difference between translating Derrida and translating Mahasweta Devi, not merely the rather more artificial difference between deconstructive philosophy and political fiction.

The opposite argument is not neatly true. There is a large number of people in the Third Would who read the old imperial languages. People reading current feminist fiction in the European languages would probably read it in the appropriate imperial language. And the same goes for European philosophy. The act of translating into the Third World language is often a political exercise of a different sort. I am looking forward, as of this writing, to lecturing in Bengali on deconstruction in front of a highly sophisticated audience, knowledgeable both in Bengali and in deconstruction (which they read in English and French and sometimes write about in Bengali), at Jadavpur University in Calcutta. It will be a kind of testing of the post-colonial translator, I think. ①

Democracy changes into the law of force in the case of translation from the Third World and women even more because of their peculiar relationship to whatever you call the public/private divide. A neatly reversible argument would be possible if the particular Third World country had cornered the Industrial Revolution first and embarked on monopoly imperialist territorial capitalism as one of its consequences, and thus been able to impose a language as international norm. Something like that idiotic joke: if the Second World War had gone differently, the United States would be speaking Japanese. Such egalitarian reversible judgements are appropriate to counter-factual fantasy. Translation remains dependent upon the language skill of the majority. A prominent Belgian translation theorist solves the problem by suggesting that, rather than talk about the Third World, where a lot of passion is involved, one should speak about the European Renaissance, since a great deal of wholesale cross-cultural translation from Graeco-Roman antiquity was undertaken then. What one overlooks is the sheer authority ascribed to the originals in that historical phenomenon. The status of a language in the world is what one must consider when teasing out the politics of translation. Translatese in Bengali can be derided and criticized by large groups of anglophone and anglograph Bengalis. It is only in the hegemonic languages that the benevolent do not take the limits of their own often uninstructed good will into

① I have given an account of this in Spivak, "Acting Bits/Identity Talk," *Critical Inquiry* 18:4 (Summer 1992).

account. That phenomenon becomes hardest to fight because the individuals involved in it are genuinely benevolent and you are identified as a trouble-maker. This becomes particularly difficult when the metropolitan feminist, who is sometimes the assimilated postcolonial, invokes, indeed translates, a too quickly shared feminist notion of accessibility.

If you want to make the translated text accessible, try doing it for the person who wrote it. The problem comes clear then, for she is not within the same history of style. What is it that you are making accessible? The accessible level is the level of abstraction where the individual is already formed, where one can speak individual rights. When you hang out and with a language away from your own (*Mitwegsein*) so that you want to use that language by preference, sometimes, when you discuss something complicated, then you are on the way to making a dimension of the text accessible to the reader, with a light and easy touch, to which she does not accede in her everyday. If you are making anything else accessible, through a language quickly learnt with an idea that you transfer content, then you are betraying the text and showing rather dubious politics.

How will women's solidarity be measured here? How will their common experience be reckoned if one cannot imagine the traffic in accessibility going both ways? I think that idea should be given a decent burial as ground of knowledge, together with the idea of humanist universality. It is good to think that women have something in common, when one is approaching women with whom a relationship would not otherwise be possible. It is a great first step. But, if your interest is in learning if there *is* women's solidarity, how about leaving this assumption, appropriate as a means to an end like local or global social work, and trying a second step? Rather than imagining that women automatically have something identifiable in common, why not say, humbly and practically, my first obligation in understanding solidarity is to learn her mother-tongue. You will see immediately what the differences are. You will also feel the solidarity every day as you make the attempt to learn the language in which the other woman learnt to recognize reality at her mother's knee. This is preparation for the intimacy of cultural translation. If you are going to bludgeon someone else by insisting on your version of solidarity, you have the obligation to try out this experiment and see how far your solidarity goes.

In other words, if you are interested in talking about the other, and/or in making a claim to be the other, it is crucial to learn other languages. This should be distinguished from the learned tradition of language acquisition for academic work. I am talking about the importance of language acquisition for the woman from a hegemonic monolinguist culture who makes everybody's life miserable by insisting on women's solidarity at her price. I am uncomfortable with-notions of feminist solidarity which are celebrated when everybody involved is similarly produced. There are countless languages in which women all over the world have grown up and been female or feminist, and yet the languages we keep on learning by rote are the powerful European ones, sometimes the powerful Asian ones, least often the chief African ones. The "other" languages are learnt only by anthropologists who *must* produce knowledge across an epistemic divide. They are generally (though not invariably) not interested in the three-part structure we are discussing.

If we are discussing solidarity as a theoretical position, we must also remember that not all the world's women are literate. There are traditions and situations that remain obscure because we cannot share their linguistic constitution. It is from this angle that I have felt that learning languages might sharpen our own presuppositions about what it means to use the sign "woman". If we say that things should be accessible to us, who is this "us"? What does that sign mean?

Although I have used the examples of women all along, the arguments apply across the board. It is just that women's rhetoricity may be doubly obscured. I do not see the advantage of being completely focused on a single issue, although one must establish practical priorities. In the book, we are concerned with poststructuralism and its effect on feminist theory. Where some post-structuralist thinking can be applied to the constitution of the agent in terms of the literary operations of language, women's texts might be operating differently because of the social differentiation between the sexes. Of course the point applies generally to the colonial context as well. When Ngugi decided to write in Kikuyu, some thought he was bringing a private language into the public sphere. But what makes a language shared by many people in a community private? I was thinking about those so-called private languages when I was talking about language learning. But even within those private languages it is my conviction that there is a difference in the way in which the staging of language produces not only the sexed subject but the gendered agent, by a version of centring, persistently disrupted by rhetoricity, indicating contingency. Unless demonstrated otherwise, this for me remains the condition and effect of dominant and subordinate gendering. If that is so, then we have some reason to focus on women's texts. Let us use the word "woman" to name that space of para-subjects defined as such by the social inscription of primary and secondary sexual characteristics. Then we can cautiously begin to track a sort of commonality in being set apart, within the different rhetorical strategies of different languages. But even here, historical superiorities of class must be kept in mind. Bharati Mukherjee, Anita Desai and Gayatri Spivak do not have the same rhetorical figuration of agency as an illiterate domestic servant.

Tracking commonality through responsible translation can lead us into areas of difference and different differentiations. This may also be important because, in the heritage of imperialism, the female legal subject bears the mark of a failure of Europeanization, by contrast with the female anthropological or literary subject from the area. For example, the division between the French and Islamic codes in modern Algeria is in terms of family, marriage, inheritance, legitimacy and female social agency. These are differences that we must keep in mind. And we must honour the difference between ethnic minorities in the First World and majority populations of the Third.

In conversation, Barrett had asked me if I now inclined more toward Foucault. This is indeed the case. In "Can the Subaltern Speak?", I took a rather strong critical line on Foucault's work, as part of a general critique of imperialism. ① I do, however, find, his concept of *pouvoir-savoir* immensely useful. Foucault has contributed to French this or dinar y-language doublet (the ability to know [as]) to take its place quietly beside *vouloir-dire* (the wish to say—meaning to mean).

On the most mundane level, *pouvoir-savoir* is the shared skill which allows us to make (common) sense of things. It is certainly not only power/knowledge in the sense of *puissance/connaissance*. Those are aggregative institutions. The common way in which one makes sense of things, on the other hand, loses itself in the sub-individual.

---

① Spivak, "Can the Subaltern Speak?" in *Marxism and the Interpretation of Culture*, ed. Larry Grossberg and Cary Nelson (Urbana: University of Illinois Press, 1988), pp. 271-313.

Looking at *pouvoir-savoir* in terms of women, one of my focuses has been new immigrants and the change of mother-tongue and *pouvoir-savoir* between mother and daughter. When the daughter talks reproductive rights and the mother talks protecting honour, is this the birth or death of translation?

Foucault is also interesting in his new notion of the ethics of the care for the self. In order to be able to get to the subject of ethics it may be necessary to look at the ways in which an individual in that culture is instructed to care for the self rather than the imperialism-specific secularist notion that the ethical subject is given as human. In a secularism which is structurally identical with Christianity laundered in the bleach of moral philosophy, the subject of ethics is faceless. Breaking out, Foucault was investigating other ways of making sense of how the subject becomes ethical. This is of interest because, given the connection between imperialism and secularism, there is almost no way of getting to alternative general voices except through religion. And if one does not look at religion as mechanisms of producing the ethical subject, one gets various kinds of "fundamentalism". Workers in cultural politics and its connections to a new ethical philosophy have to be interested in religion in the production of ethical subjects. There is much room for feminist work here because western feminists have not so far been aware of religion as a cultural instrument rather than a mark of cultural difference. I am currently working on Hindu performative ethics with Professor B. K. Matilal. He is an enlightened male feminist. I am an active feminist. Helped by his learning and his openness I am learning to distinguish between ethical catalysts and ethical motors even as I learn to translate bits of the Sanskrit epic in a way different from all the accepted translations, because I rely not only on learning, not only on "good English", but on that three-part scheme of which I have so lengthily spoken. I hope the results will please readers. If we are going to look at an ethics that emerges from something other than the historically secularist ideal—at an ethics of sexual differences, at an ethics that can confront the emergence of fundamentalisms without apology or dismissal in the name of the Enlightenment—then *pouvoir-savoir* and the care for the self in Foucault can be illuminating. And these "other ways" bring us back to translation, in the general sense.

(Spivak, Gayatri Chakravorty. *The Politics of Translation*[A]. In Gayatri Chakravorty Spivak. *Outside in the Teaching Machine*[C]. New York: Routledge, 1993.)

【研究范例】

林纾的翻译（节选）

◉钱锺书

汉代文字学者许慎有一节关于翻译的训诂，义蕴颇为丰富。《说文解字》卷十二《囗》部第二十六字："囮，译也。从'囗'，'化'声。率鸟者系生鸟以来之，名曰'囮'，读若'讹'。"南唐以来，小学家都申说"译"就是"传四夷及鸟兽之语"，好比"鸟媒"对"禽鸟"的引"诱"，"讹""讹""化"和"囮"是同一个字①。"译""诱""媒""讹""化"这些一脉通连、

① 详见《说文解字诂林》第28册2736-2738页。参看《管锥编》(三)546页。

彼此呼应的意义，组成了研究诗歌语言的人所谓“虚涵数意”（polysemy, manifold meaning）①，把翻译能起的作用（“诱”）、难于避免的毛病（“讹”）、所向往的最高境界（“化”），仿佛一一透示出来了。文学翻译的最高理想可以说是“化”。把作品从一国文字转变成另一国文字，既能不因语文习惯的差异而露出生硬牵强的痕迹，又能完全保存原作的风味，那就算得入于“化境”。十七世纪一个英国人赞美这种造诣高的翻译，比为原作的“投胎转世”（the transmigration of souls），躯体换了一个，而精魂依然故我②。换句话说，译本对原作应该忠实得以至于读起来不像译本，因为作品在原文里绝不会读起来像翻译出的东西。因此，意大利一位大诗人认为好翻译应备的条件看来是彼此不相容乃至相矛盾的（paiono discordanti e incompatibili e contradditorie）：译得矫揉造作（ora il traduttore necessariamente affetta），对原文亦步亦趋，以求曲肖原著者的天然本来（inaffettato, naturale o spontaneo）的风格③。一国文字和另一国文字之间必然有距离，译者的理解和文风跟原作品的内容和形式之间也不会没有距离，而且译者的体会和自己的表达能力之间还时常有距离。就文体或风格而论，也许会有希莱尔马诃区分的两种翻译法，譬如说：一种尽量“欧化”，尽可能让外国作家安居不动，而引导我国读者走向他们那里去，另一种尽量“汉化”，尽可能让我国读者安居不动，而引导外国作家走向咱们这儿来（Entweder der Uebersetzer lässt den Schriftsteller möglichst in Ruhe und bewegt den Leser ihm entgegen, oder er lässt den Leser möglichst in Ruhe und bewegt den Schriftsteller ihm entgegen）④。然而“欧化”也好，“汉化”也好，翻译总是以原作的那一国语文为出发点而以译成的这一国语文为到达点⑤。从最初出发以至终竟到达，这是很艰辛的历程。一路上颠顿风尘，遭遇风险，不

---

① 参看《管锥编》（三）317-318 页。

② 乔治·萨维尔（George Savile First Marquess of Halifax）至蒙田（Montaigne）《散文集》译者考敦（Charles Cotton）书；《全集》，瑞立（W. Raleigh）编本 185 页。十九世纪德国的希腊学大家威拉莫维茨（Ulrich v. Wilamowitz-Moellendorff）在一种古希腊悲剧希、德语对照本（Euripides Hippolytus）弁首的《什么是翻译?》（*Was ist Uebersetzen?*）里，也用了相类的比喻。

③ 利奥巴尔迪（Leopardi）《感想杂志》（*Zibaldone di pensieri*），弗洛拉（F. Flora）编注本 5 版第 1 册 288-289 页。

④ 希莱尔马诃（Friedrich D. E. Schleiermacher）《论不同的翻译方法》（*Ueber die verschiedenen Methoden des Uebersetzens*），转引自梅理安-盖那司德（E. Merian-Genast）《法国和德国的翻译艺术》（*Französische und deutsche Ueberset Zungskunst*），见恩司德（F. Ernst）与威斯（K. Wais）合编《比较文学史研究问题论丛》（*Forschungsprobleme der vergleichenden Literaturgeschichte*, 1951）第 2 册 25 页；参看希勒格尔《语言的竞赛》（*Der Wettstreit der Sprachen*）里法语代表讲自己对待外国作品的态度（A. W. Schlegel, Kritische Schriften und Briefe, W. Kohlhammer, 1962, Bd. Ⅰ, s. 252）。利奥巴尔迪讲法、德两国翻译方法的区别，暗合希莱尔马诃的意见，见前注 4 所引同书第 1 册 289 又 1311 页。其实这种区别也表现在法、德两国戏剧对外国题材和人物的处理上，参看黑格尔《美学》（*Aesthetik*），建设（Aufbau）出版社 1955 年版 278-280 页。

⑤ 维耐（J. P. Vinay）与达贝尔耐（J. Darbelnet）合著《法、英文体比较》（*Stylistique comparée du français et de l'anglais*, 1958）10 页称原作的语言为“出发的语言（langue de départ）”、译本的语言为“到达的语言（langue d'ar rivée）”。比起英美习称的“来源语言（source language）”和“目标语言（target language）”，这种说法似乎更一气呵成。

免有所遗失或受些损伤。因此,译文总有失真和走样的地方,在意义或口吻上违背或不很贴合原文。那就是"讹",西洋谚语所谓"翻译者即反逆者"(Traduttore traditore)。中国古人也说翻译的"翻"等于把绣花纺织品的正面翻过去的"翻",展开了它的反面:"翻也者,如翻锦绮,背面皆花,但其花有左右不同耳。"(释赞宁《高僧传三集》卷三《译经篇·论》)这个比喻使我们想起堂·吉诃德说阅读译本就像从反面来看花毯(es como quien mira los tapices flamencos por el revés)①。"媒"和"诱"当然说明了翻译在文化交流里所起的作用。它是个居间者或联络员,介绍大家去认识外国作品,引诱大家去爱好外国作品,仿佛做媒似的,使国与国之间缔结了"文学因缘"②,缔结了国与国之间唯一的较少反目、吵嘴、分手挥拳等危险的"因缘"。

彻底和全部的"化"是不可实现的理想,某些方面、某种程度的"讹"又是不能避免的毛病,于是"媒"或"诱"产生了新的意义。翻译本来是要省人家的事,免得他们去学外文、读原作,却一变而为导诱一些人去学外文、读原作。它挑动了有些人的好奇心,惹得他们对原作无限向往,仿佛让他们尝到一点儿味道,引起了胃口,可是没有解馋过瘾。他们总觉得读翻译像隔雾赏花,不比读原作那么情景真切。歌德就有过这种看法:他很不礼貌地比翻译家为下流的职业媒人(Uebersetzer sind als geschäftige Kuppler anzusehen)——中国旧名"牵马",因为他们把原作半露半遮(eine halbverschleierte Schöne),使读者心痒神驰,想象它不知多少美丽③。要证实那个想象,要揭去那层遮遮掩掩的面纱,以求看个饱、看个着实,就得设法去读原作。这样说来,好译本的作用是消灭自己;它把我们向原作过渡,而我们读到了原作,马上掷开了译本。自负好手的译者恰恰产生了失手自杀的译本,他满以为读了他的译本就无须去读原作,但是一般人能够欣赏货真价实的原作以后,常常薄情地抛弃了翻译家辛勤制造的代用品。倒是坏翻译会发生一种消灭原作的功效。拙劣晦涩的译文无形中替作者拒绝读者;他对译本看不下去,就连原作也不想看了。这类翻译不是居间,而是离间,摧毁了读者进一步和原作直接联系的可能性,扫尽读者的兴趣,同时也破坏原作的名誉。十七世纪法国的德·马罗勒神父(l'abbé de Marolles)就是一个经典的例证。

---

① 《堂·吉诃德》第2部62章;据马林(F. R. Marin)校注本第8册156页所引考订,1591年两位西班牙翻译家(Diego de Mendoza y Luis Zapata)合译霍拉斯(Horace)《诗学》时,早用过这个比喻。赞宁在论理论著作的翻译,原来形式和风格的保持不像在文学翻译里那么重要;锦绣的反面虽比正面逊色,走样还不厉害,所以他认为过得去。塞万提斯是在讲文艺翻译,花毯的反面跟正面差得很远,所以他认为要不得了。参看爱伦·坡(E. Allan Poe)《书边批识》(*Marginalia*)说翻译的"翻"就是"颠倒翻覆(turned topsy-turvy)"的"翻",斯戴德门(E. C. Stedman)与沃德培利(G. E. Woodberry)合编《全集》第7册212页。

② "文学因缘"是苏曼殊所辑汉译英诗集名;他自序里只讲起翻译的"讹"——"迁地勿为良"(《全集》北新版第1册121页),没有解释书名,但推想他的用意不外如此。

③ 歌德《精语与熟思》(*Maximen und Reflexionen*),汉堡版(Hamburger Ausgabe)14册本《歌德集》(1982)第12册499页。参看鲍士威尔(Boswell)1776年4月11日记约翰生论译诗语,见李斯甘(C. Ryskamp)与卜德尔(F. A. Pottle)合编《不祥岁月》(*The Ominous Years*)329页,又鲍士威尔所著《约翰生传》牛津版742页。

他所译古罗马诗人《马夏尔的讽刺小诗集》(*Epigrams of Martial*)被时人称为《讽刺马夏尔的小诗集》(*Epigrams against Martial*)①;和他相识的作者说,这位神父的翻译简直是法国语文遭受的一个灾难(un de ces maux dont notre langue est affligée),他发愿把古罗马诗家统统译出来,桓吉尔、霍拉斯等人都没有蒙他开恩饶命(n'ayant pardonné),奥维德、太伦斯等人早晚会断送在他的毒手里(assassinés)②。不用说,马罗勒对他的翻译成绩还是沾沾自喜、津津乐道的③。我们从亲身阅历里,找得到好多和这位神父可以作伴的人。

林纾的翻译所起"媒"的作用,已经是文学史公认的事实④。他对若干读者,也一定有过歌德所说的"媒"的影响,引导他们去跟原作发生直接关系。我自己就是读了林译而增加学习外国语文的兴趣的。商务印书馆发行的那两小箱《林译小说丛书》是我十一二岁时的大发现,带领我进了一个新天地,一个在《水浒》《西游记》《聊斋志异》以外另辟的世界。我事先也看过梁启超译的《十五小豪杰》、周桂笙译的侦探小说等,都觉得沉闷乏味⑤。接触了林译,我才知道西洋小说会那么迷人。我把林译哈葛德、迭更司、欧文、司各德、斯威佛特的作品反复不厌地阅览。假如我当时学习英语有什么自己意识到的动机,其中之一就是有一天能够痛痛快快地读遍哈葛德以及旁人的探险小说。四十年前⑥,在我故乡那个县城里,小孩子既无野兽片电影可看,又无动物园可逛,只能见到"走江湖"的人耍猴儿把戏或者牵一头疥骆驼卖药。后来孩子们看野兽片、逛动物园所获得的娱乐,我只能向冒险小说里去找寻。我清楚记得这一回事。哈葛德《三千年艳尸记》第五章结尾刻意描写鳄鱼和狮子的搏斗;对小孩子说来,那是一个惊心动魄的场面,紧张得使他眼瞪口开、气儿也不敢透的。林纾译文的下半段是这样:

> 然狮之后爪已及鳄鱼之颈,如人之脱手套,力拔而出之。少顷,狮首俯鳄鱼之身作异声,而鳄鱼亦侧其齿,尚陷入狮股,狮腹为鳄所咬亦几裂。如是战斗,为余生平所

---

① 狄士瑞立(I. Disraeli)《文苑搜奇》(*Curiosities of Literature*),《张独斯(Chandos)经典丛书》本第1册350页引梅那日《掌故录》(*Menagiana*)。

② 圣佩韦(Sainte-Beuve)《月曜日文谈》(*Causeries du lundi*)第14册136页引沙普伦(Jean Chapelain)的信。十八世纪英国女小说家番尼·伯尔尼幼年曾翻译法国封德耐尔(Fontenelle)的名著,未刊稿封面上有她亲笔自题:"用英语来杀害者:番尼·伯尔尼。"(Murthered into English by Frances Burney)——见亨姆罗(Joyce Hemlow)《番尼·伯尔尼传》(*The History of Fanny Barney*)16页。诗人彭斯(Robert Burns)嘲笑马夏尔诗的一个英译本,也比之于"杀害(murder)",见《书信集》,福格森(J. De Lancy Ferguson)编本第1册163页。

③ 例如,他自赞所译桓吉尔诗是生平"最精确、最美丽、最高雅(la plus juste, la plus belle et la plus élégante)"的译作,见前注所引圣佩韦书130页。

④ 在评述到林纾翻译的书籍和文章里,寒光《林琴南》和郑振铎先生《中国文学研究》下册《林琴南先生》都很有参考价值。那些文献讲过的,这里不再重复。

⑤ 周桂笙的译笔并不出色;据吴研人《新笑史·犬车》记载,周说"凡译西文者,固忌率,亦忌泥"云云,这还是很中肯的话。

⑥ 这篇文章是1963年3月写的。

未睹者。[照原句读,加新式标点]

狮子抓住鳄鱼的脖子,绝不会整个爪子像陷进烂泥似的,为什么"如人之脱手套"?鳄鱼的牙齿既然"陷入狮股",物理和生理上都不可能去"咬狮腹"。我无论如何想不明白,家里的大人也解答不来。而且这场恶狠狠的打架怎样了局?谁输谁赢,还是同归于尽?鳄鱼和狮子的死活,比起男女主角的悲欢,是我更关怀的问题。书里并未明白交代,我真心痒难搔,恨不能知道原文是否照样糊涂了事①。我开始能读原文,总先找林纾译过的小说来读。我渐渐听到和看到学者名流对林译的轻蔑和嗤笑,未免世态逐炎凉,就不再而也不屑再去看它,毫无恋惜地过河拔桥了!

最近,偶尔翻开一本林译小说,出于意外,它居然还有些吸引力。我不但把它看完,并且接二连三,重温了大部分的林译,发现许多都值得重读,尽管漏译误译触处皆是。我试找同一作品的后出的——无疑也是比较"忠实"的——译本来读,譬如孟德斯鸠和迭更司的小说,就觉得宁可读原文。这是一个颇耐玩味的事实。当然,一个人能读原文以后,再来看错误的译本,有时不失为一种消遣,还可以方便地增长自我优越的快感。一位文学史家曾说,译本愈糟糕愈有趣:我们对照着原本,看翻译者如何异想天开,把胡猜乱测来填补理解上的空白,无中生有,指鹿为马,简直像"超现实主义"诗人的作风②。但是,我对林译的兴味,绝非想找些岔子,以资笑柄谈助,而林纾译本里不忠实或"讹"的地方也并不完全由于他的助手们外语程度低浅、不够了解原文。

(节选自钱锺书.七缀集[M].北京:三联书店,2004:77-82.)

【延伸阅读】

1. 廖七一.诗歌翻译与经典建构[M]//廖七一.胡适诗歌翻译研究.北京:清华大学出版社,2006:143-196.

《胡适诗歌翻译研究》一书将胡适的译诗作为个案来研究,旨在描述五四运动前后中国文化环境对翻译的驱动与制约作用;揭示作为翻译主体的胡适在翻译这种社会行为中的自我意识和能动性;揭示诗歌翻译从主题到形式到语言转型,白话诗体最终成为诗歌翻译正宗的演变过程,以及白话译诗与白话新诗创作之间的互动。其中第三章《译诗与经典建构》论述了译者意图与文本功能、译诗与传播媒介、译诗与经典建构之间的关系。

---

① 原书是 She,寒光《林琴南》和朱羲胄《春觉斋著述记》都误淆为 Montezuma's Daughter。狮爪把鳄鱼的喉撕开(rip),像撕裂手套一样;鳄鱼狠咬狮腰,几乎咬成两截;结果双双丧命(this duel to the death)。

② 普拉兹(M. Praz)《翻译家的伟大》(*Grandezza dei traduttori*),见《荣誉之家》(*La Casa della fama*)50 又 52 页。

2. 滕威. 50—70 年代:被建构的拉美/革命文学[M]//滕威. “边境”之南:拉丁美洲文学汉译与中国当代文学(1949—1999). 北京:北京大学出版社,2011:1-41.

《“边境”之南:拉丁美洲文学汉译与中国当代文学(1949—1999)》在文化研究的视野中考察中国在 1949—1999 年间对拉丁美洲文学翻译与接受的历史,关注其中翻译与政治、翻译与意识形态之间复杂微妙的关系,揭示翻译与接受过程中的种种误读与错位、改写与挪用,不仅第一次全面梳理与回溯了半个世纪以来的拉美文学汉译史,同时为当代文学研究提供了新鲜的视角,作者通过细密的历史考察,再现翻译与政治之间的复杂联结,并试图在新的历史语境中恢复翻译/文学作为一种社会实践的可能性。“50—70 年代:被建构的拉美/革命文学”为该著作的第一章的内容,奠定了全书的基调。

3. 王向远. 二十世纪中国的日本翻译文学史:前言[M]. 北京:北京师范大学出版社,2001:1-12.

《二十世纪中国的日本翻译文学史》是国内外第一部研究中国的日本翻译文学史的著作,全书共五章,它将中国的日本翻译文学置于 20 世纪中国文学的大背景下,把近百年来中国的日本文学翻译划分为五个时期,围绕各时期翻译文学的选题背景与动机,翻译家的翻译观、译作风格及其成败得失、译本的读者反应及对中国文学的影响等问题,展开讨论。在该书的前言中,王向远教授首先明确了“翻译文学”和“翻译文学史”的学科定位问题,指出翻译文学并不等同于外国文学,它是文学研究的一个独立部门,翻译文学史应该是与外国文学史、中国文学史相并列的文学史研究的三大领域之一,这三者构成完整的文学史的知识体系。前言还对翻译文学研究的分类以及翻译文学史主要解决的问题进行了总结。

第五章 总体文学研究

“总体文学”源自歌德、马克思等人先后提出的“世界文学”的概念。然而它较为独立的内涵却形成于20世纪30年代法国比较文学理论的建构之中，而且最初主要是西方世界的话语符号，直到中叶以后，情况才开始改观，其特征：一是总体文学的理论构建随同比较文学的发展而提出，并在不断被关注中逐渐加以完善；二是总体文学研究的内容开始由西方拓展到东方，东西方文明的比较随之即成为其重要的研究内容。因而总体文学与比较文学有着密切的关联，但区别也较为明显。即比较文学侧重的是多“点”之间的研究，即对不同国家文学现象之间的关系进行研究，或对不同国家的文学现象作平行研究等；而总体文学则侧重于多“面”的研究，即对不同国家共同存在的某一文学现象进行全面的研究，探寻其规律性的东西。因此，总体文学是比较文学的自然延伸，反过来，比较文学的跨国家、跨学科、跨文明又是在多元的总体文学研究中得以实现的。

第一节　总体文学研究概述

总体文学，又叫一般文学或者普通文学。它由早期比较文学理论家提出，是对文学理论和文学基本原理的研究和探讨，主要涉及文学的问题、源流、运动、原则等各个方面。总体文学理论较为系统的构建经历了一个比较漫长的过程。

一、总体文学概念的提出及阐释

1788 年德国学者埃希霍恩编辑了一套名为《总体文学史》的丛书，“总体文学”概念由此提出。但直到 20 世纪 30 年代，“总体文学”概念才得到较为深刻的阐释并被广泛关注。法国比较文学理论家梵·第根在《比较文学论》中明确指出，要“站在一个相当广阔的国际视野上”，“对许多国文学所共有的事实进行探讨”；而且他认为“国别文学”“比较文学”与“总体文学”作为各具特色的三个层次，分别构成含义不同的独立学问，但三者彼此关联，相互补充，共同组成文学研究的有机整体。具体来说：“国别文学”研究一国之内的文学现象，“比较文学”关注国家之间的文学关系，“总体文学”则解决各国文学的共同发展。

十多年后，韦勒克在《文学理论》(1949 年)中提出：“比较文学应该向具有世界规模的文学研究发展，文学中的实证主义有其局限性，必须在寻求各国文学的相互联系的同时，站在国际视野的立场上使它有质的提高，在此基础上所进行的具有普遍性的文学研究。”北京大学李赋宁教授在《什么是比较文学》一文中基本上沿袭了这种定义：比较文学可以被看成是连接国别文学和总体文学的桥梁，总体文学研究是文学研究的最高目标，因为它研究的问题是文学作品的一些普遍最根本的问题。①

法国《拉鲁斯百科全书》中对于总体文学是这样定义的：“一般认为，各国文学的总和就是世界文学。总体文学的目标则是从世界文学史中提取永恒的不变的因素，总结出文学创作的普遍规律，并制定文学类型的一般理论……而总体文学则必须将文学

---

① 孙景尧. 简明比较文学——“自我”和“他者”的认知之道[M]. 北京：中国青年出版社，2003：86.

看作一个不可分割的整体,用综合的方法对文学作全面的研究。然而,这种综合的研究只能建立在比较的基础上。”①

法国学者德利耶尔教授曾对民族文学、比较文学、总体文学三者的层次和关系,打了个形象的比喻:民族文学在一国的围墙之内研究文学,比较文学跨过围墙去,而总体文学则高于围墙之上。

北京大学教授、国际比较文学协会副主席杨周翰先生指出:“我觉得不管是影响研究也好,平行研究也好,比较的结果应纳入或充实所谓‘总体文学’。‘总体文学’的概念,有人认为很含糊。我觉得美国雷马克的界说是可以接受的,即总体文学是指总的文学潮流问题和理论,或者是指美学。”②综上所述,提出总体文学的概念,其主要的意义在于对于比较文学的研究设定一个宏伟终极的目标,要求学者们能够用世界性的胸怀和眼界来研究文学史和文学理论,研究文学作品中最普遍和最根本的问题。

二、总体文学发展的三个阶段

总体文学的发展可以简要概括为三个阶段。第一阶段是它的提出,这一阶段总体文学尚未有明确的定义。此领域开创性的拓垦在德国。早在18世纪末,德国学者就使用了总体文学这一概念。1788年埃希霍恩编辑了一套名为《总体文学史》的丛书;1798年哈特曼编辑的《诗歌的总体史探讨》面世;1793年至1801年,瓦赫勒编辑了四卷本的《总体文学史探讨》。这些著作中都探讨了总体文学的问题。1827年1月31日,针对诗人马提森自负褊狭的文学观,歌德在与秘书爱克曼的谈话中盛赞中国文学,提倡文学研读的世界性视野,并指出:“一国一民的文学而今已没有多少意义,世界文学的时代即将来临,我们每个人现在就该为加速它的到来贡献力量。”③此后,歌德又多次使用过世界文学这一概念,强调文学是一种世界现象而不是一种民族现象。根据歌德当时讲话的语境,他讲的世界文学应该是指各国文学的综合。至19世纪中期,格拉塞编辑了一套规模宏大的《总体文学教科书》,在英国,蒙哥利马于1833年作了关于总体文学、诗歌等的讲演,同时,伦敦还成立了总体文学与科学系。自此,总体文学作为一个重要文学术语开始受到各国学者的认真对待。但上述学者的“总体文学”的概念时而指代一般的文学理论与批评原则,时而指代欧洲各国的文学史,显得混乱而含糊。总体文学发展的第二阶段以法国学者梵·第根为代表。这一阶段开始真正严格使用“总体文学”概念并确立其理论价值。针对当时法国比较文学界盛行的实证主

---

① 孙景尧.简明比较文学——“自我”和“他者”的认知之道[M].北京:中国青年出版社,2003:86.

② 杨周翰.建立比较文学阵地　开展比较文学研究[J].中国比较文学,1984(1):9.

③ 艾克曼.歌德谈话录[F].杨武能,译.杭州:浙江文艺出版社,2012:106-107.

义和民族主义,1931 年,梵·第根在《比较文学论》中专门用一章的篇幅讨论了总体文学理论,辨析了国别文学、比较文学与总体文学的联系与区别。总体文学发展的第三阶段以中国学者为主流。这一时期,中国学者开始大河转向,从盲目推崇西方转向对本土文学的共识,在坚守本土文化的基础上与西方强势文化和平对话。这一时期,中国比较文学台湾学派、香港学派对推动中国比较文学的发展功不可没,他们提出了要对中西诗学进行比较研究,以得出文学发展的普遍规律,这一目标与总体文学的研究目标不谋而合,也自然就促进了中国总体文学的研究。中国大陆学者曹顺庆在总体文学研究领域提出了颇有见地的观点。他重新对总体文学进行梳理,使它的概念进一步明确化,而且还对总体文学的研究目标进行了明确的划分。他指出:“总体文学研究,可以从五个方面来切入总体文学的研究领域:一是从跨文明异质性与互补性研究入手,探讨多种文明间的异质性、变异性与互补性问题;二是跨文明阐发研究问题;三是跨文明对话研究问题;四是从比较诗学到一般诗学研究;五是文学人类学研究。”①在这三个阶段的发展过程中,关于“总体文学”的概念始终存在着一些争议,而今这种争议仍未中断,而对总体文学理论的探讨仍在继续,其研究的广阔空间还有待拓展。

三、总体文学研究的特征

比较文学这一学科研究的最终目的,在一定意义上,是帮助我们认识总体文学乃至人类文化的基本规律,而总体文学正是这种文学规律得以实现的必由之路。所以总体文学是比较文学学科理论中十分重要的一环。但由于学界对它的种种分歧甚至误解,使它一直没有得到足够的重视。要想进一步促进比较文学理论研究的发展,总体文学是无法回避的一个重要领域。提出总体文学的另一原因就是当下全球化和多元文化时代所赋予总体文学新的契机。全球化当然不应该只是西化,而应当是全世界不同文明共存的文化多元化。如何处理多元本土化因素和全球化的关系,对于这些问题的研究将直接涉及总体文学和比较文学的发展。在多元文化时代的全球化语境中,总体文学具备以下几个方面的研究特征。

(一)世界眼光,民族对等

在东西方文学比较的背景下,中国学者首先强调的是世界眼光中的民族对等。这就要求同时从两个方面反对文学研究和文化交往中的“文化封闭主义”与“文化殖民主义”。由此出发,有的学者一方面赞同把比较文学视为“总体文学”迈进的中间阶段,并将印度、日本和中国等亚洲国家现代文学的形成和发展比作“世界文学总体”的

① 曹顺庆.建构比较文学学科研究新范式[J].外国文学研究,2006(2):156.

诞生标志,另一方面宣称“总体文学”的时代特征可以概括为一句话,即“交流就是一切”。在总体文学时代,交流已成为生活的同义词,封闭则是自杀的同义词。交流是生活的标志,生活是交流的总和……一切民族的生活,无不处在世界性的交流之中;一切民族文学的生产和发展,无不处在世界性的交流之中。[①]另有学者主张从世界的格局来审视包括中国在内的民族与国别的文学,提出“就目前景况而论,严格意义上的‘世界文学’并未出现,出现的只是国别文学、民族文学在世界背景中的相遇、相交和相融”。因此,略去其理想成分不论,“世界文学”的准确含义,应解释为“世界的文学”,即“文学的世界背景”或“世界的文学构成”。在这样的前提下,阐释世界文学格局,就是指“以世界的眼光”,而不是一国、一洲的眼光,对人类的文学现象作总体和历史的把握。为了做到这一点,需要跳出过去有“我”之比的中心模式,进入“第三人称”式的客观化图式。用形象的比喻形容,即从各自占有的“领海”之争,进入人类共通的“公海”境界。在这意义上,如果说“比较文学”标志的是主权尊重和族群平等的话,“总体文学”则意味着多元交汇与主体超越。[②]

(二)双向阐释,东、西互动

所谓“双向阐释”指的是同时用东西方的文学理论,去分别阐释彼此不同的文学作品。这一主张在开始阶段主要是由港台学者提出的。在此之前,文学研究领域最为常见的现象,是在西方理论“放之四海皆准”的假定下,用西方文论阐释世界各国的文学,亦即以西方“模子”单方面地套用于东方。为了改变这种褊狭,不少中国学者认为我们不仅可以用现实主义、浪漫主义乃至结构主义等来“以西释中”,同样可以调换角度,“由中释西”,即以中国文论来阐释西方文学。在这点上,一些西方学者也表达了相似的愿望和看法。其中最突出的首推萨义德对西方“东方学”的批判。根据他的分析,到目前为止,西方主流社会有关东方历史文化的阐释,实质上不过是西方自身价值的倒影、复制与延伸,在此过程中,真正的东方原貌已被误读、改变和扭曲了。按照这一观点的推论,解决这一问题的根本办法,只能是重新回到东方文化的自我起点,从东方传统的自我话语出发,“以东释东”,由此矫正“东方学”造成的失误。

(三)比较诗学,体系参照

比较诗学形成,同样关系到“总体文学”的探讨。面对世界上主要以民族、国家为单位的诸多文学及其赖以滋生的审美体系,你究竟以什么样的立场和标准去进行总体

① 曾小逸.走向世界文学——中国作家与外国文学“导言”[M].长沙:湖南人民出版社,1985:36-74.

② 徐新建.面对世界——中国比较文学学会第三届年会暨国际学术讨论会文集[M].贵阳:贵州人民出版社,1991:132-150.

判断和分析呢？单以西方为中心的做法已经过时。那么是不是改换成“非西方”的其他中心就可以了呢？显然不行。于是各国学者便开始了跨越异质文化的文论、诗学比较。目的在于通过比较，从理论的高度探寻人类文论、诗学的同一性，从而为确立“总体文学”打下基础。

前国际比较文学学会主席佛克玛站在“新世界主义”（或称理想的世界主义）立场上，主张以多元文化的眼光，进行文学基本标准方面的理论比较，同时又应充分考虑人类作为地球上的一个生物种群所具有的“共同因素”。从这点出发，他把以写作《中国的文学理论》而闻名世界的美籍华裔学者刘若愚，视为中国传统与欧美传统之间“最成功的调停人”。因为刘虽然承认文化传统之间存在的根本差异，却不认为彼此的“文化代码”，如文论、诗学“话语”不可转换。用刘若愚本人的话说，即首先是不同传统的“文本并列”，继而是在此基础上的“比较诗学，即只有通过来自两种不同传统的文本的并列，我们才能突出各自传统中真正独特的东西。……这种并列将使我们意识到那些难以表述的先决条件，即有关构成各种传统的言、诗歌、政治和阐释本质的先决条件。这就为真正的比较诗学扫清了障碍，得以超越欧洲中心主义或中国中心主义”。①

（四）文化对话，和而不同

通过从现实发展到理论体系的比较、分析不难看出，在理想中的“总体文学”尚未建立以前，人类的文学状况实际呈现的只是自成系统的“欧洲—西方文学”与“亚洲—东方文学”以及“美洲—犹太文学”“非洲—黑人文学”等多种组合与多元格局。对此，比较文学学者更多主张的是跨文化对话前提下的文学交流和互补。而进行这种交流与对话，最需要避免的是“文化中心主义”和“文化孤立主义”这两种有害倾向。从人类自“轴心时代”以来的演变进程来看，交流无疑是有利于相互沟通和互补的。

不同文化之间的交流过去已被多次证明是人类文明发展的里程碑。希腊学习埃及，罗马借鉴希腊，阿拉伯参照罗马帝国，中世纪的欧洲又模仿阿拉伯，而文艺复兴时期的欧洲则仿效拜占庭帝国。乐黛云总结说，没有互为他者的相互参照，没有从多元视角深入认识自己的可能，也就没有不同文化之间的互补、互证和互识，就不会有新文化的创建。因此为了避免冲突，实现沟通，当今世界需要的现实目标，既非“殖民称霸”亦非“自我封闭”，而是“和而不同”。“和”这一来自中国古代思想的文化主张，它的基本精神即是强调不同元素在多元关系中的和谐共处。这样，为了达到人类世界的和谐共处，使各民族文学都以平等身份进入多元格局，比较文学的重要性非但没有因

① 佛克玛.东方和西方：文化的多元化标准[J].中外文化与文论，1996(1)：95.

“总体文学”的提出而减弱，反而因那样的理想目标日益显著起来，并且在跨异质文化的中西比较中，进一步发挥其不可替代的现实作用，那就是：通过对话来解决人类在文学方面遭遇的共同问题。①

【原典选读】

总体文学、比较文学与民族文学（节选）

◉韦勒克

【导读】雷纳·韦勒克（René Wellek）（1903—1995），是20世纪著名的文学理论家。他的重要论著《文学理论》一经出版就在国内外产生了很大的影响，先后被译成西班牙语、意大利语、日本语、朝鲜语、德国语、葡萄牙语、希伯来语和俄罗斯语等十几种文字，并促进了国际学术界在文学理论研究中关于认识论和方法论的革新；而自20世纪80年代《文学理论》传入我国以来，对我国比较文学研究也产生了广泛而深刻的影响。

该书材料丰富，观点独到，结构严谨有序，由定义和区别、初步工作、文学研究的外延方法以及文学研究的内涵方法四个部分组成，其中内涵方法中的第一节“文学艺术作品的存在方式”，被国外学者认为是他对文学理论的最大贡献。本节“总体文学、比较文学与民族文学（General，Comparative，and National Literature）”就选自此部分。在这一节中，韦勒克主要阐述了总体文学、比较文学与民族文学三者之间的关系。他先是从定义入手，认为“比较文学”的定义是十分宽泛的，过去指的是明确的研究范围和某些类型问题，肯定了口头文学和民间文学的重要地位和作用，但是把“比较文学”仅仅归于口头文学不太准确；又指出，“比较文学”的另一个含义是指对两种或更多种文学之间的关系研究。文学之间的比较如果与总的民族文学脱节，会把研究的重点放在外表上，而不是事实和影响的部分；第三种观点则把“比较文学”与文学总体、“世界文学”或“总体文学”等同起来。这种定义方法也是有待商榷的。关于“世界文学”，韦勒克认为，它更偏重于全球性的民族文学共同发声；而“总体文学”研究超越民族界限的文学运动和文学风尚，“比较文学”偏重研究两种或两种以上文学之间的关系。所以一部综合的文学史，一部超越民族界限的文学史，必须重新书写。但是过分注意某一国家的本土语言，不注意“文学民族性”也是有害的。只有当我们对于上述一系列的问题有明确的回答时，我们才对总体文学、比较文学的研究更加深入，从而使“总体文学”这一跨越地域、民族的文学大同理想成为可能。

---

① 乐黛云. 比较文学与21世纪人文精神[J]. 中国比较文学，1998(1)：10-11.

“总体文学”这一定义,因韦勒克在《文学理论》中的突出强调而被广大研究者所重视,韦勒克用外部研究的宏大视角向我们阐发了总体文学、比较文学和民族文学的定义和内涵。这种提纲挈领、高屋建瓴的认识,使后来的文学理论研究者对西方文论的研究方法能从总体上获得一种整体认识;而文中提出的其他问题,也对研究者具有较强的启示性意义。但不足的是,韦勒克没有提出解决的方法,这需要我们进一步去研究、拓展。但我们有理由相信,“总体文学”终有一天会实现。■

Within literary studies, we have distinguished between theory, history, and criticism. Using another basis of division, we shall now attempt a systematic definition of comparative, general, and national literature. The term ‘comparative’ literature is troublesome and doubtless, indeed, one of the reasons why this important mode of literary study has had less than the expected academic success. Matthew Arnold, translating Ampère's use of ‘*bistoire comparative*’, was apparently the first to use the term in English (1848). The French have preferred the term used earlier by Villemain, who had spoken of ‘*littérature comparée*’ (1829), after the analogy of Cuvier's *Anatomie comparée* (1800). The Germans speak of ‘*vergleicbende Literaturgescbicbte*’. Yet neither of these differently formed adjectives is very illuminating, since comparison is a method used by all criticism and sciences, and does not, in any way, adequately describe the specific procedures of literary study. The formal comparison between literatures—or even movements, figures, and works—is rarely a central theme in literary history, though such a book as F. C. Green's *Minuet*, comparing aspects of French and English eighteenth-century literature, may be illuminating in defining not only parallels and affinities but also divergences between the literary development of one nation and that of another.

In practice, the term ‘comparative’ literature has covered and still covers rather distinct fields of study and groups of problems. It may mean, first, the study of oral literature, especially of folk-tale themes and their migration; of how and when they have entered ‘higher’,’artistic’ literature. This type of problem can be relegated to folklore, an important branch of learning which is only in part occupied with aesthetic facts, since it studies the total civilization of a ‘folk’, its costumes and customs, superstitions and tools, as well as its arts. We must, however, endorse the view that the study of oral literature is an integral part of literary scholarship, for it cannot be divorced from the study of written works, and there has been and still is a continuous interaction between oral and written literature. Without going to the extreme of folklorists such as Hans Naumann who consider most later oral literature *gesunkenes Kulturgut*, we can recognize that written upper-class literature has profoundly affected oral literature. On the other hand, we must assume the folk origin of many basic literary genres and themes, and we have abundant evidence for the social rise of folk literature. Still, the incorporation into folklore of chivalric romance and troubadour lyric is an indubitable fact. Though this is a view which would have shocked the Romantic believers in the creativity of the folk and the remote antiquity of folk art, nevertheless popular ballads, fairy tales, and legends as we know them are frequently of late origin and upper-class derivation. Yet the study of oral literature must be an important concern of every literary scholar who wants to understand the processes of literary development, the origin and the rise of our literary genres and devices. It is unfortunate that the study of oral literature has thus far been so exclusively preoccupied with the study of themes and their migrations from country to country, i. e. with the raw materials of modern literatures. Of late, however, folklorists have increasingly turned their attention to the study of patterns, forms, and devices, to a morphology of literary forms, to the problems of the teller and narrator and the audience of a tale, and have thus prepared the way for a close integration of their studies into a general conception of literary scholarship. Though the study of oral literature has its own peculiar problems, those of transmission and social setting, its fundamental problems, without doubt, are shared with written literature; and there is a continuity between oral and written literature which has never been interrupted. Scholars in the modern European literatures have neglected these questions to their own disadvantage, while literary historians in the Slavic and Scandinavian countries, where folklore is still—or was till recently—alive, have been in much closer touch with these studies. But 'comparative literature' is hardly the term by which to designate the study of oral literature.

Another sense of 'comparative' literature confines it to the study of relationships between two or more literatures. This is the use established by the flourishing school of French *comparatistes* headed by the late Fernand Baldensperger and gathered around the *Revue de littérature comparée.* The school has especially given attention, sometimes mechanically but sometimes with considerable finesse, to such questions as the reputation and penetration, the influence and fame, of Goethe in France and England, of Ossian and Carlyle and Schiller in France. It has developed a methodology which, going beyond the collection of information concerning reviews, translations, and influences, considers carefully the image, the concept of a particular author at a particular time, such diverse factors of transmission as periodicals, translators, salons, and travellers, and the 'receiving factor', the special atmosphere and literary situation into which the foreign author is imported. In total, much evidence for the close unity, especially of the Western European literatures, has been accumulated; and our knowledge of the 'foreign trade' of literatures has been immeasurably increased.

But this conception of 'comparative literature' has also, one recognizes, its peculiar difficulties. No distinct system can, it seems, emerge from the accumulation of such studies. There is no methodological distinction between a study of 'Shakespeare in France' and a study of 'Shakespeare in eighteenth-century England', or between a study of Poe's influence on Baudelaire and one of Dryden's influence on Pope. Comparisons between literatures, if isolated from concern with the total national literatures, tend to restrict themselves to external problems of sources and influences, reputation and fame. Such studies do not permit us to analyse and judge an individual work of art, or even to consider the complicated whole of its genesis; instead, they are mainly devoted either to such echoes of a masterpiece as translations and imitations, frequently by second-rate authors, or to the prehistory of a masterpiece, the migrations and the spread of its themes and forms. The emphasis of 'comparative literature' thus conceived is on externals; and the decline of this type of 'comparative literature' in recent decades reflects the general turning away from stress on mere 'facts', on sources and influences.

A third conception obviates, however, all these criticisms, by identifying 'comparative literature', with the study of literature in its totality, with 'world literature', with 'general' or 'universal' literature. There are certain difficulties with these suggested equations. The term 'world literature', a translation of Goethe's *Weltliteratur*, is perhaps needlessly grandiose, implying that literature should be studied on all five continents, from New Zealand to Iceland. Goethe, actually, had no such thing in mind. 'World literature' was used by him to indicate a time when all literatures would become one. It is the ideal of the unification of all literatures into one great synthesis, where each nation would play its part in a universal concert. But Goethe himself saw that this is a very distant ideal, that no single nation is willing to give up its individuality.

Today we are possibly even further removed from such a state of amalgamation, and we would argue that we cannot even seriously wish that the diversities of national literatures should be obliterated. 'World literature' is frequently used in a third sense. It may mean the great treasure-house of the classics, such as Homer, Dante, Cervantes, Shakespeare, and Goethe, whose reputation has spread all over the world and has lasted a considerable time. It thus has become a synonym for 'masterpieces', for a selection from literature which has its critical and pedagogic justification but can hardly satisfy the scholar who cannot confine himself to the great peaks if he is to understand the whole mountain ranges or, to drop the figure, all history and change.

The possibly preferable term 'general literature' has other disadvantages. Originally it was used to mean poetics or theory and principles of literature, and in recent decades Paul Van Tieghem has tried to capture it for a special conception in contrast to 'comparative literature'. According to him, 'general literature' studies those movements and fashions of literature which transcend national lines, while 'comparative literature' studies the interrelationships between two or more literatures. But how can we determine whether, e. g. Ossianism is a topic of 'general' or 'comparative literature'? One cannot make a valid distinction between the influence of Walter Scott abroad and the international vogue of the historical novel. 'Comparative' and 'general' literature merge inevitably. Possibly, it would be best to speak simply of 'literature'.

Whatever the difficulties into which a conception of universal literary history may run, it is important to think of literature as a totality and to trace the growth and development of literature without regard to linguistic distinctions. The great argument for 'comparative' or 'general' literature or just 'literature' is the obvious falsity of the idea of a self-enclosed national literature. Western literature, at least, forms a unity, a whole. One cannot doubt the continuity between Greek and Roman literatures, the Western medieval world, and the main modern literatures; and, without minimizing the importance of Oriental influences, especially that of the Bible, one must recognize a close unity which includes all Europe, Russia, the United States, and the Latin-American literatures. This ideal was envisaged and, within their limited means, fulfilled, by the founders of literary history in the early nineteenth century: such men as the Schlegels, Bouterwek, Sismondi, and Hallam. But then the further growth of nationalism combined with the effect of increasing specialization led to an increasingly narrow provincial cultivation of the study of national literatures. During the second half of the nineteenth century the ideal of a universal literary history was, however, revived under the influence of evolutionism. The early practitioners of 'comparative literature' were folklorists, ethnographers who, largely under the influence of Herbert Spencer, studied the origins of literature, its diversification in oral literary forms, and its emergence into the early epic, drama, and lyric. Evolutionism left, however, few traces on the history of modern literatures and apparently fell into discredit when it drew the parallel between literary change and biological evolution too closely. With it the ideal of universal literary history declined. Happily, in recent years there are many signs which augur a return to the ambition of general literary historiography. Ernst Robert Curtius's *European Literature and the Latin Middle Ages* (1948), which traces commonplaces through the totality of Western tradition with stupendous erudition, and Erich Auerbach's *Mimesis* (1946), a history of realism from Homer to Joyce based on sensitive stylistic analyses of individual passages, are achievements of scholarship which ignore the established nationalisms and convincingly demonstrate the unity of Western civilization, the vitality of the heritage of classical antiquity and medieval Christianity.

Literary history as a synthesis, literary history on a super-national scale, will have to be written again. The study of comparative literature in this sense will make high demands on the linguistic proficiencies of our scholars. It asks for a widening of perspectives, a suppression of local and provincial sentiments, not easy to achieve. Yet literature is one, as art and humanity are one; and in this conception lies the future of historical literary studies.

Within this enormous area — in practice, identical with all literary history — there are, no doubt, subdivisions sometimes running along linguistic lines. There are, first of all, the groups of the three main linguistic families in Europe — the Germanic, the Romance, and the Slavic literatures. The Romance literatures have particularly frequently been studied in close interconnexion, from the days of Bouterwek up to Leonardo Olschki's attempt to write a history of them all for the medieval period. The Germanic literatures have been comparably studied, usually, only for the early Middle Ages, when the nearness of a general Teutonic civilization, can be still strongly felt. Despite the customary opposition of Polish scholars, it would appear that the close linguistic affinities of the Slavic languages, in combination with shared popular traditions extending even to metrical forms, make up a basis for a common Slavic literature.

The history of themes and forms, devices and genres, is obviously and international history. While most of our genres descend from the literature of Greece and Rome, they were very considerably modified and augmented during the Middle Ages. Even the history of metrics, though closely bound up with the individual linguistic systems, is international. Furthermore, the great literary movements and styles of modern Europe (the Renaissance, the Baroque, Neo-Classicism, Romanticism, Realism, Symbolism) far exceed the boundaries of one nation, even though there are significant national differences between the workings out of these styles. Also their geographical spread may vary. The Renaissance, e. g. penetrated to Poland but not to Russia or Bohemia. The Baroque style flooded the whole of Eastern Europe including the Ukraine, but hardly touched Russia proper. There may be also considerable chronological divergencies: the Baroque style survived in the peasant civilizations of Eastern Europe well to the end of the eighteenth century when the West has passed through the Enlightenment, and so on. On the whole, the importance of linguistic barriers was quite unduly magnified during the nineteenth century.

This emphasis was due to the very close association between Romantic (mostly linguistic) nationalism and the rise of modern organized literary history. It continues today through such practical influences as the virtual identification, especially in the United States, of the teaching of literature and the teaching of a language. The result, in the United States, has been an extraordinary lack of contact between the students of English, German, and French literature. Each of these groups bears a completely different imprint and uses different methods. These disjunctions are in part, doubtless, unavoidable, simply because most men live in but a single linguistic medium; and yet they lead to grotesque consequences when literary problems are discussed only with regard to views expressed in the particular language and only with reference to texts and documents in that language. Though in certain problems of artistic style, metre, and even genre, the linguistic differences between the European literatures will be important, it is clear that for many problems of the history of ideas, including critical ideas, such distinctions are untenable; artificial cross-sections are drawn through homogeneous materials, and histories are written concerning ideological echoes by chance expressed in English or German or French. The excessive attention to one vernacular is especially detrimental to the study of medieval literature, since in the Middle Ages Latin was the foremost literary language, and Europe formed a very close intellectual unity. A history of literature during the Middle Ages in England which neglects the vast amount of writings in Latin and Anglo-Norman gives a false picture of England's literary situation and general culture.

This recommendation of comparative literature does not, of course, imply neglecting the study of individual national literatures. Indeed, it is just the problem of 'nationality' and of the distinct contributions of the individual nations to this general literary process which should be realized as central. Instead of being studied with theoretical clarity, the problem has been blurred by nationalistic sentiment and racial theories. To isolate the exact contributions of English literature to general literature, a fascinating problem, might lead to a shift of perspective and an altered evaluation, even of the major figures. Within each national literature there arise similar problems of the exact shares of regions and cities. Such an exaggerated theory as that of Josef Nadler, who professes to be able to discern the traits and characteristics of each German tribe and region and its reflections in literature, should not deter us from the consideration of these problems, rarely investigated with any command of facts and any coherent method. Much that has been written on the role of New England, the Middle West, and the South in the history of American literature, and most of the writings on regionalism, amounts to no more than the expression of pious hopes, local pride, and resentment of centralizing powers. Any objective analysis will have to distinguish questions concerning the racial descent of authors and sociological questions concerning provenance and setting from questions concerning the actual influence of the landscape and questions of literary tradition and fashion.

Problems of 'nationality' become especially complicated if we have to decide that literatures in the same language are distinct national literatures, as American and modern Irish assuredly are. Such a question as why Goldsmith, Sterne, and Sheridan do not belong to Irish literature, while Yeats and Joyce do, needs an answer. Are there independent Belgian, Swiss, and Austrian literatures? It is not very easy to determine the point at which literature written in America ceased to be 'colonial English' and became an independent national literature. Is it the mere fact of political independence? Is it the national consciousness of the authors themselves? Is it the use of national subject-matter and 'local colour'? Or is it the rise of a definite national literary style?

Only when we have reached decisions on these problems shall we be able to write histories of national literature which are not simply geographical or linguistic categories, shall we be able to analyse the exact way in which each national literature enters into European tradition. Universal and national literatures implicate each other. A pervading European convention is modified in each country: there are also centres of radiation in the individual countries, and eccentric and individually great figures who set off one national tradition from the other. To be able to describe the exact share of the one and the other would amount to knowing much that is worth knowing in the whole of literary history.

(René Wellek: Theory Of Literature. 6277 Sea Harbor Drive, Orlando, Florida 32887, U. S. A, Harcourt, Brace & World. 1956. 46-53)

【研究范例】

诗可以怨（节选）

◉钱锺书

【导读】《诗可以怨》是钱锺书1980年在日本早稻田大学文学教授恳谈会上的讲稿，后被收录于钱锺书散文集。这是他20世纪50年代以后发表的几篇重要批评文章之一。此文突出地显示了作者博古通今、学贯中西、议论风生的学术风格，面世以来广受好评。

作者开门见山地提出了中国古代文学批评的一个重要观点：痛苦比快乐更能产生诗歌，好诗主要是不愉快、烦恼或穷愁的表现和发泄，点出了本文要讨论的核心论点。文章从文学和心理学两条思路的角度，论述了对"诗可以怨"这个观点的理解的误区。作者先从文学的角度用古今中外的例子论证"诗可以怨"的观点提出的由来。首先对司马迁的"诗只可以怨"这种唯一功能提出了质疑。最精彩的是对钟嵘的评价。作者纵横捭阖，从谈诗打通到小说、戏剧、跨越时空、跨越国界，让钟嵘同李渔对话，让钟嵘同弗洛伊德对话，还说有时韩愈同司马迁也会说不到一处去。然后运用比喻妙言反讽钟嵘、司马迁。作者从两个方面一边比喻，一边点题，语言幽默、诙谐，嘲讽揶揄，在浓郁的艺术氛围中又不失犀利的文学批评。

节选首先从文学史的角度，指出从汉代司马迁开始，"诗可以怨"就一直是历代文人遵循的文学的正统观点，但历代文人对它的理解有历史的偏颇，有时又会犯逻辑上的错误。因为历史是由人的思想构成的，有人就会有思想的错误，也会有思想的补充和完善。不过，人们较多地注意到了历史清澈的表层，而往往忽略了经历了长期时间沉淀以后的浑浊的底层。从节选中可以看出，由穷苦之言易好转向穷苦之言才好就是历史犯的一个逻辑错误；而大多数人对韩愈"不平"含义片面的理解是历史犯的又一个错误。不仅如此，作者还从心理学的层面进一步揭示了"诗可以怨"的内在动因。

钱先生的这篇文学批评有两个显著的特点：其一，在论及中国传统文艺观念的时候，往往以西方相关例子以资佐证。其二，拆解结构主义。如《管锥编》《谈艺录》及其学术方法论就是如此。《诗可以怨》这篇文章其实隐含了"诗可以怨"所涉及的三个方面。即它侧重于"怨"之内容，怨是什么，为什么怨，以及怨的功用和怨的后果等。文中论及"诗可以怨"一方面重在"可以"——探究真正的创作机制与动因，从而引发人们思考为什么可以怨；另一方面围绕"诗可以怨"并择重于"诗"，以启发人们思考是否只有"诗"的艺术形式才可以"怨"，以及其他艺术形式如戏剧、音乐、舞蹈、绘画、小说是否也可以怨呢？文章通过严密推理和层层剖析，挖掘了"诗可以怨"的价值。这些对探讨不同艺术门类的规律和创造价值都具有重要的启示意义。■

尼采曾把母鸡下蛋的啼叫和诗人的歌唱相提并论，说都是"痛苦使然"①。这个家常而生动的比拟也恰恰符合中国文艺传统里一个流行的意见：苦痛比快乐更能产生诗歌，好诗主要是不愉快、烦恼或"穷愁"的表现和发泄。这个意见在中国古代不但是诗文理论里的常谈，而且成为写作实践里的套板。因此，我们惯见熟闻，习而相忘，没有把它当作中国文评里的一个重要概念而提示出来。我下面也只举一些最平常的例来说明。

司马迁的那种意见，刘勰曾涉及一下，还用了一个巧妙的譬喻。《文心雕龙・才略》讲到冯衍："敬通雅好辞说，而坎壈盛世；《显志》《自序》亦蚌病成珠矣。"就是说他那两篇文章是"郁结""发愤"的结果。刘勰淡淡带过，语气不像司马迁那样强烈，而且专说一个人，并未扩大化。"病"是苦痛或烦恼的泛指，不限于司马迁所说"左丘失明"那种肉体上的害病，也兼及"坎壈"之类精神上的受罪，《楚辞・九辩》所说："坎壈兮贫士失职而志不平。"

---

① 《扎拉图斯脱拉如是说》(*Also Sprach Zarathustra*)第4部13章，许来许太(K. Schlechta)编《尼采集》(1955)第2册527页。

……后世像苏轼《答李端叔书》："木有瘿，石有晕，犀有通，以取妍于人，皆物之病"，无非讲"仍瘁以成明文"，虽不把"蚌蛤衔珠"来比，而"木有瘿"正是"楩楠成瘤"①。西洋人谈起文学创作，取譬巧合得很。格里巴尔泽说诗好比害病不作声的贝壳动物所产生的珠子；福楼拜以为珠子是牡蛎生病所结成，作者的文笔却是更深沉的痛苦的流露②。海涅发问：诗之于人，是否像珠子之于可怜的牡蛎，是使它苦痛的病料③。豪斯门说诗是一种分泌，不管是自然的分泌，像松杉的树脂，还是病态的分泌，像牡蛎的珠子④。看来这个比喻很通行。大家不约而同地采用它，正因为它非常贴切"诗可以怨""发愤所为作"。可是，《文心雕龙》里那句话似乎历来没有博得应得的欣赏。

司马迁举了一系列"发愤"的著作，有的说理，有的记事，最后把《诗三百篇》笼统都归于"怨"，也作为其中的一个例子。钟嵘单就诗歌而论，对这个意思加以具体发挥。《诗品·序》里有一节话，我们一向没有好好留心。"嘉会寄诗以亲，离群托诗以怨。至于楚臣去境，汉妾辞宫；或骨横朔野，魂逐飞蓬；或负戈外戍，杀气雄边，塞客衣单，孀闺泪尽；或士有解佩出朝，一去忘反，女有扬蛾入宠，再盼倾国。凡斯种种，感荡心灵，非陈诗何以展其义？非长歌何以骋其情？故曰：'诗可以群，可以怨。'使穷贱易安，幽居靡闷，莫尚于诗矣！"说也奇怪，这一节差不多是与钟嵘同时人江淹那两篇名文——《别赋》和《恨赋》的提纲。钟嵘不讲"兴"和"观"，虽讲起"群"，而所举压倒多数的事例是"怨"，只有"嘉会"和"入宠"两者无可争辩地属于愉快或欢乐的范围。也许"无可争辩"四个字用得过分了。"扬蛾入宠"很可能有苦恼或"怨"的一面。譬如《全晋文》卷一三左九嫔《离思赋》就怨恨自己"入紫庐"以后，"骨肉至亲，永长辞兮！"因而"欷歔涕流"（参看《文馆词林》卷一五二她哥哥左思《悼离赠妹》："永去骨肉，内充紫庭。……悲其生离，泣下交颈"）。《红楼梦》第一八回里的贾妃不也感叹"今虽富贵，骨肉分离，终无意趣"么？同时，按照当代名剧《王昭君》的主题思想，"汉妾辞宫"绝不是"怨"，少说也算得是"群"，简直竟是良缘"嘉会"，欢欢喜喜到胡人那里去"扬蛾入宠"了。但是，看《诗品》里这几句平常话时，似乎用不着那样深刻的眼光，正像在日常社交生活里，看人看物都无须荧光检查式的透视。《序》结尾

---

① 参看赵翼《瓯北诗钞》七言律三《闻心余京邸病风却寄》之二："木有文章原是病，石能言语果为灾"；龚自珍《破戒草》卷下《释言》："木有刘彰曾是病，虫多言语不能天。"普鲁斯脱的小说里谈起创作，说："想象和思想都可能是良好的机器，但也可能静止不转，痛苦才推动了它们"；这也许是用现代机械化语言为"激通"所作的好比喻。

② 墨希格（Walter Muschg）《悲剧观的文学史》（*Tragische Literatur geschichte*）3版（1957）415页引了这两个例。

③ 《论浪漫派》（*Die Romantische Schule*）2卷4节，《海涅诗文书信合集》（东柏林，1961）第5册98页。

④ 《诗的名称和性质》（*The Name and Nature of Poetry*），卡特（J. Carter）编《豪斯门散文选》（1961）194页。豪斯门紧接说自己的诗都是"健康欠佳"时写的；他所谓"自然的"就等于"健康的，非病态的"。加尔杜齐（Giosuè Carducci）痛骂浪漫派把诗说成情感上"自然的分泌（secrezione naturale）"，见布赛托（N. Busetto）《乔稣埃·加尔杜齐》（1958）492页引；他所谓"自然的"等于"信手写来的，不经艺术琢磨的"。前一意义上"不自然的（病态的）分泌"也可能是后一意义上"自然的（未加工的）分泌"。

又举了一连串的范作，除掉失传的篇章和泛指的题材，过半数都可以说是“怨”诗。至于《上品》里对李陵的评语：“生命不谐，声颓身丧，使陵不遭辛苦，其文亦何能至此！”更明白指出了刘勰所谓“蚌病成珠”，也就是后世常说的“诗必穷而后工”①。还有一点不容忽略。同一件东西，司马迁当作死人的防腐溶液，钟嵘却认为是活人的止痛药和安神剂。司马迁《报任少卿书》只说“舒愤”而著书作诗，目的是避免“姓名磨灭”，“文彩不表于后世”，着眼于作品在作者身后起的功用，能使他死而不朽。钟嵘说：“使穷贱易安，幽居靡闷，莫尚于诗”，强调了作品在作者生时起的功用，能使他和艰辛冷落的生涯妥协相安；换句话说，一个人潦倒愁闷，全靠“诗可以怨”，获得了排遣、慰藉或补偿。……大家都熟知弗洛伊德的有名理论：在实际生活里不能满足欲望的人，死了心作退一步想，创造出文艺来，起一种替代品的功用，借幻想来过瘾②。假如说，弗洛伊德这个理论早在钟嵘的三句话里稍露端倪，更在周楫和李渔的两段话里粗见眉目，那也许不是牵强拉拢，而只是请大家注意他们似曾相识罢了。

在某一点上，钟嵘和弗洛伊德可以对话，而有时候韩愈和司马迁也会说不到一处去。《送孟东野序》是收入旧日古文选本里给学僮们读熟读烂的文章。韩愈一开头就宣称：“大凡物不得其平则鸣。……人声之精者为言，文辞之于言，又其精也”；历举庄周、屈原、司马迁、相如等大作家作为“善鸣”的例子，然后隆重地请出主角：“孟郊东野始以其诗鸣。”一般人认为“不平则鸣”和“发愤所为作”含义相同；事实上，韩愈和司马迁讲的是两码事。司马迁的“愤”就是“坎壈不平”或通常所谓“牢骚”；韩愈的“不平”和“牢骚不平”并不相等，它不但指愤郁，也包括欢乐在内。先秦以来的心理学一贯主张：人“性”的原始状态是平静，“情”是平静遭到了骚扰，性“不得其平”而为情。《乐记》里两句话：“人生而静，感于物而动”，具有代表性，道家和佛家经典都把水因风而起浪作为比喻③。这个比喻也被儒家借而不还，据为己有。《礼记·中庸》“天命以谓性”句下，孔颖达《正义》引梁五经博士贺玚说：“性之与情，犹波之与水，静时是水，动则是波，静时是性，动则是情。”韩门弟子李翱《复性书》上篇就说：“情者，性之动。水汨于沙，而清者浑，性动于情，而善者恶。”甚至深怕和佛老沾边的宋儒程颐也不避嫌疑：“湛然平静如镜者，水之性也。及遇沙石或地势不平，便有湍激，或风行其上，便为波涛汹涌，此岂水之性也哉！……然无水安得波浪，无性安得情也？”（《伊川语》，《河南二程遗书》卷一八）……我们也许该把韩愈的话安置在这种“语言天地”里，才能理解它的意义。他另一篇文章《送高闲上人序》就说：“喜怒窘穷，忧悲愉快，怨恨思慕，酣醉无聊，不平有动于心，必于草书焉发之”；“有动”和“不平”就是同一事态的正负两种说法，重言申明，概括“喜怒”“悲愉”等情感。只要看《送孟东野序》的

① 参看《管锥编》935-937页。

② 弗洛伊德《全集》（伦敦，1950）第14册355又433页。

③ 参看《管锥编》1211-1212页。

结尾："抑不知天将和其声而使鸣国家之盛耶？抑将穷饿其身，思愁其心肠，而使自鸣其不幸耶？"很清楚，得志而"鸣国家之盛"和失意而"自鸣不幸"，两者都是"不得其平则鸣"。韩愈在这里是两面兼顾的，正像《汉书·艺文志》讲"歌咏"时，并举"哀乐"，而不像司马迁那样的偏主"发愤"。有些评论家对韩愈的话加以指摘①，看来他们对"不得其平"理解得太狭窄了，把它和"发愤"混淆。黄庭坚有一联诗："与世浮沉唯酒可，随人忧乐以诗鸣"（《山谷内集》卷一三《再次韵兼简履中南玉》之二）；下句的"来历"正是《送孟东野序》。他本可以写"失时穷饿以诗鸣"或"违时侘傺以诗鸣"等，却用"忧乐"二字作为"不平"的代词，真是一点儿不含糊的好读者。

韩愈确曾比前人更明白地规定了"诗可以怨"的观念，那是在他的《荆潭唱和诗序》里。这篇文章是恭维两位写诗的大官僚的，恭维他们的诗居然比得上穷书生的诗，"王公贵人"能"与韦布里闾憔悴之士较其毫厘分寸"。言外之意就是把"憔悴之士"的诗作为检验的标准，因为有一个大前提："夫和平之音淡薄，而愁思之声要眇，欢愉之辞难工，而穷苦之言易好也。"早在六朝，已有人说出了"和平之音淡薄"的感觉，《全宋文》卷一九王微《与从弟僧绰书》："文词不怨思抑扬，则流淡无味"。……

韩愈把穷书生的诗作为样板；他推崇"王公贵人"也正是抬高"憔悴之士"。恭维而没有一味拍捧，世故而不是十足势利，应酬大官僚的文章很难这样有分寸。司马迁、钟嵘只说穷愁使人作诗、作好诗，王微只说文词不怨就不会好。韩愈把反面的话添上去了，说快乐虽也使人作诗，但作出的不会是很好或最好的诗。有了这个补笔，就题无剩义了。韩愈的大前提有一些事实根据。我们不妨说，虽然在质量上"穷苦之言"的诗未必就比"欢愉之词"的诗来得好，但是在数量上"穷苦之言"的好诗的确比"欢愉之词"的好诗来得多。因为"穷苦之言"的好诗比较多，从而断言只有"穷苦之言"才构成好诗，这在推理上有问题，韩愈犯了一点儿逻辑错误。不过，他的错误不很严重，他也找得着有名的同犯，例如十九世纪西洋的几位浪漫诗人。我们在学生时代念的通常选本里，就读到这类名句："最甜美的诗歌就是那些诉说最忧伤的思想的"；"真正的诗歌只出于深切苦恼所炽燃着的人心"；"最美丽的诗歌就是最绝望的，有些不朽的篇章是纯粹的眼泪"②。……上文提到尼采和弗洛伊德。称赏尼采而不赞成弗洛伊德的克罗齐也承认诗是"不如意事"的产物③；佩服弗洛伊德文笔的瑞士博学者墨希格甚至写了一大本《悲剧观的文学史》证明诗常出于隐蔽

① 参看沈作喆《寓简》卷四、洪迈《容斋随笔》卷四、钱大昕《潜研堂文集》卷二六《李南涧诗序》、谢章铤《藤阴客赘》。

② 雪莱《致云雀》（*To a Sky lark*）；凯尔纳（Justinus Kerner）《诗》（*Poesie*）；缪塞（Musset）《五月之夜》（*La Nuit de Mai*）。

③ 《诗论》（*La Poesia*）5 版（1953）158 页。

着的苦恼①,可惜他没有听到中国古人的议论。

没有人愿意饱尝愁苦的滋味——假如他能够避免;没有人不愿意作出美好的诗篇——即使他缺乏才情;没有人不愿意取巧省事——何况他并不损害旁人。既然"穷苦之言易好",那么,要写好诗就要说"穷苦之言"。不幸的是,"憔悴之士"才会说"穷苦之言"……白居易《读李、杜诗集因题卷后》:"不得高官职,仍逢苦乱离;暮年逋客恨,浮世谪仙悲。……天意君须会,人间要好诗。"作出好诗,得经历卑屈、乱离等愁事恨事,"失意"一辈子,换来"得意"诗一联,这代价可不算低,不是每个作诗的人所乐意付出的。② 于是长期存在一个情况:诗人企图不付出代价或希望减价而能写出好诗。小伙子作诗"叹老",大阔佬作诗"嗟穷",好端端过着闲适日子的人作诗"伤春""悲秋"。例如释文莹《湘山野录》卷上评论寇准的诗:"然富贵之时,所作皆凄楚愁怨。……余尝谓深于诗者,尽欲慕骚人清悲怨感,以主其格。"这原不足为奇;语言文字有这种社会功能,我们常常把说话来代替行动,捏造事实,乔装改扮思想和情感。值得注意的是:在诗词里,这种无中生有(fabulation)的功能往往偏向一方面。它经常报忧而不报喜,多数表现为"愁思之声"而非"和平之音",仿佛鳄鱼的眼泪,而不是《爱丽斯梦游奇境记》里那条鳄鱼的"温和地微笑嘻开的上下颚"(gently smiling jaws)。我想起刘禹锡《三阁词》描写美人的句子:"不应有恨事,娇甚却成愁";传统里的诗人并无"恨事"而"愁",表示自己才高,正像传统里的美人并无"恨事"而"愁",表示自己"娇多"③。李贽读了司马迁"发愤所为作"那句话,感慨地说:"由此观之,古之贤圣不愤则不作矣。不愤而作,譬如不寒而颤、不病而呻也。虽作何观乎!"(《焚书》卷三《〈忠义水浒传〉序》)。"古代"是招唤不回来的,成"贤"成"圣"也不是一般诗人愿意和能够的,"不病而呻"已成为文学生活里不可忽视的事实。也就是刘勰早指出来的:"心非郁陶……此为文而造情也"(《文心雕龙·情采》),或范成大嘲讽的:"诗人多事惹闲情,闭门自造愁如许"(《石湖诗集》卷一七《陆务观作〈春愁曲〉,悲甚,作此反之》)④。恰如法国古典主义大师形容一些写挽歌的人所谓:"矫揉造作,使自己伤心"⑤。南北朝二刘不是说什么"蚌病成珠""蚌蛤结疴而衔珠"吗?诗人"不病而呻",和孩子生"逃学病",要人生"政治病",同样是装病、假病。不病而呻包含一个希望:有那么便宜或侥幸的事,假

① 《悲剧观的文学史》16 页。

② 参考济慈给莎拉·杰弗莱(Sarah Jeffrey)的信:"英国产生了世界上最好的作家(the English have produced the finest writers in the World),一个主要原因是英国社会在他们生世时虐待了他们(the English World has ill-treated them during their lives)"。见济慈《书信集》(*Letters*),洛林斯(H. E. Rollins)辑注本(1958)第 2 册 115 页。

③ 吴曾《能改斋漫录》卷一六引王辅道《浣溪沙》:"娇多无事做凄凉",就是刘禹锡的语意。

④ 范成大诗说"多事",王辅道词说"无事",字面相反,而讲的是一回事;参看《管锥编》169-172 页。

⑤ 布瓦洛(Boileau)《诗法》(*L'Art Poétique*)2 篇 47 行。

病会产生真珠。假病能不能装得像真,假珠子能不能造得乱真,这也许要看个人的本领或艺术。诗曾经和形而上学、政治并列为三种哄人的玩意儿①,不是完全没有原因的。当然,作诗者也在哄自己。

(钱锺书. 七缀集[M]. 上海:上海古籍出版社,1994:119-121.)

【延伸阅读】

1. 北京师范大学中文系比较文学研究组. 比较文学研究资料选编[M]. 北京:北京师范大学出版社,1986.

本书共有四个部分,收录34篇文章,第一部分叙述了比较文学的一些基本问题,第二部分论述了影响研究方面的理论,第三部分论述平行研究理论和实例,最后一部分属于跨学科研究的文章。本书体例完善,全面介绍了比较文学历史沿革、基本理论和研究方法。

2. 黄维樑,曹顺庆. 中国比较文学学科理论的垦拓:台港学者论文选[M]. 北京:北京大学出版社,1998.

本书分为五个部分,包括中西文学比较,比较文学中国学派,阐发研究,类比研究,影响研究和其他。收录了台湾学者针对于比较文学理论研究的各学派思想。博采众长,眼光独到,是比较文学理论研究不可或缺的重要参考资料。

第二节　跨文明体系的总体文学研究

进入21世纪,如何跨越东西方文明的极大差异,这个问题对比较文学和总体文学的研究构成了巨大的挑战,同时也成为它探讨的重要内容。如前所述,“总体文学”的缘起又与法国学派有关,但人们并未意识到,当梵·第根指出“总体文学”是“对于许

---

① 让·保尔(Jean Paul)《美学导论》(*Vorschule der Aesthetik*)第52节引托里尔特(Thomas Thorild)的话,《让·保尔全集》(慕尼黑,1965)第5册193页。

多国家文学所共有的事实的探讨”(着重号为笔者加),[①]其中“共有的事实”的特性已明显含有了“跨文明”之意。只不过,与同时代的大多数欧洲学者受“欧洲—西方中心主义”影响一样,梵·第根同样受此束缚而不可能意识到这一点,当然更无以超越洲际本位而看到“共有的事实”中含有的跨越东西方文明的潜质。尽管如此,“共有的事实”的观念并不影响它成为跨文明体系的总体文学研究的学理依据。换言之,在某种意义上,21 世纪日益兴盛的跨文明体系的总体文学研究及其形成的诸多特征,既源于梵·第根提出的“总体文学”之“共有事实”观念,但又是比较文学发展的历史必然和本质体现。故本节将围绕此及相关问题进行探讨。

一、跨文明体系的总体文学研究的缘起和形成、发展

跨文明体系的总体文学研究的源头,可以追溯到歌德。他在谈到他的叙事长诗《赫尔曼和窦绿台》、英国理查逊的小说与中国文化精神某些相似之处时,提出了“世界文学”的概念,他说:“民族文学在现代算不了很大的一回事,世界文学的时代已快来临了。现在每个人都应该出力促使它早日来临。”[②]不错,歌德在这里明确地表达了各民族文学相互接近、交流的愿望。然而如果仅限于此,那就大大低估了他在此提出的“世界文学”的思想价值。虽然歌德在这里并没有对这一概念加以具体阐述,但他将“世界文学”的观念建立在中国文学对西方文学影响的基础之上,足以见出这个观念内含的跨文明的本质特征及其重要性。而这种观念又并非无源之水。德国早些时候的赫尔德(1744—1803)就指出,文学史应该是一个整体,应该由不同民族文学构成,应该说明不同地区、不同时代、不同作家的不同风格,应该反映文学的起源、发展、变化和衰亡。显然,歌德承袭了这样的思想同时又提升了这一观念。

与此同时,歌德的重要贡献还在于,他并非止于理论,还大力倡导融合东西文化元素的创作实践,而且他自己就在此方面亲力亲为。比如他晚年沉迷于东方文化,写有相关诗集《西东合集》;他也读过一部中国传奇(据说可能是《好逑传》),并对书中表现的中国文化赞叹不已;他还模仿中国诗歌的风格写下了 14 首抒情诗,命名为《中德四季晨昏吟咏》等。正是在赫尔德、歌德的有关思想和行为的影响下,以带有明显的跨国家、跨民族特征的民间文学的收集、整理而掀起的浪漫主义文学思潮,最早在德国兴起就并非偶然;而且由此促成的施莱格尔兄弟的有关文学批评,乃至法国的斯达尔

---

① 梵·第根. 比较文学[M]. 北京:商务印书馆,1936:206.

② 艾克曼. 歌德谈话录[M]. 北京:人民文学出版社,1982:112.

夫人在《论德国》《论文学》中提出的相关文学批评思想等,都可看作对歌德的"世界文学"观念的进一步发展。但囿于"欧洲—西方中心主义"的长期影响,上述研究者们——从最初的"耶拿派"到稍后时期的"海德尔堡派",乃至整个西方世界的学者都基本没有将研究的视野投向东方,其"跨越"也基本限于西方内部。

真正跨越东西方文明的比较文学研究,出现在20世纪50年代。当时东方和其他地区的比较文学首先在地域上突破了西欧和美国的界限,向东欧甚至亚洲、非洲、拉丁美洲广大地区发展,从真正意义上开始获得"世界性";至60年代,东欧也掀起了比较文学热潮。布达佩斯、贝尔格莱德等地先后举办比较文学国际会议和国际比较文学第五届年会;与此同时,东方的印度、日本、锡兰、埃及、以色列等国,或将比较文学引入大学课堂或积极创办杂志、发表演讲,掀开了东方比较文学的序幕;到20世纪70年代,中国港台学者成为东方比较文学极为活跃的力量,至八九十年代中国大陆学者积极参与,并在大学开设比较文学课程,积极创办学会和刊物,发表论文,著书立说,取得了一系列丰硕的研究成果。于是,中国大陆和港台学者一道,全面、深入地推进了跨文明比较文学研究,共同构建了一系列带有中国特色的比较文学理论,总体文学研究得到发展。至此,梵·第根提出的"总体文学"概念,在东西方学者特别是东方学者的努力下,终于跨越了东西方不同文明,开始了对世界范围内文学之普遍规律的探讨。

二、跨文明体系的总体文学研究的繁荣兴盛

就上述所言,跨文明体系的总体文学研究,无疑是梵·第根提出的"总体文学"之"共有事实"观念发展之历史必然。然而,在实际研究中,作为倡导者的西方学者却基本上囿于"西方中心主义"的传统,而作为响应者的东方学者却在总体文学研究及其理论构建中积极探索,促进了其繁荣兴盛。这突出地表现在以下几个方面。

(一)跨文明的总体文学研究之"东方突围"

也许连梵·第根自己都不曾想到,他所持有的"欧洲—西方中心主义"正在被他提出的"总体文学"之"共有事实"的观念所否定所动摇。但这又是不能阻止的历史的必然发展。也就是说,他们的主观持有与客观结果之间存在着矛盾,而导致这种矛盾的根本原因在于他们持有的文化帝国主义心态。爱德华·W. 萨义德对此有过尖锐的批评。他说:

> 歌德(Goethe. Johann Wolfgang von)世界文学思想——一种在"伟大的书"和全部世界文学之间模糊的综合物观念——对于20世纪初的专业比较文学家

来说是很重要的。但是,尽管如此,像我说过的那样,就文学与文化的实际意义和意识形态而论,欧洲还是起了领路的作用并且是兴趣所在。……所以,谈论比较文学就是谈论世界文学之间的相互作用。但是,这一学科是被先验地作为一种等级体系来组织的,欧洲及其拉丁基督教文学处在这一体系的中心和顶端。①

显然,一种先在的话语权利使西方比较文学学者处于“中心”,并认为理所当然;而在他们将世界文学相互作用等级化的同时,更强化了自己高高在上的地位。于是梵·第根在谈到“总体文学”时,竟以西方的彼特拉克主义、伏尔泰主义、感伤主义、自然主义等诸多“主义”来代替之;而韦勒克在讨论“总体文学”时,也不断强调冲破民族文学的藩篱仅仅使西方文化形成了一个统一体,并宣称“在不低估东方影响的重要性,特别是圣经的影响的情况下,我们必须承认一个包括整个欧洲、俄国、美国以及拉丁美洲文学在内的紧密整体”②。显而易见,这里的“不低估东方影响”几乎是故作姿态,而后面那句话才是其真谛。也就是说,他们认为比较文学学者的使命就是研究西方文学的复杂演变。尽管至今世界文学已形成“亚洲—东方文学”“美洲—犹太文学”“非洲—黑人文学”以及“欧洲—西方文学”等各具特色的不同板块,但在他们眼里,西方文学才是世界文学的代表,西方文学基本就等于“总体文学”。

因此,突破比较文学领域内的西方中心主义,将单一的“总体文学”理论革新为多元的“总体文学”理论,成了东方比较文学学者特别是中国学者自觉的学术使命和孜孜以求的学术目标。于是,从20世纪70年代甚至更早时候,他们开始了比较文学的“东方突围”,到20世纪末21世纪初东西方文学交流日趋发展,加上“第三世界文化理论”兴起,以及西方世界对自身的反省,“总体文学”的研究在跨文明体系中不断深化,其理论构建也进入一个新的发展阶段。

(二)跨文明的总体文学研究之理论构建

从上述论证已经看到,“总体文学(General Literature)”是“世界文学”概念的学术提升,也就是说,它的本质特征——“许多国家文学所共有的事实”,已被规律化和理论化。从20世纪70年代开始,中国比较文学学者就遵循世界文学“共有的事实”的基本特性,积极而踊跃地探索文学的一般规律,至20世纪末的二十余年,迎来了充分体现总体文学特征的中西诗学研究的高潮。1975年,美国华裔学者刘若愚发表的《中国的文学理论》(*Chinese Theories of Literarure*),以艾布拉姆斯提出的艺术的四要素,分

---

① 爱德华·W. 萨义德. 文化与帝国主义[M]. 李琨,译. 北京:三联书店,2003:59-60.

② 韦勒克,沃伦. 文学理论[M]. 刘象愚,等,译. 北京:三联书店,1984:44.

析了中国诗学的本质内涵及形而上学论、决定论、表现论、技巧论、审美论六种理论的融合,掀开了中西诗学研究的序幕;台湾学者古添洪、叶维廉等紧随其后,成为跨文明理论的奠基者。1976 年,古添洪、陈慧桦在《比较文学的拓垦在台湾·序》中正式提出中国学派,但它更深远的意义却在于,以"阐发"研究证实了跨文明下总体文学研究的可能性和必要性,而中国大陆学者陈敦、刘象愚等又以"双向阐述"对这一理论加以完善;深受艾氏影响又有所扬弃的叶维廉,不仅卓有见识地提出了跨文明背景下的总体文学研究的明确目标:"寻求共同的文学规律,共同的美学据点";而且提出了"两个文化模子"的理论——把"中西"两种模式看成在价值原则上两种异质的"文化模式",并进而试图参酌中西来寻求超越中西的"是"与"非"这一共同的逻辑基础,努力"寻求跨越中西文化的共同文学规律"。这是他于 1983 年出版的论文集《比较诗学——理论构架的探讨》之《东西比较文学中"模子"的运用》一文中提出的观点,其目标的设定则出自他为该书结集出版的"比较文学丛书"所作的总序。总之,叶维廉的这些观点对中西比较文学与诗学研究的理论探讨和具体实践,起到了提纲挈领的指导性作用。当然,文化模式的观点也有局限。因为它"仅仅在回到不同文化模式'本身的文化立场'上取得了较大的进展,而在对人类历史生活的元立场的讨论上面,却进展甚微"①。

大陆学者的总体文学研究的理论构建同样活跃。20 世纪八九十年代,比较文学的异质对话理论,在乐黛云、曹顺庆等的力倡下讨论热烈,而且与美国已故华裔学者刘若愚早些时候提出的异质文化融汇法相互贯通;黄约眠、童庆炳鸿篇巨制的《中西比较诗学体系》,以三编分别介绍了中西诗学的文化背景、文化的根本差异和范畴同异、西方现代诗学对中国现代诗学的影响,中西诗学异同的系统理论得以构建,开始走向成熟。伴随这些理论的出现,对文学基本观点、诗学的普遍原理、文学理论的诸多规律的讨论掀起了高潮。进入 21 世纪,新近出版的曹顺庆主编的四卷本《中外文论史》,更以其浩大的工程,为跨文明体系的总体文学研究奠定了坚实的基础。正如该书前言所说:"本书力图从总体文学的角度,向读者展示一个全面的中外文学理论发展的概貌,让读者全面地认识各国文学理论的不同特征以及对世界文学理论的独特贡献,并进一步认识世界各民族文学理论的基本规律,为建立所谓'总体文学理论(General Literary Theory)',或曰'一般的文学理论'提供若干有益的借鉴。"②

① 曹顺庆,等.比较文学论[M].成都:四川教育出版社,2002:378.

② 曹顺庆.中外文论史[M].成都:四川出版集团,巴蜀书社,教育出版社,2012:13.

三、跨文明体系的总体文学研究的特征

当今,伴随着"跨文明比较"呼声的日益高潮,越来越多的学者参与其中,总体文学研究在新的拓展中表现出了较为一致的本质特征,同时涌现出不少学术研究的典范之作。

与较早时期的总体文学研究有所不同,跨文明的总体文学研究首先主张拥有世界眼光,强调民族对等。这是因为,与世界的"交流"已成为跨文明的总体文学研究极重要的途径,而在交流中强调世界眼光中的民族对等则是第一位的。即"'以世界的眼光',而不是以一国、一洲的眼光,对人类的文学现象作总体和历史的把握。为了做到这一点,需要跳出过去有'我'之比的中心模式,进入'第三人称'式的客观化图式。用形象的比喻形容,即从各自占有的'领海'之争,进入人类共通的'公海'境界。在这个意义上,如果说比较文学标志的是主权尊重和族群平等的话,'总体文学'则意味着多元交汇与主体超越"①。这就是中国学者对总体文学研究的认识论和持有的基本态度。

其次,与较早时期的总体文学研究相比,跨文明的总体文学研究尤其强调东西双向阐释,彼此互为互动;提倡积极的文化对话,又主张和而不同。这是中国学者关于跨文明体系的总体文学研究之方法论。不论是由中国大陆和台湾学者共同构建的"阐发"论,还是他们倡导的各种形式和不同层面的对话理论,其目的都在于"立足多元文化立场,探讨不同文化体系之间的文学和文论的相互理解与相互沟通,实现异质话语的平等对话"②。实际上,这就是中国古代"和"而共处的文化思想在文学中的现代演绎。由此,梵·第根倡导的"对于许多国家文学所共有的事实的探讨"之"总体文学"研究,在东方学者的大力倡导下,不仅跨越了东西方文明,而且在"和而求同"的文化对话中向纵深发展。

总的来说,从事跨文明体系的总体文学研究,既可从创作思维的层面对东西方有关文学理论进行辨析,又可从东西方创作文本之"同"中求"异"或"异"中求"同",以揭示文学的创作规律。

---

① 曹顺庆,等.比较文学论[M].成都:四川教育出版社,2002:439.

② 曹顺庆,等.比较文学教程[M].北京:高等教育出版社,2006:263.

【原典选读】

东西方文学中“模子”的应用（节选）

◉叶维廉

【导读】叶维廉于1937年生于广东中山市，先后毕业于台大外文系，师大英语研究所，并获爱荷华大学美学硕士及普林斯顿大学比较文学博士。叶维廉在学术上贡献最突出最具国际影响力的是东西比较文学方法的提供与发明。他根源性地质疑与结合西方新旧文学理论应用到中国文学研究上的可行性及危机，肯定中国古典美学特质，并通过中西文学模子的“互照互省”，试图寻求更合理的文学共同规律建立多方面的理论架构。著有《东西比较文学模子的运用》（1974）、《比较诗学》（1983）等。

1983年他在为《比较诗学——理论构架的探讨》（1983年）结集出版的“比较文学丛书”所作之总序中，提出了跨文明背景下的总体文学研究的明确目标：“寻求共同的文学规律，共同的美学据点”，并提出了许多诗学观念。这些对中西比较文学与诗学研究的理论探讨和具体实践，都起到了提纲挈领的指导性作用。尤其是其中的《东西比较文学中“模子”的运用》一文，构建了“两个文化模子”的理论。在节选中，作者认为“中西”两种模式在价值原则上是两种异质的“文化模式”，故提倡参酌中西来寻求超越中西的“是”与“非”这一共同的逻辑基础，如此才能“寻求跨越中西文化的共同文学规律”。围绕这一核心，叶维廉论证了“文化模子”的诸多特性：其一，“模子”是结构行为的一种力量。但它又具有消极和积极的可塑性，而把握其积极性是研究者最基本和最迫切的。其二，“模子”具有重构性。即不同的甚至互相抵触的“模子”都可以重新结构、组合、判断，故不同模子之间的歧义也可因此而得以互通或被消解。其三，“模子寻根”实质就是挖掘真实。即通过“寻根”，就能从历经变异的各种文化或文学形态中窥视到“模子”的最本质之处。如中国古诗的“意”和“象”，象形字的“意”和“形”等盖莫如此。

总之，文学模子与影响它的文化模子都具有多义性。但不同文化的“模子”之“异”只是相对的，而不同文化的“模子”之“似”却是绝对的。如选文所言，它们“必有其基本的相同性相似性，因而（我们听到许多的批评家立论者说），只要我们抓住这一个基本不变的‘模子’及其结构行为的要素，便可放诸四海而皆准”。这就是文化“模子”运用于总体文学研究的理论意义。■

让我们从寓言或事件中学习：

> 话说，从前在水底里住着一只青蛙和一条鱼，它们常常一起泳耍，成为好友。有一天，青蛙无意中跳出水面，在陆地上游了一整天，看到了许多新鲜的事物，如人啦，鸟啦，车啦，不一而足。他看得开心死了，便决意返回水里，向它的好友鱼报告一切。它看见了鱼便说，陆地的世界精彩极了，有人，身穿衣服，头戴帽子，手握拐杖，足履鞋子；此时，在鱼的脑中便出现了一条鱼，身穿衣服，头戴帽子，翅挟手杖，鞋子则吊在下身的尾翅上。青蛙又说，有鸟，可展翼在空中飞翔；此时，在鱼的脑中便出现了一条腾空展翼而飞的鱼。青蛙又说，有车，带着四个轮子滚动前进；此时，在鱼的脑中便出现了一条带着四个圆轮子的鱼……

这个寓言告诉了我们什么？它告诉了我们好几个有关“模子”及“模子”的作用的问题。首先，我们可以说，所有的心智活动，不论其在创作上或是在学理的推演上以及其最终的决定和判断，都有意无意地必以某一种“模子”为起点。鱼，没有见过人，必须依赖它本身的“模子”，它所最熟识的样式去构思人。可见，“模子”是结构行为的一种力量，使用者可以用新的素材来拼配一个形式，这种行为在文学中最显著的，莫过于“文类”(Genre)在诗人及批评家所发挥的作用。诗人在面临存在经验中的素材时，必须要找出一个形式将之呈露。譬如“商籁体”或“律诗”的形式的应用，以既有的一组美学上的技术、策略、组合方式，而试图去芜存真，从虚中得实，从多变中得到一个明澈的形体，把事物的多面性作一个有秩序的包容。而当该“模子”无法表达其所面临的经验的素材时，诗人或将“模子”变体，增改衍化而成为一个新的“模子”，而批评家在面临一作品时，亦必须进入这一个结构行为衍生的过程，必须对诗人所探取的“模子”有所认识，对其拼配的方式及其结构增改时衍化的过程有所了解，始可进入该作品之实况。是故纪廉(Claudio Guillén)在其《文类的应用》(*On the Uses of Literary Genre*)一文中说：

> 文类引发构形……文类同时向前及向后看。向后，是对过去一系列既有的作品的认识，……向前，文类不仅会激发一个崭新作品的产生，而且会逼使后来的批评者对新的作品找出更完全的形式的含义……文类是一个引发结构的“模子”。①

但“模子”的选择及选择以后应用的方式及其所持的态度，在一个批评家的手中，也可以引发出相当狭隘的错误的结果。我们都知道鱼所得到的人的印象是歪曲的，我们都知道错误在哪里，那便是因为鱼只局限于鱼的“模子”，它不知道鱼的“模子”以外人的“模子”是不同的，所以无法从人的观点去想象、结构及了解人。跳出自己的“模子”的局限而

---

① Claduio Guillén. Literature as System (Princeton. 1971), pp. 109,119.

从对方本身的“模子”去构思，显然是最基本最急迫的事。

证诸文学，大家第一个反应很可能是：文学是人写的，不是别的动物写的，我们眼前的成品乃根据人的“模子”而来，是人，其有机体的需要，其表达上的需要，必有其基本的相同性相似性，因而（我们听到许多的批评家立论者说），只要我们抓住这一个基本不变的“模子”及其结构行为的要素，便可放诸四海而皆准。这一个系统便可应用到别的文化中的文学作品去。这一点假定，不只见于中西的文学理论家，亦见于其他学科的研究方法上。但事实上并不那么干净利落。首先，我们不知道所谓“基本不变的模子”怎样建立才合理？其次，我们深知人们经常使用着许许多多的各有历史来由、各不相同，甚至互相抵触的“模子”去进行结构、组合、判断。我们或许可以如此相信：在史前期的初民，如未受文化枷锁的孩童一样，有一段时间是浸在最质朴的原始的和谐里，没有受到任何由文化活动成长出来的“模子”的羁绊，是故能够如孩童一样直接地感应事物的新与真。能在结构行为中自由发挥，不受既定的思维形式的左右，不会将事象歪曲。但文化一词，其含义中便有人为结构行为的意思，去将事物选组成为某种可以控制的形态。这种人为的结构行为的雏形（文化模子的雏形）因人而异，因地而异，却是一个历史的事实。至于哪一个文化的模子较接近原始和谐时的结构行为和形式，我们暂且不论，但文化模子的歧异以及由之而起的文学的模子的歧异，我们必须先予正视，始可达成适当的了解。我们固然不愿相信有人会像鱼那样歪曲人的本相，但事实上呢，且先看下列两段话：

> 中国人在其长久的期间把图画通过形象文字简缩为一个简单的符号，由于他们缺乏发明的才能，又嫌恶通商，至今居然也未曾为这些符号再进一步简缩为字母。
>
> *The Work of the Rev. William Warbuton*. ed, R, Hurd. 7 vols. (London, 1778)111,404

鲍斯维问撒姆尔·约翰生(Samuel Johnson)：

> 阁下对于他们的文字（指中文）有何意见？约翰生说：先生，他们还没有字母，他们还无法铸造成别的国家已铸造的！
>
> *Boswell's Life of Johnson*, ed. G. B. Hill & L. F, Powell, 111, 389

好比英文字母（印欧语系字母）那种抽象的，率意独断的符号才是最基本的语言符号似的！而不问为什么有象形文字，其结构行为又是何种美感作用，何种思维态度使然。这不只是井底之见，而是在他们的心中，只以一个（他们认为是绝对优越的）“模子”为最终的依归！我们并不说象形文字是绝对优越的，因为如此说，也便是犯了墨守成规的错误了。但我们应该了解到象形文字代表了另一种异于抽象字母的思维系统：以象构思，顾及事物的具体显现，捕捉事物并发的空间多重关系的玩味，用复合意象提供全面环境的方式来呈示抽象意念，如“诗”字同时含有“言”，一种律动的传达（言，㖟，口含笛子）及“㞢”，一种舞蹈的律动(㞢的雏形是𣥂,足踏地面,既是行之止——今之"止"字——亦是止之将行——今之"之"字。)有了以上的认识,更可同时了解到字母系统下思维性之趋于抽象意念的缕述,趋于直线追寻的细分、演绎的逻辑发展。二者各具所长,各异其趣。缺乏了对"模子"的寻根的认识,便会产生多种不幸的歪曲。或说,以上二人像鱼一样,因未熟识另一个"模子",所以无辜。但对于近百年来汉诗的英译者呢?(译者可以说是集读者、批评家、诗人的运思结构行为于一身的人)他们在接触中国诗之初,心里作了何种假定,而这种假定又如何阻碍了他们对中国诗中固有美学模子的认识,我曾多次在文章中提出这个问题来,在此不另复述①,现只就与"模子"有关部分的讨论再行申述,我说:

> 凡近百年,中国诗的英译者一直和原文相悖,在他们的译文中都反映着一种假定:一首中国诗要通过诠释方式去捕捉其意,然后再以西方传统的语言结构重新铸造……他们都忽略了其中特有美学形态、特有语法所构成的异于西方的呈露方式。②
>
> 所有的译者都以为文言之缺少语法的细分,词性的细分,是一种电报式的用法——长话短说,即英文之所谓 longhand(普通写法)之对 shorthand(速记)——所以不问三七二十一的,就把 shorthand(速记的符号)译为 longhand(原来的意思),把诗译成散文,一路附加解说以助澄清之功,非也!所谓缺乏细分语法及词性的中国字并非电报中简记的符号,它们指向一种更细致的暗示的美感经验,是不容演义、分析性的"长说"和"剖解"(西方语言结构的特长)所破坏的……中国诗的意象,在一种互立并存的空间关系之下,形成一种气氛,一种环境,一种只唤起某种感受但不将之说明的境界,任读者移入境中,并参与完成这一强烈感受的一瞬之美感经验,中国诗的意象往往就是具体物象(即所谓"实境")捕捉这一瞬的原形。③

这种美感经验的形式显然是和中国文字的雏形的观物传达的方式息息相关的。对中国这个"模子"的忽视,以及硬加西方"模子"所产生的歪曲,必须由东西方的比较文学学者作重新的寻根的探讨始可得其真貌。(有关究竟中国诗如何才可以译得近乎原形而不受过度的歪曲,我在《语言与表现:中国古典诗与英美现代诗美学的汇通》一文中另有提供,在此不论)

(温儒敏,李细尧.寻求跨中西文化的共同文学规律:叶维廉比较文学论文选[M].北

① "The Chinese Poem · A Different Mode of Representation". Delos 3, pp. 62-79; Ezra Pound's Cathay (Princeton. 1969) ch. L,《从比较的方法论中国诗的视镜》,见中华文化复兴月刊四卷五期(1971 年 3 月) "Classical Chinese Poetry and Anglo-American Poetry Convergence of Languages and Poetry". Comparative Literature Studies. Vol. XI. No. 1(March 1974)pp. 21-47.

② "The Chinese Poem · A Different Mode of Representation". Delos 3, p. 62.

③ "Classical Chinese Poetry and Anglo-American Poetry Convergence of Languages and Poetry". Comparative Literature Studies. Vol. XI. No. 1(March 1974)p. 26.

京大学出版社,1987:1-5.)

【研究范例】

刘勰的譬喻说与歌德的意蕴说(节选)

◉王元化

【导读】王元化以"同"中求"异"的方法探讨刘勰的譬喻说和歌德的意蕴说,可谓从创作思维层面比较的范例。

论者首先阐述了歌德的"意蕴"包含的外在形式和内在意蕴及其相互作用;接着分析了刘勰之"譬喻"含有的"拟容切象和取心示义"的中国文化价值内涵。然而,原本在理论上以自然界作为取心示义对象的刘勰,由于其儒家思想的偏见而出现了与其价值的悖反——把自己的主观信条当作现实物质的本质,导致他在实践意义方面不可能真正做到对客观真理的揭示。正如歌德对"譬如说"的批判:"在一个探索个别以求一般的诗人和一个在个别中看出一般的诗人之间,是有很大的区别的。一个产生出譬喻文学,在这里个别只是作为一般的一个例证或例子,另一个才是诗歌的真正本性,即是说,只表达个别而毫不想到或者提到一般。一个人只要生动地掌握了个别,他也就掌握了一般,只不过他当时没有意识到这一点罢了,或者他可能在很久之后才会发现。"(《歌德文学语录》第十二节)①不过,即使歌德有如此的见解,他的"意蕴说"没有刘勰"譬如说"那样浓郁主观的色彩,但也"存在着过去现实主义理论多半具有的共同缺陷的,他对于个别与一般的关系的理解带有一定的片面性。在作家的认识活动中,他只注意到由个别到一般这一方面,而根本不提还有由一般到个别这一过程"②。这就把两个互相联结的过程分割开来,因而与他自己所提出的作家必须具有理性知识的主张形成了矛盾。

由此,刘勰的譬喻说和歌德的意蕴说,不仅互为补充而且都被文学的总体规律所匡正。值得注意的是,此文虽写于20世纪70年代,但作者并未拘囿于我国传统文论范围的束缚,而是成功运用了"文化对话,和而不同"之方法,按他自己的说法,就是解释我国古代文论的民族特色时,要"以今天更发展了的文艺理论对它进行剖析",才能"从中探讨中外相通、带有最根本最普通意义的艺术规律和艺术方法"③。■

① 王元化.文心雕龙创作论[M].上海:上海古籍出版社,1979:144.

② 王元化.文心雕龙创作论[M].上海:上海古籍出版社,1979:144.

③ 王元化.文心雕龙创作论[M].上海:上海古籍出版社,1979:69.

在艺术形象问题上，歌德的“意蕴说”也包含着内外两个方面。外在方面是艺术作品直接呈现出来的形状，内在方面是灌注生气于外在形状的意蕴。他认为，内在意蕴显现于外在形状，外在形状指引到内在意蕴。歌德在《自然的单纯模仿、作风、风格》一文中，曾经把“艺术所能企及的最高境界”说成是“奠基在最深刻的知识原则上面，奠基在事物的本性上面，而这种事物的本性应该是我们可以在看得见触得到的形式中去认识的。”（据古柏英译本迻译）歌德把艺术形象分为外在形状和内在意蕴，似乎和刘勰的“拟容取心”说有着某种类似之处，不过，它们又不尽相同，其间最大区别就在于对个别与一般关系的不同理解上。

《比兴篇》：“称名也小，取类也大”，这一说法本之《周易》。《系辞下》：“其称名也小，其取类也大，其旨远，其辞文，其言曲而中。”韩康伯《注》云：“托象以明义，因小以喻大。”孔颖达《正义》云：“其旨远者，近道此事，远明彼事。其辞文者，不真言所论之事，乃以义理明之，是其辞文饰也。其言曲而中者，变化无恒，不可为体例，其言随物委曲，而各中其理也。”从这里可以看出，前人大抵把《系辞下》这句话理解为一种“譬喻”的意义，这种看法和刘勰把比兴当作“明喻”“隐喻”看待是有相通之处的。（首先把《系辞下》这句话运用于文学领域的是司马迁，他评述《离骚》说：“其称文小而其旨大，举类迩而见义远。”这一说法也给予刘勰以一定影响。）

刘勰的形象论可以说是一种“比喻说”。《比兴篇》：“称名也小，取类也大。”《物色篇》：“以少总多，情貌无遗。”是两个互为补充的命题。“名”和“类”或“少”和“多”都蕴涵了个别与一般的关系。刘勰提出的拟容切象和取心示义，都是针对客观审美对象而言，要求作家既摹拟现实的表象，也揭示现实的意义，从而通过个别去表现一般。然而，这里应该看到，刘勰对个别与一般关系的理解，不能不受到他的客观唯心主义思想体系的制约，以致使他的形象论本来可以向着正确方向发展的内容受到了窒息。由于他认为天地之心和圣人之心是同一的，因此，按照他的思想体系推断，自然万物的自身意义无不合于圣人的“恒久之至道”。这样，作家在取心示义的时候，只要恪守传统的儒家思想就可以完全揭示自然万物的内在意义了。自然，刘勰的创作论并不是完全依据这种观点来立论的。当他背离了这种观点时，他提出了一些正确的看法。可是他的拟容取心说却并没有完全摆脱这种观点的拘囿，其中就夹杂着一些这类糟粕。例如，《比兴篇》开头标明“诗文弘奥，包韫六义”。接着又特别举出：“关雎有别，故后妃方德，尸鸠贞一，故夫人象义”作为取心示义的典范。（《金针诗格》也同样本之儒家诗教，把“内意”说成是“美刺箴诲”之类的“义理”）从这里我们可以看出，尽管刘勰在理论上以自然界作为取心示义的对象，但是他的儒家偏见必然会在实践意义方面导致相反的结果。因为在儒家思想束缚下，作家往往会把自己的主观信条当作现实事物的本质，而不可能真正做到揭示客观真理。因此，很容易导致这种情况：作家不是通过现实的个别事物去表现从它们自身揭示出来的一般意义，而是依据先入为主的成见用现实的个别事物去附会儒家的一般义理，把现实事物当作美刺箴诲的譬喻。因而，这里所反映出来的个别与一般的关系，也就变成一种譬喻的关系了。（例如：《诗小序》说："关雎，后妃之德也。鹊巢，夫人之德也。"就是这方面的一个典型例证）

歌德的"意蕴说"并不像刘勰的"比喻说"那样夹杂着主观的色彩。他曾经这样说："在一个探索个别以求一般的诗人和一个在个别中看出一般的诗人之间，是有很大差别的。一个产生出譬喻文学，在这里个别只是作为一般的一个例证或例子，另一个才是诗歌的真正本性，即是说，只表达个别而毫不想到或者提到一般。一个人只要生动地掌握了个别，他也就掌握了一般，只不过他当时没有意识到这一点罢了，或者他可能在很久之后才会发现。"（《歌德文学语录》第十二节）歌德这些话很可以用来作为对于"譬喻说"的批判。歌德反对把"个别只是作为一般的一个例证或例子"的譬喻文学，强调作家首先要掌握个别，而不要用个别去附会一般，表现了对现实生活的尊重态度。这一看法是深刻的，对于文学创作来说也是有重要意义的。事实上，一般只能从个别中间抽象出来。作家只有首先认识了许多个别事物的特殊本质，才能进而认识这些个别事物的共同本质。就这个意义来说，歌德要求作家从个别出发，是可以避免"譬喻说"以作家主观去附会现实这种错误的。

不过，我们同时也应该看到，歌德的"意蕴说"是存在着过去现实主义理论多半具有的共同缺陷的。他对于个别与一般关系的理解带有一定的片面性。在作家的认识活动中，他只注意到由个别到一般这一方面，而根本不提还有由一般到个别这一过程。《矛盾论》指出，人类的认识活动，由特殊到一般，又由一般到特殊，是互相联结的两个过程："人类的认识总是这样循环往复地进行的，而每一次的循环（只要是严格地按照科学的方法）都可能使人类的认识提高一步，使人类的认识不断地深化。"歌德恰恰是把这两个互相联结的过程分割开来。他在上面的引文中赞许"只表达个别而毫不想到或者提到一般"的诗人，以为这样的诗人在掌握个别的时候，没有意识到一般，或者可能在很久以后才会发现一般。这一看法和他自己所提出的作家必须具有理性知识的主张是矛盾的。

就认识活动的共同规律来说，由个别到一般，又由一般到个别，这两个互相联结的过程是不可分割的。作家的认识活动也同样是遵循这两个循环往复不断深化的过程来进行。事实上，完全排除一般到个别这一过程的认识活动是并不存在的。任何作家都不是作为抽象的人，而是作为阶级的人去接触现实生活的。他的认识活动不能不被他所从属的一定阶级的立场观点所决定，他在阶级社会中长期形成的阶级教养和阶级意识支配了他的认识活动，尽管他宣称自己只掌握个别而排斥一般，可是他在掌握个别的时候，他的头脑并不是一张白纸，相反，那里已经具有阶级的一般烙印了。

在作家的具体认识活动中，这一阶段由个别到一般的过程，往往是紧接着上一阶段由个别到一般的过程。在这种情况下，不论作家自觉或不自觉，他必然会以他在上一阶段所掌握到的一般，作为这一阶段认识活动的指导。因此，在这一阶段由个别到一般的过程，也就和由一般到个别的过程互相联结在一起了。作家的认识活动总是遵循由个别到一般,又由一般到个别这两个互相联结的过程,循环往复地进行着。只有这样,他的认识活动才可能由上一阶段过渡到这一阶段,再由这一阶段过渡到下一阶段,一步比一步提高,形成由低级到高级的不断深化运动。

认为作家只要掌握个别而不要有意识地去掌握一般,这一看法不仅违反了作家的认识规律,而且也违反了作家的创作规律。事实上,作家的创作活动同样不能缺少由一般到个别的过程。作家的创作活动是把他在认识活动中所取得的成果进行艺术的表现。他在动笔之前,已经有了酝酿成熟的艺术构思,确立了一定的创作意图。因此,他的全部创作活动都是使原来存在于自己头脑中的创作意图逐步体现。创作意图是普泛的、一般的东西,体现在作品中的人物和事件是具体的、个别的东西。任何作家的创作活动,都不可能像歌德所说的那样"只表达个别而毫不想到或者提到一般"。作家总是自觉地根据自己的创作意图去进行创作的。马克思在《资本论》中曾经指出人类劳动具有如下特点:"劳动过程结束时得到的结果,已经在劳动过程开始时,存在于劳动者的观念中,所以已经观念地存在着。"这也就是说,人类劳动并不像蜜蜂造蜂房那样,只是一种本能的表现,而是自觉的、有目的的能动的行为。作家的创作活动也具有同样的性质。否认作家的创作活动是根据自己的创作意图出发,就会否定作家的创作活动的自觉性和目的性。

自然,我们认识了认识的共同规律之后,还必须认识艺术思维是以怎样的特殊形态去体现这个认识的共同规律。我们应该承认,艺术和科学在掌握世界的方式上——正如马克思在《政治经济学批判导言》中所指出的那样——是各有其不同的特点的。艺术家不像科学家那样从个别中抽象出一般,而是通过个别去体现一般。科学家是以一般的概念去统摄特殊的个体,艺术家则是通过特殊的个体去显现它的一般意蕴。艺术形象应该是具体的,科学概念也应该是具体的。科学家在作出抽象规定的思维进程中必须导致具体的再现,正像《政治经济学批判导言》所说的,由抽象上升到具体的方法是唯一正确的科学方法。不过,这里所说的具体是指通过逻辑范畴以概念形态所表述出来的具有许多规定和关系的综合。科学家把浑沌的表象和直观加工,在抽出具体的一般概念之后,就排除了特殊个体的感性形态。而艺术家的想象活动则是以形象为材料,始终围绕着形象来进行。艺术作品所呈现的一般必须呈现于感性观照,因此,艺术家对现实生活进行艺术加工,去揭示事物的本质,并不是把事物的现象形态抛弃掉,而是透过加工以后的现象形态去显示它们的内在联系。不过,在艺术作品中所表现的现象形态已不同于原来生活中的现象形态,因为前者已经使直观中彼此相外、互相独立的杂多转化为具有内在联系的多样性统一。这就是由个别到一般与由一般到个别这一认识规律体现在艺术思维中的特殊形态。艺术形象的具体性就在于它既是一般意义的典型,同时又是特殊的个体。它保持了现实生活的细节真实性,典型性即由生活细节真实性中显现出来,变成可以直接感觉到的对象。在这里,由个别到一般,再由一般到个别,这两个认识过程不是并列的。作家的认识活动只能从作为个别感性事物的形象出发。在全部创作过程中,并不存在一个游离于形象之外从概念出发进行构思的阶段。因此,由一般到个别的认识功能,不是孤立地单独出现,而是渗透在由个别到一般的过程之中,它成为指导作家认识个别的引线或指针。对于由个别到一般,再由一般到个别这一认识规律,可以有两种不同的理解:一种理解是把它们截然分割为孤立排他的两个互不相干的独立过程。例如,所谓表象—概念—表象的公式,就是意味着在艺术创作过程中存在着一个摈弃形象的抽象思维阶段,而艺术创造就在于把经过抽象思维所获得的概念化为形象。这可以说是一种"形象图解论",它是反对形象思维的。另一种理解则相反,认为由个别到一般,再由一般到个别,不是孤立排他的,而是互相联结、互相渗透的。后一种理解才是辩证的观点。

(王元化. 文心雕龙创作论[M]. 上海:古籍出版社,1979:142-147.)

【延伸阅读】

1. 乐黛云. 比较文学学科新视野(代序)[M]//多元文化语境中的文学. 长沙:湖南文艺出版社,1994.

论者认为,比较文学的发展越来越趋向于一种多元文化的总体研究,而且是建立在传统的实证性研究和批评性研究之上的一种飞跃,也是对两大层次的超越。

2. 苏源熙. 全球化时代的比较文学[M]. 任一鸣,陈琛,等,译. 北京:北京大学出版社,2015.

本书反映了最近10年中比较文学学科发展的状况。收入19位当代重要的比较文学教授的论文,讨论了全球化对比较文学和文学研究的深刻影响,大学课堂内比较文学的教学实践,该学科体现的乌托邦想象,当代政治的文学研究的体制介入,以及性别、翻译、身份政治等一系列问题。

第三节 全球化时代的比较文学研究

自1965年哈里·莱文和1976年汤姆·格林(Tom Greene)主持撰写的两份美国比较文学学会学科发展报告发表以后,国际形势发生了巨大的变化。即从经济基础到上层建筑的各个领域都呈现出全球化趋势，这极大地促进了比较文学学科向纵深发展。故本节拟围绕以下问题讨论。

一、全球化趋势为比较文学学科发展提供了特殊的历史语境

在全球化趋势中，对比较文学学科发展影响最大的莫过于以下两方面：首先，经济的全球化把世界变成了真正统一的生产要素市场，各国经济的依存度越来越高。伴随着这个过程，人类的生活被纳入一个你中有我、我中有你的相互依赖和深度融合中，约翰·邓恩揭示的"人类不是孤独的岛屿而是相互联系的大陆"的人类关系的本质，从没有像今天表现得那么突出和贴切。无论不同文明、不同种族、不同国家人们的主观意愿如何，全球化都是人类历史不可逆转的大趋势，全球化生活已经成为当代人类的最主要的经验。但全球化进程的不平衡性和工业化国家主导的弊端，又引发了强烈的批判、抵抗、消解全球化的冲动。国家与国家、民族与民族、文明与文明间的矛盾凸显，国际冲突不断，文化矛盾尖锐，各种极端社会思潮涌现，全球化并没有带来人们预期的人类生活的和平整合。经济全球化、民族国家的治理结构和文化价值观的多样性，这三个人类存在的基本建构的内在冲突性，成为世界秩序重建的最大障碍。

其次，在这个历史进程中，人类的思想世界也发生了深刻的变化：西方社会进入消费社会后形成的大量"后主义"思潮，如解构主义、后现代主义、女性主义、新历史主义、生态主义、后殖民主义等，与西方社会复杂的社会运动相结合，渗透到西方文化和学术研究的几乎所有的领域，影响到绝大多数学科；而世界其他国家地区，因自身在全球化进程的位置和收益的差异，也形成了带有浓厚的民族主义和文化抵抗色彩的诸多社会思潮，或激进或温和地表达出对当代世界状态和人类前途命运的思考。这种不同文化背景、不同价值取向和不同理论路径的思想交锋，构成了全球化时代众声交响的思想背景。

而比较文学学科自身也在经历了法国学派的实证研究和美国学派的平行研究之后，面对着全球化的新形势和越来越多非西方的比较文学研究声音的加入，陷入了自身研究的瓶颈和困局，这种瓶颈和危机集中表现在以"强化作为想象的共同体民族国家身份"为己任的西方比较文学研究，遭遇到文化多元主义的挑战。歌德在一百多年前提出的"世界文学"的期许，在新的历史语境中，需要重新审视和发掘。内在于比较文学学科发生的世界主义雄心，需要重建其合法性和忠诚。比较文学何去何从？比较文学如何应对不同文化的激烈碰撞和深度对话的新语境？比较文学如何在互相交错和模糊的学术研究模式中确立自身的边界和身份？

二、全球化时代比较文学学科理论的论争

正是在这样的背景中,比较文学学科状况发生了深刻的变化。在1993年美国语言学会(ALC)学术年会上,查尔斯·伯恩海姆(Charles Bernheimer)提交了当年美国比较文学学会(ACLA)报告《世纪之交的比较文学》(*Comparative Literature at Turn of the Century*)。这份报告同其他13篇文章以《多元文化主义时代的比较文学》(*Comparative Literature in the Age of Multiculturalism*)于1994年由约翰·霍普金斯大学出版社结集出版。这份后来被称为"伯恩海姆报告"的文章对当下比较文学研究现状忧心忡忡。在报告看来,很大程度依赖西方文化传统的比较文学研究模式,已越来越不适应世纪之交的全球化现实,这种不适应表现在三个方面:第一,虽然从歌德的"世界文学"概念提出以来,比较文学的学科目标是要超越民族、国家的边界,去实现普遍的文学的共同体,但事实上比较文学的传统仍然局限在西方文化框架中,表现出根深蒂固的欧洲中心主义的偏见,这反映在比较文学研究的标准、内容、模式几乎完全建立在西方的价值系统基础上。而伴随着非西方社会的经济和文化的崛起,非西方的学者的声音不断增强,西方中心主义的自我幻觉开始破碎,但比较文学研究却没有跟上这个形式的变化。第二,西方中心主义的另一个影响是比较文学的精英主义色彩。由于对以原文进行文学阅读和研究被确立为比较文学研究合法性的基础,少数的欧洲语言文学事实上成为比较文学研究的中心领域,而对非西方文学的翻译的研究自然被边缘化。第三,伴随着20世纪60年代以来大量欧洲理论思潮的引入,比较文学也面临着理论大爆炸的冲击。解构主义、后现代主义、后殖民主义、马克思主义理论的回归、女性主义、性属研究、绿色和平运动理论等,都挤占了传统比较文学自以为属于自己的研究领域和学科优势。在这种各个学科相继理论化并且理论形态越来越近似的时代,比较文学的学科特性再一次面临着重新审视的要求。

在此分析的基础上,伯恩海姆提出了未来比较文学研究自我更新和突破的可能方向:

> 今天,比较的空间牵涉到:通常在不同专业进行研究的艺术产品之间的比较;这些专业的各种各样的文化建构的比较;西方文化传统——无论是高雅的还是通俗的——非西方文化之间的比较;殖民化的人民的文化生产的前后关联之间的比较;在被定义为女性或者被定义为男性的性属构建之间的比较,或者被定义为异性恋的和被定义为同性恋的性取向之间的比较;在种族和民族的指涉模式之间的

比较;在意义的阐释学理解及其生产和循环模式的唯物主义分析之间的比较。[1]

很明显,报告想要尽可能全面地包容比较文学研究现状所面临的诸多问题,以适应于它称之为“文化多元主义”时代的复杂现实。这样一种大包大揽的脱困思路引发了许多学者的批评和反驳。大卫·达姆罗什(David Damrosch)认为,不应该为西方学者的研究笼统地戴上西方中心主义的道德帽子,西方学者专业训练的背景决定了他们的取向,以欧洲文学为研究对象“与其说是文化帝国主义的事务,不如说是忧郁地接受不可逾越的障碍”。K. 安东尼·阿皮亚(K. Anthony Appiah)也为欧洲学者辩护:“它们(欧洲文学)本身是彼此相关的。”而周蕾(Rey Chow)则提醒:“比较文学并非可以轻易采纳或者消除的空洞空间。”而对报告的扩展比较文学空间的期待,迈克尔·里法特尔(Michael Riffaterre)则主张:“解语境化”,强调比较文学应回归文学的美学特性。彼得·布鲁克斯也不认同报告的“歉意的音调”。对跨学科的研究,阿皮亚担心会使比较文学成为“一种无法结构化的后现代大杂烩”。乔纳森·卡勒(Jonathan Culler)也指出,文化并不比文学更具有“可译性(translatable)”,以文化研究去改造文学研究是不是真正能够克服比较文学的所谓“偏见”。[2]

很明显,伯恩海姆的报告达成的共识,远远小于它引发的分歧。有关比较文学在新的历史环境如何定位和发展的问题,成了比较文学研究的中心问题。但从这些争论中,我们还是可以看出比较文学界形成了一些比较集中的问题领域。琳达·哈钦(Linda Hutcheon)就从围绕伯恩海姆的争论中提取了当代比较文学研究四个热点问题:“第一,历史上比较文学传统的欧洲中心论与目前多元文化现实之间的关系”;第二,一种持续的对以原文而不是一本进行文学阅读和比较渴望的关注;第三,今天的各种理论在学科中的位置;第四,或许可以称为形式主义者”和“语境主义者”——或者用更学术的术语——文学研究对文化研究之间的争论”。[3]应该说,哈钦对问题的总结,比较清晰地勾勒出了世纪之交的比较文学发展的基本方向。

伯恩海姆的报告,在有的学者心目中显得太过激进,在另外一些学者心目中又显得太过保守。关于报告的争论一直在延续。到了2003年,斯皮瓦克再次发难。不过,这次她对比较文学的责难远远胜过了伯恩海姆报告对比较文学研究的反思。她激进地宣告这一学科的死亡。这一年,斯皮瓦克出版了她的韦勒克图书馆讲座《学科之

---

① Bernheimer, Charles. “Comparative Literature at Turn of the Century”, *Comparative Literature in the Age of Multiculturalism*. ed. Charles Bernheimer, pp. 41-42. Baltimore: John Hopkins University Press, 1995.

② 相关内容可参见 Hutcheon, Linda. Productive Comparative Angst: Comparartive Literature in the Age of Multiculturalism, in *World Literature Today*, vol. 69, No. 2 (Spring, 1995): 299-303.

③ Hutcheon, Linda. p. 299.

死》(*Death of Discipline*)。在讲座中,斯皮瓦克指责欧洲和美国的比较文学学科,不但没有实现其超越民族、国家边界的研究承诺,相反,它通过规范和方式的设置,恰恰制造了以西方文化为中心的单一、封闭的比较文学研究体制。而全球化时代的到来,此前比较文学学科的那种自诩为完整的、明确的研究范式,表现出明显的不适应和不稳定,已经无法回应文化多元性和学科融合化的形势。斯皮瓦克提出,比较文学要想真正摆脱西方中心主义的限制,必须建构起真正的"星球视野",超越民族、国家、族群、语言、性别、"自我"和"他者"等显性和隐性的本质主义的设定,通过真正跨学科(interdiscipline)、跨文化研究,去应对全球化人类经验的挑战。①

而在另外一位年轻一辈的学者,却以相同的激进方式对比较文学的前途作了相反的论断。这个年轻的学者就是比较文学理论家、汉学家苏源熙(Haun Saussy)。在苏源熙看来,伯恩海姆的报告,远远没有把握世纪之交的人类现实的复杂性和丰富性。其"文化多元主义"的概念,带有一种非常明显的要把当代历史纳入一个单一的理论系统的企图,这种结构化的尝试注定会削弱现实本应有的生动性和悖论性。苏源熙弃用了这一概念而代之以更中性、更具描述性的"全球化"术语。按照苏的看法,全球化绝非人类大同的田园牧歌,它本身就是发达国家和西方文化主导的,这必然导致全球化的不平等和不均衡。所以,当代历史与其说是"多元的",不如说是被表象的差异掩盖了的"单极化(Unipolarity)"。伯恩海姆的报告也没有注意当今世界无论是制度还是文化都在经历惯例转换的倾向,还忽略了网络时代新媒介对文化和学术的深刻影响。

三、全球化时代比较文学学科理论的重构及实例分析

以上诸多学者对伯恩海姆报告的批评和反思,直接导致2004年《全球化时代的比较文学》(*Comparative Literature in an Age of Globalization*)一书的出版。该书的基础,是苏源熙代表美国比较文学学会(ACLA)主持编辑的学科现状报告。不同意斯皮瓦克对比较文学学科的指责,在题为《从新鲜的恶梦中缝在一起的精美的尸体:论个性、蜂窝和自私的式样》(*Exquisite Cadavers Stitched from Fresh Nightmare: Of Memes, Hives, and Selfish Genes*)这一主旨文章中,苏源熙果断地提出"比较文学已经胜利"这一命题。他强调比较文学作为文学研究的一种基本方式的有效性,强调任何国家、民族的文学都"受到不同源流的滋润"。他认为,西方比较文学研究客观存在着的文化视野的褊狭和西方中心主义的局限,不应该成为比较文学学科存废的依据,恰恰是比较文

① Spivak, G.C.. *Death of Discipline*. New York: Columbia University, 2003.

学自身更新和发展的基础。对于比较文学研究内容扩展而带来的边界的模糊，他也作出了积极的解释。他用蜂房的建筑为喻：

> 一个蜂房只能成长到一定规模，一旦其数目大到开始与其作对；接下来，它属下的居民就会带着一个新的蜂后离开，去建立它们自己的峰巢。比较文学超别的专业和学科筑巢，正是其活力的明证。①

苏源熙因此大胆地要求比较文学向当代现实的所有可能的领域敞开：不同文化，不同民族，不同语言，不同学科，不同理论，不同媒介……他还特意引用中国古语“人弃我取，人取我予”作为题词，来表达自己对比较文学学科发展的期许。在苏源熙看来，比较文学总是关注边缘、裂缝、交叉、弱者、非主流、新现象的特点，正好是传统学科的劣势和缺陷。比较文学对自己学科内容和边界的争论，也正好是比较文学活力和合法性的源泉。在一个传统的内容明确、方法确定、体制清晰的学科和专业时效的时代，恰恰是比较文学可以充分发挥自己潜能和作用的时代。在文章的最后，苏源熙甚至大胆地预言：全球化的时代也就是比较文学的时代。

苏源熙对比较文学学科的乐观主义情绪在《全球化时代的比较文学》一书中并不是绝对的，争论的声音仍然主导着相关的讨论。苏源熙自己就创造了“差异与非差异的统一体（a unity of difference and non-difference）”这一术语，来描述这部充满争议的文集。但我们不可否认的是，这些关于比较文学学科性质的争论，不仅仅没有削弱比较文学学科的地位，反而使比较文学日益成为全球化时代的真正显学。

下面选择的两篇文选分别来自《多元文化主义时代的比较文学》和《全球化时代的比较文学》两部文集。两部文集的时间跨度超过了12年，文集收集的文章代表了比较文学界在这个被称为“全球化时代”对比较文学学科现状和发展趋势的思考。这些活跃在比较文学发展前沿的理论家，从不同的背景、不同的理论视角提出的许多问题，直到今天都是比较文学研究者必须面对的基本的、结构性问题。

【原典选读】

世纪之交的比较文学（节选）

◉伯恩海姆

【导读】《世纪之交的比较文学》（*Comparative Literature at the Turn of the Century*）节选

---

① Saussy, Haun. “Exquisite Cadavers Stitched from Fresh Nightmare: Of Memes, Hives, and Selfish Genes”, in *Comparative Literature in an Age of Globalization.*, pp. 4-5. Baltimore: Johns Hopkins University Press, 2004.

自查尔斯·伯恩海姆(Bernheimer)主持撰写的美国比较文学学会(ACLA)的1993《伯恩海姆报告》。报告总结了美国比较文学学会成立以来的比较文学学科发展历程,历数了在世纪之交比较文学面临的三大困境:精英主义的画地为牢、学科交叉带来比较文学学科特性被稀释的挑战、欧洲中心主义的观念阴影,提出了超越传统比较文学的学科理论和研究范式;并以文化多元主义的开放视野,整合不同文化(跨文化)、不同学科(跨学科)、不同理论(跨专业)的成果,为此顺应了比较文学学科的又一次自我更新的要求,向前大大地跨越了一步。下面的选读部分主要分析了ACLA对当时比较文学学科所面临的问题的梳理,以及它对未来比较文学学科发展趋势的预测。这些对问题的分析和发展的预测之观点,在此后的比较文学研究中产生了广泛和深刻的影响。■

This is the third Report on Standards written for the ACLA and distributed in accordance with its bylaws. The first report, published in 1965, was prepared by a committee chaired by Harry Levin; the second, published in 1975, was the product of a committee chaired by Thomas Greene. The visions of comparative literature set out in these two documents are strikingly similar. Indeed, Greene's report does not so much articulate new goals and possibilities for comparative literature as it defends the standards proposed by Levin against perceived challenges. Together, the Levin and Greene reports strongly articulate the conception of the discipline which prevailed through much of the 1950s, 1960s, and 1970s. Many of the current members of the ACLA received their doctorates from departments that adhered to the standards defined in these reports. But the historical, cultural, and political contexts in which these same comparatists are now working, and the issues many of them are addressing, have changed so markedly from the time of their professional training that actual practices in the field have transformed it. Our report will address the issue of standards in the context of this profound transformation.

In order to clarify what we perceive to be the direction of this disciplinary evolution, we will begin with a brief analysis of the previous two reports. Both attribute the rapid growth of comparative literature in this country after World War Ⅱ to a new internationalist perspective that sought, in Greene's phrase, "larger contexts in the tracking of motifs, themes, and types as well as larger understandings of genres and modes." This impulse to expand the horizon of literary studies may well have derived from a desire to demonstrate the essential unity of European culture in the face of its recent violent disruption. The broadened perspective, in any case, did not often reach beyond Europe and Europe's high-cultural lineage going back to the civilizations of classical antiquity. Indeed, comparative literary studies tended to reinforce an identification of nation-states as imagined communities with national languages as their natural bases.

This focus on national and linguistic identities is apparent in the way both the Levin and Greene reports address the notion of standards. High standards are necessary, they argue, in order to defend the elite character of the discipline, which, says Levin, "ought to reserve it for the more highly qualified students" and restrict it to large research universities with excellent language departments and libraries. Noting that "this ideal which seemed so desirable and so feasible ten years ago has been challenged for better or worse by rapid historical change," Greene goes on to argue the case for resistance to change. "There is cause," he writes, "for serious concern lest the trends now transforming our discipline, taken in the aggregate, not debase those values on which it is founded. The slippage of standards, once allowed to accelerate, would be difficult to arrest."

The greatest perceived threat is to the very basis of comparative literature's elite image, the reading and teaching of foreign language works in the original. Greene criticizes the increasing use of translations by professors in world literature courses who do not know the original languages. The use of translations is condemned in both the Levin and Greene reports, though Levin admits that, as long as comparative literature courses "include a substantial proportion of work with the originals, it would be unduly puristic to exclude some reading from more remote languages in translation." This statement illustrates the extent to which the traditional internationalist notion of comparative literature paradoxically sustains the dominance of a few European national literatures. Europe is the home of the canonical originals, the proper object of comparative study; so-called remote cultures are peripheral to the discipline and thence can be studied in translation.

Another threat to comparative literature, according to Greene, is the growth of interdisciplinary programs. Although he says we should welcome this development, Greene's emphasis is cautionary: "We must also be alert," he writes, "lest the crossing of disciplines involve a relaxing of discipline." "Crossing" here plays the same role in respect to disciplinary rigor as does "translation" in respect to linguistic purity. There is an effort to restrict the work of comparison within the limits of a single discipline and to discourage any potentially messy carrying over or transference from discipline to discipline. Just as comparative literature serves to define national entities even as it puts them in relation to one another, so it may also serve to reinforce disciplinary boundaries even as it transgresses them.

A third major threat to the founding values of comparative literature may be read between the lines of the Greene report: the increasing prominence in the seventies of comparative literature departments as the arenas for the study of (literary) theory. Although the theory boom was fostered in English and French departments as well, the comparatist's knowledge of foreign languages offered access not only to the original texts of influential European theoreticians but also to the original versions of the philosophical, historical, and literary works they analyzed. The problem in this development for the traditional view of comparative literature was that the diachronic study of literature threatened to become secondary to a largely synchronic study of theory. "Comparative Literature as a discipline rests unalterably on the knowledge of history," writes Greene in an implicit rebuke to the wave of theorizing overtaking the field.

The anxieties about change articulated in the Greene report suggest that, already in 1975, the field was coming to look disturbingly foreign to some of its eminent authorities. Their reaction tended to treat the definition and enforcement of standards as constitutive of the discipline. But the dangers confronting the discipline thus constructed have only intensified in the seventeen years since the publication of the Greene report, to the point that, in the opinion of this committee, the construction no longer corresponds to the practices that currently define the field. We feel, therefore, that our articulation of standards can be undertaken responsibly only in the context of a redefinition of the discipline's goals and methods. We base this redefinition not on some abstract sense of the discipline's future but rather on directions already being followed by many departments and programs around the country.

The apparent internationalism of the postwar years sustained a restrictive Eurocentrism that has recently been challenged from multiple perspectives. The notion that the promulgation of standards could serve to define a discipline has collapsed in the face of an increasingly apparent porosity of one discipline's practices to another's. Valuable studies using the traditional models of comparison are still being produced, of course, but these models belong to a discipline that by 1975 already felt defensive and beleaguered.

(Bernheimer, Charles. "Comparative Literature at Turn of the Century", *Comparative Literature in the Age of Multiculturalism*. ed. Charles Bernheimer, pp. 41-42. Baltimore: John Hopkins University Press, 1995.)

从新鲜的恶梦中缝在一起的精美的尸体（节选）

◉苏源熙

【导读】《从新鲜的恶梦中缝在一起的精美的尸体》(Exquisite Cadavers Stitched from Fresh Nightmare: Of Memes, Hives, and Selfish Genes)节选自《从新鲜的恶梦中缝在一起的精美的尸体:论个性、蜂窝和自私的式样》,该文为《全球化时代的比较文学》文集中的主旨文章。该文作者苏源熙(Haun Saussy, 1960—　)曾为2009—2011年期间美国比较文学学会主席,著名汉学家。苏源熙特殊的学术背景使他对全球化时代的不同文明的对话和互释,有着更为强烈的体验和认同。他的这篇文章回应了斯皮瓦克对比较文学"学科之死"的悲观预测,提出了"比较文学已取得胜利"的相反命题,对比较文学在全球化时代恰恰可以发挥出其他学科难以取代的独特优势进行了分析,表达了他对比较文学学科发展前景的信心。但苏源熙并不回避比较文学学科的明显问题。下面的节选部分,就反映了他对困扰比较文学界的文学研究和文化研究的争论的分析。在他看来,比较文学的文学研究和文化研究的争论,其实质也就是西方中心论和文化多元主义的争论。■

The reception of the 1993 report, as evidenced in the responses from a diverse and energetic group of scholars, provides a set of mental maps of the discipline as surveyed from various vantage points. The surprising thing is how much overlap there is, how much agreement about the shape of the territory, among people who disagree about much else. The downgrading of "literature" from the exclusive focus of the discipline to the status of one mode of cultural discourse among others is read by all as a gesture directed against both the high-cultural canon of European literatures and the legacy of "grand theory," whether the respondent thinks this downgrading is a good thing or a bad one. The adoption of categories from social science is perceived as a sacrifice of disciplinary autonomy, whether "borderline suicidal" or just a recognition that "in fact, there is no central activity of the field." By their choice of examples, and sometimes by express argument, respondents indicate how styles of thought gravitate toward their elective objects. Tell me what your objects are, and I will predict your methodology. The "porosity" of disciplines registered in the 1993 report augurs a rise in status for narrative and documentary genres of writing, which are easily assimilated to biography and history and which, moreover, lend themselves to translation and thematic reading; and a neglect of poetry, which is tightly bound to language and has affinities with philosophy and logic.[57] Some see the future of comparative literature in a break with the very idea of nations and languages, so that the most comprehensive version of the discipline would be "comparative media." Those less sanguine about the report's view of the field insist on the specificity of literature, its resistance to "full contextualization in other discourses," and the need for a self-aware theory of reading.

The battle between "literature" and "cultural studies," repeatedly correlated with a battle between "Eurocentric" and "non-Western" canons of text and theory, is often announced but has trouble taking place. Once we get into the details, the big picture suffers. The front line dissolves, and the opposing forces melt into one another. One of comparative literature's totems—the close reading of literary works in their original languages—is treated as expendable by the authors of the report in a gesture that announces openness but might be read as suggesting that not all languages and literatures are equally worth the trouble of learning: "The old hostilities toward translation should be mitigated… we would even condone certain courses in minority literatures in which the majority of the works were read in translation." (The misprinting of exotic names in several essays—"Buchi Emchetta," "Vauri Viswanathan," for example—gives a further indication that close reading and multiculturalism are not yet one.)

Rey Chow observes that the integration of non-Western texts into the comparative literature canon may just mean confronting a new class of "Eurocentric" specialists in remote cultures; there is no guarantee that exposure to the alien canon will teach anyone to see it as the locals see it. Chow fires a preliminary shot across the bow of the heirs of "the great Orientalists, Sinologists, Indologists, and so forth," thus raising the question of what kinds of expertise will be considered valuable in the new comparative literature: will departments of world cultural studies have to cultivate their own specialists, uninfected by the Eurocentric virus? On all sides, the question is not *whether* to contextualize literature and admit new traditions and canons, but *how*; and asking how, quite rightly, leads us away from the delusional questions of identity and toward the pragmatic ones, away from statements such as "The proper object of comparative literature is…" and toward ones such as "What we do in comparative literature is..."

For to frame the contest between "literature" and "cultural studies" as a difference in the objects of study would make sense only if comparative literature had an essential, as opposed to an occasional, investment in a particular set of objects. An Italian department that abruptly changed its focus to the languages and literatures of Sweden would soon undergo an identity crisis far profounder than would an economics department that stopped studying Russia and turned its attention to Latin America. The historical pattern of comparative literature's declared objects of study (always migrating, always retreating) gives no reason to think that the typical objects of cultural studies lie beyond its powers. We certainly can (and should) "do" cultural research, provided only that its topics are not handed to us as ready-mades in black boxes but can be subjected to the kinds of analysis, critique, and contextualization that the discipline has taught comparatists to perform. Such reanalysis is what happened, for example, with the theory of speech acts, an immigrant from the realms of law and ordinary-language philosophy: the idea was permanently modified by its passage through literary studies, and within our field it has been one of the crucial links between the conceptions of comparative literature as "comparison of literatures" to "comparisons with literature."

There is no necessary conflict between "literature" and "cultural studies"; at most, speaking from the literary side, there is an antinomy between two properties of the object we know as "literature." (The corresponding antinomy in social science would probably be formulated as that between structure and agency.) To quote once more from an alleged arch-Formalist, "The linguistics of literariness is a powerful and indispensable tool in the unmasking of ideological aberrations, as well as a determining factor in accounting for their occurrence." Putting aside the connotations of de Man's favorite term "aberrant" (that would mean erring away from what precisely?), this formulation gives plenty of work to both cultural and historical studies (as the analysis of what "occurs" in and through the power of sign systems) and literary study (as the "unmasking" of that power by a "linguistics," or grammatical model, that accounts for the regularities in its performance).

To return to the politics of the adverb: Comparative literature is best known, not as the reading *of literature*, but as reading *literarily* (with intensive textual scrutiny, defiance, and metatheoretical awareness) whatever there may be to read. Contextualization is always a legitimate epistemological move, but let us not grant any context the final authority of the real. That would be to make comparative literature a portal for other, more meaningful, more conclusive disciplines, and so to cheat the world of the nonreductive model of critical relation that our work at its best can provide, whether in the modes of close reading, of world literature, of comparative literary history, or of interdisciplinarity. What is needed is a term similar to "literariness" but that will not suggest an exclusive focus on written texts, on imaginative "literature" (a subdivision of the written that has been current for only a couple of centuries) or, more misleadingly still, a particular canon of texts. "Culture" will not do it; culture is all about subsumption into historical identities and systems of value. What most needs to be preserved, what is at stake when we debate whether comparative literature still has a role to play or can be allowed to vanish, its work on earth accomplished, is *metadisciplinarity*: not because it sounds prestigious or guarantees our uniqueness, but because it is the condition of our openness to new objects and forms of inquiry.

(S Saussy, Haun. "Exquisite Cadavers Stitched from Fresh Nightmare: Of Memes, Hives, and Selfish Genes", in *Comparative Literature in an Age of Globalization.*, pp. 18-24. Baltimore: Johns Hopkins University Press, 2004.)

【延伸阅读】

1. Bassnett, Susan. *Comparative Literature: A Critical Introduction.* Oxford: Blackwell Publishers, 1993.

苏珊·巴斯奈特是文化翻译学派的领军人物,《比较文学批评导论》是其代表作。这本书不仅对比较文学的源流和发展情况作了全景式的描述,而且对近二十年比较文学的新貌以及方法转变给予关注。作者注意到比较文学与民族文化的密切关系,并预言作为学科的比较文学会在全球进一步地扩张,伴随而来的是,狭隘的"欧洲中心主义研究"的萎缩。本书还着重探讨了比较文学与帝国、与现代身份认同、与后殖民、与性别、与翻译等当代观念的关系。该书系为初入学科的学生而写,被哈佛大学比较文学委员会列为该学科的第一本必读书。

2. Apter, Emily. *Against World Literature: On the Politics of Untranslatability.* New York: Verso, 2013.

艾米丽·埃普特长期执教于纽约大学,出版于2013年的《反对世界文学:从不可翻译的政治谈起》是其近期代表作。如评论家 Ben Conisbee Baer 所言,这本书并不是一本明确教导比较文学翻译的教科书,而是一本开启作者关于"文学评论的政治"思辨的理论书。本书通过安排一系列"松散的、可参与的论题(loosely affiliated topoi)",来探讨传统比较文学领域具有争议性的方法论等问题。这一系列探讨看似彼此孤立,实则都直指本书的中心论题:不可翻译性。作者的探讨在一定程度上丰富了人们看待世界文学的视角。

3. Damrosch, David. *World Literature in Theory.* Oxford: Wiley-Blackwell, 2014.

大卫·达姆罗什,曾任美国比较文学学会会长(2001—2003),2014年出版的《世界文学理论》是其30年多年从事比较文学教学和研究的经验总结。本书提供了在面对今日比较文学研究中出现问题的探析。全书分为四章,分别探讨了"世界文学的渊源和原初规划""全球化时代中的世界文学""当代世界文学的争议"及"世界文学的区域研究"。其中,"世界文学的区域研究"由知名学者撰写的30篇理论文章组成,这些学者包括歌德、爱德华·赛义德、雨果·梅尔兹、博尔赫斯、斯皮瓦克等人。每篇文章附有实质性介绍和注释性参考书目，方便学生在这个变化纷繁的学科领域更进一步地理解、言说和探讨核心问题。正如哈佛大学教授 Martin Puchner 所评价的：（这本书）“带我们踏上一条探究世界文学历史和地理的精彩旅途，从而证明了世界文学是当今文学理论中富有创造性的概念”。